A Company of Tatters

by Jack Beltane

Graveworm Press

Cleveland, Ohio

A Company of Tatters
Copyright © 2014 by Jack Beltane

"Friends" by James Montgomery (1771-1854)
First published in *The Pelican Island and Other Poems* by James
Montgomery (London, 1828). This work is in the public domain.

Cover art and design by Camron Lockeby
Copyright © 2014 by Camron Lockeby

The titles are typeset using Jellyka Estrya's Handwriting designed
by Jellyka Nerevan (www.cuttyfruty.com).

For more information contact:

Graveworm Press—graveworm.com
Jack Beltane—jackofbells.com

ISBN 978-1-929309-17-7
201409P/fiction

To my company of tatters:

Matt, Suzi, Joel, Justin, Nick,

Maryann, and Gretchen

Without you, I know I wouldn't have come out half as good
as I did, if at all. I hope you can recognize the truth beneath
the fiction and will know how much you each mean to me.

And to Elizabeth

You taught me what it means to truly love someone: You are
always there, even when you aren't.

A Company of Tatters

The author thinks "A Night Like This" by the Cure, from the album *The Head on the Door*, makes a fitting epigraph to this book.

Dim the House Lights

December

There are moments that act like hinges on a door to the future—hinges you can't recognize at the time. They hide in plain sight, buried beneath all the other moments that make up a lifetime, and it's not until the door swings open and you've walked through—not until you've walked far enough to glance back and wonder how you ended up there—that you can see them, shiny and bright, glowing through the fog of years, and you wonder then how you ever missed them in the first place.

That snow day in December my Senior year of high school was one of those moments—three special, shining hinges that made up a single long weekend and held up the door to the future. I didn't know it then and would surely have been crushed under the weight of it if I had, but that weekend set up everything that came after it, like the proverbial butterfly's wings beating softly in a forest thousands of miles away. This needs to be understood because the action —the real action—always follows the hinges.

So where did this all begin? Where did the past end and the future start? Where was the moment we seized as if tomorrow would never come and our history was still only yesterday? Because when those hinges squeak and you turn back to face another closing door it's important that you can recognize it, else nothing will ever be learned, and there is no lesson more wasted than one that is willfully ignored.

The weather in Cincinnati in December is not usually the picture of white and sparkly Christmas cards. The snow doesn't fly in earnest in southern Ohio until January. If it does fly any earlier it's the really heavy, wet kind that is preceded with rain and followed almost immediately with more rain to wash it away and make a royal mess of everything. No, early winter in Cincy is a gray and muddy time, full of wet-slick tile floors in school and shiny black asphalt that makes driving at night difficult. It's the kind of climate that makes you want to stay indoors and close the blinds and watch TV until it's too dark to see that the world outside is still a sodden green-brown-yellow mess of dirt and leftover autumn leaves that are too wet to decay.

But that December, we got a snow day on a Friday, and maybe that alone was reason enough for it to be memorable: a great stretch of blue after-storm sky over crystalline waves of undulating snow carrying us into the weekend, covering all the muck and grime with its spectral whiteness, unblemished and unsullied and looking very much like a damn Christmas card. If I'd only stood in my room and looked out the window all day—at our old sledding hill and at the massive pine tree in our backyard that had served as fort and clubhouse beneath its heavy, earth-scratching limbs—I probably still would remember that day. But I didn't stand there and look at the world outside. The world outside came in to me that day—to us—and rattled us with a taste of a future we'd been trying all our lives to avoid: the one where everything ends and the only way to survive is to run away.

When we were younger, all the kids in my circle of friends, whose parents still had to go to work on snow days, got shipped off to other friends whose parents didn't have to work, and once we could all drive and stay home alone, we subconsciously kept the practice going, migrating to each other's houses once the snowplows had come through. Niz stayed with me once or twice back then, but his mom usually took a day off work, and Tobie normally ended up with Jess, who lived down the street from me back then, before her parents got divorced.

"Back then"... that's somewhere around age ten—the 'tween years when you're still a little kid who can't be blamed for poor decisions, but your parents let you go out and explore by yourself anyway. When you hit thirteen, suddenly everyone expects you to act your age—whatever the hell that means. My mom said that shit to me decades ago and I'm *still* trying to figure out how you act like a number. Part of me will forever be ten and thirteen and seventeen and twenty-something. The age I act is an accumulation of all those eras, and sometimes poor decisions are more exciting. The only difference now is that a little more thought goes into making poor decisions.

Still, by that snow day, "back then" already seemed like an epoch away: Jess now lived across town and Niz always slept in until about lunch time, like any self-respecting teenager should. I've never slept much, no matter how late I stayed up, and I expected to spend the better part of the day watching movies or MTV until my friends woke up. The unwritten rules still held fast, though, and Tobie had drifted over to Jess's only to find out Jess was sick and would have missed school regardless, so then she'd drifted over to me—it wouldn't be a snow day if we didn't end up together in some form or other, I suppose.

"Check," I said defiantly. We had MTV on in the background in my living room, but Tobie and I were playing chess.

"Except you can't move a pawn backwards," she said calmly, moving my piece back to where it had been. "You will never 'mate me with a pawn, Bells, no matter how many times you try."

"If I mated with you—"

"No," she said simply. "I'm not in the mood."

I looked at her askance but she kept her head down, pretending to concentrate on the board. I could tell she was serious—we hadn't hung out almost constantly since sixth grade without picking up a thing or two about each other's tells. Tobie got quiet and avoided eye contact when she was pretending she didn't want to talk. When she *really* didn't want to talk, she didn't come over. Still, sometimes I read her wrong.

"I thought things were going good with everyone's favorite soccer star, Greg Wilson?" I tried, cheering sarcastically in a whispered frenzy of fans going wild. She cut me a look, then swooped in and took my queen. With a pawn.

"It's okay," she agreed. "At least when he's not trying to get under my bra, which is basically all the time any more."

"Well, I mean, considering what's under there..."

"Jack," she stated simply, cutting me another look and holding my eyes, daring me to open my mouth. "Not in the mood. And like you've *ever* touched my tits."

See, Tobie Malloy had another tell: she talked kinda dirty when she was pissed off and wanted someone to know why. Normally, she was the best of us—the least likely to get into trouble and the most circumspect when it came to swearing. That's not to say she never got up to antics with us, but if there was a voice of conscience to be had in our little group, it probably sounded a lot like Tobie Malloy. She also got the benefit of the doubt because she dressed in normal clothes and exuded a genuine innocence that said whatever she did was done with the best of intentions. To be fair, it usually was. The only thing that gave people pause was that she spent so much time with us—with me. I was your basic skate rat: Brown hair in a mohawk that I rarely took the trouble to put up, so it fell in a mussed-up trail over the shaved parts of my head. I thrifted for pants and wore t-shirts —the guy least likely to win any fashion shows.

"Is he too forceful?" I asked, skipping the jokes but trying to sound casual. Not that I was a tough guy who could show anyone what-for, but I knew bigger people who'd do me a favor, if I asked.

"No," she sighed, pushing her long brown hair back over her shoulder. She cocked her head sideways and her hair fell down on her other side as she quietly took my knight (that was supposed to take her queen). "He's been really *persistent* lately. He doesn't want to just sit and cuddle with a movie on any more."

"Men," I spat incredulously, still trying to lighten the

mood. "Sooner or later, that's all we're thinking of."

Tobie was the kind of cute girl most boys didn't notice because she didn't put herself out there to be noticed. She preferred it that way, and being a guy who talked to other guys, I didn't blame her.

"Yeah, well, that's why I came over here today, so let it be a lesson to you. I didn't feel like being groped. And I really don't feel like talking about it. And... checkmate."

"Shit."

I studied the board, made a few mental moves, saw nothing.

"Dammit."

She cleared the board and looked over at me. "So now what?"

"Are you going to break up with him?"

"I said I didn't want to talk about it."

The influence of friends is great and varied. Tobie's influence on me was certainly both. We weren't boyfriend-girlfriend, exactly—that's a long story—but she was definitely my best friend, maybe even just a shade more so than Niz, who I'd hung out with since I was seven. Tobie's edge came because she was a girl, making her a best friend *and* a spy. If you're having girl trouble, who better to talk to than a girl? It really helps you get a bead on what could *actually* be going on that a male friend, even as good as Niz, can't offer. Tobie used me in the same way, but not this time. She offered me a wan smile as she dropped the chess pieces back into the box. I knew it was cutting her up.

We always made fun of each other's current steadies and pretended not to like them, but truth be told, Greg wasn't that bad... at first. He was on the high school soccer team and I thought Tobie was a bit too skate betty for him, at least by disposition, but soccer seemed to be the sport du jour for skaters, so it didn't seem to matter to him. They'd been dating for a few weeks, after he admitted to her that he'd wanted to ask her to the Homecoming dance but couldn't pluck up the courage to do it. He was shy at first, anyway— or pretended to be. Then he got more confident, and now Tobie was left trying to decide when a nice guy wasn't so nice any more.

"We should probably eat lunch," I suggested. "Wanna head to the mall? We could call Niz and Sammy, maybe Jolly and Kammy. Too bad Jess is sick—we could have a snow-day party."

She looked at me, almost dumbfounded, trying to decide what she wanted to do. I hated seeing her like that: unsure and ready to give in, not to me, but to Greg. I really wanted to say something to her about it but I held my tongue— sometimes the best intentions still come across as jealousy, which was something we'd both accused each other of before.

"I don't know..." she finally mused. "Maybe I'll just go home."

"Home?"

"You know..."

"Well, Sammy needs to get out, anyway," I decided.

Tobie stood up and straightened her clothes, prepping to leave.

"Trouble with his dad?" she guessed.

"Sort of—I don't know. He doesn't talk much. His dad mostly leaves him alone, but I guess his parents go on argu-

19

ing jags, and they're in the middle of one."

Sammy was our broken bird, the shy kid who never got exactly what he wanted, usually because he didn't have the pluck to stand up and ask for it. Or take it. The kind of kid who needed a big birthday surprise party or a Prom date with the prettiest girl in school more than any of us, but he never got them. The world just glanced over him and somehow he always managed to shrug it off and keep his head up. He had long, dirty, blond hair that was scraggly and straight, and he favored M.O.D. and Mercyful Fate t-shirts. If not for the skateboard, he could've been another stoner metalhead, and if not for Niz, he may never have talked to us.

I stood up beside Tobie and sighed. She smiled weakly again, then leaned in and hugged me—a big, long hug that tried to explain how she felt.

"You can't save us all the time, Bells," she whispered.

"What? I'm not trying—"

She pulled away and nodded. "I know."

Her eyes drifted over my shoulder, out the patio doors behind me, and she waved at someone.

"Well Sammy's here now, so it looks like your plan's already in motion."

I turned and saw him standing there, a skateboard dangling from his fingers, and I knew instantly something was wrong. He wasn't even looking at Tobie, even though she'd waved. He looked crestfallen—it's the only word that fits to describe his slumped shoulders and down-turned mouth. It would have been comical, but the eyes don't lie, and his were staring at the world with a glassy, distant look. I leaped over and opened the door and he stepped right in.

"I'm going to check in on Jess," Tobie said, not waiting for a hint to take. "You still going to the mall for lunch?"

I glanced at Sammy, but he didn't say anything, so I looked back at Tobie and shrugged.

"I'll go to Kammy's after I visit Jess," she said. "Call me later?"

"Yeah—what are you and Greg doing tonight?"

She shrugged but didn't commit, then she was gone in a swirl of brown hair and a low tinkle of car keys. I remember distinctly seeing her go because the only clear thought in my head as I watched her back disappear up the hall to the front door was that I needed her there to help me. Sometimes you could tell when something was too big to handle alone. Sammy needed friends, not just me.

"S'up, Samuel?" I asked.

He shook his head, looking for a place to begin but not finding one. Finally he looked me right in the eyes, and he looked scared. Terrified, even.

"Jack, you're my best friend. I don't know where else to go."

"Shit, Sammy, you're scaring me—what the hell happened?"

"My dad's gone," he whispered.

I admit it—and I told him later—my first thought was that he'd killed the guy.

"Gone?" I croaked.

"He was going to leave while I was at school, but we had a snow day, and he left anyway."

"Gone?" I said again, still trying to think how you beat a murder rap. It would be easy enough to prove Sammy's dad

21

didn't have much interest in him, but to my knowledge he'd never hit Sammy. Quite the opposite: he never even considered his boy. At all.

"Gone. Moved out. Packed his shit and drove off."

Relief washed over me and I very nearly said, "Oh, is that all," then caught myself.

"Shit, Sammy. I mean... I don't know... What did your mom do?"

"She's at work."

"She doesn't know?"

He shook his head sheepishly.

"You didn't call her?"

"Should I?"

"I think so, yeah."

"He didn't even look at me, Jack. He just forced his way past and mumbled something about trying not to wake me."

"Did you...?"

I was going to ask if he'd seen it coming, but that would've been both stupid and unanswerable. Of course he'd seen it coming, he just hadn't believed the signs. His parents argued all the time and his dad often stormed off in a huff, only to return the next day after work, sometimes with an apology, most times without.

"Did you... want to go skate at Niz's?" I finished, indicating his board.

He glanced at it like he'd just realized he'd brought it with him.

"Nah. Sorry about Tobie, by the way."

"She was leaving anyway."

"I thought she was going with Greg Wilson?"

22

"She is," I agreed, slightly confused. "She just dropped by—Jess is sick."

"Okay," he said, not sure he was buying it. I didn't argue; I wasn't sure he was there for a conversation.

"Speaking of Jess... You should probably talk to her about this, right?"

"Yeah?"

"Sure. I mean, her folks... you know."

He nodded sagely and chewed at his lower lip. "I can't."

"Why not?"

"She's too... *awesome*."

I didn't know what that meant, exactly. Jess was indeed pretty awesome—with her short, brown, pixie-cut hair and her rock-girl clothes and her record-store job—but she never made anyone feel out of place or anything. Sammy and I sort of stared at each other for a minute or so. I'd already run out of things to say and I wasn't going to bicker about the awesomeness of Jess, and really, now that I knew his dad was still alive, it seemed like a regular divorce, from what I knew, which wasn't much, which is why I wanted him to go to Jess.

"So Jess?" Sammy said, breaking the silence. "She's still with Niz, right?"

"Yeah. Why are you so worried about who's with who?"

He smirked and I was glad to see it.

"Sammy?" I asked with mock seriousness. "Do you need a girlfriend?"

He snuffed a laugh through his nose, dropped his board, then walked over and slumped onto the couch. I slopped down next to him.

"Sure," he sighed. "I guess that's it. My dad walked out

so I decided to come to you for love advice."

"Well, I mean..."

"Who would you set me up with, Bells?"

He was asking sarcastically but we both went along with it to keep his mind off things.

"What about Kammy? You went to Homecoming with her."

He shook his head. "She's a great person but... nah. No spark."

"No spark," I stated coldly as if I was judging him.

Now that we were on the subject of girls I was on safe ground. Well, safer ground, anyway—at least it wasn't serious stuff that I was unequipped to handle. It's good to know your limitations, and my worth ended somewhere shy of serious advice. I hoped that's what he'd been looking for: Me to get his mind off serious things, but I could tell I was wrong by his distant stare.

"Did you see it coming?" I finally asked.

"I guess, kinda," he admitted. "He always said we'd be better off without him, but he never packed his bags before."

"Do you think your mom knew?"

"Probably..." He trailed off and concentrated on the designs on the wallpaper across the room, the tinny beat of MTV through the small TV speaker drifting around us.

"I mean, she won't be surprised," he qualified. "But maybe she didn't see it happening today."

"So where's he going?"

"How the fuck do *I* know, Jack?"

I let it go; we were toeing that line between my value and my presence.

Sammy told me that his dad had only ever got him one

24

Christmas or birthday present. Sure, he was there on Christmas mornings and most of his boy's birthdays, and there were presents, but Sammy always knew that every gift he got had been bought and paid for by his mom. Except that one, five Christmases ago: A skateboard. His first real deck, age twelve, the same deck he pointed at half-heartedly where it lay on the floor. Out of all the gifts he'd ever got, that one stuck with him the most, not just because his dad had given it to him, but because it proved that at least once in his life his dad had noticed him, and had noticed him enough to know what he'd actually *want*.

"And now, after seventeen years, he just leaves?" Sammy shook his head. "I guess that's his present this year."

The full story from Sammy was that his dad had been a long-haul trucker until Sammy was about ten, when Sammy's mom finally talked him into finding work that didn't involve him being gone most of the time. If you crunch the numbers, he'd only been settled down for seven years before he left, and suddenly that seems more likely, because Sammy was right, it'd be odd to think of a guy just up and leaving his family after seven*teen* years. He wasn't a drunk or any of the usual stereotypes, he was simply unhappy all the time. Turned out he went back to cross-country trucking—a move he'd been planning, Sammy's mom admitted, though she'd been trying not to take him seriously (still hanging on to that thread of hope, I guess).

I couldn't do much but nod in the right places and ask questions that seemed meaningful without prying.

"You know, I'm not the best person to talk to about this," I eventually admitted again, trying to divert the conversation back into safer waters, not for me but before I accidentally said the wrong thing and caused more damage. "Jess, you know, her parents..."

"I *know*," he agreed adamantly. "But I like the way *you* listen."

He was sitting with his head resting on the back of the couch, his eyes shut as if he could block out the world if he couldn't see it.

"It's not you, you realize?" I checked.

It was a slight bluff, to be sure. I didn't know his dad at all—he always made scarce if Sammy had friends over, even when we ate dinner, which wasn't often but had happened a handful of times.

Sammy scrunched up his nose as if he was about to sneeze, then shook his head.

"Yeah. I never got in his way, and he never went out of his way for me."

"Maybe you should talk to your mom?"

I wasn't trying to get rid of him, even though it sounded like I was, I just wanted him to be able to talk to someone who'd make more sense than I was. He sighed heavily and opened his eyes, twisting his lips into a strange attempt at a smile.

"Maybe we should have a beer?"

I cocked my head sideways and gave him a death stare.

"Be serious, Samuel—where are we going to get beer?"

"Whiskey," he suggested, nodding seriously. "My dad left his behind and I don't think he'll be needing it now. In fact..." He sat up straight, his eyes wide and his face lit up with revelation. "I'll suggest to my mom later that we should

26

pour it out—she won't stop me. Then she'll never know we drank any of it."

I continued to stare at him, oddly awed.

"Did you just think of that right now?"

"Yeah!"

I could tell he was serious, and for good or ill, I could tell it would get his mind off things. No wonder there are so many alcoholics. But I shook my head slowly and he grinned and nodded.

"Now do you want to talk to your mom?"

"Drive me there?" he asked.

$$\acute{\mathcal{E}}$$

Niz, Sammy, and I got back to my house that night around 9:30 and my mom handed me a piece of paper with a cryptic phone message from Kammy on it.

"She called about twenty minutes ago," my mom explained. "I think she was out somewhere—it was loud, anyway. Some girl named Ally called, too, but she said she'd call back. No number."

"Ally?" I checked, glancing at Niz. "McShay?"

I'd known Ally for a while through drama club—we both worked backstage on the plays, running the props and changing the sets. I had always thought she was incredibly hot—and incredibly out of my league. She was always talking about the best concerts, that she'd gone to with her cousins, or her older brother when he visited home from college, or the hippest record stores she visited downtown on Saturdays. And she was beautiful. And she got good grades. Me? I just sat around with Niz and Sammy and watched shitty horror movies or went skating and tried to ditch the cops, or I played chess with Tobie and talked with her about nothing much of everything. But Ally lived. Ally got out there and saw all the bands we talked about. Ally found the next great band by picking through the bins at record stores that weren't a stone's throw from a fucking food court.

So there was no way Ally McShay had called me.

"Ally McShay?" I asked again. Niz shrugged in an exaggerated fashion. He was a skate rat like me and my oldest friend. He kept his dark-blond hair short and neat and parted to the side, which gave him the illusion of normalcy, but he wasn't businessman perfect—his schlubby clothes, like mine, took care of that.

"You *have* asked her to call you before."

"Yeah, but she never—"

"Maybe the message explains?" Niz said, pointing at the scrap of paper.

"Ally didn't leave a message," my mom said, then pretended to find something to do in another room.

I read the message that Kammy had left and knew exactly what it meant: *At the Wharf. Tobie says she wants to talk about it now.* I sighed heavily.

"What?" Niz asked, snatching the paper from me.

"Looks like we'll have to swing by the Wharf before we watch those skate videos."

"No! Come *on*!" Sammy pleaded, and Niz echoed his pleas with his expression.

The Wharf was a teen club that played pop music and served as nothing more than a place for pubescent jocks to act like the assholes they saw in the movies, without realizing those guys never got the girls in the end. It was loud, it was crowded, and I was quite sure Greg Wilson had dragged Tobie to it, and Tobie had dragged Kammy along. It was no wonder she hadn't called me earlier: She knew I wouldn't want to go with them.

"I gotta go," I said to them. "I'll catch up with you."

"No, we'll come," Sammy agreed grudgingly. We looked at Niz. He slumped dismally and breathed "fine" as he slogged after us.

The parking lot at the Wharf was a snowy, muddy mess, and it just got worse from there. I don't know why they called the damn place the Wharf—we were in the middle of fucking landlocked Ohio. Okay, there was a sizable river forty minutes south, but it was hardly enough to base a nautical theme on. Maybe the owner liked boats—not that anyone would notice. Inside it was dark and they piped in stage fog, which did make the swirling dance-hall lights look pretty cool. Of course, there was plenty of cigarette smoke, too, but they pretended that wasn't happening in a teen club. Come to think of it, the piped-in fog was probably a cover so they could plausibly deny knowledge.

When you walked in the front door you were at the bar, which ran all the way along the building on your left. They had a whole array of virgin mixed drinks that they served, and even some nonalcoholic beer. It was, in a word, lame, but they must've known something because they did a good trade. On the right was a big open dance floor surrounded by bar tables. Against the back wall was a stage of sorts with a DJ's booth on it (they never had live music—that would've been just a shade too cool). I don't know what the song was, but it was the one that sounds like all the others, with the heartbeat-paced bass drum and a Casio-effect garnish.

Kammy had been waiting for us. She marched over and grabbed my arm and dragged me all the way down the bar to where Tobie was standing against the wall. She looked pretty damn good, if you must know. She'd bought herself a new dress at the mall, mostly black with green accents that served both as well-placed stripes and as the straps. Aside from them, her shoulders were bare—it was one of those cuts where it has sleeves that start about mid-shoulder and go in a taut line, tight to the skin and straight across her chest. The reason I remember all this so well is because I noticed immediately that it had been carefully designed as a fortress of fabric. There was no easy way "in" to that dress—the buttons, same color as the green stripes, were big and fat and all up the back and the fabric was heavy enough to dissuade external groping. She'd bought that dress for Greg, to keep his hands off her.

"Where's Greg?" I yelled, the music pounding in time with my headache.

She didn't answer but reached out and sort of fell on me, in an approximation of a hug.

"Is she drunk?" I shouted at Kammy.

Kammy shrugged.

"Where'd she get alcohol?"

Kammy shrugged more emphatically.

"Shit."

I pushed Tobie back a bit so I could hold her up and look into her eyes. She didn't look drunk, to be honest.

"Are you drunk?" I asked her quietly. I wasn't sure she heard me, but her eyes got watery and she looked scared.

"Tipsy," she managed to say.

"Did you bring a flask?"

It was no secret that kids snuck flasks in all the time. Not a school year went by that there wasn't at least one arrest. I think the PTA had been trying to close the place down since it opened, but the truth is, those flasks ended up at school dances, too. The chaperones were only there to call the cops, and in that capacity, the Wharf employees probably did a better job—they had a business to mind, after all.

"I didn't bring a flask," she said. She sighed heavily and unnecessarily ran her hands through her hair. "I think Greg spiked my drink."

"Nice. Where is he?"

That's when she broke down. She started to cry and pointed vaguely at the dance floor. I let her go and turned around, scanning the crowd. One thing the Wharf didn't care much about was the dancing. Christ, it was like soft porn out there, and I quickly registered that one of the most egregious grinders was none other than Greg Wilson. He had apparently found some willing bimbo—probably shortly after realizing that, tipsy or not, Tobie wasn't going to put up with him.

"What an asshole," Sammy yelled over the music at me. I'd almost forgotten he was there with Niz.

31

"C'mon, Tobe, let's get outta here," I said, giving her a light tug then dropping her arm.

She kept her head down, hiding her face behind her hair, but she nodded and followed me as we walked toward the door. If it hadn't been winter, we'd've been out of there and gone before Greg even noticed, but we had to stop for Tobie's and Kammy's coats on the way out. A series of thefts had necessitated they put in a coat check, and they were slow as hell at finding coats, which gave Greg ample time to notice.

"What's going on?" he suddenly bellowed as we stood there. I had my back to him; Tobie was in front of me, but facing him. "Where you going, Tobie?"

"You're drunk," she said quietly.

He guffawed and looked around for an audience.

"You, too, sweetheart!"

"Cuz you spiked her drink," I said over my shoulder. "Why don't you go back to your new girlfriend?"

He pushed past me by shoving me out of the way and grabbed Tobie's wrist in one fluid motion. I hadn't even re-gained my balance yet before Sammy had shoved Greg back several steps and was right up in the guy's face.

"Hey!" Sammy screamed. "You don't shove my friends around, you don't spike girls' drinks, and you certainly don't get to go home with Tobie after what I saw you doing out *there*!"

Greg blanched. He backed up another step and looked around, trying to find his friends. He came up empty. Oh, the people he hung out with were there, but they backed up two steps when he backed up one. You see, we knew Sammy and we knew he was harmless, but those guys didn't. To them, he was still the sullen quiet kid in the back of math class who was either bored because he was a genius, or plotting some revenge or other. Do I think Sammy could have taken Greg in a fight? Sure. I mean, he was already pissed about his dad and when I looked over at him, the look in his eyes sort of freaked me out, too. But none of us was going to let it come to that.

"I don't think I want to see you any more, Greg," Tobie said, breaking the silence. I glanced over at the coat check girl—she looked completely unaffected. The guy behind the bar seemed to be paying closer attention and the last thing I wanted was the cops showing up, arresting Sammy, and finding Tobie tipsy.

"Let's go," I said to Sammy, touching his arm. "He's not worth it."

Sammy stood his ground, though. He only backed off when Greg finally spun on his heel and headed back into the club, flipping us off after he was safely surrounded by his friends.

"What a fucking day," Sammy sighed.

"What am I going to do, Jack?" Tobie wailed, starting to cry. I knew it was whatever Greg had put in her drink making her emotional, because Tobie was not usually so dramatic. "I can't go *home* like this!"

"Yeah..." I mused. We couldn't go to my house either.

"We'll go to my place," Sammy offered. "My mom'll be sleeping. We can hang out in the basement and watch a movie."

"Okay?" I asked Tobie. She nodded and wiped the tears away.

33

"Here's your coats," the girl behind the counter said cheerfully.

Sammy and Niz went with Kammy in her car, and I took Tobie in mine. It had sort of been her idea—I mean, she walked with me toward my car and Sammy and Niz gravitated to Kammy's car—but I felt weird. I would've liked at least one of them to come with us.

"Did you want to stay?" I asked her as we got into my car. She was still hiding behind her hair but she shook her head, waiting for me to start the engine.

"I didn't hear... Did you...?"

"No," she blurted curtly.

She'd been hiding her tears well, but I could hear them in her voice.

"I feel bad, like I ruined your evening," I said.

"This isn't about you, Jack," she said quietly.

I didn't know what to say, so I didn't say anything. I turned the key and the engine thrummed to life.

"How's Sammy?" she asked quietly, fishing a tissue out of her purse and wiping her nose. It sounded like the tears were gone, but she was still hiding behind her hair.

"He's fine, I guess," I said. "We went skating over at Niz's."

"You guys are going to kill yourselves with that set up."

It was true. Mini skateparks like Niz had built don't belong in suburban garages, but if you wanted to skate in the winter in Ohio, that's exactly where you put them. We had a rail and a platform, and they could easily be broken down and stored away. Niz built them all himself; he was a genius.

"Sammy almost did," I admitted. "He was a little more... daring than usual."

We drove quietly for several minutes, but when I've got something on my mind and it's quiet, I start to blab. I just don't know when to leave things alone.

"Why did you call me, anyway? My mom gave me the message..."

She sighed heavily and pulled her hair back over her ear so she could glance at me, then back at her purse in her lap, where she was twiddling the zipper.

"I mean..."

"I just wanted to talk," she said softly. She sounded tired. "Kammy called you before it all went to hell. He wanted me to dance, which was fine, but then he started, you know—I mean, it's one thing when we're sitting on my couch, but that was, you know, *public*. And I started to feel weird, besides— whatever he'd spiked my drink with. So I walked off and told Kammy to see if you'd come down, cuz I was ready to talk about it. I don't know why I said that to her."

She looked at me weakly and tried to smile. "Guess I needed moral support."

"Somebody needed morals out there, and it wasn't you," I quipped. She chuckled politely, but we both knew it wasn't funny.

"So by the time you got there, he'd come over and yelled at me for leaving the dance floor, so I told him to stop fuck- ing *touching* me, then he acted like it was *my* fault, cuz he was like, 'Why did you come here with me?' Then I *knew* he'd spiked my drink... Next thing was, I saw him out on the floor with that other girl—does she even *go* to our school?—

and then you guys were there."

Her voice had regained its strength while she talked. I didn't say anything else. I'd pried enough out of her and figured she'd say more if she wanted to, but she was quiet the rest of the way to Sammy's.

Sammy lived on the "bad" side of town, whatever that meant. It seemed like the only distinguishing characteristic was that the houses were smaller than the other neighborhoods and the residents were barely scraping by, so they put their money into a couple of weeks away instead of repainting the siding or dumping chemicals on their lawns for that sparkly green finish. I'm sure real estate agents have a nice way of saying that they were poor, by comparison to other areas of town, but it probably didn't include the fact that they also worked harder and deserved more than they ever got.

Sammy didn't complain, though, not about anything. His house had a side door that went straight downstairs and into the basement, or you could go forward two steps and through another door into the kitchen. We never went into the kitchen, except on the rare occasions when we ate over, and as we started down the stairs to the basement like usual the kitchen door opened and Sammy's mom poked her head out.

"Oh," she said, shocked by the girls, no doubt. Niz and I she'd expected, since we'd picked him up earlier. I think she'd seen Tobie around, and she'd certainly seen Kammy at Homecoming, so she did at least know we hadn't gone out and picked up random girls.

"Hey, Ma," Sammy said, pushing past us, back up the stairs. "I thought you'd be asleep."

"Just watching a movie," she replied. "I haven't got to

watch one of *my* movies for..." She trailed off and smiled, then changed gears. "Why don't you all come up here? I can make a fresh batch of cookies in twenty minutes."

Sammy looked at us and we all shrugged. I glanced at Tobie and she wrinkled her nose back at me and stuck out her tongue. I had no idea what that meant, but she also mouthed, "I'm not drunk," so I assume she was trying to make fun of me for what she knew I was thinking.

"Cookies sound great, Ma," Sammy answered.

He's a great guy. Yeah, sure, a little stand-offish (as my mom used to say), but he always seemed to be really in tune with people's feelings, even if he didn't always express his own. His mom could've offered us lutefisk pie and he'd've sounded as happy, because he knew that right then his mom needed someone to be with her, so we all traipsed upstairs, where Sammy introduced Tobie and needlessly reintroduced Kammy.

"Kammy," his mom said, smiling with those mom eyes that hoped this pretty young girl liked her little boy. "I'm sorry we didn't visit more on Homecoming night. You looked beautiful."

"Thanks," she replied with a blush and ducked away. Tobie had certainly told Kammy what had happened and I think she was more afraid she'd say something stupid than she was embarrassed.

"So what brings you all over here?" Sammy's mom wondered, motioning for us to sit at the kitchen table. There were only four chairs. Niz and Sammy's mom ended up standing, but she was messing around with the cookies.

"It was closest," Sammy half lied.

37

It's true, his house was closest to the Wharf, but that's not really the logic that had brought us there.

Sammy's mom got the cookie clumps spread out on the pan and shoved them in the oven, then turned to us and said, "What now?"

We all shared a look around. Tobie was keeping really quiet, despite her telling me she wasn't drunk. I widened my eyes at Sammy and looked at Tobie, trying to tell him to think of something that didn't involve, say, quick movements and fine motor skills.

"I want you to cut my hair," Sammy declared definitively.

Now Sammy's mom, she was a piece of work. She was used to doing the parenting for two and she tried to keep Sammy straight, usually with well-placed and pointed comments about his fashion sense or choice of music. She didn't seem to mind me or Niz or our other skate buddies too much, but she'd still dig on him when we were there. Never in a mean way. It was like she was trying to teach him subconsciously, like if she said the same thing subtly over and over again, eventually Sammy would wake up and do it and think it was his idea all along. Maybe that's how she tried to deal with his dad, too. My opinion of her changed that night, though, when it really hit me that she'd been shouldering the sole burden of raising her boy right, but she also hadn't wanted to do anything that might push him away—the kind of tightrope line she'd been walking all of her marriage, or at least as soon as she figured out that the man she'd married wasn't ever going to settle down. She'd honed subtle persuasion to an art form, and while she may have failed with her husband, I think she succeeded with Sammy. We knew that his hair had long been a bone of contention between them. Sammy's hair was long—shoulder length—and he didn't wash it every day, so it hung tight, not all flowy and puffy like a shampoo commercial.

"Are you serious?" she gasped.

"I'm serious," he said. "I think it's time to do something... new."

I thought the poor lady was going to burst into tears. Instead, she marched over and planted an exaggerated kiss on Sammy's cheek, then gave him a bear hug.

"But now? In front of your friends?" she checked as she let him go.

She was already planning what to do, her fingers subtly pantomiming cuts in the air. I didn't know it then, but she'd been a hair stylist before her move to office work in private medicine.

"Right now," Sammy said with a wry smirk. "I want witnesses and we've got time to kill. But don't make it look stupid."

"I do like the front," she said thoughtfully. "We need to keep that so you have something to flick out of your eyes. But we need to shorten it way up on the sides and back..."

"Why didn't you decide to do this *before* Homecoming?" Kammy asked with only slight derision.

"It wasn't the right time," he offered.

And somehow that made perfect sense.

ع

Sammy once told us that escalators have a kill switch hidden in the sidewall at the bottom, in case something went wrong. It must have been designed before they started putting those big red STOP buttons on them, and the design was carried over, because I can verify that one swift kick right in the sweet spot and any escalator will shut down— stop instantly. Sammy's dad had once been an escalator repairman or something, and Sammy explained it to us as his dad had once explained it to him, but Niz was the one who tried it. I don't think we'd believed him. Fortunately there was no one else on the stairs at the time.

*Un*fortunately, I had been sidetracked momentarily when we went down the escalator that first time Niz tried it, so I was about four or five steps behind Niz and Sammy. It's funny how they thought they were whispering to each other, but I could hear every word they said as they debated whether or not it would work and how to do it. I really didn't think it would work, and I was a million miles away when Niz's tap-tap-taps on the sidewall brought me back. I opened my mouth to make some sarcastic comment when *slam!* Niz dug his heel into the sidewall with a good, swift kick, just like Sammy had said, and the escalator stopped cold. No slow whirring to a close, but a sudden and absolute end to the movement. Niz and Sammy were as shocked as me, but when they tripped, they caught their footing on flat ground at the bottom of the stairs. Me? I stepped onto the edge of a stair and fell headlong. Sammy was on me in an instant, barely managing to ask if I was okay between gales of laughter. Niz actually looked scared. He was laughing a tad maniacally, his eyes wide and nervous.

So come that December, when I looked at Niz and growled "kill switch" the day after Sammy's dad left and we saved Tobie from the Wharf, he was more confident of his escalator-killing talent.

How we'd ended up in the mall with our skateboards was a bit more convoluted. I'd made a deal with the toy store where I worked over Christmas (they paid above minimum wage for seasonal work) that I'd work until four o'clock, then come back in at nine, when they closed, and restock until midnight. Christmas shoppers sure know how to wipe out toy stores, despite the fact that the mall I worked in was stillborn: It was built empty and it never filled up. I honestly don't know what the hell they were thinking. There were already two big malls within a half hour of our subdivision, but they stuck this monstrosity there and hoped the retailers would fill it up. They didn't.

Most of it was like a ghost town, but man, what a food court! I shit you not, the middle of the food court had a mini golf course, Ferris wheel, and carousel. At the end of it was a second-run cinema (a buck-fifty a ticket) and a huge arcade. If that's all they'd built, they'd've been fine— it was the last dying gasp of the generations that still went out to meet up with their friends and pick up girls. It opened our Sophomore year and yeah, it worked for us, but for business? Well, no. Not so much.

Anyway, I worked until four then went home, changed, and headed over to Sammy's to see if we could squeeze in some fun before I had to go back to work. Niz was already there, watching some old H-Street videos frame by frame to learn new tricks, and he was primed to go out and ride.

"Except for the snow," Sammy pointed out. It's rough being a skater in Ohio.

"All right," Niz said, cutting a slick deal with us. "Disc World opened a store at the mall, right? So we go to the mall for dinner and take our boards and cut the grip tape there. Cuz I'm telling you, Sammy, the key to *that* trick" (jabbing his finger at the TV screen) "is the grip tape."

"The *grip tape* is the key?" I begged. "And cutting it's one thing, but unless you're buying me a new deck, I won't have anything to put it on."

Sammy nodded emphatically as if he'd already been around this logic with Niz, but Niz just waved me off—he often had crazy notions that somehow ended up being correct.

"Regardless," I said. "Can't we just cut the tape here? You know, like *normal* people?"

"You have to work, Bells. We won't have time to drive up to mall, eat, buy grip tape, come back here, and cut it up. If we take our boards, we can buy the tape first and cut it into shape in the food court while we eat. It saves time."

"But my board... already has... grip tape..."

Niz waved me off again and mumbled something about getting the old tape off later, if we could just *cut* the new tape tonight.

"Okay," I agreed, giving up—he had that look in his

42

eyes and I certainly wasn't going to waste time arguing.

And so there we were, at the top of an escalator with our skateboards, heading down to the food court for a frozen Coke before they left me to work.

"Hey!" someone yelled out just as we got onto the stairs. "Asshole!"

We didn't stop or anything. I glanced around but I didn't see anyone I knew, so I assumed whoever was yelling was yelling at someone else. In a way I was right. He wasn't yelling at me, he was yelling at Sammy: Once we were about midway down the escalator, Greg Wilson popped up at the top of the stairs.

"I said, 'Hey, asshole'," he repeated.

One of his meat-head buddies appeared behind him. Now I've said it before and I'll say it again: Sammy may have looked pretty tough, but he was not a fighter at all, despite the shoving match at the Wharf the night before. When he looked at me, he looked scared. Not out of fear. It was more like a panicked look that was begging me to intervene before we were forced to find out what would happen.

"Nice haircut, pussy!" Greg called down.

That's when it struck me that he was *riding* the escalator down. If he'd really wanted to catch up and cause a scene he would have jogged down the steps and got right up on us, but he was just standing there, riding it down about ten steps behind us, yelling stupid things. He didn't want to fight, he just wanted to try and embarrass Sammy in public like *he'd* been embarrassed, but without having to test Sammy's mettle.

"Kill switch," I growled at Niz, and a grin spread across both his and Sammy's faces.

Niz jostled around so that his butt was against the wall and counted off the stairs. In the time it took him to turn sideways and count, we reached the sweet spot and he whacked the sidewall with an almighty kick. We even stumbled a bit when the stairs stopped, but Greg and his buddy spilled just like I had back in the summer. Now remember, it was Christmas, and even a dead mall gets busy at Christmas, so even though it was late in the day and most everyone had gone home, there was still extra security around, and the whack Niz had given the sidewall would have roused even the sleepiest security guard—Greg's loud cry of shock only sealed the deal.

"Hey!" some guard or other yelled, getting up from his dinner and jogging toward us.

He looked unsure, like he felt he should yell at us because he'd heard something strange, but since he couldn't say what had happened he wasn't too invested yet. In fact, he might have stopped halfway to us and turned back to his meal, except Niz and Sammy slapped down their skateboards and kicked off, in an effort to outrun Greg and his Very Big Friend. That got the security guard running, so I slapped down my board and followed suit.

Skating in a shopping mall is one of those things we always talked and dreamed about but never figured we'd do. It was fucking glorious. Those floors are so damn smooth you practically cut a powerslide just by nudging a bit to the one side. It was like hitting ice with traction. Intoxicated by the rush, Sammy tried a powerslide for real and swooped instantly out of control, crashing into an empty table at the food court. He was back on his feet before I'd even fully parsed what was happening, then he shot past me. I glanced back and expected to see a team of security guards chasing us down in a golf cart or something, but we were already out of the food court and around the corner with no one in sight. Well, no one chasing us, at least.

Niz was the farthest along and I saw him cut to the right suddenly and powerslide to a stop (having seen Sammy's wipeout, he was more prepared and managed to land grace-fully, but still rougher than usual). Sammy and I caught up and we all ducked into the record store where Jess worked.

"Hey, guys!" she said.

"Help!" Niz shrieked. She took a second to read his face, take in me and Sammy's equally panicked and flushed looks, then pointed toward the back.

"Stock room," she said simply, then called after us, "My manager's only on break, so make it snappy!"

We did. Sammy and I knew all about the delivery alleys and hallways at that mall and we sprinted straight through the stock room and out the back door.

"Right or left?" Sammy checked. Niz was completely lost. As far as I know, he didn't even get any kind of job until he was in college. Of course, that left him more time to build us skate ramps.

"Right goes back to the food court," I pointed out. "Left should head out to a loading elevator somewhere. They al-ways put those by the anchor stores."

We bolted left. Sure enough, down the hall was a freight elevator with a staircase beside it. Sammy slammed through the doors into the stairwell and we bolted up them and out onto the loading dock. It was dark and cold, but I remember

45

how bright the stars were. They always seem so bright in the winter, like the air isn't thick enough to hold them back.

Niz pulled my arm and we all dropped our boards and skated off down the dolly ramp beside the concrete steps, then off up the loading ramp to the parking lot. Either the security guard hadn't got the word out about us yet or they didn't think we'd be outside already, because we didn't see any fake police cars with those pathetic green flashing lights. To get back around to our cars we had to skate all the way behind the massive—*massive*—grocery store that was one of the other anchors (and the only store that turned a profit; it was the world's stupidest mall, I tell you) and then finally back around to the mall entrance across from it.

"I think we're gonna book," Niz said, looking at his watch.

"All right," I agreed. "I'm just gonna huck my board in my car—hopefully they didn't get a good look at us."

"Turn your coat inside out," Sammy said suddenly, starting to help me out of it.

"Wha—? Why?"

"So it looks different."

I flapped it off, then flapped some more to get Sammy to stop helping.

"All right, all right—damn kids! Leave an old man alone!"

"D'ya think Greg's pissed?" Sammy wondered.

"Gee, I don't know," Niz countered. "You knocked him on his ass *twice*, man!"

"Nuh-uh," Sammy disagreed, his eyes wild like he really thought he had to clear his name. "*You* did this one, Niz."

46

"Maybe he'll stop bugging us?" I said weakly. "Besides, I'm the one who has to go back in there and work."

Sammy smiled again, his usual mirth returning.

"Good luck," he said as he and Niz got in Niz's car.

I went back into the mall carefully, looking around like I was James Bond infiltrating a supervillain's hideout. My coat was really a too-big suit blazer I'd thrifted and inside out it looked like a blue satiny thing instead of a drab blue thing, so I wasn't sure it would help much. A blue coat is a blue coat, after all. The toy store where I worked was right at the top of the escalators to the food court, too, so I had to go back to the scene of the crime. I made it without incident— the escalator was still stopped, though—and hurried through the toy store, back into the stock room.

Steve was back there, mid-bellow as he sang in a booming voice: "Have a holly jolly Christmas...!"

He was holding a kids' Fisher-Price tape recorder and fumblingly hit stop as I walked back, the stock door waggling shut behind me.

"You're early," he said with a guilty grin.

"And you're...? Doing...?"

Steve was one of two assistant managers, who were the guys that had to share out closings and weekends so the store manager could work 9-5, Monday through Friday. I don't know what the hell was wrong with that store, but Steve was working his first job after a ten-year stint as a repo man. He was a big, muscle-bound guy with a used-car salesman look about him, and a mustache to match. The other assistant manager, Scott, worked his off nights as a male exotic dancer. So out of eighty-four managerial hours per week at a toy store full of shoppers under the age of thirteen, half of them were covered by a former repo man or a current stripper. I seriously couldn't make that shit up if I tried.

"Check it out, Jack," he said, pulling me over, away from the stock room door. "Some jackass kids fucked up the tape."

"Language," I joked.

"Yeah," he grinned. "Exactly."

He hit play and Burl Ives churned out some more of "Holly Jolly Christmas," only to be interrupted a few seconds later by a childish voice yelling and giggling, "DICK! FUCK YOU, DICK!"

The tape had been Steve's idea so we had "real" Christmas music in the toy store. He'd taken the tape recorder display model, stuck it in the middle of the front of the store, and played non-Muzak Christmas tapes. It was actually a good idea... Until those kids had swiped the recorder when it stopped playing, took it into the back corner of the store, stuffed paper in the tape-lock notch on the cassette, and recorded random obscene snippets throughout side A. To fix the problem, Steve decided to overdub the kids' obscenities with his own renditions of the damaged portions of the actual songs. So what we ended up with was a minute or so of Burl Ives or Bing Crosby serenading a classic Christmas tune, only to be interrupted by the exaggerated croon of a bellowy former repo man.

"It works, right?" he asked sincerely.

At the time, it didn't seem so bad, but in practice it was distracting, to say the least. When you're trying to ring up a line of customers twenty deep and you see them wince and

48

look around for hidden cameras every time Steve's bellow filled in a gap on the tape, it's downright hysterical.

"I don't think that's very funny," one old lady said to me as she haughtily grabbed her bag. She was wrong—it *was* very funny. *Very* funny.

"It's something," I said to Steve.

"Well, go hang out in the store," he decided, shooing me away. "I can't do this with someone watching."

Out in the store it was actually busy. Tammy and Bill were working the registers, leaving no one out on the floor (since Steve was in the back, fixing the tape). I felt bad, but I couldn't just jump on the clock and start helping out, not in my tattered skate rags, anyway. Tammy caught my eye and smiled. She was pleasant, but struck me as willfully ignorant. She was dating Scott and seemed purposefully unaware that Scott was also dating at least one other girl besides Tammy. Considering his profession, though, I suppose Scott had something to offer that most men do not.

I worked my way down the aisle toward the back of the store, straightening up the shelves as best I could without looking like I was working. As I rounded the end cap into the back aisle (it was a small, mall store—only three aisles and a back aisle connecting them) I ran into Tobie.

"Jack!" she gasped. "Thank goodness. Your mom said you were here, working or something."

She glanced at my clothes questioningly.

"Not 'til nine," I said. "What's up? I thought you were going out with Jess tonight?"

She shook her head. "No, not after last night. Besides, Jess still feels kind of sick. We're going to go over and watch

49

a movie at her house, but I wanted to catch you first."

"What? Why? You okay?"

She took my hand and pulled me back down the aisle toward the front of the store, then dropped it when she knew I was following her. She went back out into the mall. I was still a bit nervous, but a quick scan didn't pick up Greg or any security guards. I noticed some maintenance guy at the bottom of the escalator finally, trying to get it started.

"Can't talk in there," she said.

We moseyed down the mall toward the ridiculous indoor skating rink they'd put in for the holidays. Me and Jess had made a tradition of watching the rink from above on our breaks, to laugh at the people who had no business ice skating, fake or otherwise. One kid we saw was trying to be the Rhino out of Spider-Man or something, because he'd bend over at the waist, then get up a head of steam and smash into whoever or whatever was in his way. Jess and I about split our guts on that one.

"So what's up?" I asked. "We... uhhhh... You should know, me and Sammy and Niz just had a run-in with Greg."

"I know," she said. "I saw him a few minutes ago. He said to tell you you're dead."

"Good," I agreed. "That's good. That's a nice thing to say."

I looked nervously over my shoulder and Tobie chuckled.

"Greg's harmless, Bells, you know that. He talks a big game but he only acts if he thinks you're weak."

She stopped and sniffed like she was crying, even though she wasn't. She hadn't been dating Greg that long—

maybe a month at the most—but it must still have hurt. After all, he'd dumped her by groping other girls right in front of her on their date. Even the pretty girls want to be liked for something other than their cup size, and Tobie didn't even consider herself to be one of the pretty girls—she was wrong on that count, but you'd never hear it from her.

"So what's up?" I asked again.

She sighed heavily and stopped walking, moving over to one of the random benches they plop down in malls. She sat and I sat with her.

"I just felt bad about last night," she said.

"Bad? Why? You didn't—"

"Let me finish. I feel bad cuz I had Kammy call you and then when you came, I acted like you shouldn't be there. But I feel worse because of... because I was drunk."

"Well, *tipsy*, maybe," I offered. She shook her head.

"I saw him putting something in my drink. I knew he had a flask. I drank it anyway because I thought... I don't know. It was stupid."

She started to cry. Not big, out loud sobs, but the little private tears that come when no other reaction seems to fit. I scooted over and put my arm around her and she snuggled in.

"Shit," I said. "If you knew half the crap Niz and I did on sleepovers..."

She laughed a little and sat up straight, wiping her tears on her sleeve.

"I didn't hear from you all day," she said quietly. "So I started to think about it."

I gave her a squeeze and let her go.

51

"I didn't take it personally, Tobe, you know that. Of all the rotten things we've ever said to each other, last night was nothing."

"So you really have to work until midnight?" she asked.

"That's what they tell me. You saw the store—it was decimated."

"Tomorrow?"

"Noon to seven—extended hours for Christmas."

"That sucks."

"It's money. I'd like to get Sammy that CD he's been wanting."

"We should do something nice for him—how's he holding up?"

The truth is, I didn't really know, and I'll never forget the look in her eye when she asked me, as if I was the only one who *could* know; as if our whole lives depended on my answer and on the fact that Samuel Green was as unknown to me as anyone. What made it so bad is that I *should* have known. I was the one Sammy hung out with; the one he always called.

"I don't know..." I admitted.

"Jesus, Bells—it's okay. I just figured... you know..."

"I haven't asked him. I can't. I don't know how to."

That was the truth. I'd been avoiding it—not him, but *it*: the conversation. Sammy wasn't like Tobie or Niz—I'd grown up with them. I knew their silent ticks and moods, so I knew how to talk to them. But Sammy—to a large degree he was still that sullen kid we'd met in the back of the bus Freshman year: A big question mark everyone was afraid to approach. I looked at Tobie, a chill slipping over me as I re-

52

alized what could have happened to Sammy if he'd still been that sullen kid when his dad left. The part I'd missed when he came to me was that Sammy wanted to know someone still cared. He'd been dealing with his dad for years; what he needed to know yesterday was that he still belonged somewhere—and that's what friends do: They make you belong somewhere that you have no business being. There are no blood ties, no legally binding reasons, there's just a common will to be there for each other; to hang out; to help. That kind of bond isn't always there in families. Blood may be thicker than water, but sometimes I have to wonder if friendship is truly the tie that binds. After all, you don't marry family, you create a family by marrying a friend—and that's what we'd been doing all through high school: We'd been creating a family. So when Sammy's real family fell apart, he came to me—to us—to make sure everything else hadn't gone away with it.

"I think he's okay, actually. I don't think it was a big shock."

"He acts tough, though."

"I know. But he's got us. We had a good time tonight. We got to skate in the mall and Sammy took out half the tables in the food court with a wild powerslide."

"Wait... You *skated* in the mall?"

I could see her brow furrowing in a parental fashion and I was already consoling her before she even finished her thought: "I don't think acting out is going to help him cope—"

"Relax, mom. Niz pulled the kill switch earlier and tripped up Greg Wilson and his cronies. We were only trying to get away."

"*What*?" she asked dramatically. "Like, the damn escalator thing?"

I nodded.

"And you did it with Greg Wilson *on* it?"

Another nod.

"And he fell down the escalator?"

Nod.

"I can see why he says you're dead."

"Yeah."

Her smile faded and she breathed in heavily.

"Watch out for Sammy, though, okay?"

"We've got it covered. He's with Niz tonight, watching skate videos for tips."

"Sounds like he needs to learn to control his powerslide."

"What about you? You okay now?" I checked.

"Yeah. I just felt bad about last night. I didn't want you to think..." (She started to tear up again, but held it back.) "I didn't want you to think I went out drinking all the time, I guess. I don't like that image of myself in my head."

"You looked great last night, Tobie. Seriously."

She looked at me askance, her mouth gaping a bit.

"No! I don't mean drunk! I don't mean you looked good drunk or anything. I mean in that *dress*. You looked good in that dress. *That's* the image in *my* head."

"Thanks, Jack," she whispered and gave me a peck on the cheek.

"Look, I should get back," I said, trying not to blush. "I can clock in early and start sorting out the stock room—it's fucking *stuffed* back there."

"I'm going to go downstairs and find Jess."

We stood up and walked slowly back toward the toy store.

"I can't believe she's working two jobs," I said. "I mean... *why* is she working two jobs? I'd quit waitressing at that damn Big Boy."

"She did," Tobie considered—Big Boy was a sit-down burger-and-ice-cream joint, where you have a waitress. The place was always packed, especially on weekends, and Jess didn't do much but complain about it, and she was always exhausted when she got out of there. "But she worked both jobs when she gave her notice to Big Boy and she figured it wasn't that hard, and they didn't mind her un-quitting, so she went back. She still only gets five days a week between both of them."

"Yeah, but..."

"She's saving for college, Bells."

"Oh."

We looked at each other apologetically, both of us agreeing in our unwritten way to avoid talking about college. College meant leaving; college meant breaking up the family. It was best not to discuss it for now.

"No offense," she said, cutting away from me and heading down the wing where Jess's store was. "But I'm going to cut out here—toy stores and Christmas are my idea of Hell."

"Mine, too," I admitted, returning her wave and smile. "Mine, too."

Act 1

Strange Things Happen When You Throw

Hotdog Buns at Pretty Girls

January

"This one's for Sammy."

Niz glanced at me, then at Sammy. Sammy looked perplexed and a bit scared. He and I worked at a shitty little hotdog stand in the food court (after the toy store had dumped its seasonal employees). It was completely owner operated, and the owner was a white trash older woman—like fifty-five or something—who had married her daughter's boyfriend. Yeah, you read that right: her daughter's boyfriend, who was all of thirty. Better yet, her daughter was one of the assistant managers and her husband was the other. It made it pretty interesting when they were around, but also meant that most of the time none of them wanted to be there, leaving the stand to the likes of me and Sammy, unmonitored.

"What are you doing, Bells?" Sammy managed to croak, watching as I slid my hand into the bun warmer. Marcy—the owner/manager—hadn't been around all night and Niz was our first customer in about an hour. I was bored.

Without warning I whipped my hand back out of the bun warmer and let a bread projectile fly. It was a Hail Mary pass worthy of the Super Bowl, sailing in a perfect spiral right down the food court aisle until it collided with the back of the head of Donna Marie Meadows, her auburn locks shimmering at the disturbance. Donna Marie and her friend, Missy Anderson, froze. Sammy ran into the back room. Niz crossed his arms and leaned back against the service counter, appreciative of his front-row seat to the fallout.

"What the *hell*?" Donna Marie squawked back at me.

She had a curl to her lips that only girls can make, and only then for a brief window during the high school years. It was a curl that had derision, disgust, and glee worked into it, along with a healthy dose of pouting, whining, and laughter, depending on which way things went.

"I wanted to get your attention," I explained.

She emitted a teenage gasp and cocked her hip, the curl still on her lips.

"You could've *yelled* like a normal person."

Let me back up three steps: Donna Marie Meadows was the girl everyone in school noticed, and she liked being noticed. It was the only reason we were even having a conversation at that moment. Was she out of my league? Certainly. Well, she was out of my social circle, anyway. Her and Missy Anderson, both—they were the kind of girls guys like us couldn't stand but loved to watch. They wanted nothing to do with us either way, but they loved the attention.

"That's boring," I offered.

"So do you *want* something?"

She actually managed to work an eye roll into her reply. How high school girls learn to speak with and without words at the same time is beyond me. My mom never acted like that; I wondered if Donna Marie's did.

"Me? Personally? No. But my friend Sammy—he's the guy who ran into the back—needs a date to the Prom—"

Donna Marie emitted another disgusted girl gasp, turned on her heel, and walked off. Missy's gaze lingered on mine and she actually smirked before turning and huffing off after Donna Marie. Come on—it was hilarious. Some skate rat who worked at the hotdog stand in the mall winged a hotdog bun at Donna Marie Meadows' head and hit his target from fifty feet? It was impressive, if I may say so myself.

Sammy poked his head back around the doorway.

"Are they gone?"

"Yes, Samuel, I'm afraid they are. So I think that's a 'no'."

Niz began to applaud, slowly and sarcastically.

"Well done, Bells. You have ruined Sammy's prospects of *ever* finding a Prom date. And I thought we'd just decided that our mission was to do the exact opposite."

"With Donna Marie and her friends?" I chided. "Puh-leeze. Like any of us would *ever* have a chance with *any* of them. The kind of girls we hook up with will *love* this story."

Niz narrowed his eyes and Sammy finally plucked up the courage to come back and stand at the counter with me. Then he began to chuckle.

"Shit, Bells," he wheezed. "You just drilled the fucking Homecoming queen with a damn *bun*."

"Sorry it didn't work out," I replied.

By the time Monday rolled around, Donna Marie and her pal would've decided to nev-uh... ev-uh... speak... of this... again, and come lunch the event would be legendary in our circle.

61

I honestly don't know what had made me do it. It was a total whim and completely out of character. Okay, not completely, but mostly. I'm not normally that forward—I've never thrown a bun at a girl before or since—but I was bored and a little part of me truly wondered if the gamble would pay off. I sincerely wanted to make Sammy happy—he deserved it more than any of us—and I was willing to try anything, even flinging hotdog buns at hapless would-be Prom queens. That was really the only way I can explain doing it: I had seen a chance at his ultimate joy walking away from us, so I panicked to get her attention. I mean, if I got Sammy a date with Donna Marie...? It was an inspiring thought.

Niz and I had met Sammy Freshman year, sitting in the back of the school bus and looking like trouble—a defense mechanism for his shyness that perhaps the hotdog bun was also an attempt to overcome. There's no way Samuel Green would actively, consciously work toward his own happiness, you see—happiness had to come to him, exactly as it had when Niz spoke to him Freshman year. He wasn't the type who hung out with *any*one before us, which isn't to say we bestowed some great honor on the young man by lowering ourselves to talk to him or something, it's to say that Sammy may well have finished his high school career the same way he started it, if we hadn't talked to him: friendless, shy, and a little bit scary.

"That a Rodney Mullen deck?" Niz had wondered, reasonably awed.

Sammy's board was poking out of his backpack (I have a feeling the backpack was only used to transport the board). We'd seen him on the bus before, but we usually steered clear. He just put out that kind of vibe.

Sammy turned and glowered at us sullenly when Niz spoke, but he must've seen something in our eyes because his face broke out into a wide smile, and that changed everything. It made us realize that the clothes and the pissed-off stare were just a front. That, and he was used to being alone, I think. He probably didn't know how unapproachable he looked.

"Yeah! The Mutt!" he replied. "You guys ride?"

"Mostly I fall, but sure..." I said.

"I know what'cha mean..."

And there we were, three and a half years later, working side-by-side at a hotdog stand in the food court, throwing hotdog buns at girls in an effort to line up dates to the Prom. Well, I was throwing them to try and line up a date for Sammy, anyway. Niz was going with Jess—that was a given by now—but so far Sammy was flying solo. I always had Tobie as a mutual backup if no one else came along, but Sammy had no one. Kammy might go with him—she *had* gone to Homecoming with him in the Fall—but it would be an uneasy alliance. Not because they didn't like each other or didn't want to hang out, but because they both knew nothing *magical* was going to come of it. They'd only go with each other so neither of them had to go alone.

"But we *do* have to find you a date to Prom," I said with the utmost sincerity when Sammy and Niz had stopped forcing each other to laugh.

Sammy shook his head. "It's not even *February* yet, dude."

"Two more weeks and it will be," I pointed out.

63

"Sammy's right, Bells," Niz jumped in. "You're thinking about this *way* too soon."

"It's our *Senior* year, need I remind you? And that means it's our *Senior* Prom. We have to go with the right girl this time, gents, cuz this is the last one."

Neither of them responded but they were both looking at me, waiting for me to finish, so I added hesitantly, "And it takes *time* to find the right girl...?"

"I'll go with Kammy again—we had fun at Homecoming."

"*Fun*, Samuel?" I chided. "This is your *Senior Prom*. It's not supposed to be *fun*. It's supposed to be a night of enchantment and magic—"

"You know, I get enough of this crap from Jess," Niz cut in, waving us off as he began to walk away. "Come by when you get off work. And pick up a movie on the way."

We watched him wander off through the food court, no doubt working his way over to the record store where Jess worked. I poked one of the hotdogs on the rollers; it sizzled painfully and seemed to deflate in a melancholy way.

"This place is getting me down," I admitted.

"Don't worry, man—you've got Tobie," Sammy replied, misreading my statement.

I looked over at him and grinned. "No, I'm serious. I can't work here another day."

"You're on the schedule for tomorrow."

I sighed heavily.

"Let's get this shit cleaned up," I said. "I don't think we'll sell anything else tonight."

By nine o'clock we were already done breaking down

64

the place. As suspected, we hadn't had a customer since Niz left forty minutes earlier, and he hardly counted.

"We should just stay here and see a movie," Sammy suggested as he wheeled one of the thirty-gallon trashcans toward the back door. He pointed vaguely in the direction of the second-run cinema at the end of the food court.

"What's showing?" I wondered, wheeling the other trashcan up behind him. Apparently no one else took out the trash. "I think we already saw everything."

Sammy turned the knob and threw the door open, kicking a wedge under it in one deft motion. Taking out the trash was actually fun, in a way. The back hall of the mall—the delivery and employee hallway—was like a vibrant underbelly. Most all of the doors were flung open and as you walked down the hall you ran into all the other food-service people and started cutting deals for leftovers. Everybody wanted the frozen Coke from our place, but Marcy kept a close eye on that—it was certainly her best seller and she was the only stand that had it.

"So what are we gonna watch at Niz's?" Sammy asked.

"You know, they said there's a ghost boy in *Three Men and a Baby*?"

"Fuck that, Bells," he replied seriously. "I'm not sitting through that shit on a Saturday night to watch a five-second whiff of mist that may or may not be a ghost."

By this time we'd reached the neighboring stand—a pizza joint—and the dishwasher stuck his head out as we passed.

"Sammy! M'man!"

"Heya, John, what's up?"

65

"Hey, you guys wanna party later?" John asked. "I can hook you up."

Sammy glanced at me with an agreeable shrug but I discreetly shook my head and he discreetly nodded.

"Nah, s'alright—we're getting the hell outta here."

"Alright—your choice," John said apologetically, slinging a towel over his shoulder. "Can I get a chili dog anyway?"

"You still got that Who tape?" I checked. The question sort of threw him, but he nodded. "Get me 'Behind Blue Eyes' for when we get back and I'll make you a chili dog."

"Cool. Say, you want anything? Food, I mean..."

"I ate, man," Sammy said and I nodded in agreement. John shrugged *fair 'nuff* then turned and went back over to the sink to finish his dishes.

People always assumed Sammy wanted to party—and he did, more often than the rest of us—but he usually wanted to hang out with us instead. Not that we were angels, we just didn't find much of our trouble in the pot-and-huffer crowd. We accidentally backed into being straight-edge because of the trouble we *did* get into: running from cops in the middle of the night with skateboards under our arms. It's hard to run effectively if you're high. It's also hard to land a trick when you're stoned. Well, for some people it isn't, but for us it only added another layer of complexity, and frankly, we weren't up to the challenge: getting anything above a six-inch ollie kept us busy enough. So did we keep Sammy off drugs because he hung out with us and we didn't get into them? Maybe. I think Sammy's whole life had been gearing up for a drug problem—we just managed to hold it off through high school by concentrating on other mischief. I think I even knew that back then, that he could only hold his head up for so long before he gave up and gave in and looked for solace in the same places so many Americans who feel sorry for themselves do. That's why I wanted so badly to give him a win for Prom, like it would be enough to charge up his batteries and keep him straight after we graduated and weren't hanging out as much any more.

It almost worked, too.

"No love for John?" I wondered as I punched the 2 in the freight elevator. I guess the mall was built into a hillside, because you had to go up from the lower-level food court to dump the trash.

"I don't wanna talk about it right now," he mumbled. There was nothing mean or angry in his voice, like I was prying or anything. In fact, he grinned over at me. "I wanna think about the look on Donna Marie's face..."

"Man, you play this right, she just might go out with you."

"Pfah!" he spat incredulously.

"I'm serious, Sammy. She's curious now. She'll tell herself she just wants to make sure you really are as big a loser as she thinks, but look at it this way: She'll still be thinking about you."

"Bells, you've been to every damn dance with Tobie—"

"Except Sophomore year."

"Okay, but I'm not sure you're the best guy to be offering me tips on hooking up with the Prom queen."

The elevator shuddered to a halt and Sammy heaved open the wire-cage door. I pushed my bin out and he followed me.

"She's not actually Prom queen yet," I pointed out. "Since we're arguing semantics."

"Look, let's say your little plan works, Bells. Let's say you've piqued her interest. For how long? A week? Two weeks? And how far away is Prom?"

"King of Hearts," I said with stunned realization. "It has to be *her* idea. That's *it*!"

Sammy stopped short and forced me to turn back to him.

"I don't like that tone of voice, Bells," he said slowly. "It's the same tone you get when you talk about wiring bottle rockets together into a multi-stage explosive."

"That worked, though, Sammy, and so will this."

He sighed heavily, but his eyes were sparkling. No one could resist a good scheme, not when me and Niz were involved.

"What'll work?"

I stepped back over to him, selling my idea: "You might be right. You ask her to Prom, she'll say no, even if she really wants to go with you, she'll still say no. Why? Because it's not her idea. One thing you can count on with chicks like her is, if it's not their idea and it might make them look bad, then they won't do it. But if it *is* their idea, then no one can argue with them."

"I feel like there should be a logical conclusion in there," he replied coolly.

"There *is*, Samuel! Before you can ask her to Prom, you have to get *her* to ask *you* to the King of Hearts dance!"

"Do girls actually follow the rules and ask the guys to that dance?"

"I don't know... Tobie always asked me."

"Bells, your relationship with Tobie doesn't count at all."

"Fine! But you see my point."

He thought about it for a second then nodded ever so slightly. "Sure, I guess."

"So that means we have to strike while the iron is hot."

"I'll call her tonight—"

"Don't be an ass, Sammy. This is going to take careful planning."

He shook his head dismally but didn't disagree.

É

The worst sound in the world is that of the first bell on Monday morning after a weekend away from school. Scratch that. The worst sound is the *third* bell, because that meant class was starting. With the first bell, you still had a chance to get away, which is exactly what I felt like doing the Monday after the bun incident. As the first bell rang over our heads I felt a flight-or-fight response welling up in me because Sammy's face paled and his eyes widened and he muttered an "Oh" over my shoulder as he shut his locker. I turned and was prepared to swing a fist or run, but we were cornered.

"I know who you are now," Donna Marie stated unequivocally, filling up my field of vision.

She was looking at Sammy and only offered me a glance long enough to be a derisive smirk before stepping around me to confront Sammy. Missy Anderson was behind her, staring at me, so I tried to smile politely. I don't know that I've ever honestly seen the fabled "come hither" eyes directed at me, but whatever look she returned was close to what I imagine it to be.

"Me?" Sammy squeaked.

"You're the guy who punched out Greg Wilson at the Wharf before Christmas."

"*When*?"

"Not smooth," I whispered to him.

Donna Marie cut me down with another look and I went back to avoiding eye contact with her friend, which was tough, because she was really cute. Well, mostly cute. She was okay, but the fact that she was smiling at me and batting her eyes made her eminently attractive.

"I didn't recognize you with your haircut," Donna Marie was saying—carrying on a conversation with Mr. Samuel Green, dare I say.

"Until Saturday night," she added, with another look at me, but it was a touch softer this time.

"Oh," Sammy managed to push out of his gaping mouth. "Yeah. The bun."

He fidgeted with his hair a second and smiled maniacally.

"That was pretty cool, standing up for your friend at the Wharf," she continued. "He'd been hitting on every girl there all night, after Tobie told him to leave her alone."

"Good for Tobie!" I announced, then went back into quiet mode.

"You're Jack," Missy suddenly blurted. "I sit by Tobie in

physics. She talks about you all the time."

"Ah, yeah," I said, trying to sound casual. "We're really good friends. We met in sixth grade."

"Really?" she asked, way more amazed than she deserved to be.

"*Anyway*," Donna Marie stressed for her friend's benefit. "Maybe we'll see you around sometime? Maybe at the mall or something? We usually go and hang out after school, you know? Get an Icee?"

"Sure," Sammy agreed. "We go there, too. I mean, we *work* there, but we hang out sometimes, too. With me and Jack and Niz, and Jolly comes every now and again—"

"Okay," Donna Marie said, stopping him with a super sweet smile. "Then maybe we'll see you there later this afternoon?"

"You, too, Jack," Missy said as she followed Donna Marie away down the hall.

"What the hell just happened?" Sammy checked.

"The bun *worked*, my friend!" I exclaimed. "She *noticed* you! You do realize that the hardest part about dating a girl is getting her to notice you in the first damn place, right?"

"I take it back," Sammy breathed. "Maybe your relationship with Tobie *has* given you an edge."

I shook my head. "Nah. I never threw a bun at Tobie."

"But she *noticed* me," Sammy breathed. "Donna Marie Meadows just *talked* to me."

"And what was with her friend?" I wondered. "She was weird. Kinda cute, though. Sammy? Sammy, what's wrong?"

He looked really pale, maybe even short of breath. I looked around, but Donna Marie was nowhere to be seen.

71

"We're going there after school, aren't we?"

"The mall? Of *course* we are, Samuel! Donna Marie basically asked you out on a *date*, man! We're not going to let that slide."

"Second bell, gentlemen!" Mr. Miller, our math teacher, said as he hurried past.

I took his cue and left Sammy standing there, gaping, before he could argue with me.

"What the hell are we doing, Bells?" Sammy asked.

We were sitting in the food court at the mall after school. He was jiggling his knee nervously, rattling the whole table. I pointedly reached out and grabbed our frozen Cokes before they wobbled off the table and smacked onto the floor.

"We are at the mall, Samuel," I said slowly, grinning at him. "And who knows *who* we'll run into?"

"Greg Wilson?" he guessed, only half joking.

"Or a pretty girl?"

Sammy shook his head. "I can't believe you talked me into this. You said it yourself: Donna Marie Meadows doesn't hang out with guys like us."

"Sammy, I don't know what's going on—truthfully. Maybe you're right. Maybe this is some long, twisted joke cooked up by Greg to get back at us. But isn't it worth it to find out? How bad could it really be to satisfy your curiosity?"

Truth be told, I hadn't thought of the date being an elaborate trap concocted by Greg Wilson until Sammy had blurted it out in the car on the way over, and he got me thinking on it again as we waited. It did make a certain amount of sense. After the escalator incident, Greg had laid low. I really don't think he wanted a fight—there had been plenty of opportunities for that—but I also didn't think he'd given up. With the Christmas break, we'd not had much chance to run into him, and he wasn't the type of guy to risk being expelled—or risk losing a fight, anyway. Sure, he'd given us the stink-eye in the halls and maybe yelled a few lame insults, but that had been all. Then us talking to Donna Marie that morning had put us on his radar again—or we *had* been back on his radar and the Donna Marie thing had been part of his plan. I mulled it over in my head, searching for the obvious earmarks of a master plan; a scheme; a lark.

"D'ya think it's true?" Sammy asked in a dramatic whisper, mistaking my silence for fear as I reconsidered the conversation. "What Jolly said? D'ya think Greg's going to the dance with Donna Marie? That this is all a set up?"

"As *if*," an amazing caricature of Donna Marie said as a large purse plopped down on the floor beside Sammy. "Is *that* what he said?"

"Donna Marie!" Sammy squeaked. She basically ignored him and sat down. "How long were you there?"

"Just got here."

She turned and considered me distastefully and added, "I guess you're Jack?"

"Sure," I agreed.

I admit it, I was secretly as smitten as Sammy. These

73

girls were popular for a reason. It also occurred to me that what made them popular wasn't talking to the likes of us at the mall.

"Missy here can't shut up about you," Donna Marie said with a quizzical grin.

"Shut *up*!" Missy gasped at her. Then to me: "It's not true. I just think it was amazing that you managed to hit Donna with that b—"

"So!" Donna Marie cut in. "Frozen Cokes? We like Icees better."

I looked at Missy. She was practically batting her eyelashes at me again, and that's when it struck me what was really going on here. Missy was in class with Tobie. Tobie talked about me in class because we were always hanging out. Missy started to think this Jack guy sounded kinda neat. Then this Jack guy wings a hotdog bun at the Homecoming queen that she's been second fiddle to all her teen life, and that just about takes the cake. She has to meet him. She tells Donna Marie that in order to overcome the hotdog bun incident she has to *own* it, convincing her to hang out with Sammy long enough to save her valuable reputation, to make it seem like a joke between friends. Donna Marie undoubtedly saw what was really going on, but the plan made a certain amount of sense. Then when she got to school and someone asked her about the hotdog bun, she *really* decided to own it.

I felt sick. Donna Marie was doing for her friend what I was doing for Sammy: Helping her get a date, even if it meant hanging out with someone I didn't personally care for.

Or maybe, just maybe, she *was* helping Greg Wilson and not even Missy knew it.

Earlier at lunch, in school, Jolly had had two things to share with us: 1) High fives on the bun incident (despite all forecasts, Donna Marie had been telling the story herself—which was very suspicious now, I thought) and 2) a warning that Greg Wilson was gunning for Sammy again.

"Jolly" Roger Brimley was our liaison to the popular crowd. He was on the soccer team first and foremost, but he was also the kicker on the football team. The year before, he'd booted a game-winning field goal at the Homecoming game, so he was set with the guys who would otherwise have given him trouble, and because he sometimes skated with us, that respite extended to us, at least nominally. Unless we pissed one of them off.

"So what's new?" Sammy had wondered with a shrug at lunch. "Greg's been gunning for us for a month."

"Yeah, but this time it's personal," Jolly explained. "Rick saw you chatting with Donna Marie and told Greg. See, by all accounts, Donna Marie is going to ask Greg to King of Hearts."

That's what he'd said—that's exactly what Jolly had told us.

"Bullshit," I'd offered then, too hyped up thinking my plan had worked to see the fact that we were ourselves potentially being plotted against. "She was just telling Sammy that Greg was bad news—"

"Not exactly," Sammy cut in. "Believe me, I heard every word. She said Greg had been hitting on a ton of girls that night and that she thought it was cool I stood up for my friends. She never said she thought Greg did anything wrong."

"Look," Jolly said. "I just came by to let you know what I heard. If Donna Marie's going around telling everyone that you threw a bun at her, Jack, and that now she remembers when she'd seen you before, Sammy... Well, that's not a story Greg wants repeated. He's going to make trouble."

Enter Jess, slamming her books down on the table.

"Who's making trouble?"

I casually picked up my juice box, which had toppled in the tablequake.

"Greg Wilson," Jolly explained. He looked at Jess as if she could somehow stop him.

Jess was the one who always thought straight and got good grades—she was destined to either be a CSI detective or a criminal mastermind. She could figure out what was going down real quick, and she could scheme like a fiend. She routinely clobbered me and Tobie at chess, but what it really meant is that we all looked to her for the Answer (capital "A"). She kept us in line—or, more accurately, she got us out of the trouble we often backed ourselves into. At least that's how I saw it: she offered lasting solutions that paired well with my knee-jerk responses that stemmed the bleeding long enough for us to get her involved. The others often seemed afraid to ask Jess for help, I think because of the shame in-volved: We all called her Mom because even though we knew she could get us out of trouble, she wasn't above mak-ing us feel dumb for getting into trouble in the first place. Not that she was judgmental, she just didn't hide it when things annoyed her.

"Ah, yes. The Groper." Jess nodded. "I told Tobie he was trouble."

"How could you have possibly known that?" Sammy wondered. "He was a real nice guy at first. We all loved him."

"I never did," she replied simply, popping a grape into her mouth. "Seemed like an act. I wish I hadn't been sick that night. None of this would ever have happened."

No one said anything about that because we all knew it was true. If Jess had been with Tobie she'd've got her out of there the second they saw Greg hitting on another girl. Not that Kammy was a bad friend, but like I said, Jess saw things the rest of us missed and seemed to always know how things were going to end up.

"So what should I do?" Sammy asked.

He looked over at me with panic in his eyes. My plans were about to come unraveled in the face of sanity: Jess would come up with a solid solution, laying waste to the triage I'd done to calm Sammy down and—I might add—get him a date.

"What d'ya mean?" Jess wondered.

She took a bite of her sandwich then helped herself to the rest of my juice box.

"I'm supposed to meet Donna Marie at the mall after school."

"Reeeally?" she cooed suspiciously.

"But now apparently Greg has the hots for her—"

"Greg has the hots for any girl without a penis," Jess stated simply.

"So?"

I held my breath. The next words to come out of Jess's mouth would decide Sammy's fate. If Jess said to avoid Greg and the whole confrontation, then the mall trip, the dance, and Prom with Donna Marie were all shot to hell. No amount of conniving on my part could counteract the level-headed decision of Jessica Miller.

"So what?" she shrugged. "If you want to go to the mall with Donna Marie, you go to the damn mall."

And that's just what we'd done, and that's exactly where we were. I took a glance around to see if I could spot Greg and his cronies hiding behind the fake plants dotted throughout the food court, waiting only for the signal to pounce, but if they were hiding they were hiding very well.

"I've seen you skating," Missy said to me.

She smiled again and started twirling her hair. It was like a God damn teen movie or something.

"Yeah? Where at?"

So now we had me pretending to be interested in Missy so Sammy could try and hook up with Donna Marie, meanwhile Donna Marie was pretending to be interested in Sammy so Missy could hook up with *me*. Or so she could lure us into Greg Wilson's trap. Or both.

"There's a curb right by my house. I see skaters there all the time."

"You live on Carpenter?"

Except Donna Marie was honestly laughing. Sammy was like that. He was quiet and he looked mean, but he was hilarious when he got going. Like a talk show host on a great night, but that was him all the time. He could make any conversation entertaining, and I think Donna Marie was falling for it.

"Yeah. Right across the street. You're pretty good."

"Nah. I pretty much stink. But it's fun to try."

"You ever get arrested?"

I think she wanted the answer to be yes. Maybe she was trying to get back at her parents. Maybe she didn't know that I wasn't as cool as she thought I was. I was in the damn drama club, for God's sake. Didn't that make me anathema to the popular set, right off the bat?

"Nah. We always outrun the cops."

(A half truth—we hid until they gave up looking.)

"I couldn't even stand on one of those things."

"It's not that hard. I'll teach you some time."

"Really?"

(Wide eyes; big smile.)

What was I doing? She was cute, I'll be honest. I'd been dismissive before. She had a pert little nose and naturally dark skin. Her hair was short, but still long enough to put too much hairspray in. But she wasn't my type. Was she? And who *was* my type, then? Tobie? Jess? Ally McShay from drama club?

"If you want. Next time we're over there, come out and see me. I'll show you how to ride."

Actually, yes. Ally McShay was more my type. She was weird, but she was sincere. Wait. No she wasn't. She lied about having plans all the time when I tried to hang out with her. Did that make her insincere or insecure? Or did it mean that she didn't *want* to hang out with me?

"That'd be *totally* awesome!"

And why had Missy done it this way? Why not invite *me* to the mall instead of having her *friend* invite *Sammy*? This *was* all a ruse to get back at us, for Greg and for the bun! I looked over at Sammy and Donna Marie. She really did seem to be having fun. Maybe I'd got this all wrong. Like, totally and completely wrong. Maybe they both actually liked us.

"Maybe we'll go out there later and skate, eh, Sammy?"

"What?" he snapped at me.

"The curb over on Carpenter? Turns out Missy lives right across the street."

I hadn't intended to kill their conversation. We all looked at each other awkwardly for a second, then glanced off around the mall.

"Maybe we should take them to a movie first, before we take them skating?" Sammy finally said. I think if he'd thought about the fact that he was talking out loud, not privately in his head or just to me, he might not have said it. I could tell there was panic flickering behind his eyes as he realized what he'd insinuated, but he covered it well.

Donna Marie looked at me, then at Missy, then at Sammy, then she smiled quite honestly, as if pleasantly surprised.

"Okay," she said, locking her eyes on Sammy. "It's a date."

It's amazing how fragile those moments are when a first date is set. You have to let it sink in. You have to wordlessly repeat the question to each other with your eyes, with long glances and fey look-aways. Sammy and Donna Marie were doing exactly that, but for my part, I tried not to look at

Missy, not even a little bit. Well, maybe a *little* bit (pert nose), just for a second, just so she didn't think I was a jerk (dark skin, dark eyes). When our eyes met I saw defeat in them.

"You wanna double?" she asked quietly. "I mean, it's okay if you don't, I just thought... Are you seeing *Tobie*?" she suddenly realized, her face paling. "Oh... my... G—"

"No! No, it's okay. Tobie and I are just friends."

"But you were there! You got her out of the Wharf that night!"

I leaned in to her as if imparting some great secret, and she leaned in to me, too. She smelled great—some kind of perfume only young girls can pull off, but they pull it off with gusto.

"Was that night such a big deal?" I asked her. "It didn't seem like such a big deal."

"It was a big deal," she whispered back.

"Why?"

"Guys don't go to the Wharf to *rescue* girls," she said dramatically.

I winced. Could that possibly be true or was this all some teen drama she'd concocted to make her nights dancing at the Wharf seem more edgy? Is *that* what this was? Were Sammy and I "dangerous" because we rode skateboards and listened to the Dead Kennedys and 7Seconds and the Descendents?

"I didn't rescue her," I corrected. "Tobie can take care of herself. She just needed a ride home."

"Well," Missy decided, sitting back and talking in a normal voice. "I need an Icee. That's what we came here for, right Donna?"

81

"Jack and I'll get 'em," Sammy said, jumping up. "What flavors?"

"Blue," they replied in unison.

Sammy was over the moon. Any trepidation he'd been exhibiting before was long gone.

"This is going *great*," he said as we waited for the Icees. "I thought you'd ruined my chances of ever dating anyone again, and now I have a date with Donna fucking Marie. You could be nicer, though."

"Nicer?"

"To Missy. What did you say to her?"

"Nothing! We were talking about that night at the Wharf."

"So she asks you out and you ask her about that night at the Wharf?" he summarized.

I hadn't thought of it that way. I was still reeling from the whole thing myself.

"Go with us, okay?" Sammy pleaded. "Missy's cute, right?"

"Sure, she's cute. I don't know... What do I have to talk about with her?"

"Dude, Donna Marie and I hit it off. At first, I didn't even think she wanted to be here. I suddenly thought it was all about Missy meeting *you*. Then I thought it was all a set up again. Then we just started chatting. Turns out we both count the Monkees as a guilty pleasure."

"Samuel... The Monkees?"

"Asshole," he said, grabbing the Icees. "Just give it a shot, okay? Maybe they're just girls."

Maybe Sammy was right. Maybe it wasn't them who

were hung up on image and having the right friends, maybe it was *me*. Maybe *I* was the one trying to act too cool. And Sammy had seen it, too: Missy liked me. Maybe even to the point of setting this all up, like I'd thought. But not for Greg Wilson; not to help avenge her friends. And maybe that's why Sammy and Donna Marie had hit it off: They found that one tiny spark of conversation to get over each other; that shared communal joy. And Donna Marie, not having come to mall expecting anything, had suddenly found a friend. It's not hard to exceed low expectations, but it still makes you forget how little you'd expected when it turns out so well. Like how a movie you thought would suck, that's actually pretty good, always seems so much better than it really is, just because you'd expected so little to begin with and ended up with so much more.

"So, are you coming with us to the movie?" Donna Marie asked me quite pointedly as I handed Missy an Icee. She wasn't pretending to be the untouchable bitch now, she was protecting her friend.

"Yeah," I said honestly and met Missy's eyes to make it count. "It's a date."

"So, when?" Donna Marie wondered. "I don't want to wait until the weekend. I'm *so bored* with this winter! I *need* to get out of my *house*!"

"I'm off Wednesday," Sammy offered.

"Me, too," Missy said, which did honestly shock me. I really didn't think she'd have a job in the first place. Sammy was right, I was an asshole. I'd come into this completely suspicious and judgmental, and I was carrying right on with it.

"Works for me," I agreed. "What are the chances we'd all have off?"

"It's fate," Missy said, giving me the cutest damn dare-ya-to-argue smile I've ever seen.

"Fate," I mused. "Where do you work?"

"The Gap."

"Makes sense. Ever go to the Gap outlet by the airport?"

"You shop at the *Gap*?"

"Well, the outlet. The prices are great. This right here is a Gap shirt," I pointed out, yanking on the collar. "Five bucks."

"No!"

"Schya!"

It wasn't exactly the Monkees, but at least we had something.

"Okay, folks, let's get this read-through underway!"

That was Mr. K—Mr. Karkowski, the drama teacher. He lived for this shit, you could just tell, and his sustained excitement made us want to work that much harder, not for ourselves, but so we didn't screw it up for him.

"We've got six weeks until opening night, so let's shake off that Christmas vacation and get to work!"

The read-throughs at drama club were never just read-throughs. Mr. K always started blocking the play and calling out lighting ideas the second the first line was uttered.

We had what they called the Little Theatre (yes, with an "re") to perform our plays in: Three classrooms in a forgotten wing of the school that ran behind the gym, which they gutted into one big, open space. The room on one end was turned into the backstage, the middle room was the stage, and the last room was seating for about sixty people. On the plus side, we always played to a full house. It was well worn, cramped, and hot, but it was our space and we loved it. We'd never pull the crowds the football team garnered—or the attention or accolades—but we had fun working on those plays, and Mr. K knew exactly how to make sure everyone felt involved and fully invested in the drama club, not just the talent on stage.

"And this is a drama, folks, so let's get serious, eh?"

Niz was on stage, of course. Sammy worked the lights and—occasionally—sound effects. Sometimes Tobie took a bit part, sometimes she just did costumes and tickets. It was always the same, every play through high school. Niz and I had joined drama club back in eighth grade, and we sucked Sammy and Tobie in with us, sort of. Jess came to all the performances and parties and helped build the sets, but that's as close as we ever got her to joining. Why drama? Couldn't say. I'd bet it was Niz's idea.

Ally McShay and I scooted to the back row of the seating, up by the sound booth door (where Sammy sat controlling the lights). There wasn't much for us to do yet—we were both on props crew again, and with no scenes to change and no costumes, there were no props to prep—but we showed up anyway. Like I said, Mr. K had that effect on you.

85

Ally had brown hair, mostly, with bright colored streaks that framed her face, usually hot pink or cherry red or electric blue. Her lipstick always matched the streaks, too, and her eyes always pierced you from black circles of mascara and eyeliner. The fashion queens at school called her a freak because they weren't brave enough to try anything so original themselves. More than that, they weren't pretty enough to pull it off as well as she did.

"I heard you made up a new trick," Ally said to me in a low voice as we plopped into our seats.

"Not entirely," I admitted. "I started to fall, tripped, somehow kicked my board end-over-end, but *longways*, and landed back on it. I couldn't do it again. Ever."

Ally had actually skated with us once or twice. She wasn't bad—in fact, she was by far the best of us—but we'd given up inviting her to come along on a regular basis because she never took us up on it. Usually she showed up randomly wherever we were, invited or not, and hung out with us for a while. If I hadn't seen her in school every day she would've been just another skater who I saw from time to time at various spots.

She held my eyes for an uncomfortably long time and smiled.

"So how's the book coming?" I asked, simply to get her to break the stare.

"Oh," she said, ducking her eyes and turning away, covering her face with her hair. She hadn't expected me to ask, despite having told everyone she was a writing a novel. "You know... It's tough. What with homework... and plays."

She turned back and smiled.

"What's it about again?"

She shook her head slowly. "The Civil War."

"Really?" I was genuinely shocked. "You usually tell me I have to wait until it's done to find out."

"It's about a girl in the Civil War. Her dad goes off to fight for the Confederacy, but her boyfriend is fighting for the Union."

"Wow."

"Lights!" Mr. K suddenly called up. "That's where you turn on the full bank, Sammy!"

Sammy responded by turning on the lights and Mr. K smiled broadly and gave him a thumbs up, so Sammy turned them back off.

"Are you still writing, Jack?" she asked.

"Sure, I guess. Just some horror stories."

"I'd like to read them."

I smirked at her. "Do I get to read your book so far?"

"No," she giggled.

I let her divert the conversation and we talked about music instead. It was safe ground and something we definitely had in common. We both listened to the local college radio station religiously and made mix tapes for each other from time to time. She was nerdy and cool and I knew most people made fun of her, but she took it well. People like her amazed me. She was absolutely self aware and knew that people made fun of her behind her back, yet she was just as absolutely unconcerned by it all. Kammy said she dressed like she was still in middle school, and maybe she did ("Bangles—lots of bracelets and bangles," Kammy once explained), but I certainly wasn't one to talk.

Me and Sammy and Niz, we dressed like our clothes fell off the back of a truck—a garbage truck. My pants were too big, not by design but because the thrift store didn't have my size and I really wanted some of those blue work pants. This one skater we called the Toad had told me they were tougher than jeans, which I only realized later was a back-handed way of telling me that I fell and ripped my pants a lot, which I did. With Ally, though, it was a choice—she actually wanted to dress the way she did, and she took care to make sure she had created whatever image it was she was going for. I got that—Tobie was a pretty careful dresser, too—but to carefully dress in what you knew was a massively unpopular way is something I couldn't get my head around. I went thrifting for pants, wore concert t-shirts or outlet-store shirts, and wore my dad's hand-me-down flannel shirts instead of a windbreaker—not exactly the height of fashion, but I didn't exactly sit and plan it either, and it allowed me to float under the radar. Ally stood out like a beacon in the halls, her color-tinged hair like a damn flashing light that glowed "weirdo weirdo weirdo."

It really shouldn't have mattered to me, and it didn't when it came to Jess, who dressed in a similarly outlandish way (sans bangles and hair dye, and more often in jeans). It's just a weird damn thing. I guess I didn't like to draw attention to myself if I could help it, and while Jess could hide in the corner if she really wanted to, Ally couldn't. Ally wanted the attention and she wasn't bashful about grabbing for it—except when it came to the plays, then she wanted to be backstage in the shadows with me. I reckon it was because she didn't want to have to put on a costume, which is ironic.

But her personality quirks gave her that edge and made her infinitely cooler than everyone else.

She looked down at her lap and twiddled her skirt ruffles —today she was in a black skirt and mismatched stockings— and I could tell she was nervous. I felt my heart starting to pound, suddenly certain she was going to ask me to the King of Hearts dance, our school's Sadie Hawkins affair. Her bangles clinked softly as she worked the fabric with her fingertips. I was already planning how to tell Missy that for as much fun as our date had been, there wouldn't be any others.

"I have a lizard," Ally finally said.

"What?"

I admit to a heavy dose of confusion.

"A lizard. My dad finally got me a lizard. I've always wanted one."

What do you say to that? Seriously? When you'd been expecting...?

"That's cool," I said.

"Sammy! Jack! Ally! Guys—come on down here a second!" Mr. K called up. I was practically at his side before the words had stopped stirring the air, terrified she'd read my mind and know what I'd been thinking.

"We're going to have to do some pretty technical blocking to make this work," he explained. "Jack, you and Ally will actually be changing the set while the scene is still going on. Sammy, that means you'll have to make sure the stage is light and dark in the right places. Now we've got tight quarters here—do you think we can pull it off?"

"Sure we can," Sammy said for us.

"Okay then..."

And off he went, dramatically showing us where everyone would start and end up, and revealing his glorious vi-
sions for the props and lighting. I liked watching him work it
out. We all did. The man could probably have done all of our
plays as one-man shows and pulled it off better than we ever
did, but if our acting or lack of professionalism ever made
him cringe, he never let on.

Eventually, they started reading their lines, and that
meant Ally and I had nothing to do, so we headed backstage
and started to learn to listen for our set-change cues. Mr. K
decided he wanted to run through the monologues especially
("They're the *heart* of this play, kids!") so we knew we had a
lot of time before we'd be needed for anything.

"You going to the dance with Tobie?" Ally asked apropos of nothing as we slumped down on the couch backstage.

"King of Hearts?"

She nodded.

"I don't know. Not yet, anyway."

"You guys always go to the dances."

"Yeah," I agreed. "Seems that way, but we don't exactly
plan it."

"Oh..."

I thought she was going to say something else, maybe
about Missy or something, or maybe she *was* going to come
out and ask me to go with her, but she just scooted around
and lay back, pushing her feet behind me with exaggerated
vehemence. I chuckled and moved over, lying down on the
other end of the couch.

The ceiling backstage in the Little Theatre was weird.
For some reason they'd taken out the normal drop-ceiling

tiles and replaced them with cheap wall paneling, I assume for its superior acoustics or something, so it was a crappy wood-grain finish. If you stared at it hard enough, you could almost kid yourself that you were standing up, staring at the wall, instead of lying down on a ratty couch waiting for the World's Longest Monologues to be done onstage so you could change the sets. To say the monologues were long is actually an understatement. In fact, if you told me they were *still* going on today, and had been going on since I last set foot in the Little Theatre all those years ago, I'd believe you.

"Why is this scene so *long*?" Ally asked in a pleading tone.

She had her feet tucked into the back of the couch, her legs cricked and leaning over mine. I had my feet crossed, somewhere below her shoulder level.

"It looks good on an actor's resume to say they've done it."

"Seriously?"

"It's the *heart* of the play, kids...?" I questioned.

She chuckled.

"I'm going to say the playwright didn't have a clue how long he was waffling on because he never stopped and read back out loud what he'd written. So he kept going and going and going and going and go—hey!"

She whacked my legs and giggled.

We lay there silently for a few seconds. My heart rate had increased when she giggled—I always liked to hear her giggle—and I started to think again that maybe, just maybe, I should ask her out. I'd been thinking it all year, but couldn't bring myself to do it, even though she *had* called me that once, back

91

in December. She never called me back, though, and I hadn't brought it up. She constantly snubbed Jess, and the few times I had dared to half-ask her out—to go skating with me and Sammy and Niz—she'd had something else to do. I was starting to think it was just an excuse, but it honestly hadn't felt like it. She had a lot of family in town and always seemed to be with them. Plus, you could tell later that she wasn't lying, she really had done other things. Family things.

Of course, you never know.

"Ally?"

"Yeah?"

Ally was a punk-rock girl and more genuine than the rest of us. Still, I had to tread lightly. Deep down she was still just a girl, after all, and girls spook easily, I've learned.

"D'ya wanna go see a movie some time?"

A long pause. Not a good sign. Long pauses meant there was thinking, and if she was thinking, it meant she was trying to deliver her rejection softly. There was a soft rustle of fabric (I think she shrugged). I looked down the couch at her. She was preoccupied, picking at a frayed thread that had come loose from the cushion.

"Sure," she finally said.

I looked back up at the ceiling. It was suddenly very hard to breath and my legs were tingling.

"When?"

"Friday," I snapped, then rephrased it to a questioning, "Friday?"

"Can't. My dad wants the whole family to go to this lame restaurant where you eat with your hands or something —sounds *ridiculous*."

"Saturday?"

I was on a roll now. I looked back down the couch at her and she was looking at me, an odd smile on her face. She looked thrilled but somehow sad all at the same time. It confused me. For a second I thought she was about to cry.

"Is the whole gang going?" she asked softly.

I started to shake my head, then stopped. What the hell was the right answer?

"No," I finally managed to choke out.

She smiled that odd smile again then sighed heavily and looked up at the ceiling. I watched her watching the paneling. She seemed to be doing math or something, the way her brow furrowed and her eyes got an intense stare in them.

"I *really* can't," she finally whispered.

If she hadn't looked so crestfallen when she smiled at me again, I would've felt rejected. So did that mean she wanted to go, but only if the whole gang went? And why "*really* can't"? Why the stressed word? Was it an excuse or did she have something else to do, with her family or something? I mean, it wasn't exactly a "no" and she stressed the "really" and she put her hand on my calf, as if to reassure me. Then she changed the subject.

"Who's your favorite rock star?" she asked.

She held my gaze. She must have seen the confusion in my expression. She patted my leg. I felt like if I pressed her on it, she'd either tell me what she was really thinking... or she'd get up and leave rather than be put on the spot.

"Robert Smith," I answered.

"From the Cure? He's not a rock star."

"What does *that* mean?"

93

And like that, the whole thing had blown over. Ally giggled, giving me a playful pinch.

"His songs are too sappy to be rock."

"*Sappy*?" I protested. "Have you heard *Pornography*? How's that *sappy*?"

She giggled again, bringing her knees up a little.

"Okay, then," I asked defiantly. "Who's *your* favorite rock star?"

"Joan Jett," she replied without hesitation.

What could I say? I sighed heavily. She was right: if rock was power, then in a fair fight, Joan Jett would kick Robert Smith's ass to hell and back.

"So rock stars have to be tough?" I wondered.

"Sure."

"What about Freddie Mercury? Or friggin' Gary Glitter? Or David Bowie?"

"I don't know," she agreed.

I could tell by her tone she was only joking around. I glanced down at her again and realized with dawning irony that she was wearing a Cure t-shirt. I sat up and gaped at her, pointing at her shirt. She laughed a full, throaty laugh and squirmed away from me as best she could. I decided to add insult to injury and dug my fingertip into her side. She squealed and squirmed, and within seconds not one, but two, actors appeared from the wings, one each in the two doorways that led to stage right and left.

"Shh!" they both demanded.

The couch was on the wall between the two doors that led to the wings, so they got us from both sides. I wanted to remind them it was only a rehearsal—and the first read-through at that—but I couldn't be bothered. I swung my legs off the couch and sat there. Ally clambered up and sat next to me. Suddenly I couldn't believe I'd tried to ask her out. Even worse, I couldn't decide if she'd rejected me or not. I certainly didn't have it in me to try again, despite the way she was looking at me—her eyes lingered and made my heart beat faster. For half a second I was about to kiss her.

"Why did you call me?" I blurted instead.

"What? When?"

She seemed genuinely confused and I couldn't blame her. I couldn't honestly believe I'd even mentioned it, but then I guess I was feeling emboldened by the Missy and Donna Marie incident. If I could get away with a throwing a bun at a girl, then I could certainly ask a girl why she'd called me three weeks ago. It would seem just as out-of-the-blue, and judging by her expression, that's exactly what it was: a hotdog bun to the back of the head.

"A while ago," I said casually, as if it was no big deal. "That one snow day, back before Christmas...?"

"Oh my God—*then*?" She chuckled and glanced up at the ceiling again, a private smile on her lips. "I don't even remember."

"I think you do."

"Yeah? Well if you cared so much, why didn't you call me back?"

"I don't know your number."

"Why didn't you ask me in school that Monday?"

"A lot happened that weekend," I admitted. "I kinda forgot."

Her expression dropped just enough to make me feel bad and she nodded slowly.

"Yeah."

"But I'm asking now...?"

"Why?"

She looked down at her hands, twisting one of her bangles nervously.

I wanted to tell her what I suspected: That after all the lunches and hanging out at plays since school had started, she'd finally decided to call *me* and see what I was up to, which is why her rejection of our date now seemed so odd. But I couldn't be that direct—that wasn't a hotdog bun to the head, that was a bowling ball.

"Guess I just thought of it. I'm curious."

"Yeah? Well, I don't remember. Probably wanted to see if you wanted to go skating."

"Yeah?"

"But you never called back."

Somewhere in the back of my head I started to put it all together: I didn't have her number and she hadn't left it and she'd said *she* would call back... It had all been some test of my willingness to be with her or something, and I'd failed— not entirely my fault, given that weekend. But it had obviously stuck with her such that, even now, when I asked her out directly, she wondered if I was serious or just being weirdly polite.

"Can I have your number?" I asked quietly, terrified of the words even as they left my lips. It felt like a reset—or an easy way out for her. If she said no, then the rejection was real and complete.

"Sure," she said with that same private grin.

There's a certain feeling you only get when a pretty girl

gives you her number. It can't be reproduced or faked. It's like acceptance and hope and promise rolled up into a nervous bundle of joy. At least, it is when you really want her number; I think some guys get addicted to that rush, and I can see why.

She snagged a pen from her back pocket and pulled my hand onto her lap, scrawling onto my palm. It was the time-tested way of seeing how serious you were, to see if you would remember not to use or wash your hand; to see if you rubbed it off before you could call.

"Robert Smith's a rock star, too," she said softly, as if apologizing for something else. She capped her pen and pushed my hand gently off her lap.

"Thanks," I replied.

We had speakers backstage that piped the audio from on-stage to us and we heard Mr. K call us up front so he could go over some ideas with us. Ally stood up and headed out the right hand door, like Mr. K had instructed. My changes came from the left, so I stood up and moved over to my door. I glanced across and caught her eye as we both walked toward the stage. She was smiling again, the same shy smile as before.

"Ally?" I checked, not entirely sure what I planned to say.

It didn't matter. She didn't hear me. I slunk past the piles of stored props to the wings and took up my place. I looked across the stage as the scene ended. Sammy killed the lights and I had only a brief, strobe-like image of Ally pulling her hair back over her ears and glancing up at me as she took her place.

The set-change lights in the wings glowed blue and we went about our work in the darkness, with Mr. K calling the shots and pointing out directions with a penlight.

After the rehearsal, Niz and Sammy got ahead of me in the hallway—Niz in some Mr.-K-inspired dramatic retelling of a new trick—and Ally caught up to me as I lagged behind. She looped her arm through mine as we walked. My heart fluttered.

"What do you guys get up to, anyway?" she asked.

I looked at her oddly but she was watching her feet walk and didn't see me.

"I don't know. Sammy and I work at the same place, so that's fun."

"Yeah... sure."

"It's really not that bad. I hate it when Sammy's not there, but the two of us make it fun. Well, bearable."

"I have like a hundred cousins, so I usually end up hanging out with them. We go to a lot of shows."

She sighed, and I couldn't imagine that ever feeling like a chore.

"That's cool. I don't have any family around here. Well, except my brother and parents."

"Yeah."

"Bells!" Niz suddenly hollered back down the hall at us. "Step it up, soldier! I got homework to do!"

"Homework?" I called back. "Whazzat?"

He waved me off.

"See ya, Jack," Ally halfheartedly called after me as I dropped her arm and chased after Niz. I think I expected her to jog along with me, but she didn't move any faster,

98

she just kept shuffling along at the same conversational pace we'd been walking at.

"See ya, Ally!"

Niz let out an unnecessary whoop and caught my attention, so I wasn't sure if she said anything else or not.

$$\acute{\mathcal{E}}$$

In my life, some of the stupidest things I've done, I've done for girls. And some of those things I did for one girl only to fuck something up with another girl. What is it about girls that make boys fuck things up? What is it about girls that makes boys ignore their friends? Is it so hard to get a date that a fear sets in, the fear that another date won't come along so you better go with what you've got until something, somewhere breaks and everything gets shot to hell? Did a guy like Greg Wilson exist because he was so scared of committing to a girl, only to lose her, that he figured he was better off not committing at all, so he just groped whoever happened to be close by at the Wharf? Was I the anti-Wilson? The guy who'd do exactly the opposite of what his heart said in order to keep a girl he was dating? Did I *over* commit? Is that why it always hurt so much?

No, not really. Because it wasn't about commitment so much as a lack of ambition; of not wanting to go through all that shit again to get a girl. And with Missy, maybe it was about not wanting to upset the fragile balance between

Sammy and Donna Marie. Maybe that's why it *didn't* hurt with Missy. With her it was nothing but guilt and regret because I knew, deep down, I'd never been into it as much as she was, and that's a shitty, Greg Wilson thing to do to somebody.

Especially because it started out relatively well.

Donna Marie turned out to be popular because she was so much damn *fun* to be around, and she had an infectious laugh that she used at exactly the right places. She turned out to be the kind of girl you wanted to be with because you really believed you were having fun, even if you weren't, and Missy was like her sidekick; the unsung hero who had to be there for Donna Marie to play off, and was just as much fun because of it.

What's strange is, I think Donna Marie felt the same way about Sammy. I think for the first time in her life, she *didn't* feel like she had to make things fun. She felt like she could take a break and let Sammy do some of the work, because believe me, that boy *was* fun. Quiet, shy, odd—sure, those adjectives all fit, too, but that's before you knew him. Once you peeled back his veneer, you uncovered an impish little jokester ready to make you laugh.

That's why I'd been so scared when he came over to my house that snowy Friday after his dad left: The *fun* seemed to have left him. For the first time I wondered which side had been just an act: The tortured-poet exterior for strangers or the game-show-host interior for us. I mean, I couldn't imagine where he got the interior from, not with what little I knew of his family. His dad was all tortured poet, and his mom... well, his mom might have had some fun in her. It's strange how personalities form, and Sammy, like algae growing on a hot-water vent, had managed to flourish even under harsh conditions.

Perhaps that explained his penchant for the Monkees.

What it didn't really explain was why we were at Kangaroo Joe's in the mall. Kangaroo Joe's was like the anchor store of the food court: an out-of-place family pub that may or may not have been authentically Australian, but certainly was authentically breaking the law almost every day. It was apparently a closely guarded secret among a certain clique— that Sammy and I had found ourselves unwittingly entered into via Donna Marie and Missy—that Kangaroo Joe's never carded patrons. Ever. Needless to say, the place didn't last long, but it was there long enough to receive us after our dates at the mall. Donna Marie always chose a booth back away from the main mall in the half light where she said the shadows made us look older.

It wasn't really my speed, and in hindsight I think Donna Marie only went there because Missy wanted to. A date with Missy usually ended in sipping vodka from a flask somewhere, be that the mall or the Wharf or some city park after dark. It also usually ended with us making out, and that cinched it for the seventeen-year-old boy in the equation—I could put up with a lot of shit for the chance to taste her lips again; to see her eyes slowly blinking. Even so, it didn't ever feel right, only convenient, and I tried to force her into an admission a couple of weeks into the affair, sitting in a booth in the back of Kangaroo Joe's—I wanted her to admit that she felt the same way; that the shadow plays and make-out sessions would only be entertaining for so long, and it might be better to get out before we got bored.

Of course, I told myself it had to be her idea, otherwise I'd somehow ruin it for Sammy. But the truth is, I couldn't do it, not when she blinked and smiled at me, her right eyebrow twitching up in mirth ever so slightly.

"What I don't get—I'll be honest with you—is why you're here with us," I said simply.

"I'm here with *you*," Missy said dismissively.

"But you could date any boy in school..."

"I don't want to date *any* boy."

She gave me a winsome smirk and sucked at the straw in her Coke.

"But *why*?"

"Tobie told me you always overthink things, Jack, so stop. I don't think I'm as popular as you imagine."

"No, I think you are."

"Fine. Maybe I'm sick of them. Maybe I wanted to know what it was like to hang out with a guy who'd save me from someone like Greg Wilson."

She shook her head slightly and chuckled, her earrings catching the dim lights in sparkles.

"What about Donna Marie?" I wondered.

"You mean, why's she taking so long to get us a pitcher of beer?"

"Is that where she went? *Seriously*?"

Missy smirked again and cocked her head slightly to the side, considering me carefully.

"I meant, does she really like Sammy?" I asked.

"You're worried about him?" Missy assumed. "See, *that's* why I'm here with you."

"Did you ever *date* Greg Wilson?" it occurred to me.

"Yeah," she breathed, telling me with her tone of voice in that single word that it was not something she wanted to talk about. "That's why I started talking to Tobie. I wanted to warn her. He can be quite charming at first."

"He had us all fooled," I agreed.

There was an uncomfortable silence. I picked at the plate of fries we'd ordered and she tried again to suck the last drops of Coke off the ice cubes in her glass. It hadn't been a bad date. In fact, it had been a good date, one of our better dates, but I felt a weird pressure from Missy, like I had to live up to some standard I didn't know existed. In the movies, before they'd dimmed the lights, she pretended to read my palms as a way to touch my hand so she had an excuse to hold it, and she said my love line was very well developed.

"What is taking them so *long*?" Missy asked again to fill the silence, turning and glancing over her shoulder at the end of the bar.

I could see Donna Marie and Sammy laughing about something. She was using it as an excuse to lean in to him and he was soaking it up. They didn't look like they were in much of a rush to come back over to the table.

"Looks like they forgot about us," I said.

"Yeah," she agreed. "Can't be taking *that* long. This place is dead, just like the rest of the mall."

It was true. Apart from us, there was only one other couple in the bar—I mean, pub. The wait staff had us outnumbered two-to-one.

"I heard you guys skated in here once," Missy said, her eyes twinkling at me. "That true?"

"Sort of," I replied carefully. The story involved Mr. Conversation Killer, so I really didn't want to get into all of the details. "Niz stopped the escalator and we needed a quick getaway. It was more panic than fun."

"Sounds awesome," she grinned. "How'd he stop it?"

Thankfully, Sammy and Donna Marie came back during the explanation of how to stop an escalator. They were still giggling. Sammy had a bowl of pretzels, but Donna Marie didn't have any beer.

"Where's the *beer*?" Missy asked angrily.

Donna Marie shrugged and plopped into a chair. "Couldn't get it."

Missy looked at me like I was supposed to do something, but I didn't bite. I certainly wasn't going to get up and try to get a pitcher myself. One of the assistant managers at the hotdog stand had once invited us for a drink after work, and they didn't look too concerned that he took enough glasses for the two underage guys at his table, but I didn't think they'd outright sell it to someone underage, despite the rumors at school. Besides, I got the impression Donna Marie hadn't even asked for any beer, which Sammy later confirmed was true. It wasn't worth the trouble.

"But I do have this," Donna Marie said, reaching into her gargantuan purse and pulling out a slim silver flask. "Never leave home without it."

"What's in it?" Sammy asked.

"Vodka," she said, as if imparting an important lesson. "Doesn't add any flavor to whatever you put it in, so if someone does a taste test to see what you're drinking, they don't taste anything."

"Awesome, eh?" Missy grinned. "Lemme have half your Coke so I have something to pour it in," she said to me.

"Sure," I agreed, which she took to mean I wanted some, too. I can't honestly say what I would have answered if she'd asked me before she spiked my drink, and maybe she knew that and didn't bother to ask. Sammy took the flask from her and poured it in his own drink, then handed it back to Donna Marie, who spiked hers and put the flask away.

"Cheers!" she said, and raised her glass.

We clinked glasses and drank, and it was true, I didn't taste a damn bit of difference. The Coke maybe tasted a bit watered down, but that was all, and that could've been from the ice melting.

We stayed there until about ten, which would put it about an hour after the movie let out. I started to fret around 9:45 that I'd be buzzed and unable to drive home, but the drink was honestly having zero effect. The girls were laughing it up, so maybe they'd put more in their own drinks, but Sammy admitted he hadn't felt much of anything either.

Clear, tasteless, and odorless—it was probably water, in hindsight. A placebo as an excuse to act a bit a goofy and get away with it.

We took our sweet time walking them back to the car, and while Donna Marie dragged Sammy into one of those carnival photo booths to get pictures taken, Missy and I wandered over to a storefront and gazed in the window at $200 sunglasses.

"Who'd pay that much for sunglasses?" I asked.

Missy didn't answer and when I turned to see if she'd wandered off to look at something else I was surprised to find her still so close. Real close, in fact. She reached across me and took my arm and pulled me around so we were facing each other, then she pivoted up on her toes and kissed me. Not a peck, not a shy break-the-ice test, but a real lips-slightly-parted kiss. Her eyes were closed and I didn't pull away. My heart was racing and she was holding my arms at the wrists, using them to help her balance on her toes. I kissed her, enjoying the feel of her lips and the taste of her lip gloss. I wondered if Sammy was kissing Donna Marie in the photo booth. I wondered if this was really happening at all. I opened my eyes to check and she was looking right me. She broke away and plopped back down on her heels.

"Caught ya peeking," she whispered with a cute little grin.

I reached out and pulled her in to me and kissed her again, and completely lost myself to the moment and the promise I tasted on her lips.

The silver on the ring looked faded. Not tarnished, but actually *faded* somehow, as if the age and weight of time had finally had its way and infused it with a dulled glow from its core, not a simple sheen of oxidation on the surface. As I turned it in my fingers, I studied the finely cut bones, pinched in the middle and separated from each other by deep black cuts, slightly rounded, to form a perfect circle. The inside was smooth, save a maker's mark, and a glance was all you needed to see that it had been made well. It wasn't a big garish death-metal piece-of-shit like they sold at the mall. It was subtle. It was the kind of ring that made you take a second look and ask, "Are those little bones?" because the finery of it was such that you couldn't be absolutely sure. To be honest, I'm still not absolutely sure, but to me they will always be bones, even if they aren't.

"You can have it," Ally said.

I immediately handed it back to her. She wore it on her thumb, and the thought of her not having it on seemed wrong. I'd noticed it many times but had only now plucked up the courage to ask about it.

"No, no—that's not why I asked about it."

"I know. But I can tell you like it."

"Well, yeah, but so do you. Besides, I'm sure it means something to you?"

She shrugged. She was sitting cross-legged on the couch backstage and I was in a wingback chair across from her. Some teacher had been about to ditch the wingback chairs, but Mr. K had salvaged them to give us more sitting room. He'd even come up with a small coffee table that was now nestled between them. Ally twirled the ring in her fingers and looked at it. I watched how nimble her fingers looked, only realizing then that she also coordinated her nail polish with her hair highlights and lipstick. No wonder she looked so well put together—that subtle unity of color somehow made her whole, but not in a big flashy way. It's always the details that have the most impact.

She held the ring back out to me.

"No, I want you to have it. Really."

I held her gaze. She nodded impatiently and urged me to take the ring by holding it out further. I took it, if only to stop her stretching so far.

"Where did you get it?"

"I don't remember."

"Seriously?"

"Yeah—for real. I was a kid. I used to pick old boxes out of the trash. I bet it was in one of them. I never even wore it until this year."

"It's really cool."

I slid it onto the ring finger of my right hand but it was a touch too big, so I moved it to the middle finger.

"It looks good," she said quietly. "Matches your earrings."

It didn't, not really, except for the fact that the ring was a circle and my earrings were tiny hoops, but I liked the way she was smiling and I didn't feel so bad for taking it, not if it made her happy.

"Thanks."

"So, are you going to Sudsy's this weekend with Jess and Niz? My cousin's band is playing."

I looked down and twirled the bone ring on my finger, trying to avoid her stare. She was really asking if Missy would let me go because Missy had made it pretty clear to everyone who'd listen that she didn't like Ally McShay. Maybe Missy saw something in the way I looked at Ally—I don't know. I almost told her once that I'd tried to ask Ally out and she'd snubbed me, so there was nothing for her to worry about, but that's not how teenagers are wired—when it comes to the opposite sex, there is *always* something to worry about, even when there isn't.

"Yeah, I'm trying to talk Missy into going."

"Pah!" Ally spat joyfully. "I doubt she'd survive five minutes!"

"Oh, she's not *that* bad. She just hasn't ever gone to a club show."

I glanced up at Ally. She had her head cocked to the side and an expression on her face that told me not to try and pull anything over on her. She wasn't buying it.

"She made it as far as the Wharf, I hear. And so did you."

I looked away. I'd really hoped Ally, of all people, hadn't known about the lame shit I did with Missy Anderson. And the truth is, at this point I was only staying in it through the damn King of Hearts dance, so I didn't ruin it for Missy.

"We'll be there," I conceded.

"What about Sammy and the Homecoming queen?"

I shook my head. "I doubt it."

"Tobie?"

I shook my head again. She smiled sweetly when I looked over at her. It caught me off guard. There were no layers to it; no sarcasm; no wit—just a nice smile.

"Please come," she said. "For me?"

I looked down and twisted the ring on my finger, something I already knew was going to be a lifelong nervous habit.

"You have to hear the opening band," she added. "That's my cousin's band. They don't play out that much, but they're really good."

"I'll be there," I assured her.

"I guess we better get up there," she said, jabbing a thumb over her shoulder at the stage speaker. Mr. K's voice was crackling over it. "Sounds like he's wrapping up for the night."

"Hey, Ally?" I said as I stood up.

She froze and turned back to me.

"Yeah?"

"Thanks again for the ring. It was really nice of you to give it to me."

She smirked ironically.

"You deserve nice things, Bells—don't forget that."

Then she was swallowed by the shadows in the wings as she headed for the stage.

February

"Hey, Bells, how do you tell if a BB gun is loaded?" Niz wondered.

We'd set up all the platforms and rails he'd built in his garage so we could skate, and he was sitting off in a corner, taking a break, while I tried to hurt myself or pull off a good railslide, whichever came first.

"Shoot it?" I suggested.

Slap. Another missed rail. It was no use. I really wasn't that good. Compared to the videos we watched, none of us were—but we had a ton of fun failing. The next time I tried a railslide I heard a small *ting*, like I'd broken my truck or something, followed almost immediately by a loud smashing sound, like an entire patio door had shattered into pieces.

In fact, an entire patio door *had* shattered into pieces. I looked over at Niz and he was sitting gaping at me, his face pale and the BB gun pointing at the concrete floor of the garage.

"What the hell was that?" I asked, looking around.

It was a garage, so the walls were lined with junk, but I couldn't see broken glass anywhere.

"I guess it was loaded," he replied in a stunned mumble.

"Do you have spare windows out here or something?"

The *ting* had been the ricocheting BB, and clearly something had not come out well on the other end of it.

"Just a patio door," Niz replied. He finally regained his composure enough to put down the gun and get up. He walked over toward me, looking past me, and I turned and followed his gaze.

"That frame there?" he said, pointing to a brownish metal frame. "That was a double-pane door a few seconds ago."

We stepped up and examined it. Sure enough, there was a pile of glass crumbs—there's no other way to describe it—all around the bottom of the frame.

"Shit, Niz, your dad's gonna kill you," I breathed.

"I'm sort of hoping he doesn't know it's out here."

"Is that likely?"

"I don't know. How often do you need to replace a patio door?"

"Well, how often does your stupid kid shoot one out?"

Niz started to chuckle but he got over it pretty quickly.

"For the record?" I said. "That's *not* how you check if a gun is loaded."

That set him off, laughing to cover his fear. When he calmed down he managed to ask, "Do you think we should clean it up?"

"Probably," I agreed, so I helped him move the old dresser and plywood off-cuts that were in front of it. He went and found a broom and a big trash can and started sweeping the glass crumbs into a snow shovel I'd found.

"So how's it going with Missy?" he wondered.

"S'alright," I said with a shrug. "She's nice. Mostly."

"She's *hot*," Niz corrected. "Tell me again how that bun trick works?"

"Well, you see, it's like our caveman ancestors discovered: You see a pretty girl, and if you want to take her back to your cave, you fling something at her head..."

Niz was laughing, but I could tell there was something on his mind, and that hadn't been the question he'd wanted to ask. We'd known each other since we were seven or so and we'd got to know each other's ways pretty well. He was generally the better of the two of us. He worked harder at school and got better grades, and he also spent more time practicing skating, so he could do some pretty good tricks. I was more prone to watching the same movie for the hundredth time or making a mix tape if I had some time alone, and what homework I didn't get done in study hall didn't end up getting done. I took art classes and he took advanced algebra. I asked to copy off his test in physics and he let me; he earned a B, I faked a C-minus.

Niz was also the one who spent an afternoon beating down the weeds in a vacant field across from a favorite skate spot that was also haunted by the cops, so we could run off into a maze of weeds he'd created and vanish from sight. He demonstrated it for me a few days after he got done, and it was fantastic. He darted off, spiraling into the weeds, then suddenly he was gone. A few seconds later he popped up nowhere near where I would have expected.

"So we lay low until the cops get bored and leave," he shouted out.

And we did, a few weeks later, and it worked exactly to his design.

Niz was also the man who introduced me to fuzzy navels on a sleepover. The OJ hadn't been hard to come by, and I never asked where he got the peach Schnapps. It was hotter than hell that night. We sat out on his back deck in our underwear and sweated and drank fuzzy navels. Later we watched all of the *Living Dead* movies back-to-back.

"So what's up?" I wondered, watching him tug on his lower lip with his teeth as he swept up the patio door glass. "You seem... quiet."

Niz stopped sweeping and looked at me. I straightened up and gave him my attention. Had I been anyone else he would've certainly opened with, "You have to swear not to tell anybody," but it was me and he knew that's how we always did things.

"Jess and I... we... you know..." he began

"You broke *up*?" I gasped.

He shook his head vehemently. "No. The exact opposite. We... sealed the deal."

"You're getting *married*?" I shrieked. The energy flushed right out of him and he drooped down with a sigh. I had secretly been expecting (fearing?) that exact announcement for months now.

"Jesus, Bells! We *did* it! We had *sex*!"

I was speechless. Sure, we talked about girls, but we never kiss-n-told, so to speak. Maybe the exaggerated "We made *out*, if ya knowhatImean" here and there, but we didn't go into detail. We were very tactful and private in the way we shared things like that. So-and-so is a great kisser or so-

114

n-so wears sports bras all the time—enough to let the other guy fill in the blanks without having to get pornographic. So for Niz to outright say it knocked me off balance.

"Wow, uh, I mean, oh, was it, umm...?"

"It was great," he said honestly. "We didn't plan it or anything, not like in the movies where you plan a big night. It just *happened*."

"So she was okay with it?"

"Of course! But it didn't even come up, it was just... natural."

"Well *some*thing came up!" I declared, following it immediately with a mumbled apology.

"Did you and Tobie ever...?"

"No!" I cried. "I mean, you know, we've never come *close* to going *that* far."

He nodded and halfheartedly swept up some more glass. I thought it was beautiful because I could tell how much it meant to him. He'd been dating Jess over a year by that point and I knew they might actually love each other, like real, honest love. If anything, I was most amazed to find out it hadn't already happened long before. But as I said, Niz was the better of us. He glanced over at me, still standing there like a lump.

"Are you mad or something?" he wondered.

"No, no—not at all. It's great. Really. You two *should* have something like that." I tried to scoop some of the glass he hadn't swept up into the snow shovel. "I just don't know how to say that without sounding... dumb."

"I just had to tell someone," Niz replied thoughtfully. "It was so... I just needed to share it, to make it real or something. I wasn't bragging."

"Niz," I declared. "As long as it doesn't affect your ability to pull off that fancy kickflip you do, I think we'll be fine."

"Shit."

He chuckled at his own melodrama and waved for me to hold the shovel still while he swept the last of the glass shards into it. We didn't say another word about it, but he certainly seemed happier. Not that he was depressed or anything before, just contemplative. He'd been busting to tell me all night but he hadn't known how, without seeming like he was getting too personal or airing Jess's dirty laundry.

We skated for a while longer and he tried to teach me some goofy slide trick that about killed me. He managed to pull it off once—barely. I almost smashed another window in the process, when my board shot out from under me. It slammed into the wall about three inches from one of the two windows in the garage, and I'm pretty sure his dad would've noticed that one.

"So Sammy's not coming over?" he guessed at one point.

I shook my head. "Out with Donna Marie."

"*Man*—that's *twice* he's stood us up this week!"

"It's shocking," I agreed. "I didn't think he stood a damn chance with her, but there they are."

"I don't know. She always seemed kinda nice," Niz said. "And you're living the dream, too, Bells! Missy's a bit above your pay grade, isn't she?"

It was a fair question and his curiosity was born of concern. You could say it was going pretty well on the surface, but I also knew that there was no good reason for us to be going out. I'd gone along with it for Sammy, and she'd gone along with it because she had some bizarre concept of me based on conversations with Tobie. I think Tobie was actually to blame, to be honest. Not that she tried to hook us up or anything, but in hindsight, if Tobie and I hadn't been hanging out for so damn long, I doubt Tobie would be hanging out with me at all. Which isn't honestly giving Tobie enough credit. Yeah, she tended toward the popular crowd, but she had far too wide an independent streak to ever settle down there. All it really meant is that she, like Jolly, got along with the popular crowd to enough of a degree to give the rest of us a whiff of normalcy—enough so that someone like Missy Anderson would kiss me in the middle of the mall.

"She's alright," I admitted. "I think maybe I had them pegged all wrong."

I looked over at Niz, who sat considering me curiously. He rode a skateboard and dated a girl who worked at a record store when she wasn't waitressing—he was doing it the way people like me expected.

"My brother said it wouldn't last," I added.

"Really?" Niz checked. "Why not?"

I shrugged. My brother was a Sophomore in college and he'd given me a long heart-to-heart about how all the problems of high school would magically vanish when I started college; that there was some kind of Etch-a-Sketch shake that happened and reset everything. The cool people in high school were the dorks in college, he told me, and the freaks and geeks were suddenly cool. But right then, in high school? Nothing mattered more than looking and acting the right way. He said it wouldn't last because Missy would figure that out, and he told me it wouldn't matter because I only had six more months before that Etch-a-Sketch shake came and brushed it all away with gray sand.

"Do you like her?" I asked.

"Can't say as I know," he replied. "I can't wait to go to Sudsy's with you two—Jess and I never get to hang out with you any more."

"What about Tobie?"

"What about her?" he said, not trying to be mean or judgmental, just stating a fact.

"What does Tobie think of her?"

Niz snuffed a laugh through his nose.

"Shit, Bells. Tobie always worries about you, you know that."

"So she doesn't like her?"

"I think she's suspicious," he admitted. "She remembers the last time you dated a popular girl, and she knows enough to know how certain boys are just passing fads with them."

"What's funny is, I feel like she likes me more than I like her."

Niz chuckled and clapped me on the back. "Then I'd say you're okay, Bells."

"Really?"

"The fuck do I know?" he laughed, slipping into his old-man accent. "Now get on outta here, you damn kids, I got homework to do! Go on! *Scram!*"

When Missy greeted me at her door and she shrieked and was all arms and lips and soft skin and fresh soap, I basically forgot everything I'd been mulling over about her—about us. She had that effect on me.

"Jack!" she squealed, bobbing on her toes in front of me.

"You act surprised to see me."

"I'm excited! I've never got to hang out with you and the mythical Niz."

"Don't get your hopes up," I joked.

"Plus, I've never been to Sudsy's before."

Sudsy's was the the world's most bizarre concert club. Half of it was the bar and stage and the other half was an all-night laundromat. I guess the guy who ran it was catering to the local college students, and it seemed to work: Both halves were always packed. The bands Sudsy's had weren't exactly pop acts, even by college radio standards. They were the hard-working bands that toured for a few weeks then went back to their day jobs. Ally McShay had turned us on to it. One of her cousins worked there and he was always giving Ally the promo stuff for the bands that played there. It wasn't in the best part of town, but there was a parking lot a few doors down, so we didn't have to walk around much. Besides, on a Saturday night, it was stuffed with concert goers (the bigger club was across the street, that featured the college-radio acts).

119

"Hey, Jack," Missy's dad said, appearing behind her. "Missy says you're going to a concert?"

"Yeah," I agreed.

Her dad intimidated me. He was pretty big and he looked very serious all the time. I found it best not to say much, if I could help it. To be fair, though, I'd never seen him before I started to date Missy, and considering one of the best skate curbs in town was right across the street from him, that meant he'd never come out and yelled at us (like his neighbors had).

"Where?"

"Downtown, near the university."

"Who's going?"

"Me and Missy, and my friend Niz and his girlfriend, Jess."

"Same car?"

"Yes, sir."

"Who's driving?"

"Probably me."

"No probably—*you* drive, okay?"

"*Dad*," Missy protested under her breath.

"Jack?"

"Yes, sir. I'll drive."

"What time's the show?"

"Probably nine."

"Home by midnight, then—no probably."

"*Dad*! I'm seven*teen*!"

"Yes, sir."

"Have fun. Gimme a kiss, Missy."

He gave his daughter a hug and kiss, and we were off. I

120

wanted to get the hell away before he thought to ask exactly which club we were going to. The fact that he hadn't asked meant he'd either already asked Missy or he'd assumed it was the bigger club. Probably the latter. Not that there was anything wrong with Sudsy's, but it really was just a bar, and he'd certainly have figured that out. Ironically, it was probably safer than the damn Wharf—I sincerely don't think the staff at Sudsy's would have put up with spiked drinks, at least not from us. For one thing, you got carded at the door, something Missy had clearly never encountered before. That struck me as odd—you believe the movies and the popular crowd was out all night partying, sneaking into clubs and whatnot. Yet there I was, one outfit away from displaying the depths of my nerd-dom, explaining to Missy that she *had* to let the guy draw the big black X on her hand.

"How'll I get it off?" she asked in a mild panic, glancing at my hand. The bouncer kinda sorta knew us because he knew we were friends of Ally's, but he was still getting rightly perturbed.

"It'll wash off," I said confidently. "I mean, after a few days."

"A few *days*?" she gasped.

"Come on—it'll be worth it, I promise."

"Yeah, we're not leaving yet," Jess added—her tone full of tough love. She seemed so old and wise in that moment, and Missy so young and innocent.

"Come on," the bouncer said rigidly, so Jess grabbed Niz's hand and pushed past us. They didn't even bother with their licenses; we always just let the bouncer put the Xs on our hands and went about our business—it was less hassle.

121

"Nail polish remover'll probably get it off," I offered to Missy, who was still unsure and eyeing the bouncer suspiciously.

"Probably?" she wondered.

I nodded. She sighed but let me drag her back to the door. The bouncer held out his hand and she held out hers, so he grabbed it before she could pull away and slapped a big black X on it in magic marker. He winked at me and I knew he'd pressed a bit harder than necessary, to make sure it worked into her skin real good.

"Was that really necessary?" she whispered dramatically as we worked our way toward the stage.

"Yes," I said, only half listening as I looked out for Niz and Jess. "It's an all-ages show, and since they sell liquor—"

"They sell *liquor* here?" she gasped, stopping short and yanking me back.

"Yeah. It's a bar."

"You brought me to a *bar*?"

"You're kidding, right? You bring your own bar with you to the Wharf and you're worried about actually being in one?"

"That's different."

"How?"

"My dad doesn't know about that. This I can't hide in my purse."

"Look," I said, trying not to be annoyed. "It's not a big deal. Look around—half the people *in* here aren't old enough to drink! This is a *concert* club, not a *teen* club."

She was fine hiding flasks in her purse and drinking out of them, but God forbid she should legally enter a bar for an all-ages show? It didn't make any sense.

As soon as she started to look hesitantly at her surroundings I knew what she was thinking: The patrons at Sudsy's were like me and Niz and Jess and Sammy and Ally. We were the kids who sat in the back of class, listened to loud music, wore lots of black and big boots, and made fun of school-sponsored social events (even as we attended them). We were the losers, the burnouts, the skaters, the punks. This was no place for one of the runners-up to Homecoming queen. As I looked at her and watched her face change I felt horrible. She looked *scared* for Christ's sake. The Wharf wasn't just different because everyone there was fashionable and clean, it was different because everyone there was a teen, and flasks and groping or not, it was different when everyone was your own age—but I could see it in her eyes and I knew what she was thinking: There were college kids here and even grown-ups, and they all looked like the kind of people you're taught to avoid.

"Let's find Niz and Jess," I said gently, taking her hand. "We'll be fine, I promise."

As if on cue, the house DJ started to spin a warm-up set, ripping into it with "Anywhere's Better Than Here" by the Replacements. Missy would certainly have related to the lyrics if she'd been able to get past the inhuman wail that starts the song and ushered in a driving alt-rock beat. Some people started to move as if to dance—or shuffle around with a mob-like intensity, anyway—and Missy squeezed my hand tightly and tried to stay close as I pushed through toward the front. I spotted Niz and dragged her over to him.

"Where's Jess?" I yelled.

"Shitter!" he yelled back. He'd already got a big cup of Coke and I looked at it hungrily.

"So, Missy?" he yelled at her. She nodded, wide eyed. "You been here before?"

She shook her head vehemently.

"It can be overwhelming, right!" he asked as nicely as you could with a yell.

"Yeah!" she agreed.

I think she yelled, but her voice sounded so small. Next up from the DJ was "Suboceana" by the Tom Tom Club, a gentler song with a good beat. Missy visibly relaxed, or maybe it was wishful thinking.

"It'll get crowded up here!" I explained to her loudly. "Do you want to go to the back?"

She nodded.

"I'm going to try and find a table!" I hollered at Niz.

He understood and slipped off his coat, handing it to me. On the way back we ran into Jess and I took her coat, too. We always tried to find a table at the back—it wasn't as hot and it was nice to have a place to sit for a while when you wanted to. Normally we came with Sammy or ran into Ally, and since neither of them liked the press of bodies near the stage, they usually took table duty. Fortunately, we were there early enough and there was still one table open, way in the back corner. I grabbed it and smiled apologetically at Missy as she slid into the booth beside me.

"Niz is right," I said in a normal voice, but right up against her ear so she could hear me. Her hair smelled nice, so I gave her a peck on the cheek while I was close. "It's a bit much, I guess. I should've warned you."

124

I don't know if it was the kiss or my apology, but she pulled her hair back over her ear and gave me a sly grin, then leaned in and put her lips against my ear. "I think I'm over it now." I felt shivers run up my spine from her breath on my face.

"Just don't go back up there when the band starts," I said, still talking right in her ear.

"Why?"

"There's *always* a pit."

She drew her head back and looked at me with a confused expression.

"There's a pit?" I barely heard her say.

"It's sort of like dancing," I tried to explain. She drew closer again, so I playful nipped her ear lobe and she giggled. "Only it's... well, it can be pretty rough."

"Are you going into the pit?" she asked.

"Maybe for a song or two. Hey, if we can find Ally, she can keep you company."

"Ally *McShay*?" she said derisively, loud and clear, pulling away from me. "You want me to *sit* with that *freak*?"

Somebody punched my arm—hard. I turned and saw Jess standing right behind me with Ally, who had her mouth half open and looked mortified and hurt and so, so small.

"Ally!" I cried, jumping to my feet.

I stepped toward her but Jess didn't move. She glowered at me instead.

"Nice," she said, then put her drink down and stormed off.

"Ally," I said again and stepped over to her. "Hey, have you met Missy?"

125

She shook her head and for the life of me I didn't know why she was still standing there. The DJ moved on to Big Pig's "Breakaway." It was like he was picking out songs just for me.

I turned and motioned at Missy, but she was looking anywhere except at us.

"That's her!" I said lamely.

I turned back to Ally just in time to see her turn and walk off.

Now, despite what I may or may not have ever said about Ally being weird to Niz or Jess or Tobie when she snubbed us or didn't come to our parties, it was one thing coming from me and another thing entirely coming from Missy Anderson, and especially coming from Missy here, on Ally's ground. This is where people like me and Ally came so we *didn't* stand out—so we *didn't* look like freaks—and to be called out in that setting...? I felt absolutely horrible.

"So that was Ally," I said, sitting back down. "I guess she won't be joining us."

"Whatever," Missy said.

She leaned over and kissed my cheek right up by my ear. She looked much more comfortable, like by calling Ally a freak she was back on level footing.

"Just whisper something in my ear again, Jack."

See, and that was the problem: A dark table in the back where no one was looking at you? That was the Wharf's M.O. and Missy just wanted to smooch a little. To be honest, I didn't even like smooching when she took me to the Wharf, but she never seemed to care. Sudsy's wasn't really a make-out club, though. The DJ was playing the Wonder Stuff, for

126

God's sake, not whatever boy-band was the flavor of the month.

"I should go check on Ally," I said and started to move. She grabbed my arm.

"Don't," she demanded and smiled so sweetly.

But in the dim lights of the pre-show club I saw a mean girl who lacked self-confidence. I saw written on Missy's face all the jealousy and envy Tobie had warned me about earlier in the day.

Tobie and I had met up at the McDonald's down the street from my house before I went to get Missy—call it an early dinner or a late lunch. Anyway, something before the big double date with Jess and Niz. Tobie sat and sullenly poked at her fries and I could tell she had something on her mind.

"Are you sure we're allowed to hang out?" she asked sarcastically.

I scrunched my brow at her. "What? Friends can't hang out all of a sudden?"

"You know what I mean," she said evenly. "Missy seems like... the *jealous* type."

I shrugged. Tobie was one of those people I had to talk to in person—I had to see her eyes, read her face, watch her body language.

"Tobie of the Eyes," I mumbled.

"What?" She leaned in and smirked. "What did you just call me?"

"Tobie of the Eyes," I said louder. "I needed to see your eyes."

"I think you've been spending too much time with Ally

McShay backstage. You're starting to sound a little crazy."

"Don't you start making fun of Ally, too."

"I'm not making fun of her," Tobie denied. "I like Ally —and I think she likes you."

I didn't say anything. I could tell by her eyes that she was serious, and I didn't know how to respond. She smirked wryly and sat back.

"So what's up?" I wondered.

She tried to smile, shook her head, tried to avoid my eyes, smiled again, then finally sighed and tucked her hands under her thighs, sitting on them and rocking like a little kid.

"I don't think I like Missy," she said.

She paused, waiting for me to protest, to defend Missy, but I didn't, so she continued.

"At first I was all about it, you know, when she talked to me in class and asked about you? I thought I was doing you a favor."

She let out a puff and sat up straight. We hadn't really talked about Missy. It's like I'd known what she'd say, so I tried to avoid it, and Tobie let me get away with it because she thought I was happy. And I guess I was, for a while, but I'd never been able to shake the feeling that I was just doing it all for Sammy. Missy liked to kiss, and that meant we never really talked about anything, then when we did talk, she'd go on and on about gossipy things... She did seem jealous—of *every*one.

"Look, I don't know," I admitted. "She's nice enough and she's kinda fun..."

"Nice *enough*?" Tobie demanded. "*Kind of* fun? She's just another Penny Harper—"

128

"No!" I whispered harshly and stood up to leave. Tobie looked sorry the second the words dropped from her lips.

Penny Harper was a girl who had truly broken my heart the summer before our Junior year, and Tobie had been there to pick up the pieces. What hurt, though, was Tobie's insinuation that I was falling for another pretty, popular girl without thinking about what I was doing.

"If I'd've said something like that to you about Greg Wilson—that he was some average loser guy who'd cast you off on a whim—you *still* wouldn't be talking to me!"

"Jack," she whispered, tears welling in her eyes. She stood up and stepped over and hugged me, and I let her. "I just don't want you to get hurt again. You don't hear her in class."

"What does *that* mean?" I asked quietly. I pulled away from her and picked up our tray. "Look, I've got to go."

"Never mind," she said, putting on a brave face. "I shouldn't have said anything."

I looked around and sighed heavily. I plopped the tray back down and gave Tobie a hug.

"I'm glad you did," I admitted. "I'm sorry."

"I just know how these girls are."

"These girls," I mocked lightly. "Like *you*'re not one of them?"

"Fuck off," she mumbled and halfheartedly hit me, but she was smiling.

I looked into her eyes and I saw real concern for me—that was all I needed to see that she wasn't playing our usual "I hate your date" game. She was serious.

"Maybe you should learn to fall for someone who's your

type," she said. "Like Ally—"

The music at Sudsy's brought me back to the moment: "Backwoods" by the Red Hot Chili Peppers, one of Ally's favorite songs. I gazed off into the crowd where she'd disappeared.

"Don't worry about Ally," Missy said sternly, her eyes sparkling with that strange brand of arrogance that is glee. She leaned over and kissed me slowly on the lips, her eyes open the whole time.

"You peeked," she chided kindly. I couldn't help but chuckle. Maybe she was just out of her element. Maybe she was acting out to cover her nerves. Maybe she was afraid to leave the table.

"Are we going to move up to see the bands?" I wondered.

"Why? We can see them from here."

After the initial shock, Missy finally settled in well enough, but I hadn't been able to leave the table to join Niz and Jess and Ally. We all left after the second band (of three) and got back into town around 11. Jess made up some excuse to not go for ice cream, so we dropped them at Niz's and I took Missy home. It was 11:15. So the night had been a relative disaster.

"Hey, Jack?" Missy wondered in a dreamy tone of voice as I pulled into her driveway.

"Yeah?"

"My dad won't even be *awake* now—he never is."

"So...?"

I looked at her as I shifted into park and she smiled winsomely.

130

"You could stay and we could watch a movie, that's all."

"Oh. Sure. But I have to be home by one."

The night was young, but not young enough to watch a full movie.

I glanced at her and she was giving me a very strange look, then I realized where I'd seen it before, way back when she'd looked at me the first time we talked in the hall after I drilled Donna Marie with a hotdog bun. She had those "come hither" eyes again. My heart fluttered a bit.

"Let's just see what's on TV, then," Missy said.

I looked through the windshield at her house. The porch light was on and so was the light in the foyer behind the front door. It looked so peaceful and inviting.

"Okay," I agreed.

I want to say that night had nothing to do with us breaking up, but I'd be kidding myself. It had everything to do with it. Turns out I wasn't wrong about any of it: She was more into me than I was into her, and I was way more hung up on the whole popularity thing than she was. When I say she was into me, I don't mean that I made her heart pitter-patter when I entered the room, I mean that she liked me for whatever image she'd built up in her head, and I knew I couldn't live up to that. Nobody could. That left me feeling like just another one of her accessories: Here's my new sweater, look at my cool bracelet my dad got me, and—oh—here's my boyfriend, the guy who skates and listens to loud music and goes to shows at bars. That's why so many damn relationships fail, because one half or the other has a completely different idea of what the whole thing means. If all we'd wanted was trophies I wouldn't have minded, because she would have been my trophy girlfriend. It still wouldn't have ended well, once the polish wore off, but it might have lasted longer. But I wanted more than a trophy and I was so fixated on the concept that the popular crowd only wants their trophies that I couldn't ignore it. It gnawed at me and I worked at it like a sore tooth or a cut lip.

At the same time, I was an adolescent male, and when she flashed that smile and kissed me so gently, I pretty much forgot everything I'd been thinking. That's how we ended up on the couch in her basement, whatever she'd put on TV long forgotten, her snuggling on top of me. I felt her fiddling with something, and when she hoisted herself up and flipped her hair over her shoulder, her shirt fell open and I realized she'd been messing with the buttons.

"Holy shit," I gasped as I realized she'd also slipped off her bra at some point, unbeknownst to me, if she'd even been wearing one.

"You like?" she whispered mischievously. I probably stared.

"I love you, Jack," she whispered and leaned in, but she didn't kiss me. She was waiting for me to respond. When I didn't, she assumed I hadn't heard. She smiled devilishly and popped my belt, slipping her hand down my pants.

"I said I love you," she tried again, far too close to my ear for me not to have heard.

"You do?" I said.

Her hand stopped moving. She hoisted herself back up far enough to look me in the eyes. This isn't how Niz said it went. This didn't feel natural. For one thing, her damn dad was upstairs. She slipped her hand back out of my

132

pants and half pulled her shirt closed.

"Don't you want me?" she wondered.

"But your dad..."

"Is asleep. Trust me, he never wakes up."

"Yeah, but what about—"

"Protection? It's covered."

She slipped something out of her pocket and waggled it at me.

"Now," she said, leaning over and kissing me. As she did, she took my left hand and put it on her breast. "Tell me you love me."

"Oh, God," I breathed.

"I love you so much, Jack," she said.

She started to unbutton my pants as she kissed me again.

"I don't..." I managed to say between kisses.

She froze again.

"I mean, we shouldn't..." I corrected.

She looked so confused; so hurt. She swung off me and stood up next to the couch with her back to me, buttoning her shirt.

"Go home, Jack," she said. "If that's what you want."

"It's *not* what I want," I denied.

She looked over her shoulder and smiled cryptically, then turned back to me when she was done buttoning her shirt. I sat up and buttoned my pants; fastened my belt. She leaned over and kissed me again, slowly, giving me plenty of time to do something—to touch her, to start unbuttoning her shirt. I kissed her, but that was all.

"Yes it is," she decided with another smile. "I'll call you tomorrow."

É

I hadn't really hung out with Sammy for weeks. We saw each other at school and still hung out between classes and at lunch, but after school we never got together any more, except at work. He was with Donna Marie every day. Thing is, his grades had actually improved over those couple of weeks. Donna Marie was heading for valedictorian, which meant a lot of their dates were study dates, so what the hell else was Sammy going to do? He'd also toned down his attire somewhat—no doubt because he was spending so much time at Donna Marie's house, with her parents around—and with his fancy new haircut, he looked almost presentable. Sure, Missy had taken me shopping at the Gap on her work discount, and I'd picked up a couple of shirts, but Sammy had previously been the king of the off-color rock shirt. Now he dressed more like me: lame, no-logo shirts, loose fitting jeans, Chuck Taylors (with an ollie flap), a slightly shredded flannel... It was kind of weird. Thing is, for the first time since I'd known him, he also looked *comfortable*.

But I still never got to see him. I'd set this grand plan in motion and got him a date to the King of Hearts dance with Donna Marie, only the plan hadn't included Sammy never skating with me and Niz again, and never going to shows.

I slammed my locker shut more forcefully than I'd intended. The sound echoed down the hall to Tobie, who smiled in an oddly shy way and walked slowly toward me, as if expecting me to turn and run off. It was like she was trying to move up to me slowly, to see if I'd try and bite her before she got too close.

"You never called me last night," she said when she got close enough. I thought she was giving me a hard time, but she suddenly looked serious.

"Oh... Well, you know, I had to work."

"Did you talk to Sammy?"

"Sammy?" Niz piped up, slamming his locker door. "Have you heard something about our young, sick friend, Miz Tobie?"

"I'm *serious*, guys," she said. "Jolly was there, too—he said Sammy was in pretty bad shape."

I looked at Niz, Niz shrugged.

"Seems like it turned out better than the last time he was at the Wharf."

Tobie shifted her weight to the other foot and glowered at Niz, then at me.

"Wasn't that *you* at the Wharf two nights ago, Tobe?" Niz asked pointedly.

"Shut up, Niz," she growled. "I'm *serious*. Jack!"

"I don't know what to say, Tobie," I replied truthfully. "So Sammy cut loose for once... You know that his grades are actually *up*, right?"

She fixed her gaze on me and I looked her deep in the eyes. There was real concern in there, like the slow realization that everything bad you thought would happen was happening. The thing with Tobie is, she cared for everyone like they were relatives. Maybe it was her being an only child,

135

but she genuinely seemed to take on other people's pain. What I hated is when I looked into her eyes, I saw that pain and knew it was in my power to stop it.

"I'll talk to him," I finally said. "I mean, I see him at work tonight."

"Thanks."

She leaned over and gave me a light peck on the cheek, just to make sure I didn't forget.

"Shit," Niz mocked once she'd walked off. "That girl's got you wrapped around her finger."

"What girl?" Missy demanded.

She had walked up in time to see Tobie walk off.

"Tobie Malloy," Niz answered, absolutely unaware, I assume, that Missy had fire and laser beams shooting out of her eyes. I giggled nervously and put my hand on her arm. She shied away, but didn't pull back.

"He's kidding."

"I saw her kiss you."

"What? *When*?" I gasped.

"Just... right... *then*... Jack," she enunciated.

"What? That little peck—?"

"*Yes*. That little *peck*. What *was* that?"

Niz gave me a stupid screwed-up-face look over Missy's head. I chuckled and tried to turn it into an exasperated laugh of disbelief.

"She wanted me to talk to Sammy and I said I would. She was just saying thanks."

"Does she always say thanks with a kiss?"

Weird thing is, I didn't know how to respond to that. Now that she mentioned it, Tobie did often give me a peck

136

on the cheek by way of thanks, and I don't think she did that to anyone else. But she'd always done that. It was basically meaningless. Right?

"Look, I've known Tobie forever. I'm like her brother, y'know?"

Missy didn't look terribly convinced but at least she was thinking it over.

"Forever," she said quietly, giving me a suspicious look.

"Yeah. Sixth grade. Wouldn't you give your brother a peck on the cheek if he did something nice for you?"

She sighed and grudgingly nodded, but I don't think she bought it. She was trying to be nice.

"So that's all she wanted? What's wrong with Sammy?"

"Oh, you know—last night at the Wharf. We've all been worried about him since his dad left."

"His dad left?" Missy checked.

I went cold. Surely she knew that already? Jesus, was Sammy keeping that a secret? Did I just fucking blow it with him and Donna Marie?

"Yeah," I squeaked. "You didn't know?"

She shook her head, so I turned the head game around and played it back on her.

"I thought Donna Marie would've told you...?"

"Hm," she grunted. "Visit me on break at work tonight?" she said, turning on her heel.

"Sure. Of course."

"And you're going to be late for class."

She ducked into her class right as the second bell rang.

"You seem pensive," a voice said right next to me, startling me. I really had to start standing with my back to my

137

locker so no one could sneak up on me. I juggled my books, but one still fell to the floor with a slap.

"Ally!" I gasped. "Scared the *shit* out of me."

She grinned and bent down to pick up my book. Her hair was tinged red today and she'd gone extra thick with the black eyeliner and even black lipstick. She was wearing an XL concert shirt over some other shirt and had on a black skirt. Beneath that, she had knit stockings. On her right leg, she wore red and black stripes, on her left, black with red skulls. On her feet were the ubiquitous black Chuck Taylors.

"Your socks don't match," I quipped as she stood up and handed me the book, giving me a fuck-you smirk and cocking her head to one side.

"Sammy asked me to ask *you* to give this note to Donna Marie," she said, handing me a piece of folded paper.

I looked over her head, half expecting to see Sammy standing down the hall—I was slightly panicked to think he wasn't even talking to me between classes now.

"What?" Ally replied, turning to look at what I was looking at.

"Where's Sammy?"

"He barfed and went home. Rumor has it he went to the Wharf last night with Donna Marie."

"I know *that*, but—"

Ally wasn't smiling any longer. She raised an eyebrow with motherly concern.

"I thought you guys were straight-edge?"

"Well, it's just really hard to skate otherwise, and we'd rather skate. So he really did get drunk last night?"

"Rumor has it."

"Yeah, I guess that's weird."

She looked at me for several seconds, somehow making me feel worse with her absolutely non-judgmental expression. Ally wasn't exactly straight-edge either, from what I'd seen once or twice at Sudsy's, but she was certainly calling Sammy out. I got the sense it was him acting out of character that she most resented, not him drinking.

"So what's the note say?" I asked, slipping it into my back pocket. "I'm already doing Tobie's dirty work—suddenly, he's the most popular guy on campus. Maybe I should start drinking, too."

"Don't be an ass, Jack."

"Just what I was thinking," Missy said from right behind me.

I jumped again and dropped the same book. Missy looked down at it, then back at me. Ally bent down and picked it up again, sticking it back on top of the stack.

"Thanks," I said to her.

"Yeah. *Thanks*," Missy agreed sarcastically.

"Never mind," Ally replied, and walked off.

"What was *she* doing?" Missy demanded.

"What are *you* doing? I thought you were in class?"

It didn't come out right, and I knew it before I saw the look Missy cut me. It sounded like I'd planned the whole thing with Ally.

"Ally said Sammy asked her to give me a note for Donna Marie," I explained.

I pulled it out of my pocket and showed it to her and started walking slowly toward my class. At first I didn't think she was going to follow me back to hers, but she did.

139

"Sure... But why do you guys hang around with that *freak*?"

"Oh, she's all right. We're all a little weird, aren't we?"

Missy didn't smile back at me. "No. And you don't even have *lunch* with me and Donna Marie, so *when* were you supposed to give her this *note*?"

"I don't know—in the halls?"

"So Ally must be pretty *stupid*, too," Missy decided.

"Hey, don't be mean!" I protested.

She smiled warmly and kissed me softly on the lips.

"Then stop hanging out with freaks," she whispered.

"Oh," she added, stopping and half turning to me. "And don't kiss any other girls in the hall, even if they're your sister."

I think I half nodded. She ducked back into her classroom and left me standing there with my stack of books. I almost wanted to yell after her that I ate lunch with Ally every day, but I didn't. I watched Missy for a second as she sat down, flashing waves and smiles at everyone. She had a lot of friends. As I watched, I realized this was the class she had with Tobie, and Tobie caught my eye and gave me a subtle wave, mouthing, "Call me."

I nodded and refocused and saw that Missy was watching me—watching us—intently. I smiled at her and managed to waggle a finger as a substitute wave under my pile of books. She stuck out her tongue at me, not entirely playfully, as the third bell rang.

"You're late," she mouthed.

Missy was at least thorough when she broke up with me, the Sunday before the King of Hearts dance. She laid it all out very well, but what it really came down to was that she realized she wasn't as in to me as she *thought* she was in to me. I'm still not convinced she actually liked me, not *that* much. I think she liked the *idea* of me, I'm just not vain enough to believe she actually *liked* me. The week before the breakup hadn't been great, even by our standards. She'd gone to the Wharf twice, both on a night when I had to work, and I didn't feel like going over there after. Instead, I went skating, and one time I ran into Ally, then Missy caught us talking about it the next day in the halls. I think that was when it ended for her. She was clearly the type of girl who expected the sun to rise and set on her, and when it didn't, she got pissed.

"I made out with a guy at the Wharf last night," she said to me when she called that Sunday. I admit it, I felt a little sick, a little like I should've been there to prevent it.

"Oh," I replied, which was apparently the wrong answer.

"Didn't you *hear* me?" she demanded.

"Yeah, I did. So I guess you're breaking up with me? Is he taking you to the dance?"

"*Yass.*" (That's how she said it, with that teenage twang.)

Now I was pissed. She bitched at me because Tobie gave

141

me a peck on the cheek but she's out at Grope Central making out with some guy?

"Which one?" I demanded.

"Which one what?"

"Yes, you're breaking up with me, or *yass*, this guy you were making out with is taking you to the dance?"

"Look, *Jack*, you obviously don't give a *crap* about me. You'd rather go *skating* than hang *out* with me. You take me to some *dive* to see some *stupid* band. You won't stop *talking* to these *sluts* that hang all *over* you. You didn't *switch lunches* so you could *eat* with me. You don't even *wear* the nice *clothes* I got you, but you wear that stupid *ring* that *freak* gave you."

"Sluts?" I questioned when I could get a word in edgewise. It was the only thing she'd said that wasn't true. "What *sluts*?"

"Look, it's just *not* going to work *out*."

"So you're actually breaking up with me, five days before King of Hearts?"

"*Yass*."

"You're ridiculous, you know that? You think you're so *cool* and so *popular*, but deep down, you know you're *not*. *That's* why I bother you so much, because now you *actually* know me, I'm not what you *expected* and you didn't get *any* cooler by dating me."

"What*ever*. Face it, I'm the best you've ever had and you blew it."

"You're the...? I *what*?"

Silence.

"Hello?"

She'd hung up.

I slammed the phone down, then picked it up and slammed it down again for good measure. It pissed me off that *she* had the nerve to break up with *me* when *I* was going to break up with *her*, but I at least had the decency to wait until after the dance.

"Everything okay, Jacky B?" my mom yelled up the stairs. The sound of the slamming phone must have echoed.

"Fine! I'm fine!"

I sucked in a deep breath. My pulse was pounding and I felt nauseous. I may not have been overly attentive of Missy but I'd always been a nice guy. Didn't nice guys get the pretty girls any more? Or did they ever, for that matter. She was a bitch, that's all there was to it. I had to convince myself of that fact, but when I thought of her face and her round cheeks and her doey eyes and the way her lips tasted, it didn't work. She was a bitch, I was a dick, and we both deserved to be unhappy. One thing I didn't want to do was cry, so I channeled it into anger, not at her but at the fact that *I* hadn't got to break up. She really thought she was all that, and that boys only dated her at *her* whim. I really should've taken the chance to take her down a notch—make her realize that maybe *she* was the problem.

Sammy tried to help when I explained this to him the next night at work, but he'd already heard Missy's side of it from Donna Marie. Missy had spent lunch blabbing to Donna Marie, while Sammy and I, in our lunch period, had spent the time bickering about how to accomplish a trick I didn't believe was even possible using Newtonian physics (I was in an argumentative mood, of course). After school, when they were supposed to be studying, Donna Marie had filled him in, and now, here we were, the man with a date to King of Hearts with one of the most popular girls in school, and me, the world's most depressed hotdog vendor. I stabbed a 'dog meaningfully with the tongs.

"I gotta get that job at the toy store back," I whimpered. "I can't stand this place any more."

"That's just your memories talking," Sammy opined.

"No, it's not. It's the fact that I smell like a fucking grease pit when I get off work. It's the fact that our manager is a toady little shit who can't speak above a mumble. Seriously, I think he has a medical condition."

"Jack, you're just pissed—"

"Yes I am."

Sammy didn't know what to say and I'm not sure I expected him to say anything.

"I'm sorry, Sammy. I hope I didn't ruin it for you and Donna Marie."

He shook his head and smiled a guilty smile. "Nah—I don't think you need to worry. We're fine."

"I can't believe it worked out, man."

"I can't believe I porked the Homecoming queen," he agreed.

We both stopped and stared at each other, his blurted admission hanging like a bowling ball above our toes. I knew by the color draining from his face that he hadn't meant to say it, and he knew by my expression that it had struck a chord with me that I hadn't even known was there to strike.

"Look, I'm sorry you and Missy broke up," he finally said.

144

"She fucked *herself*, cuz now she'll have to go to the dance with some dateless idiot, if she goes at all. What? Why are you looking at me like that, Sammy? What do you know? Did she find a *date* already?"

He nodded slowly.

"Who?"

"Jack, look—"

"*Who*, Samuel?"

"Greg Wilson."

I flung the tongs onto the rollers and huffed into the back room, taking off my apron as I walked.

"I'm going on break," I announced.

I didn't look back at Sammy on purpose—if I had, I'd have apologized and then I'd probably have cried. I didn't blame him, but I'd be lying if I said it wasn't there: The knowledge of the cruel irony that my impromptu plan had worked, but me—the matchmaker—was now without a date, even as Greg fucking Wilson ended up with the dream date I was supposed to have.

The toy store was right up the escalators from the food court—the same escalators where Greg Wilson had taken an unexpected tumble. December felt like a lifetime ago, but there it was, still flapping around in the air of my life, taking whatever digs it could at me. As I drifted up the escalator I glanced back along the food court to the hotdog stand and saw Sammy standing there, twirling the tongs like a gunslinger. At least he didn't seem upset.

"*He* wears the clothes she buys," I mumbled to myself.

What was wrong with me? What if Missy was right? What if she was my one-and-only chance to date one of the

145

popular girls and I *had* blown it? And did that even matter? Did I want to go out with someone because they were pretty and popular? She listened to shitty music, enjoyed shitty movies, dressed like a bag of Skittles, and spent more time on her hair than her manners. She also laughed at my jokes, and not just to be polite. And she at least *tried* to find common ground, by going to see my shitty bands and letting me pick the movies every now and again.

The toy store was as dead as the rest of the mall. I stormed in and demanded loudly, "Steve!"

He poked his head out of aisle two, juggling too many Barbies in his arms.

"Jack!" He smiled at first, then he put down (dropped) the Barbies and tried to nonchalantly walk over. "You okay, man?"

"You gotta take me back, Steve," I begged. "I know it's winter and the store's dead and the Christmas season is over and all that, but I can't turn another fucking hotdog, Steve— sorry."

He held up his hands to show he didn't have any fight in him. The bulging muscles and repo-man mustache said differently. He held my gaze for a few seconds then cracked a crooked grin.

"We'd love to have ya back, you know that."

"Yeah?"

"Bobbi said I should come down and talk to you. That gal we kept on after Christmas didn't work out. You're a good worker, Jack—*great*, actually—but this *is* a toy store. Kids shop here. Moms shop here. Grandmothers shop here."

"I get it."

146

"Really, it's just your hair. If you come back, would you wear an officially sanctioned toy-store ball cap on the clock? Moms don't like mohawks..."

"Yes! Are you serious? I can come back?"

"If you wear the cap. And..." His eyes flickered over my face, gauging how far he could push me. "And if you take out your earrings."

"Done," I said simply.

Steve smiled widely with relief. "When can you start?"

"Right now."

"How about tomorrow night? Five to nine?"

I thought about Sammy down at the hotdog stand, twirling tongs by himself.

"I have to work tomorrow night, actually."

"Two weeks, then?"

I shook my head. "I won't last that long." Then I sighed heavily. "But yeah, I guess that'd be the nice thing to do."

"Glad to have you back, Jack. I'll put you on the schedule."

King of Hearts was like the middle kid of high school dances: It wasn't first, so it didn't get a parade, and it wasn't last, so it didn't get all the attention—it was stuck in the middle, a hinterland of teenage social life tacked halfheartedly to Valentine's Day (a connection so loose I didn't even make it until years later). But it was still one of the big three. I never went to a single other high school dance except the big three, and King of Hearts was as good a way as any to break up the doldrums of winter.

I went with Tobie. Niz was with Jess, and Jolly—whose dad had a big fucking Cadillac he let Jolly borrow—tripled with us with Ally. Sammy was with Donna Marie, surviving a slice of the real life with the popular set, an uncomfortable happenstance that put him in the same carpool with Greg Wilson and Missy Anderson. I guess Greg had been giving him the stink-eye all night, and Missy was giving me the silent treatment by ignoring Sammy, but they were all so enamored of Donna Marie Meadows that none of them wanted to piss her off by being openly judgmental.

"It's like a fucking teen drama on fucking TV," Sammy admitted after cornering me at the punch bowl, away from the dance floor. The punch—donated by McDonald's no doubt, with a few bags of marshmallows thrown in for good measure—was not good, but it was wet.

"How's your night?" Sammy wondered.

I tried to downplay it. He knew damn well how my night was.

"Why didn't Jolly hook up with you guys instead of us?" I asked.

"Are you kidding?" Sammy scoffed. "There's no *way* Missy and Donna Marie would've been caught *dead* with Ally McShay—no offense."

I looked over at our table. Ally and Tobie were laughing at something I can only assume Niz had said, based solely on his expression and the fact that Jess was rolling her eyes.

Jolly stuck out like a sore thumb in his Wall Street suit, but he looked good and he looked like he was having fun. Ally glanced over and caught my eye, so I smiled and she smiled back, a slightly embarrassed twist in the way she ducked my gaze.

"What's your problem? What's wrong with Ally?"

"Nothing, Jack—you know that." He looked over at her then leaned in and whispered, "Word is, she wanted to come to this thing with you."

I laughed. I honestly laughed.

"I doubt that, Samuel. Jolly's perfect for her."

"So you and Tobie...?"

"Just friends."

"Yeah? For how long?"

I glanced over at the table again and my eyes drifted to Ally. She'd dyed her streaks to match her dress, which was a deep (but somehow still bright) blue. Her lipstick matched her sleeves and tights though—black as pitch. She had on a Victorian-looking choker and I think she'd put a very small amount of glitter on her cheeks. She looked amazing, and I knew I wasn't the only guy who thought so.

"Ally McShay, huh?" I mumbled. "What about Jolly?"

"Nah—they came as friends. I think he did it to piss off Missy for breaking up with you, and Ally did it to hang out with you."

"Look at you!" I declared. "Mister 'I'm dating the Homecoming queen so I know alls about luv.' Jolly wouldn't go to a dance with a girl to piss off *my* ex-girlfriend."

"True," Sammy agreed. "And Ally *is* hot, as you have pointed out to me more than once, Mr. Beltane. Maybe he's

149

hoping he'll get lucky."

"I think your first excuse is closer to the truth, if that's the only other option. Jolly's a good guy."

"Hey, we're all dudes."

He shrugged and left it at that, splopping punch into a couple of cups before he jugglingly picked them up and headed to the other side of the gym and the table where Donna Marie was holding court. I knew Sammy and I knew he wasn't having any fun, and it made me wonder if his own motivations were closer to what he thought of Jolly's—was he with Donna Marie just to bone the hottest girl in school? And *was* she even that hot?

"They sent me to help you," Ally said, tapping me on the shoulder.

"What?"

I spun around and she smiled kindly at me.

"Tobie said I should come over and see what was taking you so long."

"Oh—I ran into Sammy."

She nodded. She knew that, and she knew that I knew that she knew that.

"Do you ever dance at these things?" she asked.

"Sure—slow dances. I'm not much of a fast dancer."

"Jesus, you sound like an old man!"

"I can't keep up with you kids!" I protested in an old-fogey voice.

She stood there and smiled at my joke, turning slowly as if trying to dance without looking like she wanted to. Man alive, but her eyes pierced right into me, clearing my mind of all worldly thoughts, Sammy's whispered comments about her wanting to come to the dance with me the only thing still echoing in my head. I didn't believe him, not really, and I certainly couldn't do that to Jolly, not right here at the dance.

"Maybe we should get the punch," Ally decided, as if I'd offered to do something else instead.

"Sure," I agreed.

As I followed her back to the table I couldn't keep my eyes off her legs and the way she moved, and I thought about Sammy's other comment, that we're all dudes. When I sat down, Tobie gave me a knowing smirk; I blushed and looked away.

"You know, Ally can hit that curb up in Harbin Park riding goofy foot?" Tobie said to me.

"False," I responded. "I've skated that curb with her and she can barely hit it regular foot."

"Hey!" Ally protested.

"It's true!" Jolly chimed in. "I was there, and you missed. A lot."

"That was my first time goofy foot!" Ally said in her defense. "But, Bells, tell 'em! I hit it all the time when it was just me and you!"

"Woah-HO!" Niz squealed. "What have we *here*? You hit *what*, exactly, Miz McShay?"

"Fuck you," she replied evenly.

"Jack just likes to hang out with pretty girls," Jolly offered. "He doesn't hit anything, though."

We all laughed, but to be fair, it was actually true. Half my best friends were girls who weren't girlfriends, and they were both pretty. Ally's gaze lingered on me as if she was trying to figure me out or was waiting for me to refute the

151

claim, but God damn Sammy had put ridiculous thoughts in my head, and now all I could think of was kissing her, so I shyly looked away.

"How often have you skated alone together?" Tobie asked without an ounce of suspicion. She looked over at Jolly and he smiled knowingly back at her.

"Not often!" Ally said quickly, turning to Tobie with mild shock. "Just a few times—right, Bells?"

"Yeah," I said. "Just a few times."

"I don't care," Tobie said slyly—there's really no other word for it.

"What's going on with you two?" I asked her, glancing at Jolly. "You're up to something."

"Nope," Tobie said, cutting off Jolly at his open mouth. "We came to dance. Right, Jolly?"

"That's right!" (He sounded like he was guessing.)

"So let's go," Tobie suggested, taking his hand and standing up with him. Jolly looked at me with a shocked expression similar to Ally's.

"We're not dating," I said to him in a clipped tone, pretending this should be obvious to everyone.

Tobie pulled him away and Niz and Jess followed them out to the dance floor.

"So you and Tobie really did come as friends."

It was a statement, not a question. Ally sighed heavily and grinned at me.

"Yeah... We always do."

Despite being alone with Ally, I was glum thinking about Missy being with Greg Wilson, and missing Sammy. I felt like I'd left a kid in the care of someone I didn't trust, and I didn't know if that feeling was for Sammy or Missy. I was afraid Sammy wasn't having any fun, and I couldn't even go over and try to spice up the evening for him, not with Missy and Greg around.

"Why so down?" Ally wondered, misreading my mood. "Are you bothered that Tobie's slow dancing with Jolly?"

"Nah..." I waved her away dismissively—I really wasn't —then it sank in, what she'd said. "Wait—*what*? Jolly's...? Aw, that sucks, Ally—I'm sorry. Lemme go talk to her—"

She put her hand on my arm and stopped me from standing up.

"It's okay, Bells—we came as friends, too."

Every once in a great while, being glum works wonders with the ladies. Case in point: I was so sore at Missy and afraid of somehow ruining Sammy's dance that I didn't think through what I said next—I was too depressed to give a shit. I just said it: "Maybe *we* should go dance, then."

"Okay," she agreed, slipping her hand into mine as we stood up. She led me to the dance floor, near enough to Jolly and Tobie that it seemed social, but not so close as to seem rude. Jolly winked at me. Tobie gave me a knowing grin that I didn't fully understand.

"What's going on here?" I asked Ally.

The music, though a ballad, was still loud, and I had to talk almost directly into her ear. She smelled good and her skin looked smooth and bright under the revolving lights.

"What do you mean?"

"I think they're trying to set us up."

"Who?"

"Jolly and Tobie."

153

She didn't look over at them. She kept her head slightly down, staring at my shoulder, her arms around my neck, my hands clasped behind her back.

"Would that be so bad?"

"I just broke up with Missy," I mumbled.

I couldn't believe it, even as I said it. Never in a million years did I think I'd be slow dancing with Ally McShay, and now I was snubbing her? Missy had been different—an accident, almost; a side effect of trying to get Sammy a date to the Prom. I'd never even considered Missy Anderson until I beaned Donna Marie with a hotdog bun and she turned around, so I'd never had the chance to think about it. But Ally? I saw Ally every day. I'd made a career out of talking myself out of asking her out, always rationalizing that she was way too good for me. Skating didn't count—I skated with Sammy and Niz, and *we* weren't dating. Plus, it didn't happen *that* often. Maybe three times. Or five. No more than seven, to be sure. But who's counting? It was always easier to go out with Tobie and the gang, and I guess in hindsight that's the real reason why Ally always stayed away, not because she had better things to do but because she thought I wanted to be with other people.

She looked up at me. "I know... I didn't mean... I just..."

"It's okay."

"Kiss me, Jack," she whispered.

"Why?"

It was seriously like someone else was in control of my body; like I couldn't control my tongue enough to form the right words. She whipped out of my arms and made a bee-line for the doors. Tobie looked at me like I'd just kicked her favorite dog, then chased after her. Jolly gave me a "this is how you repay me?" shrug, so I chased after Tobie. As I burst through the doors I caught the tail-end of Tobie ducking down the hall to the bathrooms, so I figured that's where they were going. I turned around expecting to see Jolly, but he wasn't there—probably he'd gone to tell Jess what had happened. That's what any of us did when something went wrong, especially if Tobie was involved—Jess always put things right.

I shuffled down the hall toward the bathrooms, deciding what the hell I should do. Quite seriously, I couldn't believe my own behavior and I figured I should tell her that. But then what? End with, "So how about that kiss now?" That didn't seem like a good move. I'd just ruined what to her was going to be a real moment—the start of something new. I had done to her what I was always afraid she would do to me if I ever revealed my interest in her as something more than a lunch buddy and backstage props partner.

"I can't believe you, Jack Beltane."

I thought it was Jess and was about to tell her that her voice sounded funny, but it wasn't her. It was Missy. She'd snuck up to harass me. Or, more likely, had taken the chance to harass me on her way to the bathroom.

"Excuse me?" I asked, not at all politely.

"So you come to the dance with *Tobie* and end up dancing with *her*?"

She meant Ally, of course, but I played dumb. I was not in the mood.

"Who? Ally?"

"*Yes*, Ally."

"I told you: Tobie and I are *just friends*. In fact, truth be told, she's trying to set me and Ally up, and I just blew it."

I'm not entirely sure why I said that to her. I guess I thought it might hurt her and salvage some good for me from what had suddenly become a gloriously shitty evening. I was trying to turn the knife, only it was the knife she had already stuck in me. She was obviously jealous and I was trying to use Ally to add a level of insult to injury. Because, truth be told, I still wasn't sure what had just happened, but I was starting to convince myself that Ally was being polite and going along with Tobie and Jolly's plan and I'd made a fool of her by not falling for it.

Whatever. It hadn't worked. Missy shoved me halfheartedly, then a look of revelation crossed her face.

"Tobie set this *whole thing* up!" she declared.

"What?"

"She *knew* I'd break up with you so she could set you up with that *freak*. She *never* liked me!"

I couldn't argue the last point, but the first part seemed to be a bit of a stretch. So Tobie had supposedly timed her innocent peck on my cheek perfectly to make sure Missy was watching so that Missy would get jealous and break up with me so that Tobie could set me up with Ally? Okay, actually, I could see that. Tobie was wily.

"Tobie didn't do this," I disagreed anyway.

"Do what?" Tobie asked.

Ally was hanging back behind her, looking at me sheepishly. Seeing me there, arguing with Missy, I think she realized I was in a bad place and hadn't meant anything personal by snubbing her, and it made me feel bad that she felt bad. I

156

started to turn to her, to tell her I was sorry, when Missy bumped into me as she lunged at Tobie.

"You *bitch*!" Missy shrieked.

I stepped into her path and deflected her off me, turning her around a bit.

"Hey! Keep your hands *off* her!"

It was Greg Wilson and he was closing in quickly, representing the firm fist of fate, which landed a solid blow on my left cheek and knocked me off balance and onto my ass.

"Jack!" Ally yelled, and suddenly everyone was yelling and shoving and Sammy appeared out of nowhere and Donna Marie actually *screamed* as if someone had pulled a gun or something, and all I could think was that I'd never heard Ally yell before, not like that. She sounded panicked. She swooped down and helped me up, her lip quivering and her eyes wet, though I couldn't tell if she was still crying or just starting to cry.

"Jack? Are you okay?"

Before I knew it, Jess was there and Niz and Jolly and some of Greg's friends. From what I could tell, all of my friends were trying to break it up and all of them were using it as an excuse to throw punches.

"Hey! Hey!" Jolly was yelling—probably the only guy they'd've listened to, but even he seemed to be having no luck. There was a real brawl brewing, then bodies started to fly—like, literally: Something grabbed Greg Wilson and flung him aside like a rag doll. He spun completely around and had to catch his balance bent over on his hands, but he stayed on his feet. It was a couple of the off-duty cops they hired for security. They broke it all up in about five seconds

157

flat. I recognized the one cop, and I think he recognized us—he was one of the good cops who didn't bust us for skating.

"I think you all better go back to the dance," he said. He could have easily kicked us out, but I imagine the scuffle maybe wasn't as big as it seemed in my mind. "And make sure you stay away from each other. One wrong move, and we get a paddy wagon down here."

"You guys have a *paddy* wagon?" Greg sneered. It amazed me how he and his buddies seemed completely unable to turn off being jerks, even to a cop.

"One more word and you'll find out, smart ass. I ain't some teacher who has to put up with your *shit* because they're afraid of your parents. I'm the guy who'll take you to jail, and the more you fight, the longer you'll stay."

That shut him up. Greg turned and walked off, yanking Missy after him hard enough to make her wince. I'd like to think her eyes met mine and she looked apologetic, begging me to rescue her like we'd rescued Tobie, but I doubt that's true.

"I think you're the only one who really got hit," the cop said to me. "You want an ambulance?"

"No, thanks," I mumbled with a chuckle. "It's just a bump."

"Well, I had to ask. It's my job."

He winked before he turned and walked off—he actually winked.

"I'm sorry I ruined your dance," I said to Ally. "I'm sorry I ruined *every*one's dance."

"Let's go back to my place," Sammy said. It shocked me to hear his voice. I did a double take, but sure enough, he was still there.

158

And Donna Marie was standing beside him, holding his hand, looking scared and vaguely guilty.

"Sammy? What are you doing here?"

He looked at Donna Marie for support and bit his lip. In his suit and with his haircut, he looked... well, he looked like a regular guy. The kind of guy who might date the Homecoming queen. I felt woozy.

"Greg hasn't been in a good mood all night," Donna Marie finally answered for him, as if she knew she had to be the one to say it. "Missy had just stormed off when... well, you were there, I guess."

"Look at us," I whispered.

I scanned the faces myself: Jess, Niz, Tobie, Sammy, Ally, Jolly, and Donna Marie. It was strange company for her, and I realized that maybe none of us fit in, we each just decided how much we were going to try. Ally was on one end of the scale—and I'll never forget how she looked that night—and Donna Marie was on the other end, looking totally forgettable despite how attractive she was.

"My mom said we could come over after," Sammy offered again.

"I have to get back to Missy," Donna Marie said softly.

"I can't go back in there," Sammy said. "Not now."

"I know," she agreed. "But I have to."

She let go of his hand. Panic flittered across Sammy's face.

"I can't leave you—"

"It's okay."

She smiled sweetly. She turned and looked at all of us, smiling just as brightly.

"Sorry, Jack," she added to me. "Greg sorta holds a grudge."

"No kidding."

"I *can't* leave you," Sammy interjected more forcefully. "Come with us. Who's going to notice? Or care?"

"My friends?"

It was a rhetorical question, without the slightest tone of accusation.

"Look, I'll get a ride home with Jenny and Baxter," she said. "Don't worry. We were about to leave anyway."

"Yeah," Sammy agreed dejectedly.

"It's okay," Donna Marie said. "Call me tomorrow?"

"Yeah," Sammy replied again.

This was his out, no matter how tenuous—his easy way to escape Greg and Missy and Donna Marie's other friends without looking like that's what he was doing—and he couldn't let it slip away: He wanted Donna Marie to be with him, but he didn't want to hang out with her friends for another minute, especially not after the fight.

Donna Marie turned and walked off, the *tack tack tack* of her heels like the sound of a lonely heartbeat in an empty room.

Intermission

February

"What are you doing out here?"

I turned and caught a glimpse of her as she moved between shadows. Behind her the parking lot looked abandoned, the dull orange glow of the lights trying feebly to beat back the night.

"Hey, Ally," I mumbled. "Just looking at the stars."

"I saw you sneak out."

I shrugged. "They're just playing their ad-lib games. I wasn't going to take part, anyway."

Ally chuckled and stepped up beside me, her hands dug deep into her coat pockets against the cold. She threw back her head to get her hair off her face and smiled. It was an honest smile; a good smile. A smile that said she was glad we were alone, with eyes that sparkled around a secret she had yet to share.

"Well," she agreed. "I guess there's not much for us techies to do at these things, is there?"

This weekend, the streaks in her hair were purple—subdued, she told me later, in deference to the drama club retreat we were on. It was our annual rite of passage—the time and place where the Seniors officially passed the torch to the next in line for the big roles next year; the calm and retrospective before the last play of the year.

I shrugged again, dimly aware that she might think I was being standoffish. I wasn't—I'd come outside for some air because watching everyone laugh and carry on had suddenly hit home that I wouldn't have this next year; that this was my last retreat. I don't think I'd realized how much I looked forward to them until that moment.

I turned quickly and smiled at her, probably trading a look of aloofness for one of psychosis. Truth be told, I had butterflies in my stomach that I'd never felt before when she was around. The drama retreat, Mr. K always said, was a chance to clear our heads and be ourselves—and that's exactly how that moment with Ally felt. For the first time we were completely alone, without any threat of interruption—no random skaters to happen along, no sets to change, no classes to run off to. I was never sure why we did the retreats in winter, but suddenly it seemed like the perfect time of year: The season was long and cold and no longer welcome, but the rebirth of spring still seemed very far away, hidden behind clouds of frozen air blown around by winds with teeth.

Deep winter was the pause; a time out of time.

Winter was dark and quiet and the cold air inspired huddled conferences—no colors, no sounds, no games, no distractions. The crisp focus of life is always sharpest in the darkest winter nights; the soft crunch of snow beneath your feet like a reminder of how fragile such crystalline beauty is, as your breath curls skyward toward the moon. It's only in winter that space feels so close and the end so near; that our ties to the Earth seem loose enough to break and let us drift away, silently, into eternity.

Ally tilted her head back more and looked up at the stars, and I watched in slow motion as her lips—so perfectly painted to match her hair—separated just a touch.

"I guess they invite us because they need an audience," I said casually, or so I hoped. She smiled, anyway.

"Is that Orion?"

I looked where she was pointing, moving unconsciously to her side, our breath billowing into clouds that merged then dissipated.

"Yeah," I agreed. "Kinda hard to miss, huh?"

"Yeah," she whispered.

She looked at me, her eyes twinkling in the moonlight like tiny stars in tiny black universes, a slow smile creeping across her lips. "Wanna go for a walk?"

My tongue clicked in my throat. There was no way she was serious, not about taking a walk with me, not after what had happened at the King of Hearts dance. I knew for a fact there was at least one guy much cooler than me still inside the lodge playing games, and we still hadn't cleared the air about what had happened at the dance. In fact, all week she'd been acting like nothing had happened—so much so that I had to wonder if anything even had. And yes, it was fucked up that within a week of a girl asking me to kiss her I was talking myself out of asking her out. Again.

"Sure," I replied in the only clipped tone I could muster. "Sammy and I found an old pool yesterday."

"Cool."

165

She nodded and her hair—cut close to her shoulders, right along her neckline—bobbed over her face, accenting her nose and the round domes of her cheeks.

"Did you skate it?"

"Nah. Not that kind of pool. It's just your generic shitty rectangle in the ground—no sloping sides or nothing."

We walked up the blacktop path toward the center of the camp. The place they did the annual drama club retreats was an old abandoned summer camp. Rumor was, some toxic chemical dump nearby had forced it to shut down, but since we only went up for one weekend a year, it was safe. I have to assume "safe" was in quotes, mostly because I heard that the next year they weren't allowed back—the place was sealed off for good. By then I'd graduated, so it didn't seem to matter that much to me. Now, I'm not so sure. Maybe that place was worth saving.

"So, did you have fun at the King of Hearts dance?" Ally asked casually.

I cast her a sidelong glance; she was grinning, but she didn't meet my gaze. She knew damn well it had been a train wreck. I wondered why she'd brought it up, especially now, after we'd ignored the issue all last week. I could tell by her smirk that she was trying to make fun of me or something.

"Sure...?" I said slowly. "I guess—all things considered."

"That's cool."

"You were there, remember...?" I asked sarcastically.

She sucked in a deep breath. I heard her open her mouth, then close it, then open it again.

"I was going to ask you, you know," she finally blurted. "But we didn't... you know... There was only a week between you breaking up with Missy Anderson and the dance..."

If she'd bothered to look over at me she'd've seen that I was gaping. My nerves almost instantly evaporated when I realized how much pluck it had taken for her to come out here and say that to me, which must have been why she followed me in the first place. Had it been churning in her all week, whether or not to tempt a second snub? Had she thought to say that before we ever left for the retreat? Or had it just occurred to her, right before she came outside? She did finally half glance my way, rattling me to speak before she got the wrong idea, sobbed an apology, and ran away again. I didn't think I could stand the sight of that twice.

"Are you kidding?"

Yeah, that's what I came up with: Just about the only question that could be taken the wrong way very easily. She huffed out a breath and faked a shiver.

"Forget it," she quipped. "I didn't want to go to the stupid dance anyway. Jolly just said—"

I scooted in front of her and forced her to stop walking. By now we were out of range of the dim parking-lot lights and the moon shone on her face like a spotlight on a silent-film heroine.

"That's not what I meant," I backtracked. "I would've *loved* to go with you!"

She smirked—the old, confident Ally I was used to washing back over her face.

"So—what? You were too much of a rules-hound about the girls asking the boys that you couldn't ask me?" she guessed.

167

I shook my head.

"I never even thought of it, Ally. I never would have guessed you wanted to go with me."

Her eyes narrowed quizzically.

"So did Tobie ask you or did you ask her?"

"We sort of backed into it. I don't think we've ever honestly *planned* to go to one of the dances together. It just always happens that way."

"Fuck it," she breathed. "It doesn't matter. I guess I didn't think you'd like me, not after Missy Anderson."

"She was a mistake."

"Don't say that," Ally asked simply.

She sidestepped and walked past me, so I turned and fell back into step beside her.

"I'm serious—I went out with her for Sammy, mostly."

"Sure," Ally chided mischievously, her face set and playful. "And the way she looks in those miniskirts and tight sweaters had nothing to do with it?"

"You know she's not my type," I said quietly.

"What about me?"

"I hope so. I always figured you were too cool for me."

I was serious, and she knew it. She bumped into me on purpose and giggled lightly.

"So where's this pool? I'm freezing my ass off."

It wasn't far and there wasn't much else to say about the dance or Missy Anderson. We'd said everything that mattered and we let it drop. Besides, my heart was beating so heavily I thought I might pass out, so I was concentrating too hard on not doing that to hold up my end of a conversation. Maybe she was feeling the same thing; maybe we were silent because it's hard to talk when you can't catch your breath. All of the feelings for her I'd been suppressing washed over me, weakening my knees and making me lightheaded. She'd said it, straight up: She'd wanted to go to the dance with me. *Me*. And I'd finally had the balls to tell her how I really felt about her.

Sort of.

I slipped my hand into hers, more for support than anything. She was wearing light gloves and she squeezed my hand back, offering me a quick, embarrassed smile, but she didn't let go.

We got to the pool and I sat down on the edge of it, letting go of her hand. She snuggled against me with her legs curled under her skirt and coat, me with my legs dangling into the void over the deep end, my feet banging against the side with a dull thudding as I swung them. The pool probably hadn't seen more than a few puddles of rainwater in the last decade, and the flaking paint on the sides and skittering dead leaves in the basin kind of depressed me. It was another sign of fading glory. I tried to look away, but I couldn't. The moon glowered down on the dulled white walls, creating a fading echo of the sparkling water that had once lapped against its sides.

I liked the weight of her head on my shoulder; the slow rustle of her hair against my coat. When the breeze whipped around us, I could smell her light perfume, and I understood it, I think: For all her weirdness in the clothing and music departments, Ally was just another person who wanted to look good. Just like we all were. Anyone who tells you they don't care what people think is a liar, otherwise they'd never bathe or comb their hair or wash their clothes. We all care. Sure, some of us care more than others, and some of us care in a way that makes vanity paramount to happiness, but we still care. The irony is, Ally probably cared more than any of them, and her deeper concern made her want to look more original than they did. After all, it's hard to stand out in a crowd when you look the same as everyone else.

I tried to blow a smoke ring with my exhalation and watched as the tiny cloud vanished into the starry ether.

"This is nice," she whispered.

I watched as her gloved hand—knit gloves with purple and black stripes—tugged on the bottom of her coat to close the gap between her legs and the air. She was wearing a skirt as short as her coat was long, with those heavy knitted tights underneath, and I figured she must be lying about it being nice.

"You mean nice in the way the wind actually feels like it's cutting you, or the way you can feel your eyeballs freezing?"

She nudged me as best she could with her shoulder and giggled.

"Don't ruin the moment, Jack. I've wanted this for a long time. I've always wondered what I had to do to get to hang out with you like Tobie and Jess do."

"I didn't know..."

I let the thought trail off, trying to decide if it would have made any difference. I was somewhat mortified, half wondering if I'd stepped out for a glance at the stars and had succumbed to the winter, and this was all the last dream of a man who was freezing to death. I tried to think of the signals she'd sent that I'd ignored—or, more accurately, dismissed as unbelievable. Ally McShay was a punk goddess and I don't think any of us felt worthy of her presence, which is how I suppose we'd ended up pushing her away. Though not entirely. She pushed away first; our actions were only a response.

"One thing that really cuts me is when someone calls me a freak," Ally suddenly admitted.

She shifted her weight but didn't look at me when I glanced at her. She looked so peaceful, her eyes focused on the long nothing in front of her; focused on some image in her head. I couldn't imagine ever doing anything to hurt her; she suddenly seemed so vulnerable, like all she'd ever wanted was to snuggle, but hanging out with her brother and older cousins all the time had made her tough instead.

"I may have done that before," I admitted quietly. "Or at least hung out with people who did."

She was thinking of that night at Sudsy's with Missy. She needed to know what I'd really been thinking, because what had gone on inside my head then mattered now. She narrowed her eyes—focusing, perhaps, on a very specific mental image.

"I'm sorry for what she said, that night at Sudsy's," I said softly.

Ally's head quivered in the slightest motion of negation.

"It wasn't cool and I should've called her on it in front of you. Made her say she was sorry."

Ally snuffed out a laughed and wiped her eyes with a gloved hand.

"It wouldn't have mattered," she admitted. "It wouldn't have been sincere."

"Well *I'm* sorry. I'm sorry if I ever called you that. I didn't know it—"

"It's okay coming from you," she cut in, flashing me a smile. "I know you don't intend it to be mean. It's those... *other* people that bother me."

"Yeah, well, I decided not to hang out with those other people any more."

She looked at me and smiled again, her eyes sparkling either with left over tears or with glee, I couldn't tell.

"'Freak'," she quoted. "'One that is markedly unusual or abnormal, as a person or animal with a physical oddity who appears in a circus sideshow'."

"What?"

"That's what a freak is. Am I 'markedly abnormal'? Do I have a 'physical oddity'?"

"No..."

"'Weird'," she continued to quote. "'Of strange or extraordinary character.' A weirdo is a person who is strange or eccentric."

"Okay, but—"

"Am I strange or eccentric? Am I of strange or extraordinary character?"

I didn't know what to say, how to answer, what to do. Should I get up and run? Pretend I heard them calling us back to the lodge? Change the subject?

"Yes?" I guessed, bracing myself for the blow. Instead she sat up and smiled proudly, her eyes glistening.

"'Freak' hurts because those people say it to be mean. It

172

insinuates that I'm different from normal people for reasons beyond my control. 'Weirdo' doesn't bother me because it accepts the fact that I *choose* to be different—that I have decided to be something more than ordinary; something *extra*-ordinary."

She'd obviously thought about this a lot, which made it seem... well, weird. But probably not freakish. I don't think.

"That's... pretty neat," I finally mustered in response.

"So what are *you*, Jack? A freak or a weirdo?"

"Aren't weirdos like, I don't know, sexual deviants or something?"

"Not by the book."

"The book?"

"The *dictionary*?"

"Oh—*that* book..."

"See, you have to be careful with words—you should know that. You're always writing things in that little book you carry around. Which people think is weird, by the way."

"People think that makes me weird—?"

"While words may shift in meaning over the decades," she continued as if I hadn't spoken. "The connotations usually stick. You have circus freaks, not circus weirdos. But if you saw a self-luminescent moth in the woods at night, you'd probably say, 'That's weird,' not 'That's freaky'—"

"I don't know. I might call a glowing moth frea—"

"I mean, at least weird things can be beautiful. But 'freak' is a term of derision. It's what you say when you think something is so odd it's scary to look at. It's almost synonymous with 'horrible'."

"I see your point," I mumbled.

"My dad made me look it up once," she said sheepishly; apologetically. "After I called myself a freak..."

"Oh."

Some conversations stick with you forever, and I can't say that I knew that one would at that moment, but I felt something. Ally had moved to town our Junior year and I got her to come to work on the plays when I met her in art class. She ate lunch with us, too, and fell right in with Jess, but she was one of those people you were good friends with in school, but never seemed to hang out with outside of school, unless you accidentally crossed paths. She never came to any of the drama parties, so I guess people never thought to call her when there was nothing going on. I think Jess did call her once or twice, after she first started eating lunch with us, but she always had something to do and Jess got bored of trying. And she'd shown up with a skateboard where we were skating a few times, but then never followed up on our invites to join us again later. She wasn't being snobby or anything, she was just... inaccessible. So for as odd as the conversation seemed at the time, I was glad she was letting me in on something so obviously personal.

"What is this, anyway?" she suddenly asked, tugging on my jeans.

"What?"

"These are... nice jeans..."

I looked at her and she held my gaze, waiting for me to admit what she was getting at.

"I went shopping with... Missy Anderson," I finally said.

"She picked them out?" she guessed as she stood up.

I nodded timidly. I'd said enough, and she said everything by not following up.

"I couldn't believe it when I heard you were dating her," she said very quietly.

I felt like a sellout, so I avoided her eyes as I stood up beside her. She turned and walked toward a small building behind us. I think she wanted to get out of the wind but not go back to the lodge and the others yet.

"I told you, she wasn't my type," I explained, catching up with her.

"I went to King of Hearts with Jolly to get closer to you."

If possible, considering the sub-zero temperatures, I went cold.

"Are you serious?"

She looked wistfully back across the empty pool to where the leafless trees knocked their branches in the wind against the horizon.

"He called me weird," she added with a wry smirk. "But he never said I was a freak."

"You always seemed way too cool for me—I was afraid to ask you out. Well, that and the time you rejected me—"

"Are you serious? When did I *reject* you?"

Ally looked over at me with a smirk, leaning forward so I couldn't avoid her eyes. Her smile made me laugh at myself. Truth be told, she may have rejected me that night backstage when I got her phone number, but then I'd never used it. By the time I'd plucked up the courage to call, Missy was happening. So I changed the subject back to my original statement.

"I guess I just built you up or something. I have a habit

175

of doing that, and it never ends well."

"Built me *up*?"

She said it derisively, but only because the idea that anyone could build her up seemed preposterous to her, not because she thought I was an idiot or anything. I kicked the door of the building, expecting it to be locked, but it wanged open on aged hinges and revealed a room oddly moonlit from holes in the ceiling. It was not the showers, as I'd assumed, but probably a concession stand or something. It was empty now, a big open room with a few counters at the back that we gravitated to and hopped up on to sit. Some of the area teenagers or something had dragged a couple of the old mattresses from the abandoned cabins in there and had spray painted graffiti all over the walls. It was eerie, like something out of a B-horror movie, but I didn't expect anyone to come back on a cold night like this, wielding an ax or otherwise.

"Not 'build up,' exactly," I explained, finishing my thought. "It's like, I get this idea in my head about someone, then if they don't live up to it, I act like an asshole. If they do live up to it, everything's cool. And sometimes if they end up being more than I'd expected, no matter how slightly, I completely overblow how awesome they are. I just didn't want to risk losing what we have. Or something."

I looked over at her and she was shaking her head slightly, her lips curled into a bemused expression.

"And what do we *have*, Jack?"

I shrugged.

"This is about Missy Anderson, isn't it? You built her up and she dumped you right before the King of Hearts dance?"

176

"No," I disagreed quietly, slightly amused to think of Missy Anderson having had that much of an effect on me.

I hung my head and watched my feet dangling in front of the empty cupboards, wondering why they'd bothered to remove the doors. Was that kind of hardware valuable? I sucked in a slow, deep breath. Ally didn't say anything. She didn't move. I'm not even sure she breathed. She just waited patiently for me to finish.

"Her name was Penny Harper," I finally said. "Missy didn't have a thing on her."

"Penny Harper? Does she go to our school?"

I shook my head. "Nah. She moved."

Ally reached over and rubbed my back slowly, scooching closer so she could look up into my face better and speak softly but still be heard. I hadn't meant to bring up Penny Harper, but there she was, still echoing in my head almost two years later: The perfect girl; the summer dream; the one who stuck her nose in the air and walked off the second she had to introduce me to her other friends. The one I built up so high that when she left, all I could do was fall.

"So how's that got anything to do with me?" Ally wondered gently.

I straightened up and looked at her fully.

"You seem like everything I've ever wanted in a girl," I admitted plainly. It felt good to finally admit it to myself, if not to her. It felt good to finally give substance to something that had been bugging me for months: how I drooled over Ally and spoke to her all the time but never truly asked her out. "So I figure you'll only break my heart, like Penny Harper did."

177

"I probably will, Jack, or you'll break mine..." She trailed off and grinned coyly. "Unless we plan to get married...?"

I chuckled with mild embarrassment.

"I didn't think young love was supposed to hurt," I offered.

"Who the hell said *that*?" she chided happily. "Young love *always* hurts. You think it was *easy* for me to follow you out here and tell you how I felt? I've seen you and Tobie. I know you'd dump me if she asked you to—"

"Not true," I denied vehemently.

"Funny thing is," she deflected. "If a broken heart hurt *that* much, we'd never go out with anyone again."

"Missy was really jealous of Tobie," I said evenly. "She was jealous of you, too, actually."

"*Me*? Seriously?"

"Anyway... You know, Tobie and I are just friends, and I'm sure we'll still hang out, but there's nothing there, not like that."

"It doesn't really matter, Bells," she said. "I'm not jealous if she's not."

I leaned in and kissed her. Just like that, without thinking, as if to prove a point. Not a big sloppy kiss, I just closed the few inches between our lips and kissed her, dimly aware that her lipstick tasted like apples. It was a slow, perfect kiss, the kind that said that there was really something there. And I remember the indescribably beautiful smell of her cheek against my nose, and the soft tinkle of her bangles sliding down her wrist as she touched the back of my head.

How long had I dreamed of getting lost in her eyes; of

178

touching those colorful lips to mine? She always seemed so beautiful and lonely and happy and tragic all at once: a perfect storm of poetic adjectives who raised my spirits simply by entering the room. How long had I ignored her subtle advances? How long had she been making them before I started to catch on?

The first time I met her, I was late for art class. Yeah, that was me: The guy who took art in high school. Some of the most honest people I knew took art, yet somehow the art wing got the rap as the stoner wing, inhabited by the kids who were one short step away from dropping out or being incarcerated. I mean, sure, my tablemate in ceramics made a bong and I made a set of shot glasses, but that's not the point. The point is, a lot of good people took art, the kind of people who would stand up for you in a pinch instead of running away. People like Ally McShay.

"Sit over there, please," the teacher had said to me. I forget her name now, but she was short and bubbly and deftly turned a blind eye to most of our antics. It's got to be a rough gig, trying to teach creativity to a bunch of kids who would rather be anywhere other than school.

The tables in class were all four-person affairs—it was a drawing class—and the only seat left open was at a table with Ryan Jefferson, a guy I hung out with in the stoner wing but rarely saw outside of school. We traded Pink Floyd tapes and marveled at the staying power of Fleetwood Mac and the demise of Heart, but I never could tempt him away from classic rock. Not that I tried too hard. He was grinning ear to ear and not-so-subtly indicating Ally, who had been seated next to him.

"Bells," he stated. "It was only a matter of time."

"You know, I only get about half of what you say," I replied.

"I know."

He laughed and flapped his hoodie, turning square to the table, the cloying scent of illicit cigarettes like a scarred cloud around him. I looked over at Ally and rolled my eyes for her benefit. She smiled and held my gaze, then half opened her mouth, as if speaking to me took preparation and she wasn't sure she wanted to bother.

That was the first time I noticed her lips, and not just because they were shaded blue to match the streaks in her hair. They were also perfectly formed and I very clearly thought to myself that it would be the perfect plan to stare at her if I said I wanted to draw her lips for a project for class. Thankfully, she spoke first.

"I saw you this morning," she commented. "You were hanging out with the skaters."

Ryan looked from her to me as if expecting me to deny the claim. The stoners hung out in the art wing—the 100 wing—with the hoods, not the 300 wing with the skaters and —almost inexplicably—the honors students.

"It's true," I replied, more for Ryan than Ally. "Where do you hang out?"

She shrugged, completely nonplussed. I fucking loved her already. It didn't seem like an act; she genuinely couldn't care less, but since I'd asked, she'd be polite.

"Nowhere yet. This is my first day here."

"No shit?"

"Jack!" the teacher barked with a smile. "Language."

"Sorry," I mumbled.

She let it pass and explained our daily task to us as she passed out fancy paper and boxes of artistic chalk. We were doing something about shading; it wasn't hard to follow the instructions and talk at the same time.

"Well, the jocks hang out in the 200 wing. The skaters, punks, and honors students—go figure—are in the 300 wing. And this is the 100 wing. The—" (I glanced at Ryan) "—art wing." Ryan nodded in agreement with this assessment.

"My last school was about a third the size of this one," Ally replied. "Everyone was all mixed up."

"So what do you do?" I asked. "Sports? Partying? Studying?"

"I go to shows with my brother and cousins."

"Like who?" Ryan chimed in. "38 Special? Lynyrd Skynyrd?"

She narrowed her eyes instead of being offensive and smirked privately.

"You know, small-club bands. College-radio stuff."

I nodded and listed off the last couple of shows I'd been to and her face broke into a genuine smile.

"You should come hang out with us," I offered. "There's an empty locker right by my friend's. Her name's Jess—you'll love her."

She pulled away from our kiss and smiled sheepishly, reaching out with a gloved hand and rubbing the lipstick from around my lips.

"I think they might know we were kissing out here," she said mischievously. "You look serious—what are you thinking?"

181

"Nothing. You know, the first thing I ever noticed about you was your lips? I've been wanting to kiss you since that first day in art class."

"It was obvious," she admitted. "You and that other guy —what's his name?"

"Ryan?"

"Yeah."

"So why didn't you ever hang out with us?"

"I took that locker by Jess."

"Right, but you didn't... You know... You never seemed to come along when we invited you."

"I wasn't sure I liked you."

She was totally serious, but it confused me. She smiled and tried to tell me it was okay, that she obviously liked me now, but I was still having trouble with it. I suddenly felt like I didn't know her; like she'd done her homework on me and I hadn't done mine on her.

"But you *still* don't hang out with us. I mean, outside of school and drama club."

"I wasn't sure you liked *me*," she explained.

"I don't get you," I said softly. "So, will you hang out with us now?"

"If you want me to."

"For as confident as you are, Ally McShay, you sure seem intimidated by us."

"You guys are obviously tight, Bells. I know I can't just waltz into that circle."

"Well, you *better*. Cuz I want to spend a *lot* more time with you."

"Yeah?"

She leaned in and I felt her lips on mine.

The first time she'd given me hope—extended the flirtatious branch of promise—was after the last play of the year, Junior year. She actually jogged up behind me to catch me before I drove off, her flats slapping against the asphalt of the parking lot. I turned expecting to see Tobie (Jess wouldn't have run up, she'd have yelled out to me across the parking lot) and was caught off guard to see Ally. The dumbest shit goes through your head in those moments, and I remember thinking that she was as hot as the night—it *was* a hot night, but a painfully tenuous simile.

"Hey," she said, slightly winded. "We should skate."

"What? Now?"

She waggled her head and pushed her hair back over her left ear, the smooth skin of her arm infused with the orange glow of the sunset. Those long May nights, when summer in southern Ohio is starting to get going, are magical, and with her standing there asking me to skate, it felt like a dream.

"Not *now* now, but you know, sometime."

"Yeah. Sure. Of course. Me and Sammy and Niz skate all the time—you know Harbin Park?"

She nodded.

"We're there almost all the time."

"Cool."

She sighed and looked around and I felt like I'd missed a hint I was supposed to have taken.

"What? Is there... something...?"

"Oh, no. That's all. You know, with drama ending for the year I didn't think we'd get to hang out as much."

Keep in mind that at this point, we hadn't hung out that

183

much at all, except in drama and for a few minutes at lunch for a couple of months, but that was at a table full of loud-mouths who hogged all the attention. I mention this only to be forgiven for not asking her out, right then and there, in an official way. I didn't really know her that well and I honestly always thought pretty girls were only being nice to me, not flirting. I guess I lacked self-confidence, and I guess it didn't let me see that this pretty girl had just sprinted to catch up with me before I left and had asked me to go skating with her.

I'd completely missed it, but at least she eventually learned that subtlety didn't work with me.

"What are you doing?" I gasped.

We were now snuggled up on the countertop, stretched out like it was a bed. It was purely pragmatic: It was more comfortable to kiss that way. We avoided the mattresses, though—those looked... used.

"Taking off my underwear."

She wriggled some more, pulling her lower lip with her top teeth.

"What? *Why*?"

"Got 'em!" she declared.

She actually twirled her panties on her finger before stuffing them in her coat pocket.

"Isn't that... *cold*?"

I had no *idea* how to respond. Even as my heart pounded, my head told me it couldn't possibly mean a thing—they were just uncomfortable, so she'd taken them off, that's all.

"Jack," she soothed, touching my face with a mittened hand.

She leaned over ever so slightly and kissed me full on

the lips. Kissing her felt so damn right, like it was something we'd been meaning to do for months but had never had the chance to do. Like we were finally venting something that had been stored up since we'd met, and I honestly couldn't believe she'd ever noticed me in that way—but I could tell that she had by her kisses: deep and slow and meaningful and savored.

I pulled away and lay my head down beside hers, watching her profile as she watched her breath forming clouds above her lips, the moonlight glowing on the walls around us. At that moment, it was just me and Ally McShay and the rest of the world had vanished in the blink of God's eye.

"What are you thinking, Ally?"

"I've wanted to be with you for so long."

"But we don't have to..."

"What if this is my only chance?"

"It won't be your only chance."

"Then why wait?"

She turned her head and looked at me, her eyes pulling me in. I kissed her again. She rolled over and put her leg over mine.

"We haven't even gone out yet," I whispered.

"Bells, I know you better than anyone in the world. We've dated more by talking backstage and skating than most people date in their whole lives."

"You've thought about this."

"I haven't, Bells, honest." She shook her head slowly, and I knew she was telling the truth. "I didn't plan any of this. I came out to see what you were up to. I still felt bad about the dance—"

"Don't."

She kissed me instead, and with a panicked realization I knew that this may well be about to happen and that I didn't have any idea what I was supposed to do with a girl like her. I kissed her back, trying to stretch the minutes with another lost kiss; tasting her lips; smelling her skin. She unbuttoned her coat and when I touched her stomach, she sucked in a sharp breath.

"I love you," I blurted, the words choking in my throat. I felt sure my admission would end it, the whole thing, the whole dream of Ally I had thought so far-fetched that I'd never even tried to claim it. She didn't say anything but she stopped kissing me.

"Really?"

"I—I'm sorry if that freaks you out. I just think you're really great."

She smiled widely.

"No one's ever said that to me before."

"Seriously?"

"What?" she smirked.

"You just seem so... *awesome*. I figured you'd had serious boyfriends before."

"Not really. We move too often... This is my third high school. I just hope we stay here through Prom."

As I looked at her she seemed to transform in front of me, from the cool, untouchable, enviable Ally McShay to a girl with great taste and no fear who was afraid to make friends because she was afraid she'd have to move again. I stared at her like she was an optical illusion that can be two things at once.

"*What*?" she asked, smiling.

"Nothing. I... I just... Moving so much like that... That sucks."

She dropped her eyes for a second and my heart pounded anew, sure she was going to button up and climb off me. Finally, she looked at me again: maybe it was the moon on her cheeks, or maybe there was the slightest trail left by a single, small tear.

"I think I love you, too, Jack," she said softly, almost secretively. "I should have cornered you sooner."

"I wish I hadn't been so dazzled by you."

"*Dazzled*? What does *that* mean?" she said softly. "You say the weirdest things."

"You live the life I've always wanted, and I can't imagine wanting to hang out with me if I had that."

"You're a freak."

"Hey—you know that's mean."

"Well, you *do* have an abnormality if you were dazzled by *me* and you think *my* life is worth drooling over."

She leaned over and kissed me again, sliding her hands out of her gloves and running a hand down my stomach, hooking my zipper as she moved down the front of my pants.

"I'm serious, Jack, I really want this. But if you don't, you know..."

"No... I do..."

I awkwardly fumbled in my coat pocket, my heart pounding in my neck, and my fingers finally closed on the foiled square. I pulled it out and grinned sheepishly, quite sure, all of a sudden, that I had been completely wrong about

187

her advances.

"You always carry a condom in your pocket?" she wondered curiously.

"Sammy put it there right before... Well, before the dance. He was quite sure something was going to happen."

"Whatever."

I wish I could shower you with effusive adjectives and starlight and fireworks, but the truth is, the memory is equally trauma and dream. Not because it was bad or negative—absolutely not—but because something that's such a big deal should be hard to fully enjoy the first time. I mean, we hadn't figured anything out yet. But mostly, it's such a wellspring of emotions that words can only serve to pale the real effects and render them meaningless. It was beautiful and scary and meaningful and when I kissed Ally after that night, I did so in a way I had never kissed a girl before. She was right: even without officially dating we had shared so many of our secrets with each other, but this one trumped them all. This one was ours alone, and no amount of time or space or silence will ever change it, and no amount of words can ever explain what it meant to us then and what it means to me still.

Act 2

Strange Things Happen When

You Kiss Pretty Girls

March

There are moments I will never forget. Everything is perfect: The shade of the sky, the temperature of the air, the look on her face as she smiles and turns away, pulling her hair over her ear. That's how I will always remember Ally McShay: On that quiet, blue evening in March with the soft red fire of the sun scratching a swath across the horizon. Ally, sitting on the curb on her skateboard, laughing and trying to pretend she was impressed at my attempt to pull off a trick she said would never work. Ally, the girl who stood up and and let me roll over to her, then stopped me with her upturned face and her lips and a gentle kiss. Ally, the girl who took my skateboard before she let my lips go, then turned and rolled away, pulling off the trick perfectly, her skirt billowing out around her to reveal the shorts she was wearing underneath; her hair drifting in slow motion around her cheeks; her eyes twinkling back at me in the streetlights as she grinned, enjoying every moment as much as I was. Ally, the only girl I knew who was so much more to me than any other girl had ever been before.

"You mean, you can't do that?" she asked with mock earnestness.

She flipped around and pushed off twice, barreling toward me. I didn't move and she drifted into a powerslide, the wheels graunching against the asphalt. She hopped off and the board skittered to a stop inches from my feet.

"You set me up," I observed. "You *knew* that trick would work and you psyched me out."

"Yeah?" she gazed into my eyes. "Prove it."

I kissed her—a short, lingering kiss, lips slightly open, then away—and pushed off on my board, promptly falling on my ass. Again.

"I can't learn *any* new tricks," I said sullenly. "Sammy learns new tricks. Niz learns new tricks. You *make up* new tricks."

"Come on," she begged. "It's not that hard. Put your front foot forward more—no, not *back*. You *aren't* doing an ollie—that's where you keep screwing it up. Put it *forward*, on the edge, like this."

She glided off and back around, landing the trick again.

"You flip it with your front toe, then kick it with your back foot when it's in the air. Then you land it."

"Sure," I agreed. "It's just that easy."

That giggle again, her cheeks rounded and smiling as her hair whipped across them.

"It *is*! Just try it again!"

"I don't feel like falling any more. Maybe we should stop by and see what Sammy's up to."

She nodded and picked up her board.

"How's he doing?"

192

"Okay, I guess."

Things weren't going well with Donna Marie after the King of Hearts dance, so they didn't hang out as much, leaving Sammy with a lot of time at home to mope. Sammy couldn't hang out with her and her friends because they all sided with Greg Wilson and Missy Anderson, and she was afraid to hang out with us and risk alienating everyone else she was close to. It had to give. In hindsight, I was amazed it had lasted as long as it did—or at all. But I'd never say that to Sammy.

"He won't mind me being there...?" Ally checked.

"Nah. You can show him that trick—make him forget all about her."

"Would a trick make you forget me?" she wondered with an evil grin.

"Maybe—if it was good enough."

She playfully hit me and giggled again. That sound: I will forever be able to hear that sound, the exact timbre and cadence of her laugh. I reached out and grabbed her, pulling her in and kissing her on the forehead.

"Who luvs ya?"

"Don't," she warned.

"Who's ya daddy?"

"*Gross*! I said *don't*!"

But she wasn't mad, not at all. We walked back to my car hand-in-hand, our skateboards dangling from our other hands, and I remember clearly the smell in the air—it was chilly, but also spring, so there was woodfire mixed in with freshly cut grass, and that distinct scent that always lingers in cool air: The smell of the shadow of snow.

193

"We should go out," she suggested as we hucked our boards into the trunk. "Get ice cream or something."

"Maybe," I agreed. "If he wants to."

We got in and when I turned the ignition the radio came to life, blaring the Runaways tape Ally had put in.

"Seriously—why is the Runaways your favorite band ever?"

She stuck her tongue out playfully and turned it up. I turned it back down so I could hear her.

"The *original* girl group?" she explained in a fake huff.

"The Supremes were men?"

"*Rock* girl group. The first girl group that dished out shit instead of taking it."

"Stevie Nicks didn't take shit."

"But she was part of a bigger band, with men."

One thing we loved was bickering about music. Not in the sense of being right or wrong but in the sense of talking through it and turning each other on to new music, or music we felt hadn't been given a chance before.

"So who else do we have as *real* girl groups?" I asked.

It was fully dark now—the darkness always seemed to fall so suddenly when I was a kid, probably because we stayed out so long and didn't notice until it was too late.

"L7?" I suggested. "Sinéad O'Connor?"

"Girlschool," she replied thoughtfully.

"The Go-Go's? The Bangles? Bananarama?"

She cut me a look and pulled her hair back over her ears, the red highlights shimmering by the lights of the dashboard.

"*Please*. The *Bangles*? Banana*rama*?"

"What? Pop can't be edgy?"

194

"This is my favorite song," she replied with a smirk and turned the volume up, mouthing the words to "American Nights" and daring me to turn it back down.

I loved the way she sang along to the music when we drove places—those tiny moments when she lost herself. I liked that she felt comfortable enough around me to be like that. At school she was so quiet, even at lunch with all of us carrying on, but when it was just the two of us I felt like I got to see the real Ally—the Ally who liked to sing along to the Runaways.

"Why are you staring at me?" she yelled, grinning sheepishly. "Are we going to Sammy's *today*?"

"Yeah yeah," I said and put the car in gear.

$$\mathcal{E}$$

"Let's get serious, people!" Mr. K hollered. "The retreat is behind us and we've got six weeks until we open! It's spring, it's a comedy, and it's the last play for our Seniors! Let's make some *magic*!"

Ally grinned over at me and mouthed "cheese ball." Her smile held a secret only I knew, although I think the others had probably guessed it. There was a look in her eyes now, like she was seeing me for the first time, not as that guy she hung out with backstage or in art class or at lunch, but as that guy she knew better than anyone else; that guy she'd let in, closer to her than anyone else had ever been. I felt like I could say and do anything with her, and she'd understand me. She'd been absolutely right at the pool on the retreat: It felt like we'd finally admitted to a relationship that had always been there.

After school that first day we met in art class, Jess and I helped her move her crap from her assigned locker to the empty locker by Jess. The first thing she told us was that she moved a lot. She brought it up as a joke because Jess had apologized for asking her to move after she'd just put all her stuff away.

"We move about every year or so," she explained. "For my dad's work. They need him to keep moving around, cleaning up corporate messes or something. My dad grew up here, though, so maybe we'll stay longer."

She didn't sound hopeful and we didn't press her on it. It sounded like a vague heads-up; a warning not to get too close and not to ask *her* to either.

"What do you guys do for fun around here?"

Jess and I glanced at each other. We didn't do much of anything, at least not much of anything that sounded exciting.

"We hang out," Jess said. "At the mall. At our houses. Jack and Niz and Sammy skate" (that piqued Ally's interest) "and me and Tobie watch."

"We're in drama club, too," I added. "Well, Jess isn't, really."

"Drama club?" Ally checked. "I wouldn't like acting."

"Oh, I don't either. Haven't been on stage since eighth grade, when I blew my lines. I work set design and props and scene changes."

"*That* sounds interesting," Ally said slowly. "So, you build the sets and everything?"

"Yup. You should come tonight. We just started rehearsals for the spring play."

She considered me for a long time, long enough that I started to get nervous and shared a few awkward glances with Jess. I was about to back off from my offer when she nodded and clicked her tongue.

"Sure. What time?"

"Seven to eight thirty."

"Here?"

"Yeah—let me show you where the theater is."

And there we were, a year later. Ally had worked with me on every play since, even the summer-stock play we did, when we felt like we had a bit more freedom and weren't so constrained by acceptable educational standards (or whatever thinking went into play selection during the school year). We got to pick it, in fact, instead of the teachers, so we chose *Godspell*, I think because it allowed us to have a live rock band on stage. Well, that's the part that sold me, anyway. I never thought about the religious aspect, to be honest, except that they made Jesus seem like the regular guy I'm sure he was.

Mr. K walked over to us after he'd organized everyone and handed Ally the blocking tape with a smile. I took up my spot in the seats with Sammy and watched—watched her, anyway. By now she seemed to know where to put new tape or move old tape before Mr. K even said anything. She scurried around the actors, bending down and sticking tape to the floor, her striped stockings flexed against her knees; her black skirt swooping to the floor and back again as she stood up.

"She's a way better match than Missy," Sammy said softly to me.

"Yeah," I agreed. I couldn't contain my smile. "Way better."

"How does Tobie feel about it?"

"I think she set us up. So how's Donna Marie?"

Sammy looked away from me; from the stage. He was pretending to look at the light booth, as if trying to decide if he should go up there in case Mr. K asked for lights.

"Not good," he mumbled.

"That sucks."

"I wasn't around cuz of the retreat, so she spent a lot of time with her friends."

I knew where it was going, so I didn't push it. Friends are amazingly powerful people, and groups of friends even more so. You get a good mix, and groups help balance out the crazy, but groups can also be your undoing if they turn into a hive mind. Groups can get you to do all kinds of things you wouldn't normally do. That was the problem here: Two different people with two different groups of friends, only hers were all crazy and they unbalanced Donna Marie and left Sammy the perpetual odd-man-out.

"Thanks for trying, though," he said in a defeated tone.

I let it go. We went out into the hall, ostensibly to check out the new gallery they'd put up, of pictures from all the plays the drama club had ever produced, some from twenty years before we'd started high school. It was weird to see all those faces, all those smiles, knowing that for them, it was all history, like it would be for us one day. They seemed fake, and not because the actors were in costumes and makeup and pretending to be someone else, but because pictures can't capture the emotional pull of events and so make it hard to believe that something actually happened, sometimes even when you were there to witness it: Memory turns things into dreams, and its hard later to pick apart where reality ends and romance takes over. Those kids in those pictures? They had the same problems as us, so why did it seem so hard to accept that they were real? That they were just like us, going to shows and hanging out and listening to music?

"What do you think they did?" I asked Sammy.

We'd found a roll of toilet paper the janitor must have dropped and were tossing it back and forth down the hall like a football.

"Who?"

"Those kids in drama twenty years ago? Did they have skateboards back then?"

"Sure. Maybe. I don't know. They hung out at the arcade, I bet."

"Yeah."

"They'd be our parents' age, right?" Sammy checked.

"Yeah—sure. Close enough, anyway."

"That's fucked up, Bells. Those kids could have kids our age."

"You want kids, Sammy?"

He actually stopped and thought about it. He caught the toilet roll and stood there for a second, contemplating.

"I feel ready," he finally said, tossing the toilet roll back.

"Seriously? Ready?"

"Well, I mean... I don't know. I feel like I've dated enough girls."

"No, I just meant, y'know, one day—do you want kids?"

"I guess so. What about you? You a family man?"

"Fuck that, Samuel. What I *don't* want is to start dressing like my parents and their friends and hanging out at the golf course and having dinner parties where everyone puts on ties. If I can have a family without all that bullshit, I'll be fine."

"I think it just happens, dude. I think you grow up by accident. I think my dad, he didn't want to grow up. That's why he left."

I shook my head, but he nodded that it was okay.

"Seriously, Bells. If I have kids, I'm going to act like a parent."

"I don't think you have to change to be a dad, Sammy."

"I think you probably should, though," he replied.

We tossed the toilet roll back and forth in silence for a few minutes, lost in our own thoughts. I couldn't shake the idea that those kids on the wall probably had kids that went to this school, at least some of them. Hell, probably someone in drama club right now, although no one had ever pointed out their parents to me. I couldn't help but wonder what I'd be like when I was that old. It seemed unimaginably far away.

Ally came out and joined us eventually, while the acting directions took precedence. We started to play a lighthearted game of keep away, with Ally in the middle. She tipped the toilet roll at one point and it shot straight up into a fluores-

200

cent light that didn't have a cover over it, knocking it from its mooring. It hit the floor and exploded in a shower of white powder and glass. Sammy and I bolted for cover, but Ally just stood there and waited.

"You kids break something?" I heard the janitor yell up to her—I guess he'd been right around the corner the whole time.

"Sorry!" Ally called back.

She didn't get in any trouble. She helped him clean it up and eventually Sammy and I slunk back out and helped, too.

"Thanks for bolting," Ally said sweetly after the janitor was gone.

She punched me softly in the stomach as we slumped down and sat against the wall.

"It's habit," I said in our defense. "We're used to skating around here."

"Sure," she accepted. "Hey, Sammy—you wanna go down to Egg Records with us on Sunday?"

"Can't," he said casually. "I have to work."

"What time?" I checked.

"Noon to nine. I asked for more hours."

I caught Ally's glance and we both silently agreed what that meant: He didn't want time away from Donna Marie to sit and think about Donna Marie. That, and he probably needed the money.

"That sucks," I offered.

He shrugged.

"Anything you want us to look for?" Ally asked—she'd been really great, trying to help keep him busy and keep his mood up.

"Nah... I'm saving."

"What for, Samuel?" I asked with my best salesman's voice. "A new car?"

"Actually..."

He said he wanted to find an old used hearse and deck it out. I guess his dad had called a couple of times and kept telling Sammy to get into cars because they can't outsource mechanics. It didn't mean much to me then; I was too fixated on wondering why his dad bothered to call and offer advice but didn't bother coming home.

"Guys," Mr. K suddenly said, appearing in the doorway. "We're about to wrap up for the night—can you come in here, please?"

"Sure thing, Mr. K," Sammy said and we all stood up.

Ally slid her hand into mine in the few seconds it took to walk back into the Little Theatre. We dragged our feet and let Sammy go in ahead of us so we could share even that short, private moment, trying to prove to each other, maybe, that Sammy's troubles with Donna Marie wouldn't affect us. It seemed like a natural concern in a weird way, that a friend's relationship woes could somehow rub off on others. She smiled at me as we reached the door and I gave her a quick kiss to let her know that everything was okay. Then she dropped my hand and walked through the door.

I'd been worried about Sammy since I'd started back at the toy store. He was alone down there in the hotdog stand now, and Sammy, it turns out, didn't do alone very well. He needed comfort, for all his loner ways and false bravado. It's why he was so nice to his mom—and why his dad leaving hurt way more than he let on. Me and Niz, we helped keep him straight by taking him skating, but left to his own devices, Sammy was prone to fill the dead air with noise—any noise. So when I went back to the toy store and then Donna Marie broke up with him, Sammy had plenty of time to poke shriveled hotdogs and think about how alone he was—or *thought* he was. Unfortunately, John from the pizza place also noticed, and John was the kind of guy who had bad solutions for easy problems. I mean, that was no surprise, but you'd think a guy like that would have dealt with his share of stoned friends. Instead, he also had bad solutions for harder problems.

Which is how Sammy ended up in the toy store, coming down after dropping acid that morning with John. I was straightening a display of remote controlled cars when they came in. At first I didn't recognize Sammy, partly because he was with John, and I didn't register knowing anyone he'd be hanging out with, but also because Sammy looked... blank. Sammy was never exactly mister bright-eyed-and-bushy-tailed, but he usually smiled, maybe even waved. He at least made eye contact.

"Sammy?" I checked, standing to greet them.

Sammy's eyes wavered in my direction, then he went back to staring at a hanging display of punching balloons that were slowly drifting on the air our movements created, pinging very softly as inflated rubber bounced off inflated rubber.

"What's wrong with him? " I snapped in a harsh whisper.

John shrugged. His hair was long and greasy, hanging limply down to his shoulders. I'd only ever seen him working before, so he'd always had it pulled back; he did his best to let it flop over and cover his eyes, but I wouldn't let him.

"What?" I asked again.

I glanced over to the registers where Steve was already adding up the charge receipts so he could count out the drawers quicker later. He met my eyes and I noticed he was chewing his lower lip ever so slightly, and I didn't think he was nervous about the receipts. Steve looked like he knew exactly what was going on and he was torn between helping and wanting the problem out of his store.

"Sammy?" I tried, skipping the middleman.

John was nervously eyeing Steve, so I let him believe that his scrawny ass was about to be kicked by a former repo man.

"Sammy? What's going on, man?"

He mumbled something, shook his head distractedly, then poked laconically at one of the punch balloons. It pinged softly away, drifting in slow motion. Sammy smiled.

"What the hell is he on?" I snapped at John.

"Acid," John gulped.

"Steve!" I shouted back over my shoulder. "Okay if I take my break now?"

"You bet!" he agreed.

He sounded jovial, but he still looked concerned. I hustled John and Sammy out of the toy store.

"*Offa*!" Sammy bleated, slapping at my hands as he moved. "It's so *large*!"

"Why the fuck did you bring him *here*, John?" I demanded when we were a store front away from the toy store.

"I didn't know who else to bring him to. I thought you'd know what to do."

"How the fuck do *I* know that to do? You're the damn *stoner*!"

Sammy suddenly grabbed my arm and reached out a hand toward the railing that looked down on the arcade and food court below. With absolute clarity I saw him jumping the railing and trying to fly. I pulled him back and hustled him to the escalators. He didn't fight me this time. He was staring up at the ceiling—at the dark sky lights—with his mouth agape. We managed to stumble onto the escalator. His head lolled around like a sunflower and he gazed at his feet for a second or two, as if trying to figure out how he was moving.

"So *big*!" he whispered.

At the bottom of the stairs he stumbled over the landing and I caught him and hobbled him over to the nearest bench, right beside the carousel and putt-putt golf entrance—that mall was fucking ridiculous. What I failed to realize was that

205

put him right by the ten-by-twenty-foot wall of alternating red and blue lights strobing in front of the second-run movie theater. They'd already had to tone them down once due to people having seizures or something, and now I saw that it wasn't the best place to plop a guy coming down off an acid trip.

"So what the *fuck*, John?" I demanded again. "Why didn't you just stay with him wherever you dropped acid?"

"My parents are coming home tonight!"

"Jesus Christ—don't you know how to deal with this shit?"

"No!"

"What do you mean, 'no'? What do you *normally* do?"

"I never dropped acid before!"

"*What*?"

Now I was getting pissed. The only thing that saved John from getting punched repeatedly in the face is that he looked terrified.

"So you let Sammy drop acid while you watched?"

"I was his... handler."

"Well you did a bang-up job, asshole. Bringing him to the fucking *mall*. Bringing him to a God damn *toy store* where there are *kids* around!"

He backed off a step and I thought he was going to bolt. I reached out and grabbed his wrist. Behind me the carousel started up—I felt the whoosh of air as it gained speed, the fucked-up music-box music wailing to a fever pitch, the big bass drum beating relentlessly in heartbeat syncopation. Sammy stared at the lights, mesmerized. He didn't seem to be tripping, per se, he was just not all there and easily distracted.

"You stay here, John, with him. I'll try and get off work early."

I ran back up the escalator once I was pretty confident John wouldn't leave and Sammy wasn't going to try and move. The toy store was still dead and Steve had moved on to the other drawer. He looked up at me and gave me a slight nod, his lips moving as he continued to count or add or whatever he was doing. His eyes didn't leave me, though; he could tell I had something to ask. I moved over to him and he held up a finger, then lowered it and traced down a column of numbers.

"Four cents short," he finally declared, looking back up at me. "How is a drawer four cents short?"

It wasn't worth the trouble. He dug in his pocket and pulled out some change and made the drawer even.

"That kinda shit pisses me off," he said in an angry whisper. "Did you take four cents to dick with me?"

"No," I breathed.

"Was Scott in here?"

Scott being the other manager, the stripper, who never came into the store when he wasn't working or picking up his check or meeting one of his three girlfriends—the one who seemed really sweet and innocent and, oh, so fucking clueless.

"No," I breathed again. "Look, Steve..."

"Ah, it doesn't matter. Just got short changed somehow."

I looked at my watch. It was just about 8:15. By my guess, we hadn't rung up a sale in forty-five minutes.

"Hey, Steve, c'ni leave early, d'ya think?"

His brow furrowed and he scratched at his thick, blond mustache.

207

"I got something to take care of," I added. "I didn't know about it... It just came up."

He stood straight with his arms crossed, looking like a bouncer at a nightclub, what with his bulging muscles and steely, no-shit stare.

"How far away do you live?" he finally asked.

"What? I don't know? Fifteen minutes?"

"He just needs to sleep it off, Jack. Take him home, get him in bed, and get back here. You know I'm not allowed to close up alone. I might take the money. " He grinned sarcastically, but I knew he was telling the truth. "You gotta do your count."

"Okay. Right."

"He'll sleep it off. Don't worry."

I nodded once and may or may not have thanked him before bolting back down the escalator. Sammy was still sitting on the bench staring gape-mouthed at the wall of lights by the movie theater, but John was gone. I cursed under my breath, then plopped onto the bench by Sammy.

"C'mon, Sammy, we gotta go."

"*You* go!" he yelled, and I have to say, I was glad to at least see evidence of cognitive function.

"Let's go find Niz, Sammy."

Okay, I know what you're thinking: My plan was to simply dump Sammy off on someone else so that he became someone else's problem, which wasn't true. Niz's parents were famously cool, by which I don't mean they bought us beer or anything, but that they simply stayed out of our way when Niz had friends over. They may drift in and grab some food or something from the kitchen while we watched TV, but they never tried to butt into our conversations or correct overheard behavior or offer the kind of sage advice adults always feel compelled to offer. They were there if we needed them, but otherwise, they were like ghosts. And that's exactly what Sammy needed: He could sleep in Niz's room and no one would even know he was there. We could probably have snuck an elephant into Niz's room and no one would've known.

What went on in Sammy's head that night I don't know for sure, and he was really quiet on the drive to Niz's. He had a couple of random outbursts, but mostly he held his head as if he had a really bad headache. We got him into Niz's bed and pulled the curtains and shut off all the lights, even covered the alarm clock, so there was no stimulation of any kind.

"You think he's okay?" Niz wondered. We were standing right outside the door, whispering like a couple of scared parents.

"I mean, his girlfriend just broke up with him..."

Niz cocked his head sarcastically and looked at me. "The drugs, Bells. The drugs."

I shrugged emphatically. "I never did that shit, did you?"

He shook his head. I knew damn well he hadn't. No, Niz and I were more the sneak-dad's-bourbon variety of teenage experimentation, or set off fireworks on building sites, or sneak out on sleepovers just because. We didn't stay away from drugs because we were walking the straight-and-narrow path, it just never came up. I guess it's true what they say: If you don't go looking for trouble, you don't find it. Sammy, on the other hand, had a tendency to poke around in the dark corners to see if there was anything there. He also wasn't the best judge of character. If you added up all of his character quirks and insecurities, you ended up with a kid coming down from acid hidden away in his friend's bedroom.

"So he was pretty cut up about Donna Marie?" Niz assumed.

"Yeah... I mean, he'd seen it coming. He asked what she wanted to do the other night, and she..."

"She broke up with him."

I nodded. Niz motioned for me to follow him and led me back into the kitchen where we scrounged in the fridge for a couple of cans of Coke. By the clock I had about ten minutes before I needed to leave and head back to work.

"That clock right?"

Niz turned and squinted at it, slurping Coke from the can.

"Sure," he finally decided. I double checked my watch.

Niz leaned back against the sink and sighed heavily. Behind him was a huge picture window that looked out onto a heavily wooded backyard, but now it was a massive black square reflecting us. I looked disheveled, my face drawn and worried and my shirt only half tucked in. Niz looked pretty calm but I guess he hadn't been the one trying to figure out what to do with Sammy back at the mall.

"Where's Jess?" it suddenly occurred to me.

"She went out with Ally somewhere."

"Are they coming over later?"

"I don't know. I think they were going to get Tobie and hang out—a ladies' night."

"Great—so they're going to spend all night complaining about us."

"Wow—paranoid?"

I chuckled and polished off my Coke then let rip a massive belch. Niz, not to be outdone, gunned the rest of his Coke and ripped an even bigger one.

"I'll get the scoop tomorrow," I promised. "We're going down to that record store she's always going on about."

"The one by Sudsy's?"

"Yeah... I think. You guys should come."

"Nah... Jess has to work and I don't want to be a third wheel."

He stopped with his mouth half-open, ready to form words as soon as he finished his thought. He grinned a bit and his eyes glimmered.

"You kids make a cute couple," he finally concluded, but I don't think that was what he was originally going to say.

"Thanks, Dad. I better book."

Steve didn't say much of anything when I got back to the mall and counted out my drawer. While we were straightening the shelves he made an oblique comment about man-made drugs being way worse than things you can grow. I played dumb and he let it go, but something in the way he looked at me said he knew what he was talking about. He wasn't offering advice as an indirect way to sway or dissuade me, he was simply sharing his experiences.

Sammy finally stumbled out of Niz's bedroom sometime around midnight, while Niz and I were watching some old Cheech & Chong movie (it seemed apropos— also, Niz had rented it weeks before but had lost it before we could watch

211

it, and he'd just found it again earlier in the day). Sammy slumped down onto the couch between us and stared at the TV as if he'd never seen one before, then closed his eyes, put his head back, and groaned.

"You okay?" I checked.

"Can't turn it *off*," he said quietly.

"You want the TV off?"

I reached for the remote; he shook his head.

"No, it's okay. It's just... my head. This *pressure*. I can't turn *off* my brain."

I looked at Niz for explanation, but Niz could only shrug.

"Why did Donna Marie break up with me?" Sammy wondered.

"Shit, Sammy—" Niz started, but Sammy shook his head.

"I'll tell you why..." he mused rhetorically. "She has this *charm* about her that I could never tame. You know that, right? She did it to *save* me, man. She did it because she knew, if we ended up married or some shit, she'd probably divorce me. She'd get *bored* of me and divorce me. She quit while we were *ahead*, man."

"If you say so," Niz agreed.

He cut me a look to see if it was making more sense to me. I pointed at Cheech & Chong on the TV, indicating that Sammy was still stoned. Niz giggled.

"I'm *serious*, you guys," Sammy emoted, still with his head back and his eyes closed. "She did it *now* because it hurts *less*. We can't blame our friends for everything. Fuck you, Bells. You and that God damn hotdog bun."

212

I snickered and Sammy giggled with me, then his eyes shot open and he sat up, looking straight at me.

"You fucked her, didn't you?"

"Who? *What*? Donna *Marie*?"

"No, no—Ally! You *did*."

"Maybe we should get you home," I suggested, unable to meet Niz's inquiring gaze.

"It all makes so much sense to me now," Sammy whispered, his eyes widening comically.

"What's that?" I asked against my better judgment.

"My parents split up to save each other a bigger heartache. It hurts less now so it won't hurt more *then*."

"You think *that's* why your dad left?"

"Yeah," he breathed. "Yeah, it is! It would've got worse and worse if he stayed, so he left."

Sammy was often optimistic, but his drug-infused mind seemed to have ratcheted it up to full-on hippie proportions. While it's great to think that breakups happen because someone is being altruistic, the truth is probably much less charitable. Donna Marie broke up with Sammy because she liked her friends better, just like Penny Harper had broken up with me. And Sammy's dad left because he didn't want the burden of a family any more. Saying breakups were heroic acts was nothing more than naïve justification designed to avoid the blame you rightly didn't deserve, but also not to shift it to someone you once cared for, and probably still did.

"*She's* smart, too, Bells," Sammy decided. He nodded sagely at his own observation then jumped to his feet. "Fuck it! Take me home!"

213

He sat pretty quiet most of the time as we drove to his house, mumbling off and on, sometimes with a few words audible. It's like he was thinking and over-thinking and re-thinking everything about relationships, from Donna Marie to Ally to his dad to John to Greg Wilson. At least, that's what I gathered from the bits and pieces that drifted over the music to me. By the time we pulled into his driveway he seemed to have everything figured out somehow, to judge by the look on his face: A hint of revelation with a dose of dismay, because after you'd figured out the logic of a thing there is no other way it can make sense and no other conclusion that can be drawn but the one you're stuck with, no matter how shitty.

"Is your mom up?" I asked.

"No clue. I'm okay now. Just really fucking tired. C'ni borrow that Cure tape?"

"Which one?"

"*Head on the Door.*"

I snagged my tape case from the floor at his feet and rummaged around for a second, producing the album he wanted.

"Shake dog shake," he mumbled as he took it from me.

"That's on *The Top*," I said, digging into the case of tapes again.

"No, I know—I want this one. I just get that song now..."

He got out of my car and walked steadily up the drive and into his house without so much as a glance back. I popped *The Top* into the stereo and turned up "Shake Dog Shake" and drove home. I listened more carefully, but I wasn't ready to think about whatever Sammy now got.

How do you explain the allure of a good record store to someone who doesn't collect records? I didn't have a frame of reference until Ally took me to her favorite spot, downtown by Sudsy's. To say it was a place to buy music doesn't do justice to it or any independent record merchant. You can buy music at the mall, like where Jess worked, but that doesn't make it a record store. Real record stores are like coffeeshops or bars: Places to hang out, only instead of drinks, you buy music. I had a lot of records and I'd been to music stores, but I'd never truly been record shopping before —until that day with Ally, most of my collection had come from gaming the mail-order record clubs that gave you twelve records for signing up.

Egg Records wasn't huge by square footage, but everywhere they could they'd stuffed records to sell. Album covers and posters covered the walls, and special-edition sets line the tops of the record racks like an army of rare vinyl. The bins were divided loosely by genre, sub-divided by bands, and produced a full-color swath of musical distinction. In the mall, it was a monochromatic scale of Rock to Top 40 to Rap to Soundtracks, with a bin of Classical stuck off in one corner by itself. Egg was everything Niz and Sammy and I had figured it would be as we walked past it on the way to the few concerts we attended each year: It felt genuine and, despite all the used records, it felt fresh and new and vibrant. No glaring mall lights. No cash registers beeping. No moms arguing with clerks. No bratty kids whining at their moms. And the music being played out loud at Egg wasn't whatever some corporate bean counter was trying to push that week, it was what the person watching the store wanted to hear, or what a customer wanted to hear before they bought it. Half the fun of record shopping was trying new things or being convinced to try new things, and the patrons and proprietors swapped rumors of music like the news of war. There were couches and turntables and people laughing, and everyone there seemed to know Ally, and everyone had the next best thing that she *had* to hear.

I felt immediately lost and welcome.

Ally, on the other hand, walked right in like she owned the place and left me standing dumbfounded at the door.

"Jack? Bells?"

I snapped my attention to her and she waved me over to where she was digging through new singles. I'd never been much of a singles collector, having long underestimated the value of a good B-side, but Ally quickly schooled me that some of the best bands around only put out a few singles, which were never collected onto albums and certainly never made it to CD—and forget about hearing those B-sides again if the band didn't sell well.

"That's that band I was telling you about," she said, nodding her head at the bin beside her. "With Ian MacKaye? Fugazi? That's their album."

"Who's your friend?" a guy asked, sashaying up to us and grinning at Ally.

Yes, he sashayed, which is how I knew he was jealous. I also knew he was jealous because I *know* jealous because I *am* jealous. Well, that's not entirely true—Tobie helped me get over that to a large degree—but when a girl I like ends up liking some douchebag, I still get jealous. And confused —like, should I be a douchebag if the pretty girls like douchebags?

"Bells goes to my school," Ally said.

The guy bobbed his head and shook my hand—very professional—then pointed at the single Ally was holding.

"You like those guys? We just got an album he put out with his first band."

"Really?"

I sized the guy up—he was probably out of school, but barely. Maybe he went to college in Cincinnati. Maybe this was his career move. Or maybe this was *his* store and he was older than I thought. He was wearing tan corduroys and a drab green hoodie over two t-shirts, his hair slicked back like Pony Boy from *The Outsiders*. I knew, deep down, that he was cooler than me, which made me more scared than jealous. Although, to look at him and his body language, he'd been snubbed by Ally for months. I knew *that* feeling, too.

"Bells?"

"What? Sorry—I was... I don't know. What?"

"Gary was saying Tina Weymouth came in here the other day."

"Are you fucking *serious*?" I begged.

His smile widened to epic proportions and he laughed silently, throwing his head back and everything.

"Why did she? *What*?"

217

"They played here," Gary explained. "I guess she likes to shop for records."

"Did you get her autograph?" I blurted, already painfully aware how lame it would be for the record store guy to ask for an autograph. No no—if that shit went down in your store, you got her to sign a record and then you nailed it to the fucking wall. It wasn't just an autograph—you needed more than a scrap of paper with a scribbled signature on it.

"No—but I got a picture!" he explained.

He darted off behind the counter and produced an 8x10 print of him and Tina Weymouth.

"I haven't figured out where to put it yet."

"That's so cool..."

I looked over at Ally and she was beaming ear to ear, her whole face lit up with a heartfelt warmth that only comes from finally getting to share one of your most treasured joys with someone you care about. And I realized that Gary— poor Gary—didn't have a chance with her, for whatever hidden reasons we use to decide who to date. But Gary *did* make her happy because Gary was the embodiment of the record store; the voice and face of new music, old music, and undiscovered gems. He gave emotion and meaning to the act of collecting and listening to music, elevating it from merely the transfer of dollars for vinyl to the transmission of something sacred that should be handled with care and reverence. The cash register at the front? That was nothing more than the donation plate passed between pews stuffed with records. Without Gary, Egg Records would be like the mall stores. Gary was more than a merchant, he was a curator. She came here for Gary, yes, but not because she *liked* Gary but because Gary *was* the record store. And by me and Gary bonding over Tina Weymouth she knew she'd passed on that devotion to me.

"Have you heard 'Everybody Knows' by Leonard Cohen yet?" Gary asked me, taking the picture back and tucking it away behind the counter again.

"I don't think so..."

"Ally?"

She shook her head.

"I can't believe I haven't played it for you yet..." he mumbled in admonishment to himself.

He cut off whatever was currently playing and flicked through a shelf of records behind him, pulling out the one he wanted and laying it on the platter. He got it spinning and blew ceremoniously on the vinyl once or twice, then carefully lowered the needle into place.

"This whole album is great..." he mumbled.

There are few sounds in the world as glorious as the resonant pop and click of a needle finding the groove in a record, then those long seconds of silence as you wait for the track to rotate under the stylus, and finally the opening strains of the song. But *that* song... My God, the first time that song echoed through those speakers will forever be etched in my mind as one of the most important moments of my life. Every instrument hits on the first beat, powered by a soft-edged bass that never loses its way. And when Leonard Cohen stirs the air with his breathy baritone, it's like all other noise ceases in order to make way for the only sound that counts—except that bass, that slow-pounding bass. Then slowly, Cohen makes room for high-end details—an oud, for

Christ's sake—and sultry backing vocals, underpinned with orchestral flourishes. And the lyrics... so bittersweet and painfully beautiful.

I had to own it; to have and to hold it forever.

"Jesus, can I buy that?" I breathed when it ended.

He left the record playing but turned down the volume.

"Yeah—we have another copy over there. This is my personal stash."

"I wouldn't have taken you for a fan of something like that," Ally said slyly as we flipped through the records, looking for the C-O's. "Aren't you here to look for Inspiral Carpets?"

Gary started messing around with something—pricing new stock, I think—and I understood that he had specifically come over to play us that song: nothing more, nothing less.

"That song was amazing. I like amazing. That's why I buy so many damn records—I'm always looking for moments like that again, when you first hear something so amazing that it can only have come from magic. The first time that ever happened was when I heard Zeppelin's 'No Quarter'—I must've been ten. Blew my mind."

"I'll bet. So why don't you spend more time at *real* record stores?" she asked, handing me the Leonard Cohen album with another sly smile.

"Nobody to go with, I guess."

"I'm glad you met me, Jack Beltane," she joked.

"Me, too," I agreed.

She reached out and put her hand on my back, running it down my arm and squeezing me just above the elbow before letting me go.

"C'ni go back to the singles now?" she checked.

"Yeah—this is all I can afford, but I gotta have that song."

"Ten bucks for one song?"

"Ten bucks for a *million-dollar* song...?" I retorted.

We leafed through the singles for a while, Ally pointing out everything I was missing out on—all the B-sides and remixes—and explaining who worked on which record and came from what band. It was magnificent. Gary would wander over from time to time and offer to play something Ally had picked out. It was her routine, I guess: She'd pick out a whole stack of singles then have Gary help her pare them down to the ones she could afford. Sometimes he cut stuff out with barely a glance—"the B-side sucks"—and other times he'd let her decide by playing it.

"I'm really am glad you came with me, Bells," she said while we sat on the couch in the front of the store—a well-worn velvet affair that might have come from the ruins of the last whorehouse in town—and listened to her final selections.

"This is great," I said. "Really great."

"For as much as my cousins like music, they don't like shopping for it, not like this."

"Really?"

"They usually ditch me and come back."

She chuckled and glanced over at Gary (back to pricing stock) then leaned over and whispered in my ear, "It's nice to have someone with good taste helping me pick."

Man alive, I wanted to kiss her hard, right then and there. I wanted to kiss her and lie her down on that couch and...

"Tobie misses you, you know?" she said almost glibly, sitting back.

"What?"

It certainly was not the thing I had expected her to say. She looked apologetic, like she was only reporting the news.

"Did she say that?"

"Not exactly," Ally admitted. "But while we were out yesterday... a girl can tell. She was checking up on you. Making sure you were okay."

"Well, that's Tobie for ya—she does that for everyone."

"She misses you, Bells, and I know why. You're good company."

"You're just saying that because you and I... *you know*," I finished in a whisper.

She gasped with mock offense and punched my arm.

"You ruined the fucking moment, Bells!"

"Talking about Tobie was a 'moment'?" I scoffed.

She shook her head and grinned as if she should have known better.

"It means a lot to me, you giving up a whole day to come here with me," she considered.

"Like I had anything better to do?"

"Stop! You know what I mean. I wanted to share this with you."

"And I wanted to come—this was not a chore, believe me. As long as you're there, we could sit and watch grass grow."

"Okay, now you're being cheesy."

I leaned in and kissed her then—a quick peck on the lips to let her know what I was thinking, since words didn't seem up to the task of explaining. Gary didn't see us. I think some other guy shopping for records had, but it wasn't his fault: We were being loud and Ally was the kind of girl who caught your eye.

"I really did have fun today," I said. "Seriously. I want to come back all the time."

"Good," she replied steadily, that ol' Ally smirk stretching across her lips: the look of a girl patting herself on the back for getting exactly what she'd wanted. "And we will."

$$\acute{\varepsilon}$$

Sammy's eyes widened in the darkness. It had only been a week since the breakup but he seemed more like his old self again—except for a sudden obsession he had with having heightened senses. Maybe he was trying to put a positive spin on his acid trip.

"I heard something," he whispered.

"Dude, we're in the middle of a golf course in the middle of the night. There's no one here," I tried to explain.

Ally and I had gone to his house, but he was afraid of making too much noise—it was late and his mom had dozed off on the couch. His heightened senses apparently came with a paranoid fear that his mother would figure out what had happened, and young Sammy could not be dissuaded from the fact that he was acting pretty normal—except when he tried to convince people he was normal. Anyway, he'd suggested a quick run out to the golf course by his house—a shit-ton of acres completely unfenced and dark and threaded all over with the smoothest asphalt trails anywhere. We used to go over there for hill rides because it was so smooth and effortless to get up a good speed. There was one hill that went down into a tunnel through another hill or some kind of underpass or something, and that was awesome as hell to skate—the wind on your face, then a sudden strange thrumming almost-silence as the slight sound of the wheels whooshed over the tunnel walls and bounded and rebounded all around you. It felt like you were flying, I swear, and with the slick asphalt and our fat wheels, we barely made a noise —not that you could have heard much out in the middle of the acreage.

Which is why we doubted Sammy and his narcotically enhanced senses.

"No no—I swear. Listen!"

We did. Ally snickered the second I thought I heard it, too—a sound like singing.

"I hear it!" I said with amazement.

We were standing at the top of the hill, ready to take the tunnel ride back, and we all froze. It was definitely singing —drunken singing. Apparently we weren't the only ones who had figured out how isolated the middle of the golf course was.

"Should we hide?' Ally whispered harshly.

"Sshh," I offered, holding up a hand. She hugged herself and jiggled nervously, so I added, "It's not the cops."

"Hey!" a voice suddenly yelled. "There's someone over there!"

"We should run," Ally suggested. "They could be older..."

"That's Greg fucking Wilson," Sammy declared. "I'd know the sound of that asshole anywhere."

We could see them now—four human shapes against the horizon, silhouetted by the distant city lights behind them. Greg sounded drunk and he was clearly stumbling; the other two looked fine. They were a lot closer than I'd realized.

"This is stupid," Ally said. "This kind of shit is stupid when it happens in movies because you *know* they should just *leave*. So let's *go*."

"Oh my *Gawd*," Greg bellowed. "It's a buncha fucking *skaters*."

"I'm gonna beat the shit outta him, once and for all," Sammy said defiantly. He dropped his board and ran toward them before I could grab him.

"Sammy! Wait!" I yelled, dropping my own board and taking off after him.

"Sammy?" Greg yelled in response. "Don't tell me..."

I reached Sammy as Sammy reached Greg, only dimly aware that the others were Missy Anderson and some other couple I'd seen in the halls at school, but didn't know.

"Sammy Green," Greg said sarcastically. "What are the fucking chance—"

Sammy cut him off with a solid fist to his cheek. Missy screamed. The other guy pushed his girlfriend behind him and stood there, clearly not wanting anything to do with any of this.

"Lez go, Greg," he suggested quietly.

Greg regained his balance—slowly; it was a sucker

punch—and lunged at Sammy. Sammy caught him and punched him in the stomach, yelling obscenities and maybe something about Donna Marie and maybe even something about me—it was hard to tell. I rushed over and pulled them apart, cuffing Sammy around the shoulders and dragging him back. I eyed the other guy warily, waiting for him to move in, but he didn't. If anything, he stepped back. Missy was standing with her hands over her mouth, tears in her eyes sparkling in the moonlight.

"You're an asshole, Greg!" Sammy yelled, not fighting me as I pulled him back. Greg had sobered up considerably, probably from the pain in his stomach and face.

"Fuck you, Green," he finally spat. "What did you think would happen when a toad like you dates a fucking princess? *Not* a fucking fairy tale—"

Sammy jumped, but I still had him and pulled him away.

"Let's go, man," I whispered.

Sammy sighed heavily and let me turn him around to move away. Ally dropped in with us and cast a suspicious glance back at them.

"Jack!" Missy suddenly yelled. She was crying, not from fear but from sadness, and it confused me. I stopped and turned back to her.

"Are you fucking that *freak*?" she finished.

I could barely see her face in the darkness, but she looked pained—genuinely hurt. I realized later that she'd obviously just figured it out—or thought she had, anyway—and she'd suddenly understood that Ally and I had been close for a while, which meant the whole time I'd been dating Missy, including the night I snubbed her advances, I had

226

really been with Ally. She wasn't entirely wrong, in hindsight.

But right then? No, I didn't see any of that. I saw a scared little bitch trying to hurt my girlfriend. I let go of Sammy and ran up to yell in her face, to tell her that *she* was the freak and a bitch and all the other shit I'd been wanting to vent since she'd had the gall to break up with me, but Greg stopped me with a slow punch that caught me on the side of my head, his class ring scraping my ear. I remember thinking it was odd that Missy wasn't wearing his ring, then Greg pushed me and Sammy was back by my side trying to land another punch, and finally the other guy stepped in, yelling like a God damn dad and pulling us all apart. I gave him a shove and he did nothing, he just looked at me, his face apologetic and scared and—mostly—fed up, and suddenly I felt very small and very immature.

I grabbed Sammy's arm and pulled him away again. I didn't say a word. Ally let us go past, probably to make sure we were really going and Greg & Co weren't following, then she jogged up to us and slipped her hand into mine. I dropped it and put my arm around her shoulder and hugged her to me.

"She's a jealous little bitch," I whispered, actually shaking with rage and fighting back tears, my emotions and adrenaline coming out any way they could find.

"Beltane!" Greg yelled, but we kept walking. "Jackhole! Missy says you couldn't perform, man—you can't even *imagine* what you missed, faggot!"

I may have gone back at him again with that comment, except Ally whispered, "You didn't ever sleep with her?"

227

When I looked at her, she looked pleasantly surprised.

"You knew that," I said. "I told you..."

I trailed off. Yeah, I'd told her, but that didn't make it real. Until right then, she must have still harbored a doubt, and that tiny glimmer of silver lining was enough to make me not even register whatever the hell else Greg was yelling at us. I kissed her as we walked, the shakes and rage evaporating with the simple touch of her lips on mine, and the twinkle in her eye, and the glad smile on her face.

"Do you feel better now, Samuel?"

"Little bit," he admitted. "I landed a couple of good ones. Fucking asshole."

He was still seething and I could tell it was all he could do to contain himself.

"And that fucking *bitch* Donna Marie—"

"Sammy—no. You don't mean that," Ally said softly.

"Don't fucking *touch* me, Ally. It's easy for you."

"*Easy?*"

She sounded honestly offended and the last thing I wanted was God damn Greg Wilson to ruin our night further by getting all of us pissed off at each other.

"Don't yell at *us*, man," I begged Sammy. "We're your friends—"

"Yeah?" he demanded, stopping short and reeling around to face us. I held my ground.

"Yes, Samuel. Like it or not."

He shook his head with disappointment.

"Why did I let you get me mixed up in this, Beltane?"

"Because it was fun?"

He snuffed a laugh through his nose and started walking

228

off again. We reached our skateboards and picked them up and I glanced back and caught sight of the four heads bobbing back the way they'd come, out of sight behind a rise.

"What part was the most fun for you, Bells?" Sammy wondered with quiet sarcasm. "Getting decked at King of Hearts or babysitting me while I came down?"

"I was thinking, for you, probably the first time you kissed the Homecoming queen—remember how that felt? The nerves and excitement?"

He smiled privately and turned away.

"Fuck you, asshole," he mumbled.

He sighed heavily then turned back.

"Sorry, Ally Mac—I didn't mean nothing. I was just pissed off."

"You meant *some*thing," she replied tightly.

I squeezed her hand but she didn't look at me. I suppose she deserved to know—he had made it sound pretty mean.

"I just meant—*Jesus...*"

He looked away, down the hill, at the stars, at the dry branches trying to catch the wind—anywhere but at her.

"You're *hot*, okay?" he stated. "It's *easy* for you to get a date. Not like me. I'm *sorry*. Can we fucking *go* now?"

He didn't wait for an answer. He flopped his board down and jumped on it before we could respond, howling off through the tunnel like a lunatic on night release. Ally gave me a crooked grin that said she accepted Sammy's apology but really would have appreciated getting to defend herself.

"It's not that easy, you know?" she told me instead.

"Oh, I know. You snubbed me a lot—"

"Asshole," she retorted, grabbing my board from me and

229

tossing it down the hill. She fired off a playful grin and stuck her tongue out at me.

"What the *hell*?"

"There's a difference between getting a date and *wanting* a date," she stated unequivocally. "And when you *want* a date, it's never easy—it's delicate."

"Let's just go out for ice cream, huh?" I suggested.

"Yeah," she agreed with mild sarcasm. "Let's celebrate."

$$\acute{\varepsilon}$$

You would think, since three of us worked at the mall, the last place we'd want to hang out would be the mall, but when the weather in Ohio decides to prove to you that spring is closer to winter than it is to July Fourth, you don't have much choice. Besides, the mall always seemed like the promise of something incredible happening—a new movie, or a new record, or an amazing find at the damn dollar store —so we were drawn to it despite our best efforts. There was something in the lights and sounds and the smooth, polished finish of everything that was vaguely magically—no doubt the whiff of memories from childhood, when malls were places where you got big cookies and met Santa and saw your friends outside of school or their houses. It was like, if anything happened in the world, it certainly happened at the mall, or at least started there. So we went. We went, we drank frozen Cokes, we ate big cookies, and we worried security as to whether or not they should call the cops.

"You can't be serious?" Sammy growled.

He slurped his Coke and looked up at me, sort of hunched over, but he was speaking to Niz. Jess shook her head without amusement, and Ally and Tobie sat mildly grinning, watching the show.

"If Jack's there to catch me, too, I will try acid," Niz said.

"No," I stated definitively. "I have to draw the line there. I am *not* going to be your damn babysitter."

"It wasn't any fun," Sammy admitted.

For reasons unknown to any of us, Niz flicked a french fry out into the main thoroughfare, missing a mom and her kid by inches. Jess punched him in the arm, hard, but I don't think he was aiming for them.

"No, Jack's our safehouse," Niz decided. "Jess may be our mom, but Jack's—"

"Fuck *you*, Niz," Jess protested.

"Aw, baby, I's just playing..."

He put his arm around her and she halfheartedly shrugged it off.

"Why's Jack the safehouse?" Ally wondered. "There's gotta be some stories there..."

She'd settled right in with the group and we already couldn't think of her not being there, but she was still catching up. I mean, the rest of us had been hanging out for years—me, Niz, Tobie, and Jess since we were in middle school—so Ally was always trying to figure out the hidden meaning to inside jokes or the history that had led to the present moment.

231

"Let me tell you about Jack Beltane," Niz offered, pulling his chair around as if he needed a better angle on his audience. "He and I have a long history—friends since we were in second or third grade or something—and we have a habit of cooking up some pretty dumb ideas."

"*You* cook up the dumb ideas," I corrected.

"True. I carefully plan out how not to get caught getting us *into* trouble, but Jack here is the one who figures out how to lay low long enough that you can plan to get back *out* of trouble, and that's really the most important part."

"It's true," Tobie interjected with a dour nod.

"*Seriously*?" I checked. "*That's* what you people think of me? I don't know what they're talking about," I added confidentially to Ally.

"Even John knew it," Sammy said. "That's why he brought me here."

"Bullshit. He brought you here because he didn't know any of your other friends."

Sammy shrugged.

"Well I think it's great," Ally cooed, slipping her arm through mine and pulling me closer to her. "I wouldn't mind if people thought of me like that."

How could I deny her face? I unthreaded my arm and gave her a quick squeeze-hug.

"Well, well, well, ladies!" a voice suddenly boomed. It sounded too jovial to be Greg Wilson, but that was my first thought. We all turned in the direction it came from and saw a stocky, buff kid walking toward us.

"Toad!" Sammy shrieked, and shot out of his chair to greet him.

Timmy Toderman—The Toad—was definitely the best skater around. Also the strongest. He didn't hang out with us too much, but enough to be on speaking terms. He was a year ahead of us and already in college. He was carrying a piece of pink paper and grinning from ear to ear.

"Are you the assholes responsible for *this*?" he wondered, slapping the paper down on the table. It was a crudely drawn sign that had been Xeroxed, showing a skateboard with a big "no" bar drawn through it. "NO SKATE-BOARDS" it proclaimed along the top. Then under the picture it added, "NOT EVEN TO GO TO DISC WORLD."

It seems they had completely banned skateboards from the premises, even as we sat chatting in the food court. At least, the signs hadn't been anywhere we saw them when we arrived.

"How is that *our* fault?" I wondered.

"My records indicate you were the first dip-shits to skate in this mall," Toad replied casually, his grin (dare I say?) a bit jealous.

"But not the *last*, apparently?"

"Apparently," he agreed.

"Did *you* skate in here?" Sammy asked him.

Toad shook his head.

"Pete did, to try some new wheels right outside Disc World. And I guess some other guys did..." He trailed off and we followed his gaze around to a security guard hustling toward our table.

"Break it up!" the guard called out, waving his hands uselessly.

"Break *what* up?" Jess asked, her tone flat and snide.

"Your group is getting too big!"

He stopped a safe distance away and hoisted his belt as if it were weighed down by more than a single pair of plastic handcuffs.

"Are you *serious*?" Jess demanded, somehow even more snidely.

"No loitering," the guard offered.

"We're *eating*."

Jess was handling it pretty well, so no one tried to cut in. I don't think the guard knew what to do with her. He'd been expecting lip, but not from a pretty girl.

"No more than four," the guard bleated.

He had obviously decided brevity was his best defense ("Just the facts" and all that shit). His eyes shifted nervously, planning his escape should we all stand up at once. I wondered what kind of kid he'd been in school. Probably the bully who graduated into the real world and realized he wasn't such hot shit after all, and only slightly more skilled than a head of lettuce. Or maybe he was working his way up, trying to get into the police academy. I was about to ask him —which no doubt would not have been well received— when Toad broke the uneasy silence.

"Fuck it! I was going anyway. Just dropped by to give you ladies *that*."

He jabbed a stubby finger at the flier, then spun on his heal and stalked off.

"Okay?" I asked the guard.

He shook his head.

"Fuuuuuck!" Jess drawled, standing up with a huff and pulling Niz to his feet. "We're going down to the record

234

store. See you guys in a few minutes."

Niz saluted the guard, who visibly relaxed when they walked off, though I wasn't sure if it was because Jess was gone or because we were safely down to the magic number of four hoodlums—an easily manageable number, according to the ledgers of mall-security bookkeeping.

We sat in an uneasy silence while he watched us. I glanced at Ally and she snickered, which made me giggle. That must have finally rattled him, or made him realize all his posturing didn't amount to much. He had to know we were just going to get up and walk down to the record store and hook back up with Niz and Jess. The whole thing was an elaborate shadowplay—he had to do his part to keep the mall "safe" by breaking up "gangs" of kids so the bitchy PTA moms would stop calling and whining to his boss, and we had to make it look like we cared. But by laughing at him, it stripped away the veneer and exposed the farce for what it was. There wasn't truly anything he could do, and we all knew that. If he called the cops every time a group of kids all ate at the same table, they'd fire him. But all the concerned citizens there assembled had heard the exchange and approved of the measures, and it really wasn't worth the hassle to not go along with it—and he knew that, too.

"You know what this would be good for?" Tobie asked, waggling the pink flier as the security guard finally strolled away—but not too far away.

"Burning?" I guessed.

She shook her head. "The *project*."

"What project?" Ally whispered as she saw all of our eyes light up.

"We have to get them all!" I said excitedly. "Every door, every flier!"

Tobie explained to Ally that the "project" was a year-long collection of all the fliers they put up in school. All the bake sales, school council electioneering, spirit week crap, and every other thing they plastered on the walls—we took as many of them as we could and saved them in a locker. Our plan was to put them all back up—every one of them—at the end of the year. Wallpaper the damn school with a history of fliers and handbills. And these fliers, they would be the centerpiece.

"Me and Jack will head down to JC Penney—there's an entrance down there," Ally decided.

"I'll go up by Disc World—there's *two* entrances," Sammy agreed.

Tobie smiled weakly at me, then nodded. "I'll go with Sammy—see you back at the record store? There's another entrance down there."

"Plus the parking garage on the other side of the arcade," I considered. "Yeah—we'll hook back up with Niz and Jess, then head over there."

Ally and I didn't walk fast. We were in no rush. She slid her hand in mine as we strolled, and for just an instant I saw everything in the future so damn clearly: The wife, the kids, the fact that I would be left to my own devices, as a responsible adult. No one breathing down my neck, telling me what I should or shouldn't do. No one giving me dirty looks for my hairstyle or raising their eyebrows in disappointment when they heard my music. No, I saw it all: Me and Ally would be the coolest parents on the entire God damn planet.

We wouldn't frown on our kids' decisions, we'd respect them, and we wouldn't rely on titles for respect, we'd be Jack and Ally, not Mom and Dad. I was sure of it. And I couldn't wait.

"This is nice," Ally said quietly. Every once in a while she still ducked my gaze bashfully, like she was nervous to be with me or something.

"What? The mall?"

She chuckled and looked around at all the empty store-fronts. I tell you, that mall was a vast, empty metaphor for something, but I'll be damned if I know what. It struck me—every time I set foot in the place—that something so big and shiny and well maintained shouldn't be so empty, so under appreciated, so unloved.

"No—it's nice hanging out with you and your friends."

"*My* friends?" I checked. "They're *your* friends, too."

"I guess."

She scuffed a Chuck Taylor over the slick floor, kicking imaginary rocks.

"Hey—what's wrong?"

I pulled her gently and she stopped, turning to me. She looked about to cry, but she was hiding behind her hair and I couldn't quite tell. Her colored strands were dark pink today, like the dark stripe of a candy cane; somehow red, but not quite.

"Nothing," she finally said, pulling her hair back and framing her face in color, her lips the same muted shade, out-lined ever so carefully in a deeper red. That was the face she saw every day in the mirror, and she turned it into art.

"I'm just happy," she added. "And I'm still a silly little girl."

237

She moved off before I could reply and pulled me after her, so I followed. I wasn't generally the best when it came to talking to girls—throwing hotdog buns at them was more my speed—but for once I knew when to leave well enough alone. I could see it in her eyes, anyway: She was happy. She was misty-eyed for her own, private reasons, but she was also happy.

"I'm glad I know you, Ally Mac," I said and gave her hand a squeeze.

She giggled lightly then broke into a run and pulled me along, as if to escape whatever it was that had put her in a mood. Our shoes slapped and echoed on the floor, and the whirring arcade bells and noises of the circus-like food court faded away like a distant spooky dream. The only people in the wing with us were the mall walkers—those moms dutifully putting on sweats and headbands and carrying two-pound weights as they hustled around and around the mall, maybe for exercise, but maybe because they were trying to outrun their own demons. Suddenly it all seemed too quiet and too depressing, and I sped up, urging Ally on. We dashed to the doors and ripped down the signs—one on each of the six doors—and no one saw, or no one said a word. We laughed too loudly as we stuffed them into Ally's purse, then clasped hands and ran back out, like a couple of dorks in a teen movie. I guess sometimes that shit in movies is based on real life.

When we got to the record store, winded, Tobie asked if we'd been chased. Ally and I shared a knowingly glance, unable to explain whatever it was we had both felt and had shaken, or just what it was about such a minor, insignificant thing as grabbing some fliers that had seemed so... *big*.

"No," I managed to say. "We just felt like running."

Ally laughed.

Tobie looked away.

"Hey," Tobie breathed.

I pulled my last book out of my locker and turned to her.

"Hey, Tobe. You sound serious."

"You can tell that from one word?"

"With you I can."

She wiped nonexistent tears from her eyes. I waited for her to speak again, taking my sweet time to close my locker softly.

"Still no book bag?" she checked as her way of starting the conversation over.

"I can make it to my locker between classes."

"Pff," she disagreed. "What's your next class?"

"Art—ceramics."

I looked at her and smiled and she smiled back.

"You used to be an honors student, Jack."

"What the hell does *that* mean?"

She shook her head slightly and shifted her weight.

"I like art. I need the break. I can't stand studying all the time."

"You can't stand studying *any*time."

"What the hell *is* this, Tobie? You're worse than my God damn *mom*. Seriously! She'd—"

"You spend all your time skating and hanging out at the mall and going to shows!"

"Jealous?"

She actually gritted her teeth and punched me. Not hard —nothing but a light tap on the shoulder, really, but it was the teeth and her eyes that scared me. They said she was holding something back, and I figured if it was that big, I should have got a sense of it before now.

"Getting in *fights*, Jack? Sammy dropping *acid*? You making *bongs* in art class!"

"Jesus, Tobie! What the hell is *wrong* with you? I didn't make a stupid *bong*—that was Ryan Jefferson."

She cut me a look and I didn't press the issue. Ryan and I ate lunch sometimes, and we always partnered up in art classes, so I was guilty by association, I guess. With anyone else, I would've stormed off at that point, but not with Tobie. She got the benefit of the doubt—and she had me curious.

"Is this about that *shit* Greg Wilson again? Because I am *really* sick of the way he keeps coming up."

"Everyone knows you and Sammy picked a fight with him on the golf course with Ally the other night."

"Not exactly." I sighed, glad the conversation was at least making some sense now. "He was mouthing off, as usual."

"So you and Sammy started swinging, as usual."

"Forget it, Tobie," I said. I stepped angrily away and added, "You *know* that's bullshit. You *know* none of this shit —*none* of it—happened until that asshole entered our lives."

"So this is *my* fault?" she whispered, stopping me short.

240

I watched the big wall clock for what seemed like minutes, watching the bright red second hand click from pip to pip, draining the moments until the bell rang and I would have to run to beat the last bell.

It's only later that we realize the deep significance of those stolen conversations between classes, where each word is weighted to perfection or apt to knock everything off balance. Thoughts were often left dangling in the air as we scattered for classrooms; I imagine those half-formed ideas slipping to the ground like autumn leaves, swirling with the dust and paper-wads the janitor cleaned up every night. But that action—the sudden end to conversations dictated by the bells —also seemed to dampen the fire, and while sometimes those thoughts would resurface later and well up into full-blown misunderstandings, most often they evaporated over the course of the next class, as if they had been born and died in those singular moments only, never to be thought of again.

So Tobie's observations didn't stick with me too much— I figured she was just blowing off steam because her and Greg Wilson still had mutual acquaintances that were getting harder to maintain. But later... Later I realized the full measure of what she'd said, and what she really meant. It was Ally she didn't like me spending so much time with, but that was a reason she couldn't admit, even to herself, because we all liked Ally, so she made up excuses like bongs and art classes and not doing homework. It was all bad, in other words, but the real bad, the big bad, was the girl who might finally tear me away from Tobie.

"It's not anyone's fault, Tobie," I finally said. I turned to her, but she was already walking away.

"Tobie?" I called out, she stopped and turned back, smiling weakly.

"I know, Jack," she admitted. "I just miss you."

"You *miss* me?"

It was real confusion. I felt like I saw her all the time.

"It's okay." She smiled so honestly that I believed her.

And by the end of art, it was all history—just another conversation being tossed through the halls by whatever breezes stirred it; something to forget and sweep away.

If a girl is serious about you—*really* serious—you'll inevitably end up at her house for dinner, with her family. Parents can sense that kind of thing, and they figure if their daughter is taking a relationship seriously, they better see what it's all about. More to the point, they want to know how you act and interact, whether you have manners, whether your clothes smell like smoke, what kind of car you drive—this is the gauge and measure of an American teenager. But they can also sniff out bullshit with some kind of extrasensory perception: You wear clothes you don't normally wear, or cut your hair, or try to cover up a tattoo line (drawn by someone's cousin for practice before you pulled away and came to your senses), and they'll know. They'll know, and you're done for. The only thing worse than an undesirable teenager is a faker, because with a faker they have no idea what they're up against.

Even with Ally's parents—who didn't appear to exert a huge level of control over her fashion sense, and didn't mind her hanging out with skate rats at all hours—my finger still quivered as I depressed the doorbell, illogically hoping it didn't ring too loudly and piss them off.

Her dad answered immediately, as if he'd been lying in wait. That freaked me out. I stepped back, actually poised and ready to bolt.

"Jack! Glad you could make it. Come on in. Come in!"

I'd been over to Ally's house plenty of times and her parents seemed really nice—her brother, too, the once I'd met him (he was a year older than Ally and off at college). But this was for keeps. This was the test. My foot hovered in the air above the threshold for an indeterminate amount of time, then finally dipped down, toes first, like a frightened swimmer testing the water.

"What's the shirt today, Jack?" he asked, something he always asked. At first it may have been honest curiosity, but now it was just the standard ice breaker.

My foot finally landed and carried me over the stoop, into the house. Ally's dad shoved the door and it swung silently and heavily closed. He was smiling, maybe even daring me to yell at him for slamming the door.

"Oh, uh, the Psychedelic Furs," I finally answered. "Was I supposed to dress up? Ally never said any—"

"Hell no," he cut in, slapping me on the back and ushering me into the dining room. "I think I've heard of them. Ally's always playing that new wave stuff—is that what they

243

are? Like the damn Cure. That one song is catchy—'Just like Heaven'?"

"Yeah," I agreed.

If he was trying to relax me, it was having the exact opposite effect. I knew her dad was in some high-powered corporate career something-or-other, and this all felt very polite but not very meaningful, like a business dinner. Not that he was being rude or insincere—he was trying to make me feel relaxed, which naturally made me wonder what I had to get worked up about, and so I got worked up instead.

"Jack!" Ally cried out, bouncing—yes, she veritably *bounced*—into the room. At least to me it seemed bouncy. Probably she walked, like she always did, sweeping her hair back over her ears like she always did. Probably it seemed such a vibrant step because her dad was so... not like Ally.

"Your dad likes the Cure."

That was my exact response, as if he wasn't still in the room and as if it would be news to her.

"He pretends," Ally agreed. "For my sake."

She shared a knowing grin with her dad, then pulled me back out of the dining room toward the stairs.

"Don't bother going upstairs!" her mom called out from the kitchen. "And get your brother down here!"

Ally stopped me at the bottom of the stairs and looked back down the hall, toward her parents. I could hear them in the kitchen, putting together the food, and Ally took the moment to lean in and kiss me—a slow, deep kiss that made me terrified we'd get caught. A simple peck her parents would excuse as young love, but this was one of those *real* kisses, the kind that made me want to drop to my knees and ask her to marry me. She pulled away and smiled.

"Had to get that out of the way so I could make it through dinner."

"Yeah..." I agreed.

I stepped back and she called up the stairs for her brother. I got the impression he was going to college to humor his parents. He played bass and seemed more interested in starting a band, but I guess he was studying music theory or something, and Ally said he had lots of ideas for making a career out of music that didn't all involve tours and fans. He went to school in New York City—her dad could afford to send them anywhere, one of the perks of his job, I guess—and he already seemed much less suburban than the last time I'd seen him.

"Jack," he nodded as he passed me. "Nice shirt."

Apparently that was how the McShays created small talk, although I suppose I didn't expect too many compliments for my hair—you really can't comb a mohawk, so I didn't bother; it lay over my shaved pate like a disheveled toupee.

I tried to stay quiet during dinner, only speaking when spoken to and all that. Ally's mom kept trying to include me in the conversation, which was nice, but I felt very much like the new kid at school who could only listen and smile and assume everything was an inside joke. Finally, after a lull of several minutes, Ally's mom looked over at me and smiled.

"What's your favorite book, Jack?"

"Book?"

She nodded. I sensed a trick and quickly scanned through some titles in my head, then shrugged and told the straight-up truth: "*Peter Pan*."

"Really?" her dad stressed; everyone seemed dumb-founded. "Not Stephen King? I thought all teenagers loved Stephen King?"

"I like Stephen King," I admitted. "My favorite *author* is probably H.P. Lovecraft—"

"Don't know him," her dad mumbled.

"But my favorite *book*—my favorite story—is definitely *Peter Pan*. Or maybe *A Christmas Carol*."

"Why Peter Pan?" her mom asked. They weren't being mean, they were being about as curious as you'd expect.

"I don't know. Wendy seems like a good mom."

"It's the kids, isn't it?" her dad quipped. "You like the idea of the kids running the show?"

"I like that they have friends they can count on, I guess. People they don't *have* to count on, but they do."

"Jack's had the same friends since grade school," Ally interjected, trying to help explain something I'd never really even thought about myself. I mean, why *do* we like certain books or movies more than others? What echoes are there for us in those pages, of what is or of what we want to be? It always sounds so trite when you try to put it into words, but maybe Ally was on to something. I nodded slowly.

"Really just Niz since grade school," I said.

"Sixth grade is grade school," Ally rebuffed humorously. "That's when you met Tobie and Jess, right?"

"Yeah..."

"They're just like the Lost Boys," Ally said.

"Well, no..."

"You even call Jess 'Mom'."

246

"Just as a joke," I mumbled.

"Friends are good," her dad said definitively. "But family is everything, wouldn't you say?"

I knew what the correct answer was, of course, and this time it really was a test.

"Sure," I agreed.

There was a silence that seemed to me uneasy, until Ally's brother finally broke it.

"So, Jack—what does that make Ally?"

"Huh?"

"If you guys are the Lost Boys, how's Ally fit in?"

"It's not like that," I disagreed. "I just like the story—Neverland, the pirates, adventures, *flying*. I'm not trying to live out *Peter Pan* or something."

He chuckled amiably. "Just giving you a hard time, man. I didn't remember it being a *love* story."

He looked knowingly at Ally and she blushed and turned her head down, hiding behind her hair. There was another uneasy silence, and this time her dad broke it.

"I love crime fiction. Dan Marlowe and all that."

"Why crime fiction?"

He smirked at me and I couldn't help but smile back.

"Touche." He stopped and collected his thoughts, then continued, "I think I like all the traveling they do, even if only exploring all the nooks and crannies of one town. But the bank robber ones, where they flee across the country...? I like the travel."

"That makes sense," Ally mumbled.

She glanced at her brother who looked mildly shocked, but she didn't meet her parents' eyes. They shared a glance,

247

but nothing I could really interpret. The silence didn't last long before Ally's mom announced dessert. When her parents left the room to clean up the plates, Ally slipped her hand into mine and squeezed it. She smiled with something like regret.

"Sorry if that was awkward..."

"It's fine—it felt like a test, though."

"Are you kidding?" her brother cut in. "This whole damn night is a test!"

"Shut up, Phil," Ally said nicely. "You're not helping."

"Look, Ally, they know you're old enough to move out, okay? You start college in the fall."

"So?"

I was starting to panic; feeling the first drumming heartbeats in my neck as my breath shortened. It wasn't because they were arguing—at least, not only that—it was because it seemed to be revealing a hidden conversation I hadn't been a party to. Maybe even an argument. Ally glanced at me, her eyes angry with her brother; she gripped my hand tighter, clearly unaware that she was doing it.

"So? You know?" He waggled his head a bit to indicate that the rest of his thought was self-evident, but when neither of us responded, he finished the thought himself: "They figure maybe you and Jack are going to..."

"What?" she snapped. "Elope or something?"

"Ssshh... Jesus!" I squeaked. "They'll hear you!"

Ally let go of my hand so she could jab an accusatory finger at her brother to emphasize her words.

"If they have that idea, *you* put it in their damn heads, *Phil*."

He shrugged and sat back, looking almost pleased with himself. Until that moment I had assumed they were best friends, not regular siblings. She always talked so highly of him and it sounded like they were inseparable when he was at home.

"So you haven't thought about it?" he asked pointedly. "You haven't figured that instead of—"

"*Stop it*, Phil," she begged, her face drawn down. She glanced at me with wild, apologetic eyes and I didn't like how she looked—the fear and confusion seemed to include me, but I couldn't see any direct relation, except her brother's insinuation that we were going to elope.

"Hey, cut it out, okay?" I asked him, hopefully in a relatively polite tone of voice. "Why do you want to upset her?"

He sighed heavily and looked away, shaking his head slowly. "I'm sorry, Ally—I didn't mean to upset you." He looked back at us with a sweet smile and winked at Ally. "They just know that Jack here's going to steal you away—"

"Phil, I'm serious, *you're not helping.*"

Marriage? Had they been arguing about Ally getting married... to *me*? My heart was really pounding now and I felt lightheaded. Was that even something I wanted? I mean, sure, I said I loved Ally, but when you put it into words like "marriage," suddenly the idea that I knew what love was seemed like a long shot.

"Let's go, Bells," Ally suddenly decided. She stood up and I leaped to my feet to follow her.

"Not staying for dessert?" her dad called out as we walked past the kitchen. "Chocolate mousse...?"

"No, dad—we're going to go and catch a movie."

"Which one?" he shouted down the hall as we rounded the corner to the front door. Ally snatched up her purse and fished in the hall closet for our coats.

"Doesn't matter!" she called back.

"What happened?" he asked calmly, appearing in the doorway with a pie in his hands. I kinda wanted to stay and have some, after seeing it.

"Nothing, dad, don't worry. Phil's going to say something dumb and I don't want to be here when he does, that's all."

He sighed a fatherly sigh but Ally waved him off.

"It's not a big deal. At all."

She shrugged her coat on then went over and gave him a light kiss on the cheek.

"Well, he can be a bit thoughtless at times," her dad agreed, offering me a "what can you do?" shrug.

"I had a very nice time," I replied, extending my hand to him. He juggled the pie but shook my hand firmly. "Thank you for dinner."

"Our pleasure, Jack. You'll have to come back again sometime."

"I'd like that, sir."

"Very good."

"Bye, dad," Ally said, offering him a little wave as we walked out the front door.

We got in my car and before I could pull my seat belt across Ally leaned over and gave me a long, slow kiss, her hand on my thigh.

"Sorry about that," she whispered, settling back into her seat.

"The kiss?"

250

"Shut up," she said with a grin. "My *brother.*"

"Whatever—I have a brother, too. He'd be just as dumb with you there."

She sat quietly for a minute or two, so I finally added sarcastically, "*Are* we planning to elope?"

"Why can't we be like the Lost Boys, Jack? Why can't we get away from *this* but not have to grow up to do it? Even for a little while?"

"How about camping?"

She looked at me askance to gauge if I was joking.

"Totally serious," I said. "We're going camping for spring break and you're coming. Sorry... I forgot to tell you."

She laughed and pulled her seat belt on, clicking it purposefully into place.

"Thanks, Jack."

"So what movie are we going to, anyway?"

"Just drive, Bells. Let's see where we end up."

Ally and I were watching a skate video when Tobie appeared at the back door of my house. She smiled and waved and hugged herself against the wind, but I could tell she was upset. She rarely came over unannounced, and since Ally and I had got serious, she rarely even called. Jess had told me she was keeping her distance so she didn't accidentally ruin me and Ally—which wasn't as vain as it sounds. Tobie and I had been close friends for a long time and our steady dates had mistaken our friendship as a secret romance on more than one occasion. I think she also knew that she sort of scared Ally on some level, which I didn't quite understand. Maybe I had to be a girl to get it, I don't know, but in the same conversation with Jess about Tobie staying away, Jess had also said that Ally was really quiet with Tobie when the three of them went out, like the kind of quiet you get when you're around someone you admire and don't think you could stack up to, and respect is so very close to fear. But now, standing in the doorway, Tobie was the one who looked scared. It always turned my gut to see her like that, and this didn't look like a boy-just-dumped-me look. She wasn't frowning, her face looked drawn down by the weight of the emotions she was trying to hide, and Ally saw it, too.

"Jesus, what happened?" Ally breathed. I leaped up and slid the patio door open.

"Hey, Tobe—what's going on?"

"My uncle lost the farm," she blurted.

"What?"

Tobie lived in a house on a farm owned by her uncle, out in the township. She wasn't a farm girl—most of the other fields around her house had long gone over to subdivisions, so it wasn't really a shock to find out another farm had been sold off. But she loved that house. *We* loved that house. Every summer, they filled their big above-ground pool and set up a volleyball court, and we practically lived there. Well, I did, anyway. And of course, Tobie actually *did* live there. To think of those golden fields going over to condos or cluster homes or whatever they would develop was heartbreaking. I didn't say anything, I just gave her a hug, glancing back at Ally, who was standing quietly, her fingers to her lips, unsure what to do or say.

"What are you watching?" Tobie sniffled, pulling away from me.

"Hey, Ally," she added with a smile.

Ally looked wide-eyed and uncertain—it seemed like she was afraid to open her mouth or even move. Until that moment, I hadn't fully believed what Jess had said, but now I could see it: Ally looked like the little sister caught with the wrong boy.

"You know... a skate video," she finally said with a weak smile.

"God, I'm glad you two hooked up," Tobie announced, huffing out a breath as she flopped onto the couch. "I couldn't sit through another one of *those*."

"Yeah," Ally agreed politely.

She offered me a knowing smirk—a glimmer of the Ally I knew back on her face—then reached over and picked up the remote, shutting off the video.

"Jack!" my mom called downstairs. "Jack? It's Tobie's mom on the phone—have you seen her?"

"She's here, Ma!" I called back up. "You can come down!"

"Okay," she replied, but she didn't come down. I guess she meant "okay" that Tobie was over, not that she could come down.

"So what happened?" I asked Tobie.

Her parents had put off telling her, and that's what I think hurt Tobie the most: Not just the move, but that her parents had hidden it, thereby making it a bigger deal than perhaps it was. After all, they weren't moving far ("Into town," as Tobie put it), so it wasn't like she was going to change schools or lose her friends. But hiding it only made it worse, I guess, because then she thought back to how her parents *knew* it was their last Christmas there, and she hadn't, so she hadn't done anything special. That kind of thing sticks with you, like when you don't get to say good-bye one last time.

"So when are you moving?" Ally wondered.

"Spring break."

"So we've got some time," I said brightly.

Tobie didn't buy it. She cocked her head and looked at me sourly. I pouted with a big pulled lip, and that made her smile.

"We should have one last bash there... We should have your birthday party there!" she offered. It was just an excuse, though. It wasn't about me or my birthday, it was about a send-off for her house. "You're eighteen the weekend before we have to move."

I nodded seriously. "So that means we can trash the place, right?"

This move was probably no big deal to Ally—she'd spent every year of high school in a different school, for God's sake—but she didn't downplay it. She let Tobie vent, but I figured she was three breaths away from saying, "Seriously, this isn't *that* big of a deal. You're not even leaving town!"

But she didn't because to Tobie it clearly was a big deal.

The problem is, Ally lacked our sense of history. While

Niz usually hosted the "regular" parties, the big blow-out summer bashes—with her pool and volleyball and croquet—were always at Tobie's. Her house was where we went to un-wind. We never had parties at my place, and even though we went to Niz's for parties most often, we always had the most fun at Tobie's. It was the wide open fields and massive, open yard inviting you to relax and soak it in, like you were on some bizarre vacation resort in the middle of Ohio.

And I don't know if Tobie thought of it in these terms, but it was like by losing that house, she was afraid she'd lost her usefulness or something; like we'd all find somewhere else to hang out and no one would think to call her again.

I guess it doesn't have to make sense; we all liked it out there, so that was excuse enough. Tobie and I sat for hours on her back deck, staring out over the field behind her house, talking about all of nothing. *I* felt like family at her house, and so I can only imagine how it felt to someone who actu-ally *was* family; to someone who actually lived there. Every-thing that is warm and safe and uneventful is your home—your one, true center of the universe where nothing ever changes and everything is always right and bad things don't happen.

Only that wasn't true for Ally.

It wasn't true for Sammy.

And now it wasn't true for Tobie.

Suddenly the threat of moving was all around us, and that's how something as simple as changing street addresses in the same city got blown out of proportion for Tobie. It wasn't a simple move to her or to me—it gained a greater meaning you could only needle at but never expose; some deeper weight that may or may not reveal a cold, empty hollowness if removed. So you picked at it, but not too hard.

Sometimes a place becomes bigger than itself, especially if it's the only place you've ever known. Sometimes you romanticize a place even while you're still living in it, and that's what Tobie had done. That house in the township was a symbol of something bigger than any of us could ever put our fingers on, and Tobie knew it. It was like family; it was like learning that someone you love is terminally ill.

So no, it wasn't about moving really, it was about moving *on*. It was about endings. It was about growing up and realizing that the innocent veneer of childhood has finally rubbed away; realizing that time isn't endless and that even the things you take most for granted—even something as solid as a home—can suddenly be gone.

"This must seem pretty silly to you," I said hurriedly to Ally when Tobie left the room to blow her nose or get a drink or something. We'd been playing Uno, sitting on the floor, and we'd all stood up to stretch our legs. Over cards, Tobie and I had tried to fill Ally in on all the happenings that had gone on over at Tobie's. It was like a wake in many ways, and I think we all understood that on some level. We laughed a lot, but the laughter always ended with a few minutes of quiet reflection.

"No," Ally said, giving me an unexpected hug. "I know you think I'd be over it, but moving hurts, Jack. It hurts every time."

I hugged her back and tried not to think about it. Of course it hurts to have to pack up all your stuff, pull up roots, and leave all those memories behind—because there are always memories, and there is always the fear that the new memories in a new place won't be as sweet.

There was a weight that fell that day, something like a massive apocalyptic machine being lowered with finality into place. Ally let me go and moved back to the couch, smiling sheepishly, and somewhere out there, in the blackness of the past, someone used the force and might of all their strength to move the steadfast switch into place, and the machine began to hum; the slow whir and tick of the gears began to sound.

Standing there, in my own living room, I felt alone. I knew that sound, that whir and tick, and I knew what it meant: It meant everything was going to come apart. It meant the gears would eventually grind down and the rust would cease to hold things together. It meant the house I was standing in would only be mine for a number of days I could count. It meant the childish notions of the timelessness of things—of long, hot summer days stretched into infinity before the fall—was wrong. Dead wrong.

The machine churned and hummed, vibrating back through the past and rumbling off into the future, shaking loose everything it encountered. Memories fell and smashed, places were swallowed whole, and events became blurred to the point of loss.

I looked at Ally and she was looking at me and she was crying the tears that come when you already know where the end is and the sadness is equal with relief.

"It's okay," I said.

"No," she said back and looked away.

Tobie came up behind me and lightly touched my shoul-

257

der. She tried to smile and she may have apologized. Ally said she wanted to go home; she insisted, in fact, and Tobie said she'd give her a ride. It actually made sense, rather than me leaving my house—Ally lived on the way to Tobie's, after all. Ally seemed quiet again—like Jess had said—but nodded and agreed and said she'd call me in the morning.

"You should both stay," I tried, really to try and stay with Ally a bit longer. "We can play *Sorry!* or something."

But they'd heard it, too: They'd heard that fucking machine rumbling in the darkness, and they knew it was coming for all of us. It made the most sense to scatter like rats in the daylight and survey the damage later with clearer heads.

"It's late," Ally said. "I have to get up early."

So we made plans for tomorrow. We made sure they included Tobie. We laughed at ourselves and our drama, trying to pretend that nothing had happened; that a minor move across town was exactly the small deal it should have been; that nothing unspoken had killed the conversation and the mood once the wake had ended; that everything would be exactly the same once the distorting cobwebs of late-night chats had been washed clean with the morning. Then they both made fun of me because they needed that common bond to carry them through the car ride home; to give them something to talk about to fill the silence around their thoughts.

Then they were gone.

I went to bed and had an obvious dream that something had destroyed Tobie's house, like a bomb had been dropped on it. I was screaming at Tobie that *she* was still inside, and Tobie just kept asking me *who* was.

And in the dream, I had no idea.

For saying we worked at a toy store, where the main clientele is children, we were a pretty mean staff, which is why repo men, male strippers, and skate punks don't generally end up working in toy stores.

Steve had this great idea for "theft deterrence"—he always tried to spin it—that we should put a walkie-talkie in the back corner of the store and watch the kids in the security mirror. Then, if they were about to snatch something, we could use the other walkie-talkie to call them out, all without having to leave the registers. It sounded fair, I admit, except he put the open walkie-talkie in with all the stuffed animals, not near the usually pilfered action figures and Hot Wheels cars. He would also say things into it like, "Hey, kid, it's me, the stuffed bear—can you get me outta here?"

As if we didn't already have enough screaming kids in that damn store.

Steve would shrug and point out that the little brats shouldn't be left unattended, anyway, so he was only chasing them back to their mothers.

I had been dispatched to replace the batteries in the hidden walkie-talkie, and as I came back down the center aisle a kid, maybe nine years old, stopped me.

"Hey, mister, do you have any skateboards?"

"Sure," I said. I led him back to the shitty pre-packaged

boards we sold and handed him one, but I couldn't help myself: "But y'know, if you're serious, kid, you need to get a *real* board—"

"*Joey!*" a mother barked. The kid and I both froze.

"Joey? What is that?"

The kid looked at me then back at his mother. "A board."

"And what's on the other side of it?" she asked.

"Wheels—but it's not a skateboard!"

Yeah, he actually said that. She didn't buy it either. She grabbed it from his hands and thrust it into mine, then hurried the poor pup out of the store.

"Well played, Jack," the stuffed bears squawked at me. "Way to make the sale."

I turned and flipped off the nearest mirror, almost poking Tobie in the eye.

"Christ! *Shit*... Tobie. Where'd you come from?"

"Home. I thought no one could ever sneak up on you?"

"You must've practiced. What are you doing here?"

"My parents are packing. I had to get away. When's your break?"

I glanced at my watch. "Oh, right about now."

I walked back up to the front of the store. Steve looked from me to Tobie, grinned evilly and winked, then said, "Taking your break?"

"Yeah—if it's okay?"

"Sure it is," he agreed. He even clicked his tongue at us.

"This is Tobie," I added in some weird effort to make it not seem so creepy.

"I recognize her," he said. "What's your girlfriend's name?"

"Ally."

"Right."

He clicked his tongue again and winked, so we left.

"What the hell was that?"

I shook my head. "He's just being Steve. His last job was a repo man, so that should tell you something."

She shrugged, admitting that it told her exactly nothing, and we hopped on the escalator down to the food court. The one thing I missed about working at the hotdog stand was the frozen Cokes. I was addicted to the damn things, and still got one almost every day I worked.

"He's just excited because Jess came by on her break," I explained. "He was trying to give me tips on juggling two girlfriends."

"Eww," Tobie balked. "Are you serious?"

"And I'd bet he's talking from experience."

"Gross. Totally gross. So what did Jess want?"

"She's worried about you," I said. "You want a frozen Coke?"

I didn't actually wait for her to answer, I just ordered two.

"Worried about me?"

"Yeah, you know... the move."

Tobie tried to blow it off, but not very hard. We got our drinks and sat down at a table with a nice view of the carousel. Once, Ally and I rode that stupid carousel in the empty mall, side-by-side on massive golden horses, all smiles and glee. She looked like a little kid again, and I'll bet I did, too. I've always loved carousels.

"You want to ride it?" Tobie asked.

"Huh? Oh... No." I smiled bashfully. "Ally and I rode it... I was just thinking—anyway. So, yeah, Jess is worried about you. Me, too."

"You? I hardly see you any more. That's why I figured I'd catch you on break."

I reached out and touched her hand, not liking the drawn look on her face.

"Hey, what's wrong?"

"Nothing. Forget it."

She looked away, then back, a smile flickering across her lips.

"I was just thinking about last summer, sitting with you, watching the crows in the field."

"You're afraid I won't come and hang out with you now?"

"Where are we going to hang out, Bells? My living room in the condo?"

"Sure?" I guessed.

"It won't be the same," she said glumly, slurping her frozen Coke.

I looked at her. Her hair looked flat, like she'd not even bothered with it, and her t-shirt and jeans were decidedly un-coordinated, at least for Tobie.

"It'll be fine," I assured her. "Maybe we can go and hang out at the park?"

"That's too much like a date. And you have Ally for that."

"Shit, Tobie—this isn't about Ally, is it?"

She shook her head slowly. "Of course not. Ally's great."

She was lying, and I could see that; could read it plain-as-day in the lines writ along her furrowed brow, daring me to doubt her veracity. Not that she was lying about Ally being great—Ally was, and Tobie thought so, too—but that her present doldrums weren't about Ally. Well, Ally and me. The move was traumatic for her, I have absolutely no doubt of that, but it was also an incredibly convenient hook to hang her fears on—her fears that Ally was going to replace her. I watched her slurping her Coke and I could tell this was different. Somehow we always knew each other's relationships were going to end, but this time I don't think either of us was so sure.

I'd felt that way about her once, when we were sixteen.

"Tobie..." I started.

She looked up and smiled devilishly, cutting me off. "We tried to hook you two up, you know?"

"Who did?"

I'd suspected something was going on back at the King of Hearts dance, but I also hadn't believed it because it would have meant either too many people were involved, or someone had been set up to get hurt at the dance. Tobie nodded, smiling widely for the first time all evening; glad to be rebuilding her part in me and Ally, as if this meant she couldn't be locked out.

"Jolly and I cooked it up."

"*Bull*shit. *Jolly* was in on it?"

"It's true, Jack of Bells. Ally was in on it, too."

"*What*?"

Now that much *was* news to me, more shocking even than Jolly having had a hand in it. Although it did make me feel better, as it would have been his broken heart if the dance had gone as they had apparently planned and Jolly *hadn't* been in on it. Tobie smiled proudly and sat back, sucking her straw in her best imitation of a spoiled brat.

"So how ya like *that*?"

"But I'd already asked her out!" I protested. "She blew me off!"

"Which is why she figured you'd never ask her again. And then with Missy—well, she didn't want to seem like she was too excited you broke up. So I suggested we all hang out at the dance and, you know, you never know what magic might happen then. Or could be *made* to happen, anyway."

We gazed at each other for several long seconds. It was a weird thing for her to be jealous of a girl she'd wanted me to be with, which made me wonder if she'd thought it wouldn't work out. Maybe her plan had worked too well, and now she regretted it. Or maybe she'd just expected to have someone of her own by now, and as each day passed with no one new, it cut deeper and deeper that I wasn't there to hang out with her.

I knew how *that* felt, too.

"So this condo," I finally said. "Does it have a back patio, at least?"

She gave me a pathetic look and nodded slowly. Clearly "patio" needed to be in quotes.

"There's the park behind it. Harbin Park."

"So see? We can hang out there!"

"If you're not too busy," she accepted.

"When was I ever too busy to hang out with you?"

She smiled, but she didn't answer.

The streetlights formed yellow circles like stage lights down the street. Ally, Niz, Sammy, and I stood at the top of the hill looking down, to where Jess was waiting. It had been Niz's idea, to ride the hill in the dark. He said it would make it easier, because we wouldn't really be able to tell how fast we were going. He was trying to prove a point to Sammy, that all tricks are equal parts physics and mind-over-matter. If you *believed* you could do the trick—if you could shut off the nagging voice that said you couldn't—then physics would take over and it would work.

Niz always had theories like that. I think he bought them, too. We usually told him *once* that he was full of shit, then went along with it. He wasn't exactly the best skater, so as far as I was concerned, that meant either he could never shut off the nagging voice or physics was wrong—or his whole idea was wrong. So this hill, this was a test of sorts.

The hill was over by Niz's house and wound up into a cul-de-sac that was separated from another cul-de-sac by a stretch of woods. The other cul-de-sac was right by my house, and as the crow flew—or the boys walked—it was faster to go up the hill and cut through the woods than it was to take the streets that led to my house from Niz's. We'd been hoofing it up that hill for a decade, and as soon as we started to skate we started to egg each other on to ride it.

Once, we stopped about halfway up and tried it. It was fast—*really* fast. My board started to wobble in a way I'd never felt and next thing I knew I was launching off up the curb, over some guy's tree lawn, and landing on the sidewalk. I cut up my knee pretty bad—it still buckles on me, from time to time—and we'd never plucked up the courage to try it again, despite the fact that Niz had completed his run unscathed.

"So this is the fabled hill?" Ally said slowly.

"It'll be fine in the dark," Niz repeated uncertainly.

"It was a *long* walk up," Ally said thoughtfully.

"I'm not buying it, Niz," I chimed in. "It wasn't *your* knee that got gashed open last time."

"You hit a rock," he explained, waving me off. "It was just bad luck."

That wasn't true and he knew it, but I let it go.

"Let's just do it," Sammy finally decided. "All you gotta do is ride off up the curb and into the grass to stop. No problem."

I glanced at Niz. He looked serious but said nothing, telling me with his eyes that he'd back out if I really wanted to.

Ally's board flopped down, as did Sammy's. Niz suddenly looked like he wished he'd never brought it up. I dropped my board. He couldn't back out now. His board hit the asphalt and we all pumped once—there was really no need to pump at all—and began the ride. I had a much better board, I kept telling myself—better wheels, firmer trucks, wider deck—so there was no way this one would wiggle. The last time we'd tried this I'd been on some piece-of-shit department-store deck I'd got for Christmas, when my parents thought skateboarding was just a phase.

The wind was ice cold against my face and my eyes started to tear up. I swiped at them with my shirt sleeve and saw a car come into focus, rounding the bend at about the halfway mark. A white car, with something on the roof.

"Shit," I heard Niz spit beside me.

"Cops!" Sammy bellowed.

To the cop, it must have looked almost beautiful: Four skaters rolling down the hill in a relatively tight formation, clothes and hair flapping behind them, then the formation suddenly splitting off, two going to each side at slightly different angles, like one of those dandelion fireworks that makes the thick tendrils like spilled salt over the sky.

The curb was exactly as difficult to get over as I remembered. It was one of those C curbs that curves up from the street to the grass, so you didn't really have to jump it—but we should have, at least at the speed we were going. I felt my knees crumble under me like a skier hitting the moguls, and there was no way I was keeping my balance. As I was jettisoned from my board, two things struck me simultaneously: Ally and I had gone off the same side of the road, and when the lights on a cruiser pop on in the dark, it's really fucking bright. The cop also twiddled the siren for one short *whoop*, as if we hadn't seen the lights.

I landed roughly but got straight to my feet and found my board, then spun around and saw Ally scampering into a stand of trees that separated two houses. She saw me see her and waved frantically for me to follow. I caught up to her and she took my free hand, pulling me deeper into the trees. Niz's street bordered on the biggest park in town, so there was nothing back in the woods except a creek at the bottom of a pretty steep hill. Niz and I had spent hours "exploring" that creek; I swung around and took the lead. Ally squeezed my hand tightly. I looked back at her, her face pale in the moonlight, and I could see that she was scared. Ally—the coolest girl I knew, who hung out at bars with her cousins and liked bands that named themselves after rotting food or anything that could injure, maim, or kill you—was suddenly truly afraid. She was starting to freeze.

"Come *on*," I whispered harshly.

"We should go back."

"What? *Why*?"

"We didn't do anything wrong. He'll just give us a warning."

"Bullshit," I disagreed. "Ask Timmy Toderman how many boards of *his* the cops have impounded. Can *you* afford a new board?"

She jigged for a second, undecided, caught in the perfect balance between doing what she'd always been told and doing what she knew was acceptable, all things considered. Because she was absolutely right: We'd done nothing wrong, for some reason they just really hated skaters. I mean, the cops knew to leave us alone when we skated at the high school, which meant the very authority figures we suffered with every day as teachers and principals had taken a stand for us somewhere along the line—they even let us bring in makeshift ramps and quarter-pipes for the annual field day at the end of the school year. So the way I figured it, if the adults who were forced to hang out with us because they were our teachers didn't see anything wrong with it, then I didn't see why I should lose my board for riding down a damn hill.

"Get down," I blurted, yanking Ally down beside me just as the cop's searchlight scanned over us. This guy was serious. Usually they just flashed the lights and chased you away. Maybe some other skaters had been causing actual trouble somewhere, and he assumed it was us. I heard a car door open.

"Fuck... Scoot," I ordered, waving deeper into the woods and down the hill. "There's a creek at the bottom."

She let go of my hand and pushed leaves and sticks in front of her, copying my half-sitting, scooting descent. We made it down in one piece, boards and all. It was really dark in the woods, the moonlight like a fading memory somewhere above us. As our eyes adjusted we could discern darker shapes against the darkness, and a flash every now and again as the cop scanned the woods with his flashlight. If he pointed it down, he'd see us. I glanced into the darkness and I knew exactly where we were: Niz and I called it the Y—a spot where two creeks came in and fed the larger creek, leaving a wedge hillock between them. I took Ally's hand in mine and gently pulled her in the rough direction of Niz's house. If we took the right branch of the Y, we'd not only be behind another hill and thus hidden from view, we'd also be on a direct course for Niz's backyard.

My heart was pounding from nerves and exercise. Once I was sure we were hidden I stopped and turned back to Ally. I was expecting to see tears reflecting the moonlight, but she was grinning ear to ear.

"What's so funny?" I whispered.

She shook her head lightly, then reached out and grabbed my face with both hands, planting a firm kiss on my lips.

"Nothing," she whispered.

"Shh..." I cautioned.

Her hands dropped back to her sides and we both froze. There was the soft crackle of sticks broken under weight, but it sounded too rapid to be a person walking.

"Raccoon," I guessed.

I stared back the way we had come, searching for any glimmer of the cop's flashlight. There was nothing, and several seconds later we heard a car door slam and the telltale sound of an engine being gunned as a pissed-off cop drove up into the cul-de-sac to turn around. Moments later the engine sound came back and sped past us.

"You weren't kidding about the cops, were you?" Ally said breathlessly.

I realized I'd been holding my breath and let it out.

"No... I wonder where Niz and Sammy are?"

I didn't expect a response and she didn't offer one.

"Come on," I said, taking her hand again and leading her down the creek to Niz's house. We emerged from the woods at the same instant Niz and Sammy came sprinting around the corner of his house from the driveway; we all scared each other and jumped, then burst out laughing. Jess jogged up a few seconds later.

"You assholes are good," she said with admiration. "I didn't even see you go past me!"

"Where were you?" Niz wondered.

"I ducked into the trees when I saw him coming down

the road. I yelled 'cop,' but I guess you didn't hear me."

"We were too busy listening to Professor Niz tell us how riding in the dark made it easier," Sammy explained.

"Somebody must've done something," I figured. "I mean, he was looking for someone."

"Nah," Niz said dismissively. "He's just got a bone to pick—probably a jock in high school. Can you imagine if Greg Wilson ends up as a cop?"

Niz turned and slid back one of the patio doors and we all went inside. Niz's house was a sprawling ranch, so he and his brother basically had one side to themselves and his parents stuck to the other side, with the kitchen and dining room in the middle. The TV was on, just as we'd left it. His dad was getting a drink in the kitchen and he flashed us a big smile as we tumbled in.

"Getting a little air?" he asked innocently, but you could tell he knew damn well that we'd been doing something he'd not entirely approve of.

"Yeah," Niz said.

"Close the door," he replied, pointing at the patio. "It's supposed to dip into the 40s tonight." Then he was gone, back to his half of the house.

"Where's Tobie?" Ally asked as we slumped onto the couch.

I glanced at Jess—I hadn't talked to Tobie for a couple of days, except briefly at school.

"She had to work," Jess said. "I told her to switch with someone, cuz we'd all be here... She said she'd drive by after she got off, but she doesn't get off 'til, like, eleven or midnight or something, so..."

"You still want to go to that record store tomorrow?" Ally asked Jess.

"Hell, yes! As long as they have what I'm looking for."

"They do. You still working?" she added to me, nudging me in the ribs.

"Yeah. Full shift, nine to five."

"Just the girls, then?" Ally asked Jess.

"I could go," Niz pointed out.

Jess smirked joyfully and shook her head at him.

"Just the girls," she agreed. "Tobie has off, too."

I remember the way Ally smiled at Jess as she pulled her hair back and tied it in a loose ponytail. She felt me looking and glanced at me with mild embarrassment, but when she saw my smile she grinned back until I turned away.

Out of all the hijinks we got up to, I think our single greatest achievement was wallpapering the 300 wing with the outdated debris of a hundred school dances, bake sales, pep rallies, and school elections, exactly as we'd planned. As soon as the day of an event passed, we nabbed the fliers pasted to the walls or tacked to the bulletin boards and we saved them up. We filled an empty locker with them—no exaggeration. The only reason we decided to pull the trigger on our plot before the last day of school was because the locker was too full.

I had finally remembered to add the NO SKATE-BOARDING fliers we'd nabbed from the mall, and as I pulled the crumpled pile out of my backpack and stuffed them in the locker, it became obvious that we had an unexpected space issue.

"Maybe if we'd stacked them in there neater..." Jess considered, chewing the inside of her lip thoughtfully.

"Well, nothing to do for it now but empty it," Niz pointed out. "I grabbed tape from Mr. Fence's room."

He waggled the two tape dispensers menacingly.

"So how do we do it?" Ally asked, her eyes shining gleefully. She even rubbed her hands together in anticipation.

"Grab a stack," Niz demonstrated. "Grab a tape dispenser. Tape 'em back up on every blank wall you find."

It was an amazingly simple plan. The whole thing had started because Niz had posted an unauthorized flier in support of Miss Piggy for Homecoming queen that had been summarily removed. So he put it back up, and it got taken back down. So we printed a bunch and stuck, like, twenty of them up—all removed before the first bell. Long story short, we figured there'd be nothing against us posting authorized fliers, albeit it months after the events they were advertising, and we figured we could slip in a few votes for Miss Piggy to boot (now for Prom queen).

The reason it was such a great achievement is because as soon as we got going, everyone in the hall started to chip in. Suddenly there were kids I didn't even know asking me for instructions, grabbing stacks of fliers, and going to work. We taped them on every square inch of wall, we taped them together and made chains strung across the hall, we taped them over doors and on the steps... All these people coming together for the single purpose of re-posting expired fliers. It was glorious. Even the teachers who happened by seemed unconcerned, or else wisely decided that they'd just survived the world's softest riot and were unwilling to press their luck. And like magic, when the bell rang for first period, everyone scattered to class and no one seemed to know who had started it.

First period I had history—a "futurism" class that predicted future events by studying history—with Tobie. I was still chuckling when I sat down at my desk by hers. She looked at me morosely.

"What's so funny?"

"We did the flier thing," I whispered. "Where were you?"

"*What*? I thought that was the last day of school?"

She looked hurt and it knocked the laugh right out of me.

"The locker was full. Niz wanted to do it right away."

"You couldn't wait another day? You couldn't *tell* me?"

"Well, where *were* you?"

She sighed heavily, crossed her arms, and slumped in her chair. She stared at the blackboard, a look in her eyes I'd seen before: she was holding back rage or tears or both.

"My mom packed my clothes," she mumbled. "I had to find something to wear."

"*All* of them? Already?"

"The ones I *wanted*," she growled. "Who helped you?"

"Everyone," I said sadly. "It was great. Everyone in the hall helped."

"You know what I mean."

"Well, you know, Niz and Sammy and Jess and Ally."

Her head snapped around and she glowered at me.

"So, everyone but *me*."

"Jesus, Tobe. We didn't mean it like that. Niz started it off—he swiped tape from Mr. Fence's room—and suddenly we were all chipping in to help."

I felt sick about it, seeing her sitting there. She was in a black skirt and a dark green top; I remember thinking that this was the outfit she'd just *had* to find, that had made her late, that had made her miss the wallpapering. I hated that outfit. I hated it because it was easier than hating myself for not thinking of her; for not telling everyone to wait. After all, Tobie had collected as many fliers as the rest of us—she had every right to be mad.

"I'm sorry, Tobe," I whispered.

"Forget it," she spat as the teacher walked in, right with the last bell, and closed the door roughly to mark his entrance and get our attention. I glanced at Tobie, but she was pretending to find a page in her notebook.

After class she got up without a word and dashed out into the hall. I pushed my way after her, but I picked the wrong guy to be rude to: Greg Wilson shoved me back.

"Watch it, *faggot*," he growled, looking around for someone to share his laugh. No one did, they just backed up and gave him room.

"Looks like your girlfriend's mad," he added in a baby-talk voice.

"She's not my girlfriend," I replied angrily, losing sight of Tobie as she wove down the hallway. Greg puffed out a laugh.

"That's right. Because freaks only date *freaks*."

"*Fuck* you, Wilson, you fucking retard."

He shoved me back against the lockers hard, my books dropping to the floor and my head slamming back with a cold echo. You'd think a teacher would have heard and come running, but they always seemed to drag their feet. Half of them probably sided with Greg Wilson, anyway—figured he could teach the kid who took study halls and art classes a thing or two about straightening up his act.

I tried to shove him away from me, but he was stronger than I'd expected. I guess seeing Tobie pissed must've irked him or something, or else he'd finally seen his chance to get me back and that got him fired up. He had my clothes gathered into the balls of his fists at my shoulders and he managed to slam me back again. That was when I realized he wasn't actually going to do anything: He was too afraid to let go of my clothes long enough to even try and punch me.

Or he could rear back and try a headbutt.

"Is there a problem here?" someone said just as Greg seemed ready to come at me with his forehead. It hadn't sounded like a teacher, and it wasn't: It was Ryan from art class, with his towering hulk of a friend whose long, Slash-like hair hid his face from view most of time. I'd talked to him in ceramics, too, but never caught his name—he was actually so soft-spoken that I often missed what he said, and now he just stood there silently, looking at us with eyes like menace.

Greg let me go and stepped back.

"Fucking freaks," he spat as he turned and stormed off. I watched him go and finally saw a teacher poke his head out of his classroom, then duck back in.

"Thanks," I said to Ryan.

He chuckled kindly and punched me on the shoulder. His friend actually saluted me.

"Bells," a voice said calmly. I felt a hand on my arm. "You okay?"

I turned to Jess. She looked mortally concerned.

"What's wrong with Tobie?" she asked. "I saw her bolt—"

"The stupid fucking fliers," I said angrily, bending down and picking up my books as best I could without drawing attention to the fact that I'd dropped them. "She wasn't *there*, Jess."

"*Shit*... Are you working tonight?"

"Yeah."

"I'll come by on my break."

She vanished into the press of bodies changing classes. Somebody bumped into me and apologized profusely—like I cared.

It's funny how such minor things end up being such a big deal. I know Tobie didn't blame me, not really, not any more than she blamed any of us. If I had a guess, she blamed Niz. She knew I went along with Niz more often than I should, but I was the one she'd be pissed at because she could be; because she had to be openly pissed at somebody, and we'd been openly pissed at each other so many times since the sixth grade that it didn't even bother us any more. Come tomorrow, she'd be fine, I'd apologize anyway, and it'd be like nothing had happened. That's how it always went. That's why we were such good friends.

I figured Jess understood this. Then again, it makes as much sense that she didn't. She never got the way Tobie and

I were: the way we were always there for each other but just as often the cause—however indirectly—of each other's pain. Sometimes I wonder if Tobie and I didn't do shit to each other on purpose, to make sure the other one still cared and would still be there to pick up the pieces.

"Jack," Jess said very dourly on our breaks that night. "Tobie is *really* fucked up about this move. You *have* to be more careful of her feelings."

"Why am *I* the one who has to be more careful?" I said flippantly. "I don't see what the big deal is."

"You *know* what the big deal is, Bells. That's her only house and we're her only friends. She's losing one and now she figures she's losing *both*."

We were sitting on one of the annoying plastic benches between two massive fake potted trees, right in front of the girl store (as I'd always called it)—the one that was almost one-hundred-percent pink and sold a bunch of cheap-ass earrings and shit. When we were kids, Tobie loved that fucking store. We'd get our parents to go to the mall and we'd meet up and run off. She'd always have to stop there, and I always had to stop at the movie-poster store. We were twelve, maybe thirteen, so we could never buy anything—maybe once or twice, if one of us had saved enough allowance—but that wasn't the point. It's how I knew that she liked animals with big eyes (frogs, owls, koalas) and it's how she knew I loved horror movies.

"You know Tobie's my best friend," I mumbled.

"I know you two have been driving me *nuts* since we were kids, yes," Jess agreed. I grinned sheepishly at her.

"So what do you want me to do? This isn't about the fliers, is it?"

Jess shook her head slowly. "Sometimes I can tell that she wants to talk to *you*, Bells. Not me, but *you*."

"She knows she can call me anytime—"

Jess was shaking her head.

"Or come over?" I tried.

She shook her head. "Not this time, Bells. She's afraid of how Ally would take it."

"*Ally*? Why would Ally care? She knows I'm friends with Tobie."

"Look, girls talk when you're not around, okay?"

"I don't know what that means," I admitted.

"Never mind. Just call her, ask her to meet you for pie over at Big Boy or something."

"She doesn't like Ally?"

Jess laughed kindly, as if I was the biggest simpleton on the planet trying to do basic math.

"She loves Ally, Jack. We all do. But she needs you to herself again right now, just for an hour. Okay?"

"I should've told Niz to wait."

"Would you shut up about the fucking *fliers*, Jack? Seriously. She just needs to know you're still there for her, like you always were."

What was I going to say? No? Huh-uh, not to Tobie. That'd be like Niz calling me from jail and me telling him to get lost. No, no matter how skewed her thinking may have been that got her into this slump, now was not the time to abandon her or assume that she'd come around by herself. I was a stupid fucking teenager, but I wasn't *that* stupid.

"I have off tomorrow," I finally said. "And I hope Ally understands."

"Thank you, Jack," Jess said sincerely. "Do you want me to talk to Ally?"

I looked at her and chuckled. "No, *mom*, I can talk to my girlfriend all by myself."

Jess shook her head and punched my arm—she had a hell of a swing—pursing her lips playfully.

"If you two didn't need constant mothering, I wouldn't hang out with you. It's too stressful."

"Thanks," I agreed and stood up.

On my way back to the toy store I stopped for a frozen Coke and wondered what Tobie was doing.

April

Jess had been very clear that I shouldn't mention the move before Tobie did, otherwise it would seem like a set-up. Which it was. But we had to pretend it wasn't. I almost asked Tobie what instructions Jess had given *her*, but I didn't. We sat at Big Boy and I watched her push her pie around the plate with her fork—pecan, like I knew she'd get. The only thing that allows me to consider pecan as an acceptable pie is that Tobie liked it so much. I had coffee and Key lime pie—Tobie felt about coffee the way I felt about pecan pie, but my parents had been letting me drink it every morning with breakfast for as long as I could remember. People are always shocked to hear that, but coffee has less caffeine and *way* less sugar than pop, so I'm not sure what the big deal is.

I could tell Tobie was glum, but she was trying to ignore it. She was pretending to be happy for me, and pretending that she didn't know this wasn't my idea. I felt a twist of nausea that it had taken Jess to make me call Tobie. We had *always* dealt with stuff for each other before— from the Greg Wilsons to the Penny Harpers to the random things that get normal people down—and if I wasn't there to help her, what good was I?

I felt a low breeze coursing out of the hole that had formed the night she first told me she was moving; the hole carved out of the past by the future. It was cold and dark in that hole and Tobie looked resigned to it, her head down, watching her fork spin around her plate, trying to shoulder the burden of keeping it together while things fell apart.

"I'm going to try and write a real story," I said softly.

She stopped pushing her bite of pie and stabbed it, sliding it into her mouth as she looked up at me.

"What do you mean, a real story?"

"You know—not horror."

I'd grown up on Stephen King, Clive Barker, Dean Koontz, and Peter Straub, so it was natural that my fiction would try to emulate them. My last story had been about a bunch of teenagers who got picked off, one by one, by a mattock-wielding madman in an abandoned summer camp. It was a way to try and capture the drama retreat in fictional amber, as well as to entertain myself. I'm sure there was some latent psycho-analysis there, too, about punishing bad kids and all that...

"Horror isn't real fiction?" she wondered. Her face cleared almost imperceptibly and I knew she was glad to be thinking of something else.

"I don't know. I mean, it is, but I'm not sure I like to write about killing."

"That's probably a good thing. So what *are* you going write about?"

"I don't know. Probably still dark stuff, but maybe more

psychological, like *Cujo* or *The Dead Zone*. I have this idea about a serial killer who interviews his victims before he kills them, to help them come to terms with their deaths."

Tobie stopped eating again and stared at me. I raised my eyebrows expectantly.

"How is that *not* horror?" she asked.

I laughed. "Maybe I should just write about this?"

"What?"

"The shit we got up to in high school."

She shook her head slightly. "That's boring. Or, well, it *can* be if you don't do it right. You should read some Kerouac if you're serious—that's kinda what he did."

"The beat poet guy?"

"Yeah—*On the Road*. Miz Williams said I'd like it and I read it over the summer. It was pretty good, but it was like that: like a fictional diary or something."

"Yeah, like that," I agreed thoughtfully. "Kerouac..."

"And you might need to live a little first," she added. "I mean, what've you done worth writing about?"

"What has anyone *really* done that's worth writing about?" I returned.

She smiled defiantly. "All I've got is this stupid move."

And there it was: It was a non sequitur, but she'd finally broached the topic. I hadn't meant to guide the conversation that way, but I had figured if I got her talking instead of pushing her pie around, it would come up eventually. It's all that was on her mind, after all. You could tell.

"How's it going, with the move?"

She sighed heavily and tears moistened her eyes. She stared out the window, then around at the other patrons, all

283

families or older couples. I wondered if anyone else there was having a serious conversation, and I bet they were. Somehow coffee and pie and being in public makes serious conversations easier.

"It's fine," she sighed. "It's stupid that I'm this upset. I'm going to miss it, that's all."

"No, it's not stupid," I said quietly.

"I know." She smiled weakly and held my gaze. "I just can't imagine you coming over if we can't sit out on my porch and sip lemonade."

"Well, I *will* come over, wherever you are—you know that, right?"

"I guess."

"I'm serious, Tobe. How could that even worry you? You think I come over to sit in your chairs or talk to you?"

She looked away. I would've reached out and taken her hand, but she had them folded in her lap.

"It's not just that," she admitted, looking back at me. "Everyone's going away to college, and I'm staying here, and now I don't even have my old room any more."

"Sammy's staying in town," I offered weakly. She cocked her head slightly and smiled sympathetically, as if she knew I was trying my hardest but was still coming up short.

"I like Sammy, but he's not you or Jess or even Niz. He won't call me."

"You make him nervous," I deflected, and she allowed herself to take the bait.

"How do *I* make him nervous?"

"Because you're pretty and smart and not a skate rat like Jess or Ally."

284

"Jess doesn't skate," she protested, but she smirked happily.

"She may as well," I offered.

"Yeah..." She looked away again briefly then grinned and turned back. "Why *do* you hang out with me, Bells?"

"I like you," I said simply. "And I've always hung out with you."

"So I'm a habit?" she asked with feigned offense.

"I really can't imagine you not being around—it'd be ugly."

"Thanks, Jack," she accepted, finally digging into her pie.

What we'd avoided discussing again is that she was right: soon we'd all be scattered to different colleges in different states, and habit or not, soon we'd all have to live with not being able to hang out with each other. For her, it was the move that she hinged that realization on. For me, it still seemed far away and unreal because I had nothing tangible to mark it with—no hook to hang my coat of past years on as I left the room. For me, college was way off in the fall, and I still had to survive the rest of Senior year. But for Tobie, with the move, it seemed so much closer. For Tobie, she was moving on already, and nothing puts a fine point on it like literally packing up boxes and covering up all those things you'd accumulated over the years. For me, even though I'd have to pack up and go away to school, most of my shit was staying behind, preserved in the static reality of my boyhood room.

Ally had said moving always hurts, and I believed her, and I could see it in Tobie, too, but until you actually have to leave somewhere for good—leave an empty room behind where once so much life had existed—you can't understand that weird twist of heartache. Even if you *want* to move, it still singes; you still look back one last time and let the memories wash over you and drip off a silent smile, full of optimism and fear.

So we avoided it completely. We spent the rest of the time talking about the petty things that we always used to hide our true feelings, like stupid teachers and too-hard homework assignments, and whether so-n-so was really sleeping with what's-his-name or if it was just a rumor. Then we sprinkled the small talk with a dash of remembering old times, and maybe that ounce of flavoring was too much: Recognizing that things had changed and there were times long enough ago to call "old" was too close to the truth. We lapsed into silence and stood uncomfortably at the registers to pay the bill, like an old married couple that's sick of talking to each other.

"I get it, Tobie—a little," I said as I held the door to the parking lot open for her. "You feel like we're all going away —like *every*thing is going away."

"It is."

I shook my head. We walked across the parking lot toward our separate cars. I was being very careful not to say "goodbye" or "good night" or even "see ya later"—nothing that had an ounce of finality in it, as if this moment could stretch with us into the rest of time.

"Bells, this is the end—"

"Don't quote the Doors to me, Tobe."

She chuckled.

"But it *is*, Bells. The end of high school, the end of num-bered grades—we've grown up, Jack. We're all going to leave... I'm not ready."

She started to get misty and tried to hide her face but I forced her into a hug and held her and let her cry silent tears against me. I wasn't ready either, and as I stood there I could feel it nipping at me, that damned future that didn't necessar-ily include my friends. I'd been able to hold it at bay because the present—my present, with Ally—filled my view. And maybe that's how it should always be: Maybe the present *should* always fill our view and leave the past for the dying and the future left unsaid.

But it's not like that. It never is.

"We haven't grown up," I whispered. "Not if we don't want to."

Tobie stood on tippy toes and gave my cheek a peck. Her eyes lingered on mine and she very lightly took my hand in her fingertips, then let it go.

She was smiling, but I wasn't convinced.

Down the one side of their driveway the Malloys had a very long curb that was painted black. One scuff, and it looked like shit, but it had long been a dream of ours to skate that curb. Painted curb, after all, can be a skater's best friend —not always, but often enough to try. Out of deference to

Tobie's parents, we had never asked to skate it, but standing there, the weekend before spring break, knowing that in another week the Malloys would have moved, it seemed like the right time to finally broach the subject.

"You ask her," Sammy ordered, his eyes flickering wildly like I was about to ask a hooker for a blow job.

I looked over to where Tobie stood with Kammy, Barb, and Jess. She had a big red cup in her hand, her elbow resting on her hip, and she was trying to laugh at their jokes, but not doing a very good job of it. The weather was pretty nice for Ohio in April, and that was about the only good thing about the party so far—everyone seemed to be treating it like a damn funeral.

"I don't know," I wavered, not taking my eyes off Tobie. She looked somehow out of place, or maybe her posture wasn't right. She didn't look comfortable, anyway, and this was her home.

Was.

I looked around at the others—Niz, Sammy, and Ally—and could see that last-chance whiff of desperation etched on their faces. How many times had we begged each other to hit that curb *once*—just *once*—to see what it was like? Ally stepped over and kissed my cheek.

"Please?" she asked coyly.

"Your seductions won't work on me," I lied.

She put her arms around my waist and looked up at me, her mouth hanging slightly open, a grin in her eyes.

"Get a room," Sammy mumbled nervously.

I winked over Ally's shoulder at him; he shook his head and looked away. Niz did not. He was grinning ear to ear.

Ally reached up and turned my chin back to her, then kissed me slowly on the lips, her other hand maneuvering into my pocket and fishing out my keys. She skipped back and held them up.

"Now, how did I get these keys, boys? And I wonder what's in Jack's trunk?"

I don't want to ruin the surprise, but our skateboards were in my trunk. Niz, still grinning, cleared his throat.

"Hey, Ally?" he wondered innocently. "Me and Sammy have our boards in my trunk. Wanna get *my* keys, too?"

"No," she snipped with a smirk.

"So go ask Tobie already," Sammy suggested again.

I looked back over at her and she was watching us. She smiled weakly and moved her pinky beneath her big red cup. I sighed and tromped over.

"Hey, Tobe."

"Heya, Bells. Having fun over there?"

"Yeah, but... you know... we were wondering—"

"Jesus, Bells, not the *curb*?" Jess blurted. "Are you *shit*ting me? Is that *all* you retards think about?"

"Well, that's not very nice," I groused mockingly.

"You can skate the curb," Tobie cut in. "Scrape it all to hell—I don't care."

She took a big swig of her drink and raised her glass to me, her eyes willing me to jog back over to the others and give that curb a ride—or stay with her and talk.

"Your parents won't care?"

She shook her head slowly. "My dad and uncle spent all week axing snow fences and shooting beer bottles in the barn with pellet guns. What do you think? This is going to be turned into a fucking gated community, so tear it *all* to hell, for all I care. Every bit of it."

She looked away angrily, trying to hide her face from me. Jess shot me a menacing look then ushered Tobie away toward the house with Kammy and Barb in tow. I'm not sure why I was supposed to feel like shit, but I did. I didn't try to go after them, though. I walked back over to the others and shrugged defeatedly.

"She said we can—"

"Yes!" Niz and Sammy hollered in unison.

Ally practically ran to my car and grabbed our boards, and before I knew it, I had been lulled into the rhythm and slap of wood on painted curb. Sammy kept trying to grind—convinced it would be as good as the time we'd pulled grinds on the slick, polished steel of a railway track—but he didn't fare so well. Turns out the curb wasn't anywhere near as good as we'd imagined, because it was all full of notches and chips that had been painted over, but we tried again and again and again anyway. Ally hit it pretty well a couple of times, sending us all into gales of cheers and applause, but that was the high point. Truth be told, we were pretty shitty skaters, except for Ally—she was great.

"How *did* you get so good, Miz McShay?" Niz wondered after one particularly good tail slide.

"I've had hours to practice," she said with a shrug. "Not much else to do in the summers."

"Does your brother skate?"

"Nope, just me."

"But why skating?"

"It's the only solo sport out there," she replied. "My parents never wanted to sign me up for any league sports, just in case we had to move."

Niz glanced at me apologetically. We'd all picked up skating because we rubbed off on each other—it was a very social activity for us, despite Niz also spending hours practicing by himself. With us, we only practiced alone to have something to show everyone else later—skating all alone seemed weird, like if you pulled off a mean trick and there was no one there to see it, did it really happen?

"What are you guys talking about?" Tobie asked from behind me, walking up to us with Jess.

"Skating," I replied.

Jess rolled her eyes; Sammy hit a rock and tipped from his board, sprawling out behind Niz as his board ramped away; Ally collapsed in a fit of laughter.

"Having fun?" Tobie checked.

"Sure—this curb's great."

"Cool. D'ya wanna come sit with us on the porch? Watch the sun set?"

Tobie looked right at me, I turned and looked at Ally, Ally shrugged.

"We kinda told Ally's parents we'd be back for dinner."

"Oh."

There are few moments in my life I would truly change, given the chance, but that one tops the list. It's hung there forever since that day, a canker sore I can't stop pushing with my tongue: a deep, sharp pain that whips blood from my skin and hurts the same amount every time, no matter how fleeting or suddenly it's gone. My stomach still turns and I squirm for that ghost of my past, watching uncomfortably

291

again and again as I make the wrong decision.

The weird thing is, I think we all felt the same thing, not just me, only they were all spectators. That single syllable falling from Tobie's lips set into motion a series of events that didn't need to happen, that didn't ultimately change the outcome of anything, and that really only served to taint the rest of the year. What would it have hurt to sit for another half hour with Tobie? The McShays ate dinner late—it wasn't that we didn't have time, it's that my parents were out and my house was empty and Ally and I had plotted to stop off there and, well... you know. But the look in Tobie's eyes as she looked from me to Ally, it haunts me still. It said everything to me even then, but I was powerless to stop it. When you're eighteen, the promise of sex with a pretty girl far outweighs anything else. When you're eighteen, you understand that sunsets come and go and you deeply believe that pretty girls are fleeting. Maybe they are, but the problem is a lack of depth in that perspective: There certainly are more sunsets than pretty girls who like you, but every sunset is unique, and that one was more so than any of the others.

God, what I wouldn't do to have that single sunset back: to sit with Tobie when she most needed me to sit with her, even if I would have had my arm around Ally. By not staying, I had silently spoken some deeper utterance: that I'd rather be somewhere else than with one of my best friends when she wanted to enjoy a final sunset with me; with all of us.

But instead of listening to the prophetic echoes, I ignored them and carried on, and Ally and I went back to my house and put on some stupid old movie and screwed, then went to her house for dinner.

And Tobie sat with all of her other friends feeling rejected in the worst way: rejected because the person she'd thought would care the most turned out not to care at all. Or so she thought, because I did care, a lot—I just cared too late.

I realized it consciously that night, trying to get to sleep. I shot up in bed, feeling sick, and called Tobie, completely unmindful of the hour.

She didn't answer.

That, more than anything, cost me everything.

"Thanks for helping, Bells," Tobie said.

We were sauntering through the park behind her new condo—I'm sure we'd driven past these condos a hundred times before without looking at them. All the boxes had been taken out of the truck and stacked in empty rooms and her parents were getting the beds ready. A week ago we'd all been out at Tobie's house for one last fling, and now it was gone. Now all we had was the darkness of the park. Somewhere out in that darkness were the Roots—a tree's root system exposed over an old, dry creek bed Tobie and I had discovered on some field trip or other, back in middle school. It had become something like a fortress to us over the years, a magical place where all of our secrets were trapped by the roof of roots as we sat underneath them and talked.

"I wanted to help," I replied. "I'm glad you called."

"Really?"

I chuckled. "Yeah—I'm always glad."

"Still, I didn't think you'd come. I figured you'd be busy."

"Well I *am* supposed to be working."

She laughed and slipped her hand into mine, pulling me off to the side.

"I think there's a gazebo over here, or a bandstand or something."

She was right, there was an old gazebo at the top of a slight rise. In the darkness it looked ghostly, glowing dimly in the light of a slight moon. We walked up to it, our feet clomping on the weathered wood. I climbed up on the bench and looked back the way we'd come, only to discover we were still pretty close to the condos. I guess we'd been walking really, really slowly. I turned back to Tobie and sat down on the railing, my feet on the bench. She climbed up next to me and snuggled in against the chill in the night air.

We sat there and talked for a while, about everything and about nothing. About Niz and Jess, and Sammy's problems, and how sorry she was for bringing Greg Wilson down on us. She was sad and trying hard to hide it, and I did all I could to pretend I didn't notice. It had been a while since we'd sat and talked like that, and I missed it, and I told her so. That seemed to make her feel better.

I can't say I didn't think of Ally while we were there, but I do remember that neither of us mentioned her. I don't think it was a conscious choice or a plot or anything, but I think we both knew that if we said her name, she'd be there in some way. It was a sin of omission. I should have dropped Tobie off and gone home and called Ally, but I didn't because I'd already abandoned Tobie once and I wasn't going to do it again. And I didn't mention Ally because I was afraid —because I didn't want Tobie to think I wasn't *there* with *her*. Tobie needed to believe that, right then, I didn't want to be anywhere else in the world, and the truth is, she was right: Right *then*, I *didn't* want to be anywhere else. I wanted to be with her, to give her comfort, to put my arm around her and hug her and smell her hair. I wanted to hear her laugh and look into her eyes, which seemed to glow blue even in the moonlight.

But Tobie had her own need of proof. I started to move away when she said she was tired, figuring it was my cue to go home, but she put her hand on my knee and stopped me.

"I want you to kiss me," she said.

It wasn't a question or a request, she was simply stating what she was thinking, but she knew the full weight of what it meant and how time has a way of slipping at the most important moments. Everything else in relation to the moment seems so far away, back in the mists of almost forgotten, or off in the future of never-will-be. It's easy to believe there is nothing around but the darkness and the wind cutting through a gazebo in the park. It's easy to lose hold of the vision we require to make sure we don't hurt other people— but if you take your eyes off what matters for even a second, you're sunk.

"Me, too," I admitted.

"So why don't you?"

"You know why."

"Ally," she agreed.

And there she was, real and between us, as she should be, bringing my vision back into focus.

"I really like her."

"I do, too."

She held my gaze and I didn't look away. If I turned away, it was the sunset all over again. At least, that's what I thought then. I thought she needed to see that I still cared; that I had to *prove* to her that I still cared.

"It's just one kiss..."

There was a pleading lilt in her voice that hurt to hear, as if this one kiss could change her life; as if everything hinged on what I would do. And in that moment, with that swell of friendship or love or whatever you want to call it, I thought it was a pretty petty thing to give her, to help her believe that everything was going to be just like it was before. It seemed such a small token to ask for, to help her sleep at night; to make her feel as wanted as I knew she was. It seemed like the cost I had to pay for that damn sunset, for turning my back on her before. There was nothing to it, for me, is what I'm trying to say. It was just something that had to happen so I could try and put everything right.

So I kissed her, once, maybe longer than I intended, and when we parted I couldn't tell if she was happy or about to cry.

"I better go," I stated.

I stood up before she could protest and shook my legs. We hadn't really moved for at least an hour. I filled the silence with stupid get-the-blood-flowing noises so that she wouldn't have the chance to ask me to kiss her again.

When she walked off without a word I followed her down the rise, jogging to catch her at her back door. She slipped in and half closed the door, as if trying to escape from the moment.

"Thanks again, Bells," she said, her face a wedge of brightness in the dark.

"See ya later, Tobie," I replied with a wave as I turned and walked back to my car.

It was the start of Spring Break and we very purposely hadn't made any plans.

It really seemed like spring break of our Senior year should have been more exciting. We should have saved all through high school and had a big blowout celebration some-where—most likely *not* Florida or Mexico or any of the places newly minted eighteen-year-olds go to get drunk and kid themselves that they're acting like grown-ups. Sammy had this plan that we should go to California and find the spots where our favorite skaters pulled off tricks in the videos we always watched. It was a great plan, and since we all knew it was never going to happen, we planned for it any-way. What actually happened is that we went camping, but not the whole gang. Tobie and Jess stayed home, leaving just me, Sammy, Niz, and Ally.

"They're pulling away," Niz said when we first claimed

our campsite and were ambling around, collecting sticks, Ally and Sammy had wandered off in opposite directions looking for kindling.

"Who is? Jess and Tobie?"

"I don't know... They know we're all heading off come fall. I think they're trying to remember what life was like before us."

I laughed incredulously. "*Before* us? *Was* there a life before us—before the four of us?"

He stopped walking and looked at me sidelong. The sun was cocked just above the treeline and it turned him into a silhouette when he shifted his weight and blocked it with his head.

"Maybe not for you and Tobie. But for me and Jess...? Yeah, there was a lot of life before us."

"Niz?"

"Yeah?"

He started walking again, but having him alone like that reminded me of something I needed to tell him. I reached out and grabbed his arm, turning him back to me. I had to tell someone, and it had to be him. He could see it written on my face and he moved around, watching me, waiting for me to speak. The wind seemed cold despite the sun and I huddled into my jacket.

"Niz, I kissed Tobie on Saturday, after I helped her move."

He didn't say anything for several seconds, letting it sink in, then, "What?" he finally asked.

"'Just one kiss'," I laughed harshly. "That's what she said, and that's all it was, but I kissed her."

298

"*Why?*"

"She needed me to," I whispered angrily, though I'm not sure who I was upset with. "I ignored her at the party... And the way she asked, it was like asking for a hug..."

I met his eyes. He licked his lips slowly, considering. The wind ruffled his hair and he looked off into the distance, as if bidding it to go away. Eventually he looked back at me.

"Did you tell Ally?"

"She's here, isn't she?"

"Then don't—don't tell her." He held my gaze, even when I tried to dodge it. "She doesn't know how long you and Tobie have been rattling around. You're right, too—for you, life started when we met Tobie and Jess at that dance in sixth grade. I saw it in your eyes. And as long as it doesn't happen again—I mean, you know what it meant and what it didn't mean, right? Do you still like Ally?"

"Hell yes."

I didn't even hesitate. The question was ridiculous and we wouldn't even be having the conversation if I'd stopped liking her. If that was the case, I'd have made out with Tobie and we'd be on-again and I'd break up with Ally. But that's not even close to what I wanted. "I just wanted Tobie to know she still mattered, and she asked, and it seemed... okay."

"Is it weighing on you?" he wondered.

I shrugged—and I think that was the worst of it. I didn't really feel bad or guilty because it had meant so much to To-bie. To me it *had* been like a long hug, but to other people kisses mean everything, and for good reason. Kisses peel back the hidden feelings and expose the raw heart of the matter—but it didn't change how I felt about Tobie, and it didn't change how I felt about Ally.

So it meant nothing, it meant everything, and it meant I could never explain it to anyone.

"I didn't even think of it until just now—honestly. But when you said they were pulling away... I don't want to lose Ally over this, but that's why I did it, right? So she wouldn't pull away? Tobie?"

I sighed heavily. Clearly it had been bubbling below the surface after all, if such a small scratch could let it out.

"Look," Niz said. "Five months from now we won't be anywhere near each other. You did something to help a friend that another friend won't really understand—and I *mean* that," he added, staring me down for emphasis. "I know we don't want to think about it, but whoever we're with at the end of summer, well... eventually, they'll just be friends. *Friends*, right? So just ride it out and forget about it."

"That's either the best advice or the worst advice you've ever given me. And it's certainly the most depressing thing you've ever said."

He looked off into the wind again, considering something else.

"I think Jess is going to break up with me," he finally admitted.

"Are you shitting me?" I blustered. "But you *can't*! You've been dating *forever*!"

"A year and a half." He weighed the words carefully and nodded. "But we're not going to get married, Bells." He turned to me again and smiled widely. "So I'm just going to ride it out. And I'm going to enjoy it."

That night we sat around the campfire and told jokes and stories and laughed and got reflective and stared into the fire. We talked about college and where we'd be in five years, and Niz was right: none of us said, "I'm still going to be hanging out with you guys." You could say that we all figured we would be, so it wasn't worth saying out loud, but I think we knew; we all knew the truth of what Niz had said to me. We *felt* it viscerally, and we ignored it, and that made it so much easier to ignore the kiss, as well. Sitting with my friends—poking embers and watching sparks drift up into the starry sky—the last thing I needed was to ruin it any sooner than time itself would do, so I buried it. I buried it and I threw more dirt over the hole every time Ally snuggled against me or snuck a kiss or smiled or looked at me. I buried it for exactly the same reason it existed: Because it seemed like such a small thing to do to protect someone I cared for and to keep her happy.

Later, alone in our tent, Ally and I made love—slowly, sweetly, and without the fear of being caught. For the first and only time, it was just us without the lingering fear of interruption; her soft breath in my ear and the warm scent of her shoulder under my nose. As I pressed my lips against her neck and heard her breathe my name, the farthest thing from my mind was kissing anyone but her. With Ally, it had never *just* been a kiss; there had never been any question over the intent or purpose or meaning or depth. With Ally, it was always clear: a bright, white cloud floating in a dried blue sky, moving and billowing in its own easy way.

I enjoyed that clarity and it allowed me to suppress the rain. But it did weigh on me, I was wrong about that. I under-

stood Niz's advice at a higher, objective level of reasoning—
that we'd soon only be friends, regardless, so one little kiss
shouldn't be allowed to derail what we had left—but at the
lower, gut level, it didn't feel right at all. Maybe that was me
being objective, too, but it seemed a lot like lying—the bad
kind of lying, where you're not trying to spare the other person's feelings but are actually trying to keep yourself out of
trouble. That kind of shit always weighs on me. I don't even
like playing poker because I'm actively trying to fool my
friends so I can walk away with their money. There is nothing more horrible than lying to people, especially your
friends, for personal gain—*nothing* more horrible—and Ally
was way more than just a friend to me.

The other problem was that part of me thought Niz was
wrong: I truly believed that Ally and I were going to stay together forever. I believed—as I still believe—that if you
truly love someone, then time, space, and hardship can't separate you, not for long. That made the kiss feel like one of
those stupid, meaningless mistakes that could end up ruining
my entire life, and when weighed against each other, I
started to convince myself that it *was* a white lie, after all—a
lie of kindness to protect someone's feelings or prevent injury. Did I really want to let a single kiss unhinge our future?

Still, what kept me quiet after we got back from camping
was that nagging little voice that told me Niz was probably
right—he usually was—and *that* made it a bad lie again.
That made it selfish, to allow me to have what I wanted and
not risk losing something that meant everything to me. Time
and space would come to test us soon enough, and I wasn't
ready to see how we'd fare against a hardship like infidelity,

no matter how small and no matter how good the intentions.

So it weighed on me. It weighed on me heavily, and Ally noticed almost as soon as we drove back into town after our overnight jaunt in the woods. Out in the woods, it had been easy to ignore—there was no one else around and it was easy to pretend it would always stay that way; that the entanglements and lives of the rest of the world didn't affect us. But when we got back to familiar surroundings it crashed down on me. Ally sensed it, too, almost immediately. Maybe my face changed. Maybe I didn't kiss her as willingly when I dropped her at home. Maybe I forgot to say I'd call her later. Maybe I didn't call her at all because I didn't know what to say. And maybe I wanted to call Tobie to see what *she'd* say, but I didn't do that either, so it festered. It festered and it made me sullen and withdrawn; it made Ally ask me if there was something wrong when I was with her. I shook my head and looked away, and so she *knew* that something was wrong. That only served to make the kiss bigger and more meaningful than it was: Trying to hide it gave it a whiff of importance that it didn't deserve.

But the fear of losing her before I was ready to lose her kept me quiet.

The last Sunday of spring break I went over to Niz's and found him riding his ramps in the garage, spilling out into the driveway. He looked angry, but his eyes glimmered with relief when he saw me walking up.

"Ally with you?" he checked.

I shook my head. He nodded and hit a truck stop with excessive gusto. I was about to say something about needing to talk, but he beat me to it with, "So I guess Jess and I broke up."

I dropped my board down and let it dribble across the driveway toward him. He stopped and grinned over at me, trying to put on a brave face.

"Just like I figured..." he added.

"But why now? I mean, if at all, but why not wait until... until...?"

I couldn't finish the thought. I couldn't let myself think that there was any fitting moment for a clean break in the very near future—the day after Prom or after graduation or after the summer stock play or right before we left for school. No, I was trying to avoid thoughts of logical breakups in an effort to make the future seem infinite; in an effort to make hardships worth working through.

"We're still going to Prom," Niz explained, as if that either made sense or was the only thing of any concern. "And we're still going to hang out. We're just not going to do anything... else."

"I don't get it."

Niz slammed down from an ollie, then bent over and scooped up his board, violently flinging it into his backyard with a maniacal roar. He plopped down on one of the platforms he'd built and sighed heavily.

"I don't either, but that felt really good."

"Did you argue with her? Tell it was a dumb idea? Tell her that you could pull it off—you've been dating almost *two* years!"

"Yeah, I argued. I mean, I didn't yell at her or anything. I think what she's really saying is that she doesn't want to marry me."

"Do you want to marry *her*?"

"How the fuck do *I* know? I'm eighteen."

"Maybe you should ask her—let her know you're serious. Maybe she broke up because she thinks *you* don't want to be with *her*?"

Niz laughed without mirth and lowered his head to watch his fingers fiddle with his shoelaces.

"Do you know how awesome it would be for you two to get married this summer?" I asked.

For a second, I really thought I was convincing him, too. Then he looked up at me and snuffled in a deep breath.

"That would be stupid," he said evenly.

"What? *Why*? Don't you love her?"

"No, she's right," he agreed indirectly. "Is it love or a habit at this point? We have to figure that out. So if we can hang out without being intimate, then maybe it's not love. Maybe it's just a habit we need to break before we head off to college."

"I don't think it's that easy," I offered. "Believe me. I think I have both."

"Love?" Niz spat with derision. "I *know* you've got a habit, but you think you have *love*? Then tell me, oh sage one—answer the age-old question for me: What the fuck is love and how do you know?"

He wasn't trying to be hurtful. He was working through his own problems, trying to balance things so that the answers would make sense. And he was right: I had nothing intelligent to offer to the conversation going on in his head, but he mistook my silence as defeat, not as the current output of my own churning thoughts. Maybe if we'd hashed it out run it through the usual mill of self-deprecating jokes and analogies to skate tricks—maybe we'd have been able to nail something down and save both our minds. Instead, I shut down because what I wanted to say—about Ally and about lying—wasn't going to help him any. I was arguing for love —for suffering through a relationship in the rough spots because the thought of being apart was worse than anything else—even as I understood that maybe, with true love, the rough spots shouldn't involve kissing other people, no matter who they were, and that if Jess was right about her and Niz and the inevitable breakup, then maybe the rough spots aren't even worth mentioning, just like Niz had suggested.

So nothing happened. We cracked some jokes about Niz being able to chase tail at the mall again, then went out back and shot up some Coke cans with our BB guns. By the time we got back to skating, the whole thing had blown over and I still didn't know what to do.

Turns out Tobie and Jess may have been having a similar conversation.

I'd guess Tobie was trying to figure out how to make me confess to Ally so that she—Tobie—could apologize and help us smooth it over. But Jess, I'd bet, was playing the pessimist and telling her not to bother—just like Niz had told me. But I think that's where we were heading, me and Tobie. We were heading for a confession, to each other and to Ally, and we were hoping the way Ally and I felt about each other would win out over the ways old friends show they still care. We both needed that. Tobie and I both needed to believe that we helped each other more than we hindered.

But it chewed on me. I should've apologized to Ally the night it happened, then asked Tobie to try and help me explain, if Ally would allow it. But I didn't, and there it sat, like a demon on my chest stealing my breath, and Ally saw it so she knew, later, how long I'd been lying to her and how big I had let the lie become by trying to ignore it.

Sometimes there are no words. Sometimes there is only that look in her eyes, the one that tells you that you did exactly what she'd expected, and exactly what she'd fooled herself into believing you wouldn't do. There is anger, but it's at herself, and in the end, that's what hurts the most: The fact that you acted out a story she'd already known the ending to; the fact that she was let down by her own faith; the fact that you lived up to the worst, most pessimistic views of humanity and gave her fresh evidence for those views to exist; the fact that you couldn't be the person she wanted you to be; the fact that you were the one to prove to her that she'd let herself down.

Sometimes, the look in her eyes says all of that and tells you that she wished she could go back, not to before you hurt her, but to before you met, or at least before she decided to let you in. You know that myth about the vampire? The one where he has to knock and he has to be invited in? That was actually a warning from mothers to daughters about people like me: About the ones you let in. About the ones who bleed you dry. About the ones who turn on you and make you lose your faith.

When I looked into her eyes, that's what I feared the most: Not that I'd ruined it for *us*, but that I'd ruined it for *her* and for the one man she could have eventually loved. I feared she'd become a vampire. I feared she would only be happy if she drained men from here on out, because once upon a time she had let the wrong one in and he had turned her into a vampire. And that seemed like such a horrible thing for Ally and for the world to be denied the person she had once been.

"What does that *mean*?"

Her teeth gritted; her hands balled into fists; her back rigid, but her shoulders pulled down; her hair hanging in her face, the blue dye reflecting in her tears.

"I don't know..."

"You don't *fucking know*?"

We were at a drama club meeting the week after spring break. Ally had gone to look for Tobie to ask if I was okay; to see if there was something wrong that was making me sullen toward her. It was the exact logical thing to do—everyone knew that Tobie knew everything about me—but she had no idea. She turned the corner just as Tobie said to Jess, "Jack kissed me the day I moved," and that's all Ally needed to hear. It didn't matter that she hadn't heard the setup or the explanation or the excuses. She'd heard everything that mattered.

"Ally, I'm sor—"

"*Don't!* Don't fucking *say* it until you fucking *mean* it, Jack!"

"Tobie's just a *friend*, I swear."

"I can't believe I'm saying this, Jack..." She sounded calm suddenly. Too calm. Her fists unclenched, her posture relaxed. "But Missy Anderson was right. She knew *exactly* what was up between you and Tobie fucking Malloy."

"No—don't hate Tobie."

"Don't hate *Tobie*? Are you fucking *kidding* me?"

I felt a tear stripe my cheek. There were a thousand

308

thoughts in my head and not one of them would land on my tongue. The only things that settled were the things I knew I couldn't say: Sorry, love, don't, please. Words that no longer held a meaning when I said them out loud. She didn't need my setup or explanation or excuses. Her tears and rage said it all, and they were tears and rage I'd been trying to hide from myself for over a week, so I let them come out of Ally for both of us. I heard every word she yelled echoing through every thought I had, and her words sounded so much better than my thoughts—so much more true—so I stood silently and let her go.

The next day at lunch I saw her sitting by herself, at a table far away from us, and I saw what I had really done to Ally. I saw the girl most other people saw: the girl who sat alone and didn't talk to anyone and didn't make friends.

And I was the reason why.

Jolly came in that day and sat with her, unaware that we were all at a different table. He must have thought no one else was there yet. I could see him telling her a story that was probably hilarious—Jolly was a pretty funny guy—but she wasn't laughing. He realized that and he reached out and touched her arm. She pulled away. Then she stood up and walked off.

"No," I said to Sammy.

"What?"

"You guys hang out with *Ally*, not me."

It all sounds so damn heroic, but it really wasn't. A hero would have got up and apologized to her. A hero would have told her how he was going to try and put things right, not between them, because they were broken, but between her and

309

her other friends. A hero wouldn't have quietly slunk away, leaving other people to try and clean up his mess. I was no hero. I saw me exactly as Ally had seen me in the hall the night before, and I hated what I saw.

"I just wanted to get through Prom," she'd said quietly, right before the rage came back. "You broke my fucking *heart*, Jack!"

She forcefully slammed my shoulders back, pushing me away with all her strength, and the bang of my body against the lockers surprised me. She didn't hold on. She let go, and I slid like dead weight to the ground. Her shoes made only a whisper as she ran away, her skirt rippling around her mismatched stockings.

Tobie and Jess rounded the corner seconds later, both panic-stricken.

I just lay there where Ally had let me fall and said to Tobie, "Get the fuck away from me."

So she did. Jess had already run off, looking for Ally.

The tile floor was cold against my cheek, and I deserved it. Every moment I lay in discomfort was a moment I knew would fade, so I tried to stack them up in the hopes they would reverberate forever.

I suppose it worked.

I still remember that night in April so very fucking well. I remember the cold tile floor. I remember the exact shade of blue in the highlights of Ally's hair; a blue so perfect it hurt to look at it, and I wanted to tell her—I wanted her to know how well she had colored it, and how beautiful she looked— but her face was inches from mine and I couldn't hear my thoughts for all her shouting.

But I remember the blue and how it was reflecting in her tears.

I lay on the floor and watched Tobie, blurred by my tears, trace the same path as Ally had moments before. I lay there and let the coldness seep in and I hated myself more than I'd ever hated anyone in my life.

There is a certain stillness that only spring nights can bring. It's not the same as a winter stillness, when everything is hiding or dead. And it's not like a summer stillness with its low whir and drone of insects, nor the quiet calm of an autumn night when leaf smoke plays in the storm fronts that eventually bring snow. Spring is the quiet strain of growth—muscle and fiber flexed against the hardship of weight. And at night, that whiff of life is omnipresent, bringing a warmness to the air that never seems as cold as the fall. I'm glad it happened in the spring. Heartbreak in the spring doesn't seem as lonely, just reflective. The future still holds promise in the spring, if only because of the season.

I needed to feel that promise around me—to smell that whiff of the future—so I left my house after dark and told my parents I was going to see Niz, back by ten, all that happy-kid stuff. I didn't drive, since Niz lived right around the corner. They didn't know yet that Ally and I had broken up, though I'm sure they'd guessed something was going on.

Only I didn't go to Niz's. I went up to the park—the one spot in town where you could almost fool yourself there was no one else around. No one to hear you sigh. No one to see you smudge tears from your eyes with the heels of your hands. I would have gone to the Roots but I knew that if my parents found out I wasn't at Niz's they'd call Tobie, and Tobie would find me at the Roots. It was our spot, after all. So I went to the wall, all the way at the other end of the park, at the top of a massive sledding hill that overlooked the city center below. The wall was maybe three feet tall—more a safety rail than a wall—and I sat on it and watched the lights twinkling, the mass of dark forest between them and me like a spill of black ink over the landscape. There was life down there in the lights. There was fun and regret and people being too serious to take it all in.

I pulled in a long breath and huffed it out slowly, a whisper of a cloud curling from my lips and dissipating in the air. It was a clear night and the stars winked in tandem with the lightshine below. I looked up at them and wished only that my head would be as clear, or at least that I could see the bright points of light in the darkness. I knew there had to be some left, but seeing Ally alone at lunch had damn near gutted me. The only thought that kept me going was that I deserved the pain, for me and for her: I had to live to serve my punishment.

"Just! One! Kiss!" I cried out, slamming my skateboard end down into the mud at the base of the wall. It felt good. It felt like I was doing something about it by being alone and angry. I had been angling for Ally since the first day I'd seen her, and I'd forgotten her in the way Tobie's lips parted when she breathed.

Everything was falling apart, and the best thing seemed to be to remove myself from it all. The rickety wheel was spinning too fast and thick shards of the past were whirling off and flying away, waiting to be discovered later when they'd lost meaning. It was all going to be gone soon—all of my friends, my life, my childhood—everything that had ever mattered, especially Ally, would soon be gone. No use dragging it out. I felt a strange, internal plodding—walking, not running, like I was afraid that if I made too much noise it would awaken the creatures and cost me my life. I felt a pulling back, an almost physical sensation, like I was leaving a dark and wild forest and I knew that as soon as I was out of earshot of the beasts in the underbrush, then everything would be okay.

If only I could quiet the night before it got to me.

I narrowed my eyes at the city center, concentrating on something that wasn't there. I simply didn't care any more, that was all there was to say about it. Nihilism was a damn sight easier than concern, and Ally had made plenty of friends to help her through it. That thought made me laugh— as if she'd need help getting over some asshole who had kissed another girl, just like she'd always known he would do. No, Ally was better than that. Or smarter, anyway.

I pounded a few more rivulets into the mud with the tail of my skateboard. Stopped. Considered the mud, the slow-wavering grass (almost as black in the darkness as the sky was), the odd pebble that had been carried up here in the treads of boots or tucked in the runners of sleds. Pounded again. Stopped. Then I gave up and screamed "No" at the top of my lungs, howling against every past action so it could

313

echo into my future emptiness and give me something to look forward to.

That's when I noticed the brightness—a harsh whiteness cutting into me and leaving only my shadow on the hillside. I turned slowly and had to shield my eyes, barely managing to distinguish the unmistakable shape of a light bar on the top of a cruiser.

"Park's closed, man," the cop said.

He lowered the spotlight and turned it off, then walked over to me. I'd been so lost in thought I hadn't heard him pull up or get out of his car.

"Sorry," I mumbled.

He ambled over, none too concerned, and when he got to the wall he turned and sat down on it, facing the opposite direction from me. It was the cop from the dance—the one who never gave us a hard time for skating. He usually made sure we weren't hurting anyone or anything then let us go about our business.

"You're that kid from the dance," he said as if he'd finally figured it out.

"You remember that?" I asked, honestly amazed. He chuckled.

"There was only one fight that night. Had a rough day?"

I looked over at him, the solitary street light behind me lighting up his face. He'd always seemed old to me because all people over a certain age look the same, grown-up age (at least until they get to be grandparents). It's the stark filter enforced by nature so the kids know who's who—or who's a kid, anyway, because the rest of them don't matter and they don't understand. Only this guy, suddenly he didn't look so

314

old. In fact, he looked downright young.

"Yeah, you could say that."

He glanced at me and nodded. "It's a breakup—I get it."

"Is it that obvious?"

"No—it's a safe bet. You were yelling pretty loudly."

I couldn't help but laugh and stumble through another apology as I did it.

"Ten years ago, I was right there, man," he said. He sucked a breath in through his nose and looked about ready to agree with himself. "She was the prettiest girl I'd ever seen."

"What happened?"

"Not a lot—we just broke up. I mean, *yes*, at the time...? At the time it seemed like a lot, but not now it doesn't."

"It really hurts," I admitted, looking away and cutting off my words so he wouldn't see me getting misty. "I screwed up."

He let my words hang in the air for several seconds, out of deference to the admission, then finally said, "We all screw up. Every one of us. Does she know how you feel?"

"I don't think it matters how I feel."

He let the words settle again, drifting to the ground and spreading like dust into my thoughts.

"It probably matters more than you know," he offered.

"I think I better go home."

He stood up, arms crossed, and took a step toward his cruiser. "Let me give you a ride."

"Am I under arrest?"

He laughed incredulously. "No. But I can't let you stay here, in the park, and I don't feel like following you in a car

315

to make sure you leave—that would be weird."

"Okay," I accepted. "Fine. Whatever."

"Get in the front," he said as I clambered off the wall. "The back's a tight squeeze."

We didn't say another word in the two minutes it took for him to drive me back to my house. I had him stop out of sight of it so my parents wouldn't freak out if they saw me being dropped off by a cop, and he seemed fine with that approach.

"Thanks for the ride," I said as I got out.

"No problem—be careful out there..."

"Jack," I filled in for him when he looked at me expectantly.

"Jack. Be careful."

"Okay, sure... G'night."

"Night, Jack."

I figured out how to miss lunches so that Ally and the others could have their old lunchtime back. It's not hard to convince teachers that you're studying for exams, apparently. Either that, or Mrs. Brishel, the librarian, could see it in my eyes that I'd had enough and needed to collect my thoughts. And when Jess came into the library looking for me mid-week, Mrs. Brishel didn't say a word. She looked up from her book, watched with mild disapproval for a second or two, then went into the back room on a made-up errand so we'd be alone.

"You and Tobie: always breaking each other's hearts, one way or the other," Jess proclaimed, plopping down in the chair across from me. "Is it so you have a reason to hang out again and put the pieces back together?"

"I came here to eat alone, *mom*."

"Look, Bells, it's none of my business, but if you want Ally back, avoiding her—and us—isn't the way to go about it."

I glared at her. She had the same logical smile she always had when she was explaining something to us. How she always managed to cut through the shit and tell it like it was I'll never know—but if Jess offered you advice, you'd be wise to at least listen, if not take it.

"You really think she'll take me back?"

Jess shrugged. "Tobie talked to her."

I cut her a look. "Bullshit," I said. "It's not that easy."

Jess nodded sullenly. "I think Ally needs to hear it from you."

"She doesn't want to talk to me."

"How do you know that?"

"You heard what she said to me in the hall—I *know* you did. And she's right: I set it up to fail because I was afraid it wouldn't last."

"Now you know *that's* bullshit, Bells. That's the whole damn *point*, isn't it? You *didn't* think about what you were doing because you thought everything would be there forever."

"It didn't even mean anything," I mumbled.

"What? *Ally* didn't mean anything?"

317

"No! The stupid kiss. Tobie. I was just trying to make her feel better."

"You're an idiot," Jess decided simply. "You know, you and Tobie should've just figured this shit out Sophomore year instead of having this long, drawn-out affair. I don't like seeing either of you hurt, and for as much as you're there for each other, did you ever stop to wonder why you both get hurt so much? If you guys want to be together, then just *be* together."

"I *don't... want...* to be with her!" I stressed. "We're just *friends*."

She huffed out a sigh and look away; if a sigh can have a defeated tone to it, hers had it.

"Is she going to Prom? Ally? She said she just wanted to go to Prom."

"I don't know, Jack. Maybe?" She paused and offered me a weak smile. "Look, we're planning to skip school tomorrow. You should come with us—just the four of us, like old times. We'll just hang out."

I didn't say anything. I looked away, like I was trying to figure out what Mrs. Brishel was up to. Jess reached out and lightly touched my arm, drawing my attention back to her.

"You know, this hurt Tobie a lot, too," Jess said softly. "She likes Ally and she likes you and she likes you and Ally together, and she's terrified that she lost it all—you, Ally... She actually *threw up* that night thinking about it."

I met Jess's eyes; she wasn't kidding.

"Don't you at least want to know what Ally said to her?" Jess asked plainly.

"Fine," I blurted. "So what's the plan?"

318

The plan, it turned out, was more like an intervention. That's how it felt, at least. There was me, and there were my friends, and my friends were trying to convince me I should try and get Ally back. We started out over at Niz's playing Foosball, and the whole time they planted not-so-subtle digs about how awesome Ally was and how smart and understanding. It was weird. I finally called them out on it and asked them why she wasn't with us and they all looked at each other guiltily. It ruined the moment—if there had even been a moment—and I felt bad, I guess. Sure, they'd had it coming, but I was supposed to be playing along and acting like this whole thing hadn't been cooked up as a way to get me and Ally in the same room. I mean, if that's what they'd wanted then they really should have invited her along.

"Where the hell is Sammy, anyway?"

"It's just supposed to be us," Tobie said quietly. "The four of us—"

"Like old times. Yeah. Great. Let's go eat."

I was pretty pissed and Tobie knew it. I drove mostly so I could pretend I had to pay attention to the road instead of them. Tobie fiddled with the radio until I snapped at her to stop.

"Sorry," she mumbled.

"Since when were you such a big Runaways fan, Bells?" Jess asked pointedly.

I glanced in the rear-view mirror at her and she held my gaze in the reflection, staring me down—daring me to say it out loud: Since Ally.

"I *like* the Runaways," I said defensively.

It was true, but she knew who had introduced me to them. She let it drop.

We went to the mall for lunch and got frozen Cokes and saw a movie and had fun trying to avoid the security guards, who would undoubtedly call the cops. You could tell everyone was giving us the stink-eye, wondering why we were there and knowing damn well that we'd skipped school. For some reason, that made me feel better—that short-term adrenaline rush of getting away with something made everything seem better. And they'd been right, after all: It *was* nice to be just the four of us again. I didn't realize how much I'd missed that until that day, sitting in the mall and digging up all our old, favorite stories. We'd had a lifetime together and it had been a really good one. It hadn't been so long ago we were kids hunting for fossils in the creek by Niz's house, and now we were adults, at least on paper. Only I didn't feel very grown up, and I think that helped a lot, as well. For that day I felt like a kid again, but a weird sort of kid who was old enough to do whatever the hell he wanted. There aren't many days like that, days where you literally don't have a care in the world—or rather, can pretend you don't by hanging out with a group of enabling friends. We were still irresponsible teenagers, and that seemed like excuse enough to screw up and not be held too accountable for it, which made it very easy to forget school and broken hearts.

I have a theory that the body may derive energy from food, but the soul derives energy from emotions, and that's just as important. Spending time with friends recharges that battery, or seeing a great movie, or going to a great concert. Those are the days and moments all that "seize the day" bullshit is about—those carefree spans of time when nothing matters but exactly what's happening. As you grow older, those spans grow shorter and further apart, which only makes them all the more important to seek and tend. Living in the moment is the most freeing stance you can take—but it's also a terribly thin tightrope across a yawning cavern of doubt. All it takes is one moment—one misstep—and you may lose the chance for all those other moments in the future to come. The trick is to balance that responsibility with the childlike wonder of the world, and to a child the world exists only for the exact time they are experiencing it. That's why kids can seem so selfish and dramatic, because the *now*—the *moment*—is all they've got, and if something is in danger of screwing that up, they truly believe there will never be another moment like it. "Object permanence" the shrinks call it: The knowledge that shit still happens even when you aren't around, or that things don't change; don't go away.

But they do. That's why those moments are so hard to find as adults, because we know the kids are right: If you can't see it, taste it, or feel it then it might very well be gone forever.

That's what hit me when I was walking Tobie across the condo parking lot to her door at the end of the afternoon: It was almost over—the day, the school year, life as we knew it. I'd walk into my house in another thirty minutes and my parents would yell at me for skipping school, and real life would come crashing back in, and with it the certainty of what I'd done to Ally.

"Why so pensive?" Tobie asked timidly.

I shook my head and laughed humorlessly.

"You really should talk to her—"

"No."

321

"Why are you so *stubborn* about this?"

"Why do you think it's so easy to *fix*?"

"I talked to Ally."

"I know—Jess told me." I wasn't pleased and I didn't hide it.

"*You* should talk to Ally."

"She deserves better than me," I replied softly, looking away.

"She doesn't *care*," Tobie retorted. "She's moving, you know. She told us."

"Really? *When*?"

"She wouldn't say. Sometime this summer, I guess. Before you leave for college."

"So what's the point?" I wondered. "If Niz and Jess figure they can't pull it off, what chance do me and Ally have?"

"Is this really how you want to leave it?"

"It's better that she hates me," I decided.

"I don't believe that. And I don't think *she* believes that."

"Look, it's not that easy, okay?"

"*Why*?"

"No." I stopped her and turned her to me.

"Jack, don't be so angry..."

I didn't really hear her.

"No! Listen! I figured it out. You wanna know who *I* go to to get me out of trouble? I go to *me*. I'm the fucking safehouse, right? And I'm fucking *telling* you, this isn't trouble I can get out of. I *fucked up*, Tobie. And this is what I get."

I stormed ahead of her and she lingered back, barely

322

keeping up with me. I reached her doorstep and swept my arms sarcastically to indicate she should go inside. She stopped short and looked at me. I reached for the door knob and Tobie jumped forward and stopped my hand.

"Bells, wait," she begged. I turned to her and she looked so scared. She was holding herself, using her arms as a barrier to stop anyone getting close.

"Give me a hug," I said.

She practically dove at me, and we hugged like we should have hugged that night in the gazebo, and she cried like she should have cried then, too. Instead, in the gazebo, we tried to cover the fear and regret with a kiss... but not this time. This time we hugged and I rested my chin on her head like I always did, to be funny, but she didn't notice.

"I'm so sorry, Jack," she mumbled. "I ruined *every*-thing."

"No you didn't," I soothed. "I didn't have to kiss you."

"But I knew you would," she admitted. She pulled back and sniffled in a deep breath, wiping at her eyes with the heels of her hands. "I don't know why I wanted to kiss you so badly. After that shit with Greg Wilson there was no one... but there was you. There's always you, Bells."

"It's okay."

"You *do* always fix our problems."

"No I don't. It just seems that way cuz I'm always around."

"You *do*. So let us try and fix this one for *you*, huh? You want to know who your safehouse is? It's me. It's *us*. And you *know* that."

"It's no use," I said definitively. "I mean, what's she

323

thinking right now? She knows we all skipped school. She's not an idiot—she's knows we're together. And I can't stop being friends with you, Tobie, not for anyone. And that's what I'd have to do, to make it work."

Tobie laughed out a few tears and shook her head.

"Don't, Jack. Don't."

"I'm serious, Tobie. If I saw you hurt and sad like that again, I'd still kiss you to make you feel better."

"I was just *jealous*," she said sternly, fresh tears sprouting in her eyes. "I was just so fucking *jealous*, and I *ruined* it for you!"

I didn't know what to say, so I hugged her again and let her cry. I'd kissed her because I'd wanted her to know I still cared, and that I cared deeply. I'd wanted her to know that nothing was going to change, that no matter where she lived or who we were seeing, there was still us and I'd still be there for her. So if I could do all that to Ally then—and could imagine doing it again, if needs be—then what good did that do any of us? Did I want to see Ally again? Of course I did, but I knew that wouldn't be fair, not to her. It really was trouble I couldn't talk my way out of because deep down I knew I'd done it to convince *myself* as much as Tobie that nothing was going to change. Ally had been right: I set it up to fail rather than let it coast to an end. I preferred the fiery close with explosions and blame instead of the slow walk into a sunset. Somehow, that made sense.

"Let's go to Prom," I suggested to Tobie. "Me and you and Niz and Jess, just like our Junior Proms. Just like we were today."

She held me tightly and whispered, "I'm not going to

324

kiss you again, Jack."

"Ever?"

"Ever."

"If you think that'll change my mind, it won't."

She laughed lightly and let me go, turning and pulling open the front door.

"I think you should ask Ally," she said.

"I can't," I replied.

"Not for you, Bells. Do it for Ally."

"I can't... lose her again. If she said no it would just..." I trailed off.

Tobie smiled.

"Then do it for me, to make *me* feel better," she said softly, but I pretended not to hear her.

Ryan was molding something out of clay that approximated a vase. He was attempting "hand-molded wheel-tossed," which meant he was trying to effect a wheel-tossed design without the wheel. This actually followed the curriculum: We were in advanced ceramics now. Of course, all that meant was that the teacher didn't spend any time teaching and we were free to make whatever the hell we wanted, however the hell we wanted.

"Another bong?" I guessed. He stopped and grinned over at me.

"I broke the last one. Say, whatever happened to that girl, Ally?"

"What do you mean?"

He shrugged, working the clay with his fingers. "She used to meet you after class, and now she doesn't. She was nice."

"I guess we broke up."

"You *guess*?"

"We did."

He stopped molding and sat up straight, shaking his head slightly. Ryan was the kind of guy I always wondered why we didn't hang out more, like outside of school. I knew we ran with different crowds, art class aside, but he was still a good person. A bad kid—drugs, skipping school, parties—but a good person.

"She was *hot*, man—that was a mistake," he considered.

"No shit."

"So what happened?"

"I don't really want to talk about it."

"You should, though."

He smiled knowingly and poked at his bong, to make it look like he was working. I was wasting time making a coiled-clay monstrosity—ceramics was not the best of motivators for a guy a few weeks away from graduation. I'd never honestly thought of Ryan as any kind of confidante. Sure, we hung out in art class and in the halls, maybe ate lunch a few times and traded tapes—but nothing more meaningful than that.

"She found out I kissed another girl," I tested. He let out a low whistle and held up his hands, begging off being any kind of assistance after all.

"Shit, Jack... Who'd you kiss?"

"Forget it—it's complicated."

I looked over and he was smirking, fully aware that I was not going to blow him off so easily or I wouldn't have said anything at all. He wanted to see how serious I was, though, and deftly changed the topic, to see where it would lead me. If we got back to the Ally question, then he knew I couldn't back out twice. All this time we'd been chummy in art, and maybe I should've been talking to him more often. He was a lot smarter than he let on.

"So what's up that one guy's butt, anyway?" he asked.

"Which guy?"

"Dude that slammed you into the locker a while back...? I never did ask you what that was about."

"Oh, that..." I laughed. "His current girlfriend is my ex."

"Why's that so funny?"

"Because *his* ex-girlfriend is the girl I kissed."

And there it was—full circle. Score one for Ryan, who had successfully navigated the conversation back around to what was clearly bugging the hell out of him: What did I do to lose a girl like Ally McShay?

"I figured it was about a girl," he replied. "So why did you kiss his ex-girlfriend? To piss him off?"

"She's sorta *my* ex-girlfriend, too."

"So was she your ex because of him?"

I laughed lightly. "No... Her name's Tobie. We go way back."

"Tobie? Chick with the long dark hair?"

I nodded. I didn't know he'd ever been introduced to her.

327

Maybe at lunch or something? I tried to remember, but couldn't. Tobie was so ever-present for me, it could have been anytime.

"Well, she's hot, too," he decided, as if that made it okay. "Maybe not *as* hot—"

"Look, forget it, okay?"

He shrugged and went back to molding his bong. I worked on my monstrosity a bit more, silently stewing over everything again. Since Ally and I broke up, it felt like something was missing, and I'd never really felt like that before. It felt like a memory of summer on a blustery February day: Something you knew had happened and knew was nice, but you couldn't for the life of you pin down the essence any more, because the current reality was so different... But it felt like you should be able to, and maybe a certain song or something would trigger that memory from time to time, and suddenly it would feel like summer all over again. Suddenly you could smell the fresh-cut grass or the summer rain on the wind; hear the low rumble of a distant storm; see the eerie flashes of heat lightning play across the clouds. That's how it had been since we broke up: Ally was my summer memory and my fear was that winter would last forever.

"My friends think I should talk to her—try to get her back."

Ryan stopped working and looked at me, but didn't sit up or anything. After a few seconds he went back to his bong, pushing the clay with his fingers. I had to admit, it was starting to look pretty impressive.

"Why bother?" he wondered.

"I think I love her."

"So you're going to marry her?"

"Can't I just love her and not marry her?"

"No," he said simply, cutting me a quick glance and a half grin. "You go back, you tell her you love her, then you'll have to follow through."

"Fuck that, Ryan. I told her I love her lots of times."

"But you never went *back* to tell her, did you?"

"I guess not—I don't really know what that means."

He stopped what he was doing and gave me his full attention. I got the sense most of his philosophy, at least regarding love, came from Deep Purple or Black Sabbath or something, but I'd heard what my other friends had to say, and they seemed just as uninformed. Why not give the stoner a chance? I nodded, urging him to continue.

"Look, I don't really know either, man," he admitted. "But going *back* is like leaving the room by the back door then coming back in through the front door. It says you never meant to leave. People have expectations, y'know? Even if you just say you forgot something, then it's this big deal, to see what you came back for. So with Ally, y'know, if you go back, you gotta be ready to tell her what you came back for. And I'm not sure a shrug and 'I don't know' will cut it. She'll expect more."

"I don't think so. She's moving."

"When?"

"Summer...?"

"So she wanted a clean break?"

"I don't know what she wanted."

"You know what'll help?" he asked very seriously. I shook my head and he indicated his bong with his eyes. "Let's get baked, Jack. Figure this shit out."

I chuckled. "I appreciate the offer, but I think I'll just try and forget her."

"Really?"

He could tell I was lying. He could tell there was no way I was ever going to forget Ally McShay. But what he'd said rang true: What was the point in going back to her if nothing big came out of it? So we could date for—what?—another month or so before she moved?

"I don't know, Ryan. But I don't think pot will help."

"You'd be surprised, man."

"Did you ever go back for a girl? Did you ever smoke up and decide you should go back?"

"Yeah," he admitted. "I did."

"And?"

He shrugged and smiled with defeat. "She expected something bigger, man. But we just fell into the same rut and I made the same stupid mistakes all over again. And I think that made it worse."

"So you didn't marry her?" I joked.

"No," he laughed. "No I did not."

May

"Well, Sammy, here we are again."

Sammy glanced at me, lined up his shot, and let the model plane go. It was one of those big Styrofoam gliders that flies awesome two or three times, then either snaps a wing on impact or gets stuck in a tree. We were indoors at the mall and had been doing pretty good, though. Sammy had been tossing the plane back-n-forth with a guy working the putt-putt golf in the food court below the toy store, across the way. Sammy threw it down, and the guy threw it back up. Amazingly, it hadn't gone off course yet.

"Yeah," Sammy agreed, sighing mournfully.

After Donna Marie broke up with him, he'd had enough of the hotdog stand, too. I talked the toy store into hiring him, and there we were.

"We gotta get you a Prom date, Sammy."

He laughed and hucked the plane back down.

"So you and Tobie are going?"

"Yeah. I guess."

Sammy caught the plane then lowered it and looked at me, a serious glint in his eyes.

"So, you know, Ally asked Jolly to go with her—just as friends."

I nodded. "I'm glad. Is he taking her?"

"Yeah."

"At least she didn't hook up with Greg Wilson," I quipped, trying to lighten the mood.

"Shit—he doesn't care about us any more. He thinks he *won*."

"You think?"

"Sure! He's convinced he broke you and Missy up, and I bet he takes credit for me and Donna Marie, too."

"What a fucking year," I breathed.

"Seriously," Sammy concurred.

The blurring line is how it all shook down, and the closer things get to that line, the fuzzier they become. Ally was my dream date to my Senior Prom, and now I'd ruined it. Then the blur sets in, because nothing made more sense to me than taking Tobie to Senior Prom. She'd always been there, for everything I could remember that mattered; she was my best friend. But I saw Ally's smile, imagined her warmth against me, and the blurring line got fuzzy again. Best friend or maybe my worst habit. Tobie. Something entirely new, like I'd never felt for a person before. Ally. Someone I wanted to make happy, above all else. Al-bie. Jesus, I was fucked. Why couldn't it be more clear? Tobie had been right to be jealous because Ally *had* replaced her—not entirely, no more than girlfriends ever replace old friends, but enough. Of course, Ally had been right to be suspicious, too—she was the blurring line and it made it difficult to see clearly, because I knew that eventually Ally *could* have completely replaced

Tobie, but that was still in a future I was fighting off even as I ran to embrace it. I wanted to hold on to Tobie even as I was prepared to let her slide away for Ally. It *should* have been more clear and it pissed me off that it was easier to pretend nothing had happened than it was to try to work for something meaningful—because that "something meaningful" would be gone when Ally moved away.

So why not stick with old habits? New habits could be dangerous; the unknown was something to fear, not welcome. Right? I sighed heavily.

"Well, we're done," Steve said from behind us. I loved it when he closed because he was so lax with us. "Why so glum? I did the vacuuming for you."

"You do know it's weird that you *like* to vacuum, right?" I checked.

Steve grinned devilishly.

"Anyway," he said. "All that's left is for one of you to count my drawer. The place is *dead*. I'm willing to risk you guys calling it a night. I'm not trying to stiff you outta pay..."

He held up his hands in submission, perfectly willing to let us stay.

"How long do we have?" Sammy wondered. "Like, a half hour?"

Steve glanced at his watch. "Yeah, about that."

"I think I'll head out."

"Me, too," I agreed.

Sammy counted the drawer then we clocked out and headed downstairs to the record store. Sammy had brought me to work, and the plan was for Tobie to take me home after we went to a movie. Me, Niz, Sammy, Jess, and Tobie, out for a night on the town.

"Do you know what Ally's doing tonight?" I asked as we walked, trying to sound casual.

I took off my toy store uniform shirt and stuffed it in my backpack with the hat they made me wear. Underneath I'd worn one of my regular t-shirts, and at least the place let us wear jeans. Sammy did the same, and by the time we got to the record store, we looked relatively normal. Well, normal for us.

"I think she was going to a show with her cousin. She's not home moping, if that's what you're asking."

"I didn't figure, Sammy. I just feel bad."

Sammy pulled me back and we stopped short of the record store entrance.

"I lied. She *is* home moping," he said earnestly. "Do you want me to call her?"

"Would it matter? Would she really want to come down and hang out with me and Tobie?"

"And me? And Niz and Jess?"

"Yeah, but..."

"I know." Sammy sighed heavily. He looked up and down the mall, like he was trying to spot the spies before they spotted us.

"Do *you* want her here?" he finally asked. "Does *Tobie*?"

"Tobie set us up in the first place—you know that!"

"What happened, Jack?" he asked seriously. "What *really* happened?"

"Tobie needed me."

"And you?"

"Do we have to talk about this?"

334

The last thing I wanted was to be forced to put into words the swirling morass of emotions that I had. I missed Ally more than I had ever missed anyone in my life, but I didn't even try to get her back—no begging, no pleas for mercy.

"She wasn't surprised," Sammy offered, trying to prod me into talking. "I mean, she was disappointed, but only because she was hoping she was wrong about you and Tobie."

I looked at Sammy thoughtfully. He was curious, I know, but I wasn't an idiot. Ally wanted him to talk to me; she wanted to know if everything she thought was true *was* true.

"Tobie and I go way back," I mumbled.

"What happened in the gazebo, Jack?"

And how do you tell him that the amassed weight of seven years had happened in the blink of an eye? That when someone you've cared about for that long is sad and alone, you want to make them feel better, period? That sometimes a kiss is just a kiss? What had happened in the gazebo wasn't important, it was how it made Tobie feel that mattered to me. And as soon as I realized that I was more concerned about that than how it made *Ally* feel, if only for that moment, then I knew I was no good for Ally, so it took the fight out of me. She didn't deserve me. That's why I didn't fight back. That's why I slid down the lockers and lay there on the floor watching her run away. It was an easier position to maintain when I assumed she was done with me; when I got the pain I deserved.

"It was just one kiss, Sammy," I said softly.

He raised his eyebrows. "You're an asshole."

"I'm sorry, Sammy."

"Why can't you tell *Ally* that?"

He sounded pissed.

"Because she might forgive me!" I snapped.

I hadn't thought of it before, but that was the God's honest truth. The reason I could let it go was because I figured, deep down, she hated me; that when we politely avoided each other with a smile backstage or at lunch, we were playing parts to get through the rest of the school year in a civilized manner, then we'd go to different colleges and never see each other again. But if I apologized and she forgave me...? Well, then there was no reason to not get back together, and that would fuck up everything all over again, or at least introduce the potential for a colossal fuck up later, because I was quite certain that I would do something stupid despite my best intentions, and another fuck up would be devastating. It seemed better to quit while I was only a bit behind rather than too far gone.

"You know, I don't get you," Sammy said. I'd never really seen him angry before, at least not at me, and I couldn't understand what was getting him so pissed off. "Tobie got between you and Missy—"

"She didn't get between us. I never liked Missy that much."

Sammy sucked in a heavy breath, his gaze locked on mine. "And now she's got between you and the only girl I've ever seen you *loopy* over, except stupid fucking Penny Harper, back in tenth grade."

"Look, Sammy... Did she put you up to this? I really don't want to—"

"She didn't put me up to it, man. I'm curious. Ally is

perfect for you—you know that." He paused, changing his tempo. "You know how you said you wanted to get me a Prom date cuz you wanted me to be happy? Well, same thing, Bells. I want you to be happy."

"Tobie makes me happy."

"*Bullshit*. Not like Ally did, and you know it."

"*Tobie needs me!*"

That stopped him. Stopped him cold. I felt ambushed, but I could see it in his eyes that he meant well; that he was trying to help; that he was trying to straighten out my mind. So I tried to give him a glimpse of that weight—next to Niz, Tobie was my oldest friend. And if something truly bizarre had happened, and Niz needed me to forget Ally—no matter how much it hurt me—I'd do the same thing for him.

Maybe.

No, I probably wouldn't.

But I mean, Ally *was* the new girl, and as much as we tried to make it not be true, we all knew it. Deep down I think Sammy knew it, too. It's a shitty thing and a bitter reality, but there it was. Friendship cuts deep, but those cuts are only as deep as the life you've spent together, and no tie binds better than the friends you forged your first moments of independence with in your 'tweens, and still managed to keep when the dust of puberty settled. Those were the ones you knew you could always count on because they'd never left your side, not for any reason. Other friends just as close may come along, yes, because it's the weight of the years together that matters, not the number, but Ally wasn't there... yet. What I couldn't admit is that I knew Ally was on the fast track to supplanting them all—in a future that *could* happen

337

but most likely wouldn't. Still, given the options, with all the cards on the table, it was safer to fold than to gamble.

"Tobie has *always* been there for me!" I tried to explain. "No matter how *stupid* or *fucked up* the thing I got myself into was, she was *there*. She needs me more than *Ally* needs me."

"You think *Tobie* would believe that?" he snapped back. "Because *I* don't. You think the move was rough on Tobie? You don't think *Ally* wants some stability?"

"What does it fucking matter?" I yelled, done with the conversation. "We're *all* moving! I'm going to O-U, Ally's going to some school out west—we're going to break up, anyway, Sammy! Tobie's not going anywhere, *and* she needs me, so I have to make a *choice*, Sammy."

"So this is because Ally's moving? It's easier to dump her than fight for her? So I should stop hanging out with you because you're going to college in the fall?"

I cut him a look and started to walk off. Sammy and I had never had a real fight before, and I didn't like the way it felt. I also didn't like the fact that he was right; that everything I'd been trying to hide was right there, out in the open, whether I said it out loud or not: What I was really avoiding was having to break up with Ally again and, more than that, finally breaking up with Tobie, for all that meant. If I went back to Ally, I would be dumping Tobie, and I didn't know if it would be worth it in the end. It was selfish, but it made it easier for me to put all that pain on the new girl, no matter how much I loved her—and I did love Ally, with everything I understood to be love at that time—rather than face an uncertain and potentially painful future with no one at all.

Sammy was right: I was an asshole and Tobie would *not* have approved.

"Wait," he said, hooking my elbow and turning me back to him. "I have seriously never heard you talk about a girl the way you talked about Ally. *Think* about that, man. Isn't she worth it?"

I shook free and glared at him. "I'm going to find Tobie, then I'm going home."

I didn't look back as I walked off.

$\mathcal{E}$

Now it all seems so ludicrous, but back then we were young and trying to be carefree. Niz and Jess had broken up because it made sense somehow, because we were all being forced apart. The future was a pin too big being shoved into the wheel, and the spokes were cracking from the pressure.

Me and Tobie, we should have known better; we should have recognized that our bond was different. When we were fifteen, we had officially dated, and we'd officially broken up, and we'd officially still continued to hang out. That had been a rough year for both of us, for different reasons, and only the fact that we'd had each other—some anchor to a past that seemed simpler and more innocent—had got us through. So I hung on to Tobie because she still seemed more permanent than anyone else. She was still my anchor. Only anchors can be a blessing and a curse: mooring you in the harbor so you don't accidentally float into dangerous waters, or holding you back by not letting you move on. But couldn't they do both? Couldn't they let you float off but not away?

And then there was Ally... The girl who taught me so many things because she'd been forced to grow up faster than the rest of us, her constant relocations making her see the world through more adult eyes and gaining her the insight that, in the end, everything is transitory. In the end, everything fades or dies, but the trick is to remember that everything is a loop—a long, slow spiral to a point in the center, the final dot, the moment when we take our last breath and the moments that made up our time are extinguished forever. The secret, she knew, is not letting the little endings weigh you down until you're past them; until after the exposed nerves have grown scar tissue and the red blemishes have faded to a color that almost matches your skin, so that when people ask about it you can be almost cavalier when you tell them it was nothing.

"You know, this doesn't have to be awkward, Bells," Ally said quietly. I stopped and turned back to her and she smiled. "We don't have to keep hiding out in opposite wings."

We were down to the final dress rehearsal for the spring play—it was the week of the performances. We'd been too far in for either of us to drop out, but more important, we didn't want to drop out; we didn't want to let Mr. K down. So we'd struck up a truce of silence, imposed mostly by my decision to stay in the wings on my side so we weren't together backstage. She had also started hanging out in the wings on her side, across the stage from where I was.

"But it *is* awkward..." I mumbled.

"But it doesn't *have* to be."

I'd caught her looking across the stage at me a few times, just as I looked across at her. It was dark and I couldn't really see her, except when the light shone correctly, illuminating her face for an instant; a small flash of beauty holding back the mighty press of shadows around her, if only for an instant.

I didn't say anything. I stood silently and looked at my shoes as I scuffed the floor. She didn't say anything either, but I could feel her looking at me. I knew I could just apologize and she'd forgive me, but I wouldn't let myself. It was too close to Prom now to ruin it for Tobie. I looked at Ally and it hurt me to see her expectant smile willing me to apologize. One small word that would make her happy...

But I couldn't do it: Not to her and not to me. Not when I knew it would all be over again when she left with her family and then went to college on the other side of the country. And not when we both knew my feelings for Tobie hadn't changed. It would take focus and commitment to repair that kind of damage, and while the will was certainly there to give it another try, we still only had enough time left to attain a level of trust and comfort that could be used as the foundation for something more meaningful that would most likely never have time to actually happen.

"I don't know what to say," I finally admitted, glancing up at her.

She looked so God damn beautiful. She'd started to let

her hair grow out and had it pulled back in a pony tail, her eyes bright, her lips as enticing as always. It struck me suddenly that we'd never officially broken up. I mean, we'd never said it; we'd never said we didn't want to see each other any more. All she'd said was that I shouldn't tell her sorry, not until I meant it... but I still wasn't sure I would mean it. I'd be saying sorry to get her back, but I needed to be sure I was getting her back for *her* not *me*. She didn't deserve it if it was for me; if it was nothing but an attempt to be forgiven for my sins.

"Remember when you said I deserve nice things?" I wondered. She nodded slowly, maybe even hopefully. "Well here—take your ring back. I don't—"

Her hand shot involuntarily to her necklace, the one I had given her, her fingers loosely touching the tiny golden heart.

"Does that mean you want this back?" she whispered, her lips drawn down, close to panic. I stopped trying to get her ring off my finger and looked at her, and really *saw* her, and I knew exactly what she was thinking: That I wanted to give it back and with it the memory of everything we'd shared.

That I wanted to forget her.

"No—I want you to keep it."

"And I want you to keep the ring, Jack. I don't want you to for—oh, forget it."

"Forget what?" I asked.

"That you deserve nice things."

"You do, too."

She looked down at her shoes and chuckled lightly. I was

struck by the fact that I couldn't remember ever seeing her like that before. Normally when she looked down, her hair hid her face, but with it pulled back, I could still see her, and I could see that she was smiling.

"You know... Tobie told me everything."

"I know," I admitted. "I mean, she told me you guys talked, anyway."

"We miss you at lunch, Jack."

"I miss you... guys, too."

She seemed to be prodding me to say something, almost as if she'd been told I had something to say but would need gentle persuasion to actually say it. I didn't know what she and Tobie had talked about—I hadn't let Tobie tell me—and I wracked my brain trying to think of the right thing to say now, all the while knowing there was only one word that she wanted to hear. One word that would fix everything.

If I meant it.

If I meant it wouldn't ever happen again, if we got back together. If I meant I could be certain of that and could make that promise.

But I simply didn't know—the blurring line was too wide—and it hurt my head trying to figure it out in what could well be our last conversation.

"I never see Sammy any more," she said. "How's he doing?"

"Good. He's taking Melissa to the Prom."

"I don't think I know her."

"Yeah... She's a friend of a friend, I guess."

"So you're going with Tobie?"

"As friends, yeah—as friends. Sammy said you're going with Jolly."

"Yeah. As friends."

"Jolly's cool. I'm glad you're going."

"My mom said I shouldn't miss my Senior Prom," she laughed. "Got in a big fight with my dad over it. She said it's supposed to be special."

"No pressure, right?"

"Yeah."

She laughed, the sound of her chuckle bringing back everything in a wash: How much I missed her, how much I needed her, how long I'd pined for her. I couldn't take it any more. I couldn't be so close and not have her.

"Ally, I—"

She looked up at me.

"I think we better take our places. The scene's almost over."

"Yeah," she agreed quietly, the smile fading from her eyes before it even left her lips. She turned and walked slowly into the wings, the beaded safety pins on her Chuck Taylors rattling lightly.

She looked so good—so young and so wise. It hurt like hell to think of her, so I ducked into my wing and tried to forget. But when I looked over toward her she held my gaze and I waved and she smiled and waved back and then it was dark.

People come and go. We can't hold on to all of them forever; our hands are too small and our grip isn't strong enough.

The four of were standing at the top of a huge set of escalators: Me, Niz, Jess, and Tobie. Jess and Tobie had gone all out for Prom—they both looked amazing. But it wasn't just their Prom gowns or fancy hair—they looked at ease; completely comfortable and *alive* in the way you can only be with your friends.

Friends.

That's all we were, four friends, and it made everything so much easier.

"Think we can stop it?" Niz asked, straightening his bowtie for the hundredth time. We might have felt at ease, but tuxedos are probably the world's least comfortable clothing: bowties, cummerbunds, tailored pants, hard shoes with no treads—it was hell in clothing.

"Are you serious?" Jess asked hopefully, grinning ear to ear. "This thing's gotta stretch three floors!"

It was true. Senior Prom was at the fancy convention center downtown, and the escalator had been designed to take you from the ground floor to the ballrooms without having to stop at the floors of meeting rooms in between. When we went up it at the start of the night we'd considered stopping it, and now that we'd been at the dance and got bored, we'd decided to see if it was possible. Tobie had suggested it, as we sat and nibbled finger-foods, sipped weak fruit punch, and listened to the kind of music they played at the Wharf. Jess had smirked and nodded, so there we were.

"Hey! You kids! *Scram*!" a voiced yelled, followed by the hollow clicks of people running in dress shoes.

"Sammy!" Tobie called out happily. "You made it!"

"Jolly—what's up?" I added.

Sammy and Jolly had doubled, and to be fair, I hadn't gone out of my way to find them, since Jolly had brought Ally. I didn't want to ruin their evenings with our awkwardness.

"Where are your dates?" I tried to ask discreetly, but nobody bought my "not that I care" tone.

"Going to the bathroom or getting snacks or something," Sammy replied. "We figured we'd see what you assholes were up to."

"Niz wants to stop this escalator," I explained.

Sammy nodded approvingly. He looked over at Tobie and nodded very slightly, his lips curling into a grin. I assumed he was excited to show off his escalator-stopping skills.

Sammy stepped onto the risers and winked and Niz tumbled on behind him. I started to jump on, but Tobie grabbed my arm and spun me back.

"Jack—hold on."

I looked from her to the escalator and sighed. "What's up?"

She pulled me away from Jolly and Jess and over to the windows that looked out on the downtown cityscape beyond, glowing golden in the streetlights and headlights. A bus

346

belched into gear, thundering against the windows for a second before moving on.

"Jack?" Tobie said, and I knew she was serious when she used my real name. "I think you should go and talk to Ally."

I huffed out a sigh. "Shit—*Tobie*! No—"

"*Please*, Jack."

"One: Why? And two: I can't do that to Jolly again."

Tobie held my gaze, calculating, then grinned bashfully and decided to come clean.

"We set this whole thing up again," she admitted.

"What? What whole thing?"

"Me and Jolly... and Ally."

I narrowed my eyes suspiciously. "What does *that* mean...?"

"It means we couldn't prod you into asking Ally to Prom, so we had to make sure you hooked up here anyway."

I shook my head slowly. "No, Tobie, she doesn't—"

"She *does*," Tobie cut it in. "I'm telling you, we set it up with *her*. She wants to talk to you. She's not in the bathroom, she's waiting for *you*, and she'll be absolutely *crushed* if you don't show up. Is that what you want? Her to remember you as the guy who crushed her at Prom, just like—"

"I get it," I held up my hands to stop her from digging up the Ghost of Junior Proms Past. "She really forgives me? Why? Why should she?"

Tobie shrugged. "The rest of us haven't been avoiding her for the last two weeks like you have. I think she understands what happened, but I also think she wants to hear it from you."

I shook my head again. "What about you, Tobie? This is

347

our Senior Prom—our *last* Prom."

"And I came with you, just like always. I've had plenty of dances with you, Bells. Let her have this one. She deserves it."

I wanted to argue with her but I couldn't. Her eyes caught the light and dazzled me, and her smile sealed my fate. She wanted this and she knew *I* wanted this. More than that, the thought of Ally sitting at a table, her heart pounding like mine was, wondering if she was going to get to dance with me at her Senior Prom—that was the thought that swayed me. It would be hard for me to go in there, but I wanted to see her again and I wanted to see her happy again —and I wanted to be the source of that happiness.

I was doing it for her, not me.

Well, not entirely for me.

"But she's moving in the summer..." I protested weakly; my last fear and my only excuse.

"But she's here *now*," Tobie said. "Live *this*, Jack. Worry about the future when it gets here—who knows where this will lead?"

She was right, of course. Who the fuck cared if we'd break up at the end of the summer? Maybe we wouldn't. Maybe we'd see that we were truly perfect for each other, like Sammy said, and we'd make it work, even across three thousand miles of America the Beautiful. We could take awesome road trips and meet up in Colorado, like Kerouac and his friends always did.

And if it didn't work out? Then maybe Niz and Tobie were right: Enjoy the ride while you're on it instead of worrying about when it will end. So if this ride included another chance with Ally McShay—a girl who, by rights, should never have wanted a schlub like me in the first damn place, and certainly shouldn't want to give an asshole like me a second chance—then I'd be a fool not to get on and enjoy it.

"You guys have been setting this up for a while," I mumbled.

Tobie smiled but said nothing. There was a great resounding *whang!* followed by two whoops of delight and the distant yell of Niz shrieking, "It fucking worked!"

"That's your cue," Tobie said. She stretched onto her tip toes and kissed me softly on my cheek. "And that's for making tonight perfect."

She let go of my hands and walked off before I could change my mind.

É

She looked like a movie star, that was all I could think. Her hair was pulled up and back in a loose bun-like thing, with just her highlighted strands twirling down on either side of her face—a deep crimson that matched her dress. She was smiling timidly, as if unsure whether to laugh or cry. Her hands were clasped delicately in front of her, holding the smallest purse she could find. The dress was strapless, her face separated from the fabric by her unblemished shoulders. It was tastefully cut straight across her chest, revealing a form beneath the fabric that her sloppy t-shirts hid too well.

It stretched down to her knees in one piece, ending in an asymmetrical spiral. Her legs were bare right down to her red slip-ons—of course Ally McShay was too smart for heels.

"I'm sorry," I said. "I'm so sorry. I'm so sorry I hurt you."

Not "You look great" or "It's nice to see you." No, I said what I'd been meaning to say for weeks; we skipped the small talk, just like we always did. She smiled sweetly, her eyes glistening.

"Kiss me, Jack," she whispered.

She took me in her arms, clasping her purse behind my neck. I leaned in and kissed her, the rush even greater than the first time we'd kissed, back in the concession stand on the drama retreat. This was different. This was the kiss I had known and felt sure I would never know again; a sweetness I'd tasted but thought I'd never taste again. It felt like winning and cheating and *home* all at the same time; like the sudden release of a weight removed. She opened her mouth slightly and we kissed deeper, eyes closed against the past and uncaring of the future.

And we swayed. And the music seemed like a distant noise, from a place and time so very far away. And the room seemed empty, the soft shuffle of other feet a sound made by wind and leaves, not people.

When our lips parted, we hugged, a tight hug that said we didn't want to let go.

"I really am sorry," I whispered. "I didn't want it to end like this."

"It's okay," she said. "I missed you so much. This is exactly how I wanted it to end."

That's when I realized she was crying. I pulled back and looking into her eyes. She was crying about us, but not about me, not about what I did.

"What's wrong?"

"I'm moving tomorrow, Jack."

"*What*?"

It felt like a gunshot. I recoiled against the weight of it.

"My dad says this is the last time, but who cares? I'm going to college."

"Wait... No... *What*? School isn't even done yet! You *can't* move before summer!"

"I graduated early. My mom and me, we made him wait until after Prom."

"Why didn't you tell me?"

She shrugged and avoided my eyes.

"Ally? How long have you known this?"

She sniffled and smiled a watery smile. "Since February."

I didn't reply. I gaped, my mind recalibrating a thousand things I had thought were true.

"That's why I didn't fight back," she admitted, looking me in the eyes. We moved slowly, dancing to a rhythm that didn't match the music. I felt lightheaded, and I was holding her as much for romance as to keep my feet.

"I don't understand..."

And I didn't, I truly didn't. I felt like the stooge who had been set up and the luckiest man alive, all at once. I wanted to hug her and hold her and never let her go, and I want to push her away and run and scream. So she'd had a secret,

351

too, only her secret wasn't her fault. Her secret had been to fight the future and live in the moment for the greater good of us both. Her secret had been to make the ride enjoyable before the brakes whooshed and the carriage came to a neck-breaking stop.

I slumped against her in imitation of a hug, but I was weak and my knees wouldn't hold me, it seemed.

"When were you going to tell me?" I asked into her hair, my face buried against her neck, breathing in the cool, even scent of her perfume—always just enough to only be smelled if you were lucky enough to be that close to her.

"I wasn't."

"What?"

She hugged me back, her lips against my neck, her tears wet on my skin.

"It made it easier when I hated you, Jack. But I couldn't do it. I couldn't leave without being with you one more time. You mean too much to me. That's why I let you in to begin with."

"So this isn't us getting back together? This is... good-bye?" I whispered.

"You're a good friend, Jack." She pulled away and smiled and smudging at her cheeks with her fingertips. "It gets you into trouble."

I laughed ironically. "But what if... What if we hadn't broken up?"

"I don't know, Jack. I hadn't planned that far. I didn't want to think about it."

"So this is it? This is our last dance?"

And there it was, that smile I'd come to love, that little

twist and the glint in her eyes. She parted her lips just enough to give them a quick lick.

"You know what I've always wanted to do?"

I shook my head.

"Skate in a Prom dress."

I smiled with her, then leaned in and kissed her again.

The glint of gold in the dimple on her neck where her shoulder bones met, a floating sparkle of light caught in the luminescence of her skin, gliding weightless above the fine-line cut of her Prom dress: A tiny golden heart I'd bought for her in a whim of normalcy that said I understood that beneath the skate rags and goofy shoes, she was still a girl. A tiny heart she wore for the same reason. I saw her, frozen in the moment, perfectly balanced as she slid along a grind, with that tiny ember burning on her neck on its smoke-thin chain, her face and eyes smiling in one motion: bliss. Pure bliss.

Ally skittered off the end of the curb—a bright yellow hump about six inches tall that ran the length of the high-school parking lot, to denote throughway from parking spots —and scraunched to a stop in front of me in the groan and whine of her wheels on asphalt.

"If I can do that in this dress and these damn shoes, you can do *something* in that tux."

"If I could skate half as good as you, I would."

She grinned maliciously then reached around and pinched my butt. I squealed and let my board flop down, hopping on it as much to escape as to try any tricks. I rode away from her, then turned back and assessed the curb. The paint job glinted in the streetlights, and at the end of it stood the most beautiful girl I knew, smiling and goading me on.

Nobody minded that we cut out of the dance early to skate (though I think Sammy and Tobie both thought we had other plans). Sammy had nodded and grinned and shook my hand and slapped me on the back, like we'd closed a massive real-estate deal. And Tobie said she'd cover for us if anyone asked. I could tell she was a happy, though. Her and Jolly stood there, arms around each other, grinning at us like proud parents.

"You still have to go to the after-Prom," Tobie cautioned. "If you don't, they'll call your parents."

"The cops," Jess corrected dourly, she of the disapproving approval, not wanting us to ruin a good night by getting into trouble. "They'll call the cops."

"Seriously?"

Then Ally tugged my hand lightly.

"Come *on*," she pleaded. "We're just going to the high school—it's practically on the way."

Which it wasn't at all. Prom was downtown, and between us and the high school was our massive, empty mall where the after-Prom was being held, with a full run of the mini-golf, rides, games, and movies.

But of course, I wasn't going to quibble.

"We'll be there before you are," I assured them. "Tobie...?"

"I'll be with Jolly," she finished. She smiled for real. "Be careful."

I didn't want to think about it as I stood looking at Ally from the other end of that curb. If I thought about any of it for too long, I'd cry: about what my friends had done for me—for us—and what Ally meant to me and how having only the memory of her, that I could already taste, would sting. So I pushed it all aside and pushed off, mounting probably the single best railslide I've ever accomplished. I came off the end perfectly and waggled the board around, tripping to a stop against her. She hugged me.

"Now wasn't that fun?"

I kissed her, slowly and meaningfully.

"I really, really am sorry about—"

"I know, Bells," she cut in. "Stop saying it. It doesn't matter now. I get it. The only thing that's making this easy for me is that I know you'll have her to go back to."

"It's not like that," I tried.

She shook her head and smiled and kissed me to stop me from talking.

"I thought this was it," she admitted.

She slid out of my arms and flipped up her board with a kick, catching it in one hand (the lamest of lame skate tricks) while she took my hand with the other. I flipped up my board, too, and we giggled at the inside joke of its lameness as we wandered back to my car.

"What do you mean? What's 'it'?"

"I thought we'd stay here. This is where my dad grew up —did you know that?"

355

I shook my head.

"Yeah—that's why I have so many cousins here. That's why I figured he'd finally stop moving."

"Why *do* you guys move so much?"

She sighed heavily. "Dad has a great job, so we follow the money. He says it's all for us, so he can buy us nice things and send us to nice colleges. But I never wanted things. All I ever wanted was a place to call home."

She grinned weakly at me and I put my arm around her, hugging her in.

"What kind of work does he do again?" I asked, sincerely curious so I could avoid it at all costs and never, ever do that to my kids.

"Some corporate bullshit. He goes in and straightens out troubled companies or gets them ready to be sold or something, so he's always moving, not just traveling."

She watched her feet walking for a few seconds and when I glanced at her I could see that her brow was furrowed against something, a thought she couldn't decide whether or not to voice.

"There is just one thing about Tobie, actually," she admitted slowly, gripping my hand tighter and swinging my arm nervously.

"Yeah?"

She stopped short and dropped my hand, forcing me to look at her. I reached out and moved one of her red strands of hair over her ear, but it was a meaningless gesture; I knew it would flop right back into place.

"Did you guys... Did you and Tobie ever...?"

"*God* no!" I protested. "It was just that one kiss, I swear.

356

We've *never*, you know, *been* together. *Ever*."

She smirked apologetically.

"Seriously, Ally," I said. "Sometimes I feel like kissing Niz cuz he's my best friend, but I don't, cuz he's a guy."

"That's the weirdest thing *any*one has *ever* said to me."

I offered her a guilty smile and tried to rephrase it; to say what I meant. Because she was right, I would go back to Tobie when she was gone. I knew it, she knew it, and Tobie knew it.

"I get it, Bells, really," she said. "I just had to make sure, you know, because that was special for me—for us."

She turned away and slipped her hand back into mine, pulling me toward my car.

"Now where?" she checked, cutting off any further conversation; she'd wanted to know but she didn't want to talk about it. "What time is it?"

I glanced at my watch. "Nine-thirty."

"We've still got awhile before the after-Prom check-in starts..."

"Don't go," I blurted, stopping and hugging her far too roughly. She didn't protest. She dropped her board and hugged me just as hard, her back hitching against tears.

"Stop it," she begged. "We're both leaving for college, anyway."

It was true, but it didn't make my heart stop pounding; it didn't take away the anger and confusion; it didn't take away the fact that she was there with me, my nose in her hair, her scent on my skin, her tears on my shirt.

"Fuck you, Bells," she murmured as she pulled away, pawing her face to wipe away the tears. "I told myself you wouldn't make me cry. I've done this a hundred times before."

"Really?" I checked. "You've left other boys—?"

"*No*," she confessed, angry with herself. "That's just what I have to tell myself so this is no big deal."

And that was it. That was the closest we got to a big goodbye—our strongest protests and arguments against the future.

We picked up our boards and walked hand-in-hand to my car.

And we talked about music instead.

É

Ally's hair moved over her shoulders, her eyes shut, her bottom lip stretched between her teeth, the soapy smoothness of her arms holding me down. She moved and I moved with her.

We'd stopped at my house so I could get changed before the after-Prom, even though I never did change. My parents were gone—actually, they'd volunteered to work at the after-Prom, which was okay, I guess. And since Sammy had invited everyone over for breakfast after the festivities, Ally needed to call her folks—she didn't want to go home before she had to, to tell them or even to get changed. I was exhausted and back-flopped onto my bed while she used the phone. It must've been thirty seconds, but I dozed off. I woke up when I felt her weight over me and her lips, very gently, on mine.

"Aren't you going to ask me what I'm doing?" she whispered with a light giggle.

That giggle.

Later, when she straightened up from fixing her makeup in the mirror and turned to me with a wide smile... God, I wanted her again. I couldn't believe I'd wasted the last two weeks without her, because that's what it had been: Wasted time. All that time we could never have back.

I stood up beside her and collected my tux from the floor. I didn't feel like changing into something more comfortable, not with her looking so well formed in her dress. I wanted to feel like I deserved her, and my skate rags suddenly didn't seem to fit the bill.

"I never really hated you," she said thoughtfully as I pulled on my pants—a private thought she'd said out loud. "I always knew I was only borrowing you."

I started to shake my head. She smiled happily and gave me a lingering kiss.

"I will always be jealous of Tobie," she admitted cryptically. "And Niz and Sammy and Jess. Jealous that you have that and that I was never a part of it, not really."

"You *are* a part of it," I disagreed. "The *biggest* part."

She sighed heavily. "But jealousy is what got me here, so...."

"What does *that* mean?" I wondered with mild panic, afraid she was alluding to Tobie again and that the moments we'd been living would suddenly expire.

She grinned, laughing sympathetically at herself and imparting a secret she now found amusing: "Seeing you with Missy Anderson finally made me do something about you. I wanted to prove that I was a better girl for you than she was. I just couldn't stand seeing you with someone like that."

"But...?" I blurted, trying to reconcile her admission with what I had expected her to say. "So wait... that night? At the retreat? That would have happened anyway, even if Missy and I...?"

She smiled slyly. "Maybe."

"You said you hadn't planned it!"

I didn't mean to sound accusatory and she didn't take it that way.

"I *hadn't*. I mean, I was trying to figure out how to get between you and Missy, sure, but I hadn't thought of anything specific, and then you broke up, anyway."

"Well it would have worked," I said softly. "Anything you did, I would have dumped Missy in an instant for you."

"It doesn't matter," she decided. "It's just funny how jealousy is such a prime motivator of our worst sides."

I didn't respond; she didn't expect me to. It was as close as she was going to get to telling me she didn't really fault Tobie for our breakup, or me. It just was.

"I don't understand why you can't stay at least another month," I said instead.

"We were supposed to leave last week. We had a long talk. I made them stay for Prom. I mean, my mom made my dad stay, for me..."

"You could stay with... with Jess."

She shook her head. "It would just prolong it, and it wouldn't really matter. There'd be too much pressure. We'd fuck it up."

It made sense, as much as I hated to admit it. As much as

360

I wanted her to stay and knew *she* wanted to stay, it would be awkward now. Every minute we weren't together we'd feel like we were spinning our wheels, holding ourselves back from something grand; something memorable. And then when we were together, there'd be the unspoken desire to use every little thing to try and form a new lasting memory; to do something meaningful. It wouldn't work, not for more than this one night. Sometimes when you try too hard, you end up getting the wrong results, and that wasn't a chance she was willing to take. What we had now was as close to the perfect memory as we were going to get. Best just to let it go; let it fossilize and stay unchanged.

"*I'd* fuck it up," I finally agreed. "But this hurts way more than you hating me."

"I don't believe you," she said evenly. She kissed me, letting her lips stay on mine; the warmth of her cheek on my nose; the soft weight of her hair on my face.

"I wish we'd hung out more," I said when she pulled away, thinking back to all the time we'd known each other in school, but never on the weekends. All those hours and weeks and months we could never get back: Unformed memories clinging to the bones of a doomed romance. Instead of dry humping Missy Anderson, I could've been out on the town with Ally McShay. Instead of doping around the mall with Niz and Sammy, I could've been skating with Ally McShay. Instead of playing chess and snuggling with a girl who wasn't mine, I could've been cozied up with Ally McShay. But it was too late now, and the echoes of all those moments-that-had-never-been swept over me, buckling my knees and turning my stomach into knots.

"I wish we had, too," she agreed. "But we've got all night before I have to be home. So let's go hang out. Let's go get coffee at Big Boy."

We didn't have time for coffee, not really, but I agreed and we got it anyway. We got it because we wanted to sit across from each other and talk and watch each other, as if we had all the time in the world. That's what friends do, after all: they carry on like there's always a tomorrow.

I liked the way she nodded and smiled and watched the steam curl up from the surface of her cup as she talked; the way she rested her elbow on the table and fiddled with the hair over her ear as she listened; the way she laughed with her whole mouth and eyes, her cheeks glowing like perfect domes. I liked the way she pointed when she was excited and sat on her hands when she was thinking and watched the little kids with their parents, because you could tell she missed her family.

That's when it struck me: She didn't hate her dad for moving. Her mom, her dad, her brother—they were family *and* friends to her. They were the only constants she had in the whole world, and they meant everything to her. She couldn't stay because she didn't want them to go without her. They were driving across the country to turn moving into a big family vacation, she'd explained—perhaps their last—and I hated myself for putting her in the position of having to choose, because of course she wanted to leave with her family just as much as she wanted to stay with me and everyone else. It wasn't fair, but she made the right choice. She always did—that's why she was so amazing.

Later we went for one last skate, halfway to the mall and

362

the after-Prom. One last hill ride, but we didn't even get to the top before we saw a cop come around the bend above us. I'd bet a hundred bucks the cop didn't see us—or care—but we bolted anyway. We dashed between two houses, cut through a backyard, and headed back toward the cop (so he'd pass us sooner than he expected and not catch sight of us), then back toward the street between the next two houses, finally stopping under the cover of a massive bush. The cop kept going without even touching his brakes. Ally giggled and I shrugged.

"They don't *always* care."

She leaned in and kissed me, holding my face in her hands, pinning me there as if she would never let go, and I held her and kissed her and prayed it would never end.

"It was special to me, too," I said when we sat and gazed into each other's eyes.

"What was?" she asked softly.

"Before, when you asked if me and Tobie... if I'd... I just want you to know: What we had was special to me, too. *You're* special. There's never been anyone like you."

"Thanks," she said, a single tear slipping out of each eye and streaking her cheeks.

"I'm going to miss you so much, Ally."

"God, I'll miss you, too."

"I'm glad you picked me."

"What do you mean?"

"You could've spent this time with anyone—or no one— but you picked me."

"I figured you'd be worth it, even if it was just that one night at the retreat," she said with a wry smirk, another tear

363

running into the corner of her mouth as she smiled. "Even though it would hurt later. I *wanted* it to hurt, so I knew it was real. All my other friends—I just let them go. But I wanted to *feel* this. After all these schools, I wanted to know what it really means to leave. I *wanted* you to be my problem. Sounds dumb, doesn't it?"

"No, not really."

"No, it is," she admitted, nodding and shaking her head in mild dismay. She looked back up at me and held my gaze, running her thumb over my cheek with a sigh. "It's dumb because I think I even wanted you to screw up, because no one has hurt me before, because I never let anyone get close enough before. I wanted to know what that felt like, too. You hurting me like that—it proved how much this meant."

"I'm sorry," I whispered. She threw her arms around my neck and hugged me and I held her.

"We need to ride this hill and get going," she whispered in my ear.

She let me go and leaned back, smiling happily again.

"I'll never forget you, Jack."

"Bells," I corrected quietly.

"Bells," she agreed, then stood up and pulled me to my feet.

Ally had been right: for as much as she meant to me, she never really got to be one of us, and she should've been— that's the thought that keeps me up at night. I had a chance to do something great and meaningful for someone who deserved it when I first met her, and I blew it. I blew it because I assumed she didn't care, and maybe she didn't then—or didn't let herself, anyway. Maybe she didn't hang out with us because she didn't want to get too close, because she knew it would end, one way or another. Then it became real. Then her dad sat her down and told her they were moving, and this time she reacted differently. Instead of closing in on herself and shutting us all out, she opened up. She allowed herself to glimpse the one thing she'd always wanted as much as she'd feared: A tight circle of friends. She did it knowing more than any of us that it would end, and her anger at our breakup was directed more at me cutting short her plans than it was at me kissing Tobie.

But it also worked, well enough.

"Hey, kids!" Niz bellowed as we signed in at the after-Prom and got our wrist bands. "You two didn't manage to crawl home and change?"

I glanced around. We weren't the only ones still in our Prom clothes, but we were in the minority, and I understood with a flash of panic the cliché that the best-dressed people at the after-Prom had probably all been doing something else when they should have been getting changed.

"I didn't feel like it," Ally said, hooking her arm through mine. "This is my last night, and I wanted to look pretty, and Jack went along with it. Can't a girl want to look pretty for a night?"

He didn't argue, but I caught Niz's eye and glowered at him. I knew he'd picked up on her "last night" comment, but I didn't think it was worth mentioning—at least, not yet.

Ally slipped her hand down and took mine in hers. She gave me a brief, sheepish glance, full of mischief, and I squeezed her fingers. Then the music broke out. They'd hired the actual DJ from the Wharf to come and play, and the pop-infused drum machines and loops of whatever hit he was playing echoed off the cold tile of the food court like sonic ping-pong balls. Most of the popular crowd took to the floor and started dancing, but they looked out of place—probably because it was a mall, not a club—and out of time. It was like watching them dance with the sound off, somehow: Just bodies moving in random ways, and none of them paying the least attention to anyone else.

For us, it was like the return of the conquering queen when we found the others, because everyone loved Ally, especially Tobie, and I know Ally understood that cold irony; remembered that Tobie had helped set us up; recognized that Tobie had gone with me to two dances but had actively facilitated me leaving with another girl, the same girl, both times, both Ally McShay. So there were no angry looks or jealous glances because in the end everyone got what they wanted.

In the end.

The sky was a deep purple—the deepest purple I'd ever seen, at least in the sky. I have no idea what strange atmospheric conditions colluded to form it, but looking out the backstage door of the auditorium where we performed the annual variety show, I got lost in it. That, and the soft blanket of humid air that descends in late May in southern Ohio, and doesn't let up until October, was draped over me. I miss those long, hot summer nights with the cicadas droning in time with the grasshoppers and the stars fuzzing out above the moisture-filled air. Over to the west it was darker still—a storm rolling in, pushing that purple sky in front of it.

Someone tapped my shoulder. I had my headphones on —it was *Led Zeppelin III* on an endless loop for me these days. I needed it to supplement the Cure albums I'd used to prop up my broken heart. Ally had been gone a week. I pulled my headphones off and turned around.

"We're up next, Jack."

It was Kammy. She smiled nicely and hopped on her feet, like a little kid who has been asked to get Scary Uncle Joe and tell him the food was ready.

Every year, right at the end of the year, the high school did a variety show, where the cheerleaders could revisit their best routines, the jocks could warm up for a future of frat-boy Vaudeville antics, and the drama club could perform a few scenes from a play no one there had bothered to come and see the first time around. That left me doing the set changes and props for the whole thing, a job I should have been doing with Ally.

"Okay," I agreed.

Kammy—looking slightly relieved—nodded once and bobbed off. It was just a rehearsal—the big show was the last weekend in May, then we graduated the weekend after that.

Only I wasn't as excited as everyone else. These things that seemed like such a big deal months ago—landmarks of becoming my own man—now only seemed to reinforce things I'd rather forget, or pointed the way toward them, at least.

Ally was one thing, but the good thing I'd got going—all the planning, plotting, and friend-making over the last twelve years in school—came to a head Senior year, and now Senior year was almost over. It suddenly felt like a lot of work only to pick up and leave and have to start all over.

Or maybe it *was* just Ally, because let's face it: I still had three months of summer to go with my other friends, so it was hardly the end of anything. But it still felt that way.

"There you are, Jack!" Mr. K beamed. He knew—of course he knew, since he was down one stagehand—but he was a good actor and he acted like nothing was wrong. I think the shrinks call that "positive reinforcement."

"I'm here," I agreed.

"We aren't going to do the full scene changes now, but I want you to—"

"Walk through it like the performers walk through it," I finished for him. "I know. Stagehands need practice, too."

He put his hand on my shoulder and met my eyes.

"Stagehands are the most important thing, Jack. Without sets and costumes and makeup and lighting, the people on stage are just talking in a dark, empty room. Naked."

He chuckled and I couldn't help but laugh with him.

"Sure, Mr. K."

"Okay!"

He clapped me on the back and corralled me to the wings, where he handed me a roll of blocking tape. Setting out the marks had been Ally's defacto job.

"I'll tell you what to block," he explained, and then he was off, clapping his hands and rallying the troops. He hadn't picked the best scenes from our play, per se; he'd picked the scenes that guaranteed everyone in the cast had a line in the variety show. Mr. K just wanted all his kids to be happy.

"Hey, Jack," a girl said from behind me. I turned and saw Donna Marie. She was doing a solo song—I think Missy and a couple of other girls were singing backup—but I hadn't expected her to say anything to us, least of all to me.

"Hey, Donna. Congrats on Prom queen and all that."

"Thanks. I guess it's pretty dumb."

"No, it's not dumb. You deserved it—you *earned* it."

"How's Sammy?"

"Holding up."

"Missy was so pissed that he went to Prom with Ally McShay."

It hurt to hear her name and be reminded of her, so I deflected my feelings to anger. Fuck Missy Anderson—who the hell did she think she was? And she was wrong, anyway —Sammy had only doubled with Ally, but he'd gone to Prom with Melissa.

"He didn't go with *her*," I corrected. "He doubled with Jolly."

"Whatever."

"And why the hell would Missy care who *Sammy* went to Prom with?"

But even as I said it, I knew: Missy got pissed just to draw attention to the fact that Ally hadn't gone to Prom with me. I know Donna Marie hadn't come over to indirectly make that point; it was small talk. She wanted the dirt on Sammy.

"Sammy's in the booth working the lights," I added before she could respond. "He'd love a visit, I'm sure."

Donna Marie shook her head and laughed nervously. "I can't."

"Why not?"

She looked at me and said simply, "It would hurt too much. Anyway..." She straightened up. "I heard about Ally moving away and, I don't know... I just..." She huffed a sigh and chose her words carefully. "I just thought you should know that you made the right choice. I never minded Ally."

"Thanks?" I checked.

I wasn't entirely sure what she meant, but I could tell by her tone and the set of her head and the light smile she wore that she was being kind and conciliatory and confessional all at the same time.

"Mr K's waving at you," she added, pointing over my shoulder.

I told Sammy about it later and he tried to shrug it off. It had been almost three months, after all—three months of seeing her in the halls with other guys; three months of him dating other girls for a week at a time. He'd learned long ago to shrug it off, but I could tell it still hit him, to know that she still cared enough to ask. I knew exactly how he felt and I think it made him realize how *I* felt. As I got into my car after rehearsal that night and rolled the window down, another car roared up beside me: Sammy's big piece of junk.

"Hey!" he hollered and Frisbeed something across his car, through my open window, and into my lap—it was a hell of a shot.

"What's this?" I squawked as I picked it up.

"You need that!" he yelled. "Track three!"

Then he gunned the engine and puttered off.

It was the Smiths, *The Queen is Dead*. I wasn't a huge fan at the time, and Sammy knew it, but he also knew me. I put it in and did as Sammy ordered, and for the first time in weeks, as I drove home alone through the dark streets of my hometown, I didn't feel so very alone at all. Sammy had done this. Robert Smith had filled whole albums with love and loss. Morrissey had done it, too—and they'd all survived.

It didn't make it go away, but it gave me some perspective—the kind of perspective teenagers lack until it matters. It's ironic that the age group who gets to run wild and fall in love and get hurt and do stupid things is also the least capable of dealing with it. You ask me, I think it fits, though: If we were never teenagers—always on the brink of disaster (be it real or imagined)—we'd never gain that perspective we need. You can't grow up if you don't know what it means to be a kid; if you don't recognize that half your wounds are self-inflicted.

All through high school I'd dreamed about being older, about not having curfews, about us all being on our own recognizance. The most cruel irony is that when I finally achieved that goal, we'd all moved to college, and the friends I'd intended to share that day with were no longer there to enjoy it with me.

That night, as I drove home, I realized that it was my hometown, but it was most likely not where I was going to live for the rest of my life. None of our parents had grown up there, after all. Suddenly everything looked odd and I felt like a stranger on streets I knew so well.

The part of me that lived there was over, and that thought hurt more than anything else.

É

Scene changes are never perfect—they always seem rushed and imprecise no matter how many times you've done them. But moving the props around without Ally there —without her rolling her eyes at me or sharing a giggle or looking serious when the change was more complex—was too fucking hard to stomach. I couldn't do it without her. Any of it. By the time we hit the final rehearsals, I was close to having a panic attack.

"Are you okay, Jack?" Mr. K asked quietly as he helped me push the set pieces to the same wing one night.

I'd tried to run from one side of the stage to the other to get props, but Mr. K cut that off pretty quickly and suggested we move all the props to the same side, rather than trying to run back and forth.

"Sure."

He looked at me like he wanted to say more, then said, "Do you need help?"

"Help?" I barked in a harsh whisper; Mr. K visibly re-coiled.

"I mean with the sets. We could ask Tobie or... or Jess..."

"Nah, that's okay, Mr. K," I said gently. "I don't need any help."

"Okay," he agreed.

"Okay," he repeated as he glanced at me over his shoulder and walked back onto the stage, clapping his hands.

As Sammy dimmed the house lights and brought up the stage lights, I glanced over into the darkness of the opposite wing. I honestly expected to see her face fade out of the shadows like it always had: round and perfect and smiling at me. But of course, it didn't. It was dark over there and it would remain dark—dark and empty. Everything she'd ever touched was piled up around me like the remnants of an earthquake or a flood, and the opposite wing was a wide open swath of darkness and drafts.

That first play with her, spring of Junior year, had seemed so magical. Usually the other props people were the kids who hadn't made the cast, and they were bitter and jealous and they wouldn't come back for the next play. But Ally was there, like me, because she *wanted* to be the person hiding in the wings—the person near the stage but out of the spotlight. I knew she'd be back, from the first time we both tried to move different chairs into the same spot, and she giggled then looked away, almost afraid, it seemed, to be caught having fun.

The darkness across the stage caught the memory and tore it away. I could hear the scuffles and shuffling of the performers waiting for their cues, their hushed whispers like winter winds fighting with tree branches. The thing about darkness is, you eventually get used to it. Your eyes and heart adjust and you see things where things shouldn't be. You see shapes and shadows—something slightly darker against something a shade more gray.

The day before opening night I got a postcard from Ally, from the Grand Canyon.

"I can't wait to get to our new house so you can write me," she wrote. "I hope you haven't forgotten me. When I looked out at the Grand Canyon, I thought, 'That's how it feels, big and empty.' How dumb is that? Sounds like something you'd say! I miss you, Bells. I'll write you when we get there. —Ally Mac"

Dumber than what she thought is the fact that I put that postcard in the opposite wing opening night and every performance of the variety show after that, so that she was there, in some small way. So that when I looked over into that darkness, it felt like I was looking at something that mattered. And I hoped she could sense that I wanted her there with me even as I shunted the props alone.

August

Niz's family had a houseboat on a lake in southern Kentucky. Over the years, I'd been there a few times with Niz and his family, and Sammy had come a couple of times, too. There wasn't much to it—no five-star accommodations or vibrant nightlife—but we always had a ton of fun. Days went by in stretches of reading sci-fi paperbacks, waxing intellectual about whatever came up, swimming, and water skiing. Once you were out on the lake on the houseboat there was literally nothing else to do, which inspired a forced relaxation and gave a timeless quality to the day. Nothing was defined by opening or closing hours or days of the week—it was just stretches of daylight to fill, broken up with darkness to sleep through.

It took four or five hours to get there from Cincinnati, and the car trips were half the fun. The summer after we graduated we *all* went, the whole gang, as a final send-off to our lives together. Unfortunately, I wasn't in the mood for fun that trip, and I didn't join in with most of the jokes. Tobie rode with me, of course, and Sammy and his current girlfriend—Melissa, from Prom—also rode with us. Niz and

Jess were in another car, loaded down with all the crap we'd dragged along. Maybe I could feel us splitting up already; tiny cracks that, left untended, would fracture and split in irreparable ways.

Later, I was sitting on the roof of the houseboat—moored out in a cove a half day's putter away from the dock—with my legs dangling over the side, resting back on my arms, when Tobie finally decided to catch me alone. Beneath me, in the August-blue water, Sammy and Niz and Jess and Melissa were splashing around. I think they were playing catch, bobbing seated in life jackets worn like diapers, but with all the splashing and yelling, it was hard to tell.

I heard someone flip the tape in the old boombox by the ladder to the water, the soft hiss of the wind-in replaced with the opening strums of Tom Petty's "Free Fallin'"—the music floating up to me with a strange, isolated sound as it echoed off the hills that surrounded the cove. I knew she'd be looking for me. I knew the second I only counted four heads in the water that she had come back aboard. So when I heard the soft tinny ring of her hands sliding along the hollow aluminum of the ladder to the roof I called out, "Heya, Tobe" and stayed where I was.

"Never could sneak up on you," she chuckled.

By the pad of her feet I could tell she was barefoot, and the tell-tale drip of water off her hair and bikini said she'd just got out of the water.

"What are you doing, Bells?" she asked. "You were so quiet in the car—I figured you were just tired."

"I was," I agreed. "I didn't get much sleep."

She sat down next to me and flipped her legs over the side. "Why not, Bells?"

I glanced at her, at her smiling eyes and sun-touched skin; no makeup on and no style to her wet-now-drying hair, and she still looked so beautiful. It actually hurt to look at her, so I turned away. I sat forward and rested my forehead against the railing.

"Because you should be Ally."

"Jesus, Bells," she breathed. She wasn't angry or upset, only distraught. "I thought...? You haven't mentioned her for a while."

"I called her," I admitted.

"And?"

"I saved up enough money to fly out and visit her. Only then we put this trip together, so I called her and told her I'd send her the money so she could join us."

"And she said no?"

I blurted out a single wash of tears, then swallowed it back and breathed deeply. Tobie put her hand lightly on my back, her fingertips tickling me like dandelion puffs. It was a touch waiting for me to react. I turned to her and grabbed her and buried my face in hair, and she held me. Tobie was always there to hold me, but suddenly it felt like goodbye all over again. The downside of us always starting over, again and again, was that it also meant we kept ending, again and again. In another week I'd be at college, and it scared me to think I wouldn't know where to turn; that for the second time I had to say goodbye not because I wanted to but because that was how time and fate had twisted, and destiny will never be denied.

"She sent me a mix tape a while back," I said.

Tobie pulled away and forced me to look at her, her eyes glistening with empathy.

"Yeah?"

"It was all breakup songs. All songs about loss, about not wanting it to end."

"She *didn't* want it to end," Tobie said. "She just knew that it had to. She's a smart girl, that's why I liked her. That's why *you* liked her. But would you *really* give up everything to be with her?"

I laughed ironically and gazed down at the others. Niz yelled something up to us about lovebirds. I ignored him.

"I couldn't even give *you* up," I agreed.

And maybe that was it. Maybe I'd wanted Ally to come because I needed her there so I wouldn't have to say goodbye to Tobie. Because with Ally there, it would have been all about her, but now it was about Tobie instead, and about my friends, and about *everyone* leaving, not just Ally. Losing one girl that way had been rough enough, but what I feared most was losing all of my friends the same way.

And I finally understood what Tobie had been feeling when her parents lost the house in the township.

"Tobie? What's going to happen to us?"

"What do you mean?"

"I'm not sure I can talk to Ally again now..."

"Jack, don't say that."

"She told me I should treat it like a breakup."

"She didn't mean it. She'll still love to get your letters and mixes."

"I know," I chuckled lightly. "She was crying when she said it. She said she didn't want to come because then she'd have to leave all over again."

"I told you she was smart."

"So what's going to happen to us? Does that mean we have to treat this like a breakup?"

"I think you and I can keep going along like we always have, Bells. If you want to send me money to come for a visit, I'll take it."

I could feel my eyes stinging again. She touched my face and smiled.

"Thanks, Tobie."

"Let's go for a swim, Bells," she whispered.

The moments that make us great are fleeting. Our time boils down to the days, the hours, that shape our will. We are great only in those moments—or less, if we let the sadness define us. Choose those moments carefully when you're deciding who to become.

Curtain Call

May

There are three things about Prom night that stick with me, like frozen slides exposed and projected on the wall. Three things I keep coming back to, when certain songs come on or when the late-spring breezes echo a certain way around my house, mirroring those moments when the cuts were healing and still throbbing and I lay awake thinking of her, wondering where she was and what she was doing, and hoping that, above all else, she was happy. I'm sure if I thought about it, I could remember more—could probably write an entire book just from those last twelve hours we spent together—but Ally was right about that: If we leave the memories untouched, they will stay perfect forever. As soon as we try to build on them, they'll crumble to dust like parchment and no one will be able to have them again.

The first thing is the movie at after-Prom. I can't remember what we saw or if we even cared. We were tired, the theater was dark, and the darkness gave us a strange sense of privacy. I remember the weight of her head against my shoulder and the careless way she played with my fingers. Every touch seemed like a blessing; like another stolen second when we were close enough to feel each other's skin. We dozed off. I remember waking up and feeling her lips on my neck—a light kiss, like the kind you give a dying man; the kind you give someone when you don't want them to know that you understand it may be the last time. I think about the scent of her hair and the way her dress still looked red, even in the near-darkness, and I wonder how I managed to hold it back.

The second came when we all crashed at Sammy's before breakfast, sprawled out on the basement floor like a company of tatters. Ally and I snuck off upstairs, into the living room, and snuggled on the couch. She caught me looking condemned, so I tried again: "You really could stay. Stay all summer..."

"Bells," she whispered—the sound of that single word etched in my synapses like deep-cut runes in stone, and just as magical. "Don't."

"We're both eighteen."

"So what?"

"So we can do whatever we want. You don't *have* to follow your dad's stupid jobs any more."

"And then what?" she asked. "You drop out of college and follow me, or I follow you?"

"One of us could transfer."

"And?"

"And *what*?"

She sighed heavily. "Jack, do you really think we'd get married?"

"*Married*? Who said anything about married?"

"It's either that or we break up again, right? So which is

more likely? I mean, we *already* broke up once."

She was right and I knew she was right and I hated that she was right. I swallowed heavily and sighed.

"It hurts less now so it won't hurt more *then*," I mumbled, remembered exactly what Sammy had said about his parents as he came down from his trip.

"Let's not break up again," Ally whispered.

"So I *should* follow you?" I wondered hopefully.

"No, Bells. I mean, if we still want to be together later, we'll figure out a way. Let's leave it like this for now. Let's leave it perfect."

And I suppose we did. We cast the relationship in amber and stuck it on a shelf. She had an unfair advantage, of course, because she'd moved many times. I know she'd never left a serious boyfriend, so she wasn't lying about that. But I'm sure there were guys—there *had* to be—and other friends. Or maybe not. Maybe she always made excuses not to hang out with people from school, wherever she went, so that she wouldn't have to go through the pain of leaving over and over again. It kills me to think at what age she learned that lesson; what age she learned to live a guarded, closed life so that she'd never have to say goodbye to anyone close to her. This time had been the exception. She'd realized that just this once the heartbreak was worth it for the memories, because it certainly was for me. I don't regret a moment of it, except those moments we didn't spend together.

Which brings me to my last memory of that night: My very, literal last memory of Ally McShay. She took my face in her hands and kissed me, kissed me hard and deep and I tasted the tears as they ran down her cheeks. She never said goodbye; she never said that word. Never once. Not on a night like this.

She opened the car door and got out, slamming it behind her like she had done a hundred times before, jogging up her front walk as best she could in her rumpled Prom dress, barefoot, her shoes dangling with her ridiculously small purse from her delicate fingers.

She stopped when she got to her front stoop and turned back to me. She blew me a kiss and laughed a real, happy laugh—at the ridiculousness of the gesture, and how well it fit—and then she waved, still smiling, a little girly wave, her left hand at shoulder height, bending her fingers up and down in unison.

Her front door opened. I saw her dad standing in the shadows in the hallway. He didn't look out. She hopped over the door frame and fell into his arms; hugged him tight; buried her head in his chest, and he held her and the door slowly closed between us.

She was going to be an incredible woman and I just wanted to be with her to witness it.

But I never saw Ally McShay again, not in person.

Of all the precious memories I tend, my favorite one is simply this: No one else in the world has ever seen her pull off a railslide in that heavenly glamorous Prom dress. I like to think she skated in her wedding dress, too—that she married a guy who would let her and want her to—but that Prom dress was mine.

No one else can have that but me.

Beyond the flight of Time,
Beyond this vale of death,
There surely is some blessed clime,
Where life is not a breath,
Nor life's affections transient fire,
Whose sparks fly upward to expire.

"Friends" by James Montgomery

Acknowledgments

A very special thanks to Jeanne, Kristin, Elizabeth, and Kay—my esteemed proofreaders who suffered through this book before anyone else, to help smooth out the wrinkles, correct my oversights, and catch the typos. Any mistakes left after they've gone through it are all mine.

Massive thanks and props to Camron Lockeby, who worked with me right up to the wire to get the cover tweaked to perfection. He took my stick figure of a girl skating and somehow created a masterpiece that pulls out the essence of this story and truly allows you to tell a book by its cover.

And a sincere thanks to you, the person reading this, who spent your money on this book when there are so many other, more worthy things you could have spent it on. Without the random, unsolicited comments from strangers like you about my books I would certainly have given up writing long ago.